The Kreutzer Sonata Variations

The Kreutzer Sonata Variations

LEV TOLSTOY'S NOVELLA AND COUNTERSTORIES BY SOFIYA TOLSTAYA AND LEV LVOVICH TOLSTOY

Translated and Edited by

MICHAEL R. KATZ

With a Foreword by

EKATERINA TOLSTAYA

and an Afterword by

ANDREY TOLSTOY

Yale UNIVERSITY PRESS/NEW HAVEN & LONDON

Published with assistance from the Louis Stern Memorial Fund.
Introduction, editorial text, and translations of *The Kreutzer Sonata, Whose Fault?*,
Song Without Words, Chopin's Prelude, "The Wife Murderer," and selections from Lev
Nikolaevich Tolstoy's letters and diary copyright © 2014 by Yale University.
Foreword copyright © 2014 by Ekaterina Tolstoya.
Chya vina? [Whose Fault?] and *Pesnya bez slov* [Song Without Words] copyright © 2010
by State Museum of L. N. Tolstoy, Moscow. Used with permission.
Epilogue to The Kreutzer Sonata copyright © 2014 by Hugh McLean.
The Diaries of Sophia Tolstoy copyright © 1985 by Cathy Porter. Excerpts used
with permission.
The Truth About My Father © 1924 by John Murray Press. Excerpts used with permission
of Hodder and Stoughton Limited.
Tolstoy: A Life of My Father copyright © 1953 by Harper and Brothers Publishers.
Excerpts used with permission of HarperCollins Publishers.
Afterword copyright © 2014 by Andrey Tolstoy.

Yale University Press books may be purchased in quantity for educational, business, or
promotional use. For information, please e-mail sales.press@yale.edu (U.S. office) or
sales@yaleup.co.uk (U.K. office).

Designed by Mary Valencia.
Set in Adobe Caslon type by Westchester Book Group,
Danbury, Connecticut.

Library of Congress Cataloging-in-Publication Data
The Kreutzer Sonata variations : Lev Tolstoy's Novella and counterstories by Sofiya Tolstaya
and Lev Lvovich Tolstoy / translated and edited by Michael R. Katz ; with a foreword
by Ekaterina Tolstaya and an afterword by Andrey Tolstoy.
pages cm
Includes bibliographical references.
ISBN 978-0-300-18994-0 (cloth : alk. paper)
1. Tolstoy, Leo, graf, 1828–1910. Kreitserova sonata. I. Katz, Michael R., translator, editor.
II. Tolstaia, Ekaterina, 1972–, writer of preface. III. Tolstoy, Andrey, writer of added
commentary. IV. Tolstoy, Leo, graf, 1828–1910. Kreitserova sonata. English. 2014.
V. Tolstaia, S. A. (Sof'ia Andreevna), 1844–1919. Ch'ia vina? English. VI. Tolstaia,
S. A. (Sof'ia Andreevna), 1844–1919. Pesnia bez slov. English. VII. Tolstoi, Lev L'vovich, graf,
1869–1945. Preliudiia Shopena. English. VIII. Tolstaia, S. A. (Sof'ia Andreevna), 1844–1919.
Moia zhizn? Selections. English. IX. Tolstoy, Alexandra, 1884–1979. Tolstoi. Selections.
English. X. Tolstoi, Lev L'vovich, graf, 1869–1945. Vérité sur mon pére. Selections. English.
PG3366.K7 2014
891.73'3—dc23
2013051138

A catalogue record for this book is available from the British Library.

Contents

CONTENTS

Foreword

EKATERINA TOLSTAYA

SOFIYA ANDREEVNA TOLSTAYA lived a grand, rich, and tragic life—but a happy life as well.

Lev Nikolaevich Tolstoy and Sonya Behrs were married in 1862. The two joined their fates: at age thirty-four, he was already a well-established man with considerable life experience and a well-known writer; she was a young woman, age eighteen, dwelling in a world of girlish hopes and dreams, surrounded by boundless parental love in an atmosphere of friendship and support.

After their marriage the young couple settled on Lev's estate at Yasnaya Polyana, which became the primary location of their family life for the remainder of their lives. The young Sofiya Andreevna found life at the estate unfamiliar, but her love for her husband and his encouragement helped her become the genuine mistress of Yasnaya Polyana. She learned to take pleasure in everyday affairs, creating comfort and warm surroundings for her entire family.

Sofiya Andreevna was a splendid wife and mother. She experienced both the happiness of motherhood and its deep tragedy: five of her thirteen children died in childhood. She assumed responsibility for the demanding everyday domestic work at Yasnaya Polyana. Lev Nikolaevich was an excitable man, often carried away with unusual domestic projects: breeding a particular species of Japanese pigs or Indian hens, for example, or planting a special variety of chicory; when he encountered difficulties or failure, he would just as suddenly abandon his latest scheme. Each day she had to serve her growing family the best and most nutritious food possible; she had to see to it that the soil was worked, that flowers, apple trees, and gardens were planted, and that the forest was cleared and renewed.

A feeling of family happiness reigned in the Tolstoy household; guests took great pleasure in their visits. At times as many as forty people gathered at the estate. Sofiya Andreevna carefully planned all the details to receive them and provide for their needs. Documents surviving in the archive show the importance she attached to domestic life. It was Sofiya Andreevna who brought to life the traditions that united them, made them—children, friends, relatives, and grandchildren alike—strive to maintain the family seat for the future. Like her husband, she devoted her life to serving other people, her friends and family, who were in need of her caring and her warmth.

Sofiya Andreevna also helped her husband in his literary work. Able to decipher his handwriting extremely well, she copied his manuscripts and prepared them for publication. Tolstoy worked on his novel *War and Peace* for seven years, rewriting it and making many corrections; Sofiya Andreevna recopied the epic work several times. She served as the prototype for many of Lev Nikolaevich's characters. She took on numerous tasks and was successful in all of them. The Russian poet Afanasy Fet, a great friend of the Tolstoy family, described her as "industrious as a honeybee."

Sofiya was imbued with many talents. She could draw exceedingly well; she was a fine musician; she left the world hundreds of unique and original photographs; she had a fine appreciation for words, and she herself was a writer. During her lifetime she published a collection of children's stories called *The Skeleton-Dolls* (1910); in recent years a volume of her memoirs, *My Life,* and two novellas, *Whose Fault?* and *Song Without Words,* have appeared in print. In these works Sofiya Andreevna demonstrates both talent as a writer and genuine humanity, revealing to the reader her soul and her life experience. At last we can comprehend the life and tragedy of her family as seen through her eyes.

Let scholars continue to debate whether Sofiya Andreevna was the great Lev Tolstoy's "evil genius." She was undoubtedly the worthy companion of his life, a faithful wife, the loving mother of his children, and the affectionate grandmother of his many grandchildren. Almost one hundred years have passed since Sofiya Andreevna's death, and today a large family of Tolstoys lives all over the world, including some in Russia and even at Yasnaya Polyana. And that is her most important and lasting legacy.

Acknowledgments

I WISH TO ACKNOWLEDGE the unstinting support and advice during work on the various phases of this project from my dear friend and distinguished colleague Stephen Donadio, Fulton Professor of Humanities at Middlebury College and editor of the *New England Review;* Aleksandra Baker, Lecturer Emerita in Russian at Middlebury, who meticulously checked my translations; Galina Alexeeva at the Museum-Estate of Lev Tolstoy in Yasnaya Polyana and Natalya Kalinina at the Tolstoy State Museum in Moscow; Vadim Staklo, Eric Brandt, Erica Hanson, and Dan Heaton at Yale University Press; my two readers, especially Hugh McLean, Professor Emeritus at the University of California at Berkeley; Edwina Cruise, Professor Emerita at Mount Holyoke College; the Mellon Foundation for its generous funding of my research through the Emeritus Fellowship Program; Middlebury College for its valuable support of my postretirement career; and finally my spouse, Mary Dodge, who heard, read, revised, argued, disagreed, approved, and encouraged, as only a lifelong partner can do.

To avoid confusion I have standardized the spelling of Russian names throughout.

Introduction: *The Tolstoy Family Story Contest*

MICHAEL R. KATZ

> I never expected that my train of thought would lead me where it
> did. I was horrified at my own conclusions, wanted not to believe
> them, but it was impossible not to.
> —L. N. TOLSTOY, on *The Kreutzer Sonata*

> You have not written anything stronger than
> this work, nor anything darker.
> —N. N. STRAKHOV to Tolstoy, on *The Kreutzer Sonata*

LEV TOLSTOY'S CONTROVERSIAL NOVELLA *The Kreutzer Sonata* (1889) is a
fictional narrative that takes the form of a heartrending confession by a
conscience-stricken Russian aristocrat. Years earlier the hero Pozdnyshev
had married a much younger woman, partly to satisfy his intense physical
desires; over time he becomes pathologically jealous of her relationship—not
physical, but deeply emotional—with a musician. In a fit of fanatical rage
Pozdnyshev murders his wife, and he is subsequently condemned to recite a
brutally frank account of his crime to any interested listener. In Tolstoy's telling of the tale, the reader is the captive listener, figured as a fellow railway
passenger addressed by Pozdnyshev on an all-night journey.

Publication of Tolstoy's scandalous work was initially prohibited by the
Russian censors. The tale was read aloud to a group of Petersburg intellectu-
als at the house of Tolstoy's own sister-in-law.[1] The following day it was
shared at a major publishing house, where it was decided to divide the manuscript into sections and copy it by hand. Soon more than three hundred copies
of the story were circulating in the capital. *The Kreutzer Sonata* was finally

---

1. This gathering was depicted by the Russian realist painter Grigory Myasoyedov; the
original (1893) hangs in the Institute of Russian Literature (Pushkin House) in Saint
Petersburg.

published in volume 13 of the author's *Collected Works* (1891), but only after his devoted wife, Sofiya Andreevna Tolstaya, made a personal appeal to Tsar Alexander III to grant his permission. He announced his decision:

> Yes, as part of the collected works it can be permitted; not everybody can afford them; it won't be a matter of a large circulation.[2]

His Excellency was wrong. As we would say now, *The Kreutzer Sonata* went viral.

When it was translated into English, in 1890, the story was barred from general distribution in the United States. An assistant attorney general in the Post Office Department declared it to be of "indecent character."[3] Shortly afterward, peddlers in New York loaded pushcarts with copies of the work under signs reading SUPPRESSED, "conspicuously displayed to attract custom." The peddlers were arrested and brought before a judge, who read through the highlighted passages and declared that he found "nothing likely to affect public morals."[4] Later that year a vendor in Philadelphia was also indicted for selling an English translation of the tale. The presiding judge, however, declared that in his view, the work was "not obscene" and possessed "very little dramatic interest or literary merit":

> Count Tolstoi's "Kreutzer Sonata" may contain very absurd and foolish views about marriage. It may shock our ideas of the sanctity and nobility of that relation, but it cannot on that account be called obscene libel.

The judge concluded his opinion with a rhetorical flourish:

> The court was reminded . . . that the Czar of Russia and the Post Office officials of the United State have condemned this book as an unlawful publication. . . . Without disparaging in any degree the respect due to these high officials within their respective spheres, I can only say that neither of them has ever been recognized in this country as a binding authority in questions of law or literature.[5]

---

2. Peter Ulf Møller, *Postlude to "The Kreutzer Sonata": Tolstoj and the Debate on Sexual Morality in Russian Literature in the 1890s*, trans. John Kendal (Leiden: E. J. Brill, 1988), 75.

3. "Tolstoy's Tabooed Book," *New York Times*, August 2, 1890.

4. "'Kreutzer Sonata' in Court," *New York Times*, August 8, 1890.

5. "Count Tolstoi Not Obscene," *New York Times*, September 25, 1890. See also Dawn B. Silva, *Banned Books: Literature Suppressed on Sexual Grounds* (New York: Facts on File, 2006), 96–98.

This widespread unofficial circulation of Tolstoy's story, followed by its official publication, launched a spirited debate about the so-called "sexual question" in Russian culture during the last years of the nineteenth century and the first decade of the twentieth. The debate prompted an examination not only of sexuality itself but also of the meaning of love, the institution of marriage, the structure of the family, and conflicting views of adultery and fidelity. In his unsettling story, Tolstoy had given full voice to his cherished convictions on all these subjects, as well as on the topics of masturbation, contraception, prostitution, women's education, and the prevailing double standard of morality for men and women.

Moreover, *The Kreutzer Sonata* also provided insights into the author's exploration of his own sexual identity. The initial description of the musician-intruder Trukhachevsky is highly erotic and suggests that Pozdnyshev himself might have found him sexually attractive:

> He had almond-shaped, damp eyes, reddish smiling lips, a little waxed mustache, the latest, fashionable hairstyle, and a commonly pretty face . . . and he had particularly developed buttocks, like a woman's, or as Hottentots are said to possess.

Pozdnyshev's violent murder of his wife in the dramatic conclusion of the story is described in similarly suggestive sexual terms:

> I knew that I was stabbing her below the ribs and that the dagger would penetrate. . . . I heard and recall the momentary resistance of her corset and of something else, then the penetration of the knife into something soft.

By the end of the tale, and stated explicitly in the author's dogmatic "Epilogue to *The Kreutzer Sonata*," Tolstoy reached the remarkable conclusion that the only acceptable alternative to man's powerful sexual drive was total abstinence and uncompromising chastity.

From the moment of its initial publication in Russian and speedy translation into English and other European languages, the story attracted an enormous amount of critical attention, including lavish praise as well as fierce condemnation. As early as 1890, in a lengthy interview published in an American newspaper, the preeminent French writer Émile Zola was quoted as saying that Tolstoy was "a compound of a monk of the Middle Ages and a modern Slav" who had stolen his best ideas from French authors. *The Kreutzer Sonata*, Zola argued, was a "nightmare . . . born of a diseased imagination," which proved beyond any doubt that "its author is cracked" (*il y a une petite fêlure dans sa tête*).[6] The controversy has still not abated: well over a hundred years later a respected British Slavist in a recent biography of Tolstoy characterized the work as a "shrill indictment of human sexuality":

> Pozdnyshev's lunatic diatribe goes on for twenty-eight senseless chapters. . . . This piece is tedious, unsubtle, unrealistic and anti-human. . . . A work of absurdity, insulting to the intelligence and artistically inept, *The Kreutzer Sonata* is among the worst things ever to come from Tolstoy's pen, and it deserves nothing more than oblivion.[7]

Other modern critics have added significantly to our understanding of this complex novella. In first place is the extraordinary book by the Danish scholar Peter Ulf Møller, *Postlude to "The Kreutzer Sonata": Tolstoj and the Debate on Sexual Morality in Russian Literature in the 1890s.* Møller analyzes the tale and discusses the history of its publication, the controversy it aroused, the public debate in Russia, and the literary responses it inspired. Møller's work is without doubt the starting point for anyone interested in the subject and its range of implications, and I am deeply indebted to his scholarship.

As anyone pursuing the questions raised by the work would soon discover, the number of articles focused on *The Kreutzer Sonata* is immense. I cite here only a few of the sources I consider to be among the most stimulating and original. Richard Gustafson calls attention to Pozdnyshev's powerful state of intoxication, a combined result of the tobacco he smokes, the strong tea he drinks, and the hypnotic motion of the train as he narrates his tragic tale; Rosamund Bartlett discusses the enormous impact of the work of Dr. Alice Bunker Stockham (1833–1912), an American obstetrician and gynecologist, whose principal work, *Tokology: A Book for Every Woman* (1886), influenced Tolstoy's thinking about sexuality and the role of women; Lawrence Kramer makes a credible connection between Pozdnyshev and Coleridge's "Rime of the Ancient Mariner" (1798):

> Remorse over the murder has transformed him into an uncanny figure. He has become a charismatic stranger on a train, Coleridge's Ancient Mariner as a chain-smoking modern neurotic, complete with verbal tic, a strange tale to tell, and glittering eyes that rivet the listener-victim to the telling.

6. *New York Herald*, August 24, 1890.
7. Anthony Briggs, *Brief Lives: Leo Tolstoy* (London: Hesperus, 2010), 85–86.

Ruth Rischin explores the symbolic significance of Beethoven's *Kreutzer Sonata* in the tale, as well as Tolstoy's general opinion concerning the risks involved in listening to classical music. Ronald LeBlanc, in his study *Slavic Sins of the Flesh*, makes explicit the libidinous connections between food and sexual appetite in both the story and the "Epilogue." He points out that when Pozdnyshev returns from his business trip, he catches his wife and the musician in flagrante delicto: not engaged in sexual intercourse, but finishing a romantic supper.[8]

Tolstoy's wife of almost fifty years, Sofiya (Sonya) Andreevna Tolstaya (née Behrs) (1844–1919), repeatedly and laboriously copied her husband's story each time he made revisions to satisfy the Russian censors. She also pleaded with him to modify the character of the heroine. In the earliest versions of his tale, there was no doubt whatever about her infidelity, but Sonya wanted Tolstoy to make the wife innocent of any wrongdoing. The author came around to yielding to her wishes, but some readers at the time—and some even now—remain convinced of her guilt.

Sonya wrote extensively about *The Kreutzer Sonata* in her own letters and diary, and in her voluminous autobiography (*My Life*). She disagreed markedly with Tolstoy's emphases and conclusions at almost every turn; moreover, she was deeply embarrassed that the reading public had construed the story as a reflection of her own marriage to the famous writer.

But in a most extraordinary and intriguing twist of events, in an effort to work out a response to her husband's story, Sonya turned to writing fiction herself. She composed her own original literary challenge to *The Kreutzer Sonata* in a text that remained almost unknown until quite recently. For more than one hundred years Sofiya Andreevna Tolstaya's novella, in accord with her family's wishes, had been concealed in her archive at the writer's country estate in Yasnaya Polyana. In 1994 it was finally published in a Russian journal,

---

8. Richard Gustafson, *Leo Tolstoy: Resident and Stranger* (Princeton, N.J.: Princeton University Press, 1989), 352–55; Rosamund Bartlett, *Tolstoy: A Russian Life* (New York: Houghton Mifflin Harcourt, 2011), 324–33; Lawrence Kramer, "Tolstoy's Beethoven, Beethoven's Tolstoy: The *Kreutzer Sonata*," *Critical Musicology and the Responsibility of Response: Selected Essays* (Aldershot, England: Ashgate, 2006), 145–61; Ruth Rischin, "Allegro Tumultuosissimamente: Beethoven in Tolstoy's Fiction," *In the Shade of the Giant: Essays on Tolstoy*, ed. Hugh McLean (Berkeley: University of California Press, 1989), 12–60; Ronald D. LeBlanc, *Slavic Sins of the Flesh: Food, Sex, and Carnal Appetite in Nineteenth-Century Russian Fiction* (Hanover: University of New Hampshire Press, 2009), 134–38.

but little notice of it was taken at the time. It was republished in 2010 in a splendid edition with a print run limited to one thousand copies, edited by the former director of the State Tolstoy Museum, where it appeared along with the text of *The Kreutzer Sonata*, as well as another of Sonya's stories (about which more presently), and one by their son Lev Lvovich Tolstoy.[9]

Entitled *Whose Fault? Apropos of "The Kreutzer Sonata,"* Sonya's "counterstory" was written in black-and-white school notebooks (purchased in the closest town, Tula) sometime during the period 1891–94. In it Sonya expressed her profound disagreement with her illustrious husband's long-held ideas about the nature of women, the institution of marriage, and the causes of adultery. Although she read and circulated the manuscript of her story among family members and close friends, she chose not to publish her work. Tolstoy himself refused to read anything his wife wrote. Their son Lev Lvovich heard his mother read the story aloud and wrote to caution her against publishing such a "badly written novella," for fear of tarnishing her reputation as a "faithful wife and mother." It was this view among the Tolstoy descendants that prevailed and was largely responsible for keeping the story concealed for a century.

Sonya's notebooks contain a curious collection of alternative titles for her story, all emphasizing the same theme of the husband's culpability and the wife's innocence:

"Is She Guilty?"
"Murdered"
"Long Since Murdered"
"Gradual Murder"
"How She Was Murdered"
"How Husbands Murder Their Wives"
"One More Murdered Woman [or Wife]"

Some of these rejected titles bear the subtitle "A Woman's Tale." The most explicit challenge to Tolstoy's literary authority comes in the margins of Sonya's notebooks. There she includes brief excerpts from her husband's original story, against which she polemicizes in her counterstory. These citations are essential to understanding the context of her own tale and the point-by-point refutation it articulates. I have included the Kreutzer passages in question in italicized footnotes to my translation, indicating precisely where Sonya's marginal notations were placed.

9. *Oktyabr'* 10 (1994), 6–59; *Kreitzerova sonata, Ch'ya vina?, Pesnya bez slov, Prelyudiya Shopena*, ed. V. B. Remizov (Moscow: State Tolstoy Museum, 2010).

The male characters in Sonya's story are based on real-life figures drawn from within the intimate Tolstoy family circle: Prince Prozorsky, whose name derives from the Russian word *prozorlivyi*, "perspicacious," is an egotist obsessed with writing, who fancies himself a great "philosopher," although his wife questions the originality of his thought. He is, moreover, depicted as having a voracious sexual appetite, not only with his wife as the object: his wandering eye never misses a pretty peasant lass. Prozorsky is almost certainly based on the man Sonya lived with, whose intellectual aspirations and personal foibles she knew all too well.

Placed in contrast to the prince is his old friend Bekhmetev, a quiet, unassuming "intruder," portrayed as an ideal man: he's capable of genuine friendship with a woman and eager to form a spiritual union with her. He possesses a range of artistic talents and demonstrates a sincere interest in the heroine's children. Physically weak and unattractive, during the course of the story he becomes increasingly ill. It is most likely that the character of Bekhmetev was modeled on Tolstoy's friend and chess partner Prince Leonid Urusov, the vice governor of Tula, the man who first introduced Sonya to the works of the Roman Stoics Seneca and Marcus Aurelius. Tolstoy became jealous of his friend's attentions to his wife and tried unsuccessfully to restrict his visits. Urusov succumbed to his serious ailments in 1885.[10]

Although Sofiya Andreevna chose not to publish her counterstory, in 1898 their son Lev Lvovich (1869–1945) wrote and published his own response to his father's *Kreutzer Sonata*. Entitled *Chopin's Prelude*, it was a well-intentioned but rather heavy-handed piece criticizing in no uncertain terms his father's most controversial pronouncements. In the end Lev Lvovich advocates early marriage as the only viable solution to the problem of male sexual drive. After reading her son's story, Sonya noted in her diary: "He does not have a large talent, but a small one, sincere and naïve." His father read his son's work, too, and his view was much less charitable: Tolstoy noted in his diary that his son's story was "stupid and untalented."

It has recently been established that Sofiya Andreevna wrote a second unpublished novella, also included in the 2010 edition in Russian. Entitled *Song Without Words* (1898), it explores the relationship of a talented composer and musician with members of the Tolstoy family. In fact, Sergei Taneev (1856–1915) had studied composition with Tchaikovsky and piano with Nikolai Rubenstein. During the summers of 1895–97 he visited Yasnaya Polyana; Sofiya Andreevna developed a deep attachment to him that evidently embarrassed

10. See Alexandra Popoff, *Sophia Tolstoy: A Biography* (New York: Free Press, 2010), 141–44.

her children and enraged her husband. Taneev himself, it seems, was more attracted to men than to women, and remained largely unaware of the nature and intensity of Sonya's affection.

The male characters in *Song Without Words* are not very well developed: the husband is depicted as a simple, down-to-earth man—in fact, so down-to-earth that he seems to spend all his free time digging in his beloved garden. As for the musician, he is a shadowy figure: a distracted egotist, preoccupied with his music, he is intent on preserving his equanimity, and is both flattered and bewildered by the heroine's attentions. She herself is the most intriguing character in the work: highly intellectual and deeply spiritual, Sasha is captivated by music, and quickly drawn to the talented composer who takes up residence in the neighboring dacha. His virtuoso musical performances, combined with his eccentric personality, supply her with new zest for life. In spite of her belief that art should remain pure, unspoiled by human passion, Sasha finds herself falling deeply in the love with the man who produces such marvelous sounds. In time, when the composer fails to respond positively to her amorous advances, the heroine gradually sinks into mental illness and in the end has herself committed to a clinic for the insane.

This story reveals a deep psychological understanding of and a profound sympathy for the plight of a woman suffering more and more extreme emotional distress: depression, obsessive-compulsive behaviors, and suicidal tendencies. It also describes in rich detail the world of a Moscow composer, and in particular the masculine milieu of a music conservatory; it hints suggestively at the unacknowledged relationships between teachers and students, calling attention to an element of strong homoerotic attraction. This was a taboo subject at the time, yet one of great personal importance to Sonya, given her long-held suspicions about her husband's sexual proclivities.

In these two fascinating counterstories, Sofiya Andreevna, wife of the renowned "great writer" Lev Tolstoy, was daring to elevate herself to the status of an author in her own right. Not only that: she presumed to disagree with his well-established views and to express in literary form her own ideas about male-female relationships, boldly challenging what remains her husband's most controversial achievement.

In so doing, Sonya was clearly participating in the late-nineteenth-century debate on women's rights. She was situating herself in relation to the leaders of that contemporary struggle, including the Nobel Prize–winning Norwegian writer Bjørnstjerne Bjørnson (1832–1910), whose play *The Gauntlet* (1883) had attacked the double standard of morality and asserted that before marriage men should be obliged to remain as chaste as women if they are determined to insist on retaining the stamp of social approval known as "respectability" for themselves. The equally provocative plays of another Norwegian, Henrik Ibsen, are of course still widely recognized as a highly influential forum in which these sexual issues and the status of women are openly discussed and debated.

Of the writings assembled here, three are centered on pieces of music, by three composers, Beethoven, Mendelssohn, and Chopin. In a brief article published in English during the 1950s, one of Tolstoy's daughters described the importance of music in the Tolstoy household and in the writer's life:

> There was always music in our house. . . . Our entire family was musical. . . . Father played the piano and even studied the theory of music when he was young, hoping to become a composer.[11]

Alexandra then quotes her father's views of the nature of music itself, both its power and its perils:

> "What is it?" he would say, "Why is it that a certain combination of sounds impresses you so much, stirs your emotions, sometimes brings out the best spiritual forces concealed in your soul? I can't explain it."

On the other hand, Tolstoy expresses his worries about the impact of music (and art) on man's desire:

> "And what has become of art and music? . . . It is devoted to excite, stimulate all kinds of sexual feelings. Think of all the filthy operas, operettas, songs, romances, which are thriving in our world, and involuntarily you come to the conclusion that contemporary art has one definite aim—spreading corruption as widely as possible."

Although the four stories that make up this collection resonate with larger cultural developments, they also resonate with one another. This unique combination of competing literary texts within one family seems to me unprecedented in world literature. Not only do these counterstories by Tolstoy's wife and son convey their deep disagreement with the "great man's" views, but they also passionately strive to undo the message of the original.[12]

11. Alexandra Tolstoy, "Tolstoy and Music," *Russian Review* 17 (October 1958), 258–62. The following two quotations also come from this article.

12. Perhaps only Zelda Fitzgerald's semiautobiographical account of her marriage to F. Scott Fitzgerald, *Save Me the Waltz* (1932), and Klaus Mann's short stories and novels exploring the difficult relationship with his father, Thomas Mann, can in some ways be compared.

In addition to the counterstories by Sofiya Andreevna and Lev Lvovich, translated, annotated, and presented here for the first time, the letters, diaries, notebooks, and memoirs of the Tolstoys contain provocative comments about their own works, about those of other family members, and speculations about the others' underlying motives. I include relevant excerpts from these texts, Lev's and Sofiya's, hoping to provide a comprehensive collection of contradictory views within this one family, as well as presenting the reader with a case study of the extraordinary power of ideas in Russian society.

Tolstoy's "Epilogue to *The Kreutzer Sonata*" was written as a nonfictional response to the many letters he received after the appearance of his tale. It was intended to clarify the main themes of the story, but succeeded only in inflaming the controversy that followed the novella's publication. In his retrospective reflections he summarizes his views on sexual morality by presenting five theses and providing practical instructions as to how a man can lead his life according to the ideals of Christianity—including, of course, the ideal of sexual abstinence. The "Epilogue" repeats and restates the arguments of the narrator, Pozdnyshev, but it adds one new provocation: since the Christian ideal with regard to sexual morality is absolute chastity, Tolstoy argues that the concept of a "Christian marriage" is an untenable self-contradiction, invented by the church to make sexual contact permissible and not sinful for Christians.[13] The "Epilogue" became Tolstoy's major contribution to the fierce debate on sexual morality that his dark tale had set in motion.

A disquieting fragment of an unfinished story from the late 1860s is also included here in its first translation into English. Entitled "The Wife Murderer," this tale was broken off, and Tolstoy never went back to it; he returned to the theme of a husband's insane jealousy and resulting uxoricide only years later, when he began writing *The Kreutzer Sonata*.

The last two documents are excerpts from memoirs by two of Tolstoy's children who survived him: Lev Lvovich, who wrote and published *Chopin's Prelude,* and Alexandra Lvovna (1884–1979). Lev Jr. was least like his father and most resembled his mother. As the first sickly child in the family, he was nurtured lovingly by his mother, who developed a lifelong attachment to him, and he repaid her with uncompromising loyalty. His memoir, *The Truth About My Father* (1924), can be read as a passionate defense of his mother. In stark contrast, Alexandra (Sasha) was, of all the Tolstoy children, the most alienated from their mother. She wrote two memoirs about her father, *The*

13. See Møller, *Postlude to "The Kreutzer Sonata,"* 181–87.

Tragedy of Tolstoy (1933) and *Tolstoy: A Life of My Father* (1953). Her adoration of him was so unqualified that she devoted her entire life (all ninety-five years of it) to his well-being while he was alive, and then to the service of his ideals, with the establishment of the Tolstoy Foundation in Valley Cottage, New York.

Excerpts from the memoirs of Tolstoy's children are followed by a selected bibliography of works in English by and about the two principals: Lev Niko-laevich Tolstoy and Sofiya Andreevna Tolstaya. The literature dealing with him is vast; works devoted to her are relatively few, but in the twenty-first century their number has increased and their value has improved significantly. Those readers who do not know Russian are invited to sample the sources available in English. They will be well rewarded, perhaps even inspired, as I was, with the longing to learn, in the words of the nineteenth-century novel-ist Ivan Turgenev, the "splendid . . . majestic" Russian language.

Part One

THE STORY AND COUNTERSTORIES

The Kreutzer Sonata

LEV NIKOLAEVICH TOLSTOY

But I say unto you, that whosoever looketh on a woman to lust
after her hath committed adultery with her already in his heart.

(MATTHEW 5:28)

His disciples say unto him, if the case of the man be so with his
wife, it is not good to marry. But he said unto them, all men
cannot receive this saying, save they to whom it is given. For
there are some eunuchs, which were so born from their mother's
womb: and there are some eunuchs, which were made eunuchs of
men: and there be eunuchs, which have made themselves
eunuchs for the kingdom of heaven's sake. He that is able to
receive it, let him receive it.

(MATTHEW 19:10–12)

I

IT WAS EARLY SPRING. We had been traveling for two days. Passengers
going short distances kept entering and leaving the train, but three people,
like myself, were going the whole way: an unattractive woman, a smoker, no
longer young, with a weary expression, wearing a mannish overcoat and cap;
her acquaintance, a talkative man about forty years old whose things were neat
and new; and a gentleman of medium height with brusque gestures who kept
to himself; he was not yet old, but his curly hair had obviously turned gray

prematurely and his unusually glittering eyes darted quickly from object to object. He was wearing an old overcoat made by an expensive tailor: it had an astrakhan collar and he wore a tall astrakhan hat.[1] Under his coat, when he unbuttoned it, he had on a tight-fitting jacket and an embroidered Russian shirt. Another peculiarity of this man consisted in the fact that from time to time he emitted strange sounds, similar to clearing his throat or to a laugh begun and then broken off.

During the entire journey, this gentleman assiduously avoided making the acquaintance of other passengers. In response to his neighbors' overtures at conversation, he replied curtly and abruptly, or else he read; or, staring out the window, after first taking out some food from his old bag, he smoked, or drank tea, or ate a snack.

He seemed oppressed by his loneliness; several times I wanted to engage him in conversation, but each time our eyes met, which happened frequently since we were sitting opposite each other, he turned away and either picked up his book or looked out the window.

Toward evening of the second day, when the train had stopped at a large station, this nervous gentleman went to fetch some hot water to make himself tea. The fellow with the neat new things, a lawyer, as I subsequently discovered, went to have tea in the station with his neighbor, the lady in the mannish overcoat, the smoker.

During the absence of the gentleman and the lady, several new passengers entered the car, including a tall, clean-shaven, wrinkled old man, obviously a merchant, wearing a coat of mink fur and a cloth cap with a large peak. He sat opposite the lady and the lawyer, and immediately entered into conversation with another young man, apparently a merchant's clerk, who had also boarded at this station.

I was sitting diagonally across from him and, since the train was standing still, during those moments when no one was passing through the car, I could overhear snatches of their conversation. The merchant first announced that he was traveling to his estate only one stop further; then, as usual, they began talking about prices and trade; they spoke, as always, about how business was in Moscow these days, and then started chatting about the trade fair in Nizhny Novgorod.[2] The clerk began telling a story about the drink-

---

1. Made from the tightly curled wool of very young lambs from Astrakhan, a city on the Volga.

2. A major urban center along the Volga River where an important trade fair was held every summer.

ing bouts of some wealthy merchant with whom they were both acquainted, but the old man didn't let him finish; instead, he began describing his own past binges at Kunavino.[3] Obviously he was proud of his participation and described with obvious delight how once, together with this same rich merchant, he had gotten drunk and played some prank that could be talked about only in a whisper; the clerk burst into laughter that filled the entire train car; then the old man started laughing, too, exposing two yellow teeth.

Not expecting to hear anything interesting, I stood up to walk along the platform until the train departed. At the door I met the lawyer and the lady, who were talking about something excitedly as they approached.

"You won't have time," the sociable lawyer said to me. "The second bell's about to ring."

And sure enough, hardly had I managed to reach the end of the train when the bell rang. When I returned, the lawyer and the lady were still engaged in lively conversation. The old merchant was sitting opposite, staring ahead sternly, from time to time chewing his lips in disapproval.

"Then she plainly informed her husband," the lawyer was saying with a smile just as I passed, "that she was both unable and unwilling to live with him, since . . ."

He continued, saying something else that I couldn't hear. Two more passengers came on after me; then the conductor went through, a porter rushed in, and there was so much noise that I couldn't make out their conversation. When everything had quieted down and I could hear the lawyer's voice again, the conversation, obviously, had moved on from a particular case to more general considerations.

The lawyer was saying that the question of divorce was now occupying public opinion in Europe and that similar cases were occurring more and more frequently in Russia. Having noticed that his voice was the only one audible, the lawyer stopped speaking and turned to the old man.

"Those things didn't happen in the old days, did they?" he said, smiling pleasantly.

The old man wanted to make some reply, but at that moment the train began moving and the old man took off his cap and started crossing himself, whispering a prayer. The lawyer looked away and waited politely. After finishing his prayers and crossing himself three times, the old man put his cap back on, pulled it down low, settled into his seat, and began speaking.

3. A small town north of Nizhny Novgorod.

"They did happen, sir, but less often," he said. "Nowadays it can't help from happening. People have become so educated."

The train, gaining speed, rattled over the rail joints; it became hard for me to hear, but I was interested, so I moved closer. My neighbor, the nervous man with glittering eyes, apparently also took an interest; without getting up from his place, he, too, began listening.

"What's wrong with education?" the lady asked with a slight smile. "Would it really be better to marry as in the old days, when the bride and groom had never seen each other?" she continued. She was replying, as is the habit of many women, not to her interlocutor's actual words, but to those she thought he would say. "They didn't know if they loved each other or could love each other; they married whoever happened along and suffered all their lives. Do you think that's better?" she asked, evidently addressing me and the lawyer primarily, least of all the old man with whom she was talking.

"People have become so educated," repeated the merchant, looking with contempt at the lady, leaving her question unanswered.

"It'd be interesting to know how you explain the connection between education and marital discord," the lawyer said with a slight smile.

The merchant wanted to say something, but the lady interrupted him.

"No, those days have passed," she said. But the lawyer stopped her.

"No, allow him to express his thought."

"Foolishness results from education," the old man replied authoritatively.

"Marriages are arranged between people who don't love one another, and then everyone's surprised when they don't get along," the lady hastened to add, looking at the lawyer and at me, and even at the clerk, who rose from his place. Leaning against the seat, he was listening to the conversation with a smile. "It's only animals that can be paired up as the owner wishes; people have their own inclinations and attachments," she said, obviously wishing to irritate the merchant.

"There's no reason to talk like that, madam," said the old man. "Animals are beasts, but man has been given law."

"But how can one live with a man when there's no love?" the lady hastened to express her views, which she probably thought were original.

"People used not to talk about such things," the old man said in an emphatic tone of voice. "That only happens nowadays. Something occurs and right away the wife says, 'I'm leaving you.' This fashion's caught on even among our peasants. 'Here,' she says, 'take your shirts and trousers. I'm running away with Vanka. His hair's curlier than yours.' What can you say? The first thing a woman should have is fear."[4]

The clerk glanced at the lawyer, the lady, and at me, obviously suppressing a smile, prepared to deride or approve the merchant's words, depending on how they were received.

"What sort of fear?" the lady asked.

"Why this: she should fear her hus-s-s-band! That sort of fear."

"Well, my dear man, that time has passed," the lady said with a measure of anger.

"No, madam, that time cannot pass. Just as Eve, a woman, was created from man's rib, so she'll remain until the end of time," said the old man, tossing his head so sternly and triumphantly that the clerk immediately concluded that victory belonged to the merchant and he laughed loudly.

"That's the way you men think," the lady said, refusing to yield and glancing at us. "You've given yourselves freedom, but you want to lock women away in a tower. Then I suppose you'll permit yourselves everything."

"No one has to grant permission; it's just that a man doesn't bring any offspring home after his exploits, while a woman is a frail vessel," the merchant continued to insist.

His impressive tone, obviously, vanquished his listeners; even the lady felt crushed, but still didn't give up.

"Yes, but I think you'll agree that a woman is a person and has feelings just like a man. So what should she do if she doesn't love her husband?"

"Doesn't love him!" the merchant repeated loudly, knitting his brows and pursing his lips. "She'll love him, she will!"

The clerk in particular liked this unexpected opinion and produced a sound of approval.

"Oh, no, she won't," said the lady. "And if there's no love, it can't possibly be forced."

"Well, and what if a wife betrays her husband, then what?" asked the lawyer.

"That's not supposed to happen," said the old man. "You have to be on the lookout."

"And if it does, then what? You know, it happens."

---

4. Tolstoy uses the Russian word *strakh* (fear, terror, awe). Saint Paul, in the Epistle to the Ephesians, which is read at Orthodox marriage services, urges that "the wife fear (*boitsya*) her husband" (5:33). The King James Bible has: "see that she reverence her husband."

"It happens to some, but not people like us," said the old man.

Everyone fell silent. The clerk stirred, moved even closer, and, apparently not wishing to be left behind, said with a smile:

"Yes, sir, there was quite a scandal with one of our young men. It's also very hard to resolve. It involved a loose woman. She began acting like a devil. The young husband was steady and mature. At first she went after an office clerk. The husband tried kindness. She wouldn't stop. She did all sorts of nasty things. She began stealing his money. And he beat her. But she just got worse. She even carried on with an unbaptized Jew, if I may say so. Well, what could he do? So he threw her out. Now he lives like a bachelor while she walks the streets."

"Because he's a fool," said the old man. "If he'd given her less leeway right from the start, if he'd disciplined her as he should've, she'd still be with him, she would. You can't give 'em freedom at the outset. 'Don't trust your horse in the field or your wife in the house.'"

Just then the conductor came in to collect tickets for the next station. The old man handed his over.

"Yes, sir, you have to rein in the female sex, or else all's lost."

"Well, weren't you just saying how married men misbehave at the fair in Kunavino?" I asked, unable to restrain myself.

"That's a different story," said the merchant and sank into silence.

When the whistle sounded, the merchant stood up, took his sack from under the seat, buttoned his coat, doffed his cap, and left the carriage.

2

As soon as the old man left, several voices rose in conversation.

"A papa right out of the Old Testament," said the clerk.

"He's a walking Domostroi," said the lady.[5] "What a strange idea he has of women and marriage!"

"Yes, indeed. We Russians are far from sharing the European view of marriage," said the lawyer.

"The main thing that such people don't understand," said the lady, "is that marriage without love isn't really marriage, that only love sanctifies marriage, and the only true marriage is one sanctified by love."

The clerk listened and smiled, wishing to commit to memory for future use as much as he could from this clever conversation.

---

5. The Domostroi was a sixteenth-century Russian set of household rules based on very conservative principles.

In the midst of the lady's remarks we heard behind me something like the sound of broken laughter or sobbing; turning around, we saw my neighbor, the lonely gray-haired man with glittering eyes, who, during the conversation, which obviously interested him, had moved closer to us unnoticed. He stood, resting his arms on the back of the seat, evidently in great agitation: his face was flushed and one of his cheek muscles was twitching.

"What kind of love . . . love . . . love . . . sanctifies marriage?" he asked, stammering.

Seeing the agitated state of her interlocutor, the lady tried to respond as gently and fully as possible.

"True love. . . . Only if this love is present between a man and a woman, is marriage possible," said the lady.

"Yes, ma'am, but what do you mean by true love?" asked the man with glittering eyes, timidly and with an awkward smile.

"Everyone knows what love is," said the lady, obviously wishing to end the conversation with him.

"But I don't," said the gentleman. "You must define what you mean . . ."

"What? It's very simple," said the lady, but stopped to think. "Love? Love is the exclusive preference for one man or one woman over everyone else," she said.

"Preference for how long? A month? Two days? Half an hour?" asked the gray-haired man and then laughed.

"No, excuse me. You're obviously talking about something else."

"No, ma'am, I'm talking about the same thing."

"She means," the lawyer intervened, pointing to the lady, "that marriage must follow, in the first place, from attachment, or love, if you like, and if that exists, then only in that case does marriage constitute something sacred, so to speak. Thus any marriage lacking in this natural attachment—love, if you like—has nothing morally obligatory about it. Do I understand you correctly?" he asked, turning to the lady.

The lady indicated her approval of this explanation of her view with a nod of her head.

"Thereafter," continued the lawyer, but the nervous gentleman with eyes now burning as if on fire, obviously restraining himself with difficulty, didn't let him finish, and began again:

"No, I'm talking about that same preference of one man or one woman over everyone else, but I only ask: preference for how long?"

"How long? For a long time, sometimes one's whole life," said the lady, shrugging her shoulders.

"That only happens in novels, never in real life. In life this preference for one person over everyone else can last a year, which is very rare, more often only months, or even weeks, days, hours," he said, obviously knowing that he'd astonish everyone with his opinion and feeling pleased by that fact.

"What are you saying? No. Excuse me," all three replied in one voice. Even the clerk emitted some sound of disapproval.

"Yes, ma'am, I know," the gray-haired man outshouted us, "you're talking about how things are supposed to be, while I'm talking about how things really are. Every man experiences what you call love for every single beautiful woman."

"Oh, what you're saying is awful; isn't there among people a feeling called love that lasts not just for months or years, but for one's entire life?"

"No, not at all. Even if we grant that a man prefers a certain woman for his entire life, then the woman, in all likelihood, will come to prefer another man; that's how it's always been on earth and how it really is," he said. He reached for his cigarette case and began to light up.

"But it may be mutual," said the lawyer.

"No, sir, it can't be," he objected, "just as in a cartload of peas two identically marked peas can't possibly lie next to one another. Besides, not only is it a matter of improbability, but also most likely a question of satiety. To love one woman or one man for one's entire life—is the same as saying that one candle will last a whole lifetime," he said, inhaling the smoke greedily.

"But you're talking only about physical love. Don't you grant the possibility of love based on the identity of ideals, on spiritual affinity?" asked the lady.

"Spiritual affinity! The identity of ideals!" he repeated, emitting his sound. "In that case there's no reason to sleep together (excuse my rudeness). Or is it that people go to bed together as a result of this spiritual affinity?" he asked and laughed nervously.

"Allow me," said the lawyer. "Facts contradict what you're saying. We see that matrimony does exist, that all people, or the majority of them, live in wedlock, and many of them live a long married life honorably."

The gray-haired man laughed again.

"First you say that marriage is based on love, while I express doubt in the existence of love other than sensual; then you prove the existence of love by the fact that marriages exist. Marriage these days is pure deception."

"No, sir, allow me," said the lawyer. "I'm merely saying that marriages have existed and do exist."

"They do exist. But why do they? They have existed and do exist among those people who see something mysterious in marriage, a sacrament that binds them before God. Among some people marriages exist, but not among us. Here people get married without seeing anything in it other than copulation, and the result is either deception or coercion. If it's deception, then it's easier to bear. The husband and wife merely deceive people that they're in a monogamous relationship, while both engage in polygamy. It's vile, but it still works; but when, as happens most often, the husband and wife have accepted the external obligation to live together for their whole life, and have come to hate each other by the second month, and wish to divorce, but still live together, then this results in that terrible hell when people drink themselves to death, shoot themselves, kill, or poison themselves or the other person," he said, speaking faster and faster, without allowing anyone to insert a word, and getting more and more excited. Everyone was silent. It was very awkward.

"Yes, undoubtedly critical episodes occur in married life," said the lawyer, wishing to end this shockingly heated conversation.

"I see that you've discovered who I am," the gray-haired gentleman observed quietly, with apparent serenity.

"No, I haven't had the pleasure."

"It's no great pleasure. I'm Pozdnyshev, the one to whom that critical episode occurred to which you're referring, that episode in which a man killed his wife," he said, glancing quickly at each one of us.[6]

No one knew what to say and everyone remained silent.

"Well, never mind," he said, emitting his sound. "However, pardon me! Ah . . . I don't want to intrude."

"No, no, please," said the lawyer, not knowing himself what the "please" meant.

But Pozdnyshev, not listening to him, quickly turned aside and returned to his seat. The gentleman and the lady began whispering. I sat down next to Pozdnyshev and remained silent, unable to think of anything to say. It was too dark to read, so I closed my eyes and pretended that I wanted to snooze. We traveled in silence to the next station.

There the gentleman and the lady moved into another car, having arranged it with the conductor. The clerk made himself comfortable on the bench and fell asleep. Pozdnyshev kept smoking and drinking the tea he'd made himself at the last station.

When I opened my eyes and glanced at him, he suddenly addressed me resolutely and with irritation:

6. The surname Pozdnyshev comes from the Russian word *pozdno*, meaning "late."

"Perhaps you find it unpleasant to sit with me, now that you know who I am? If so, I'll leave."

"Oh, no, please."

"Well then, would you like some tea? It's very strong." He poured me a glass.

"They talk. . . . And they always tell lies . . ." he said.

"What are you talking about?" I asked.

"Always about the same thing: this love of theirs and what it is. Do you want to sleep?"

"Not at all."

"If you like, I'll tell you how that love led to what happened to me."

"Yes, if it's not too painful for you."

"No, it's more painful to keep silent.[7] Drink some tea. Or is it too strong?"

The tea was really more like beer, but I drank a glass. Just then the conductor came through. Pozdnyshev followed him with his angry eyes and began speaking only once he'd gone.

3

"Well, then I'll tell you. . . . You really want me to?"

I repeated that I very much wanted him to. He was silent, rubbed his face with his hands, and began speaking:

"If I'm going to tell you, then I must begin at the very beginning, how and why I got married, and what I was like before then.

"Until my marriage I lived like everyone else, that is, those of our circle. I'm a landowner, a university graduate, and a marshal of the nobility.[8] Until my marriage I lived like everyone else, that is, in depravity; and, like everyone of our circle living a depraved life, I was certain that I was living just as I should. I thought of myself as a charming fellow and a completely moral man. I was not a seducer, had no unnatural appetites, and didn't make depravity the main goal of life, as many of my peers did; I practiced it moderately, decently, for my own health. I avoided those women who could burden me by giving birth to a child or becoming attached to me. However, there may well have been both children and attachments, but I acted as if there weren't. And I not only considered that moral: I was proud of it."

He paused and emitted his sound as he always did when some new idea occurred to him.

---

7. Cf. Coleridge's "Rime of the Ancient Mariner": "Since then, at an uncertain hour, / That agony returns: / And till my ghastly tale is told, / This heart within me burns."

8. A noble elected to manage the affairs and represent the interests of the gentry.

"And there lies the central abomination," he exclaimed. "Depravity doesn't reside in anything physical; no physical outrage constitutes depravity. Depravity, genuine depravity, consists precisely in freeing yourself from any moral relations to a woman with whom you've engaged in physical intimacy. And I gave myself credit for this freedom. I remember how upset I was when I didn't succeed in paying a woman who'd given herself to me after probably falling in love with me. I calmed down only after I'd sent her some money, having shown her that I didn't consider myself morally obligated to her in any way. Don't nod as if you agree with me," he suddenly shouted at me. "I know what you're doing. All of you, and you, too, in the best case, if you're not the rare exception, you hold the same views as I used to. Well, never mind, forgive me," he continued. "The point is, it's terrible, terrible, terrible!"

"What's terrible?" I asked.

"That abyss of delusion we live in concerning women and our relations to them. Yes, sir, I can't talk about it calmly, not because this 'episode,' as that fellow put it, happened to me, but because since this episode occurred, my eyes have been opened and I've come to see everything in a different light. Everything's upside down, upside down!"

He lit a cigarette; resting his elbows on his knees, he continued speaking.

I couldn't see his face in the darkness; but above the rattling of the train, I could hear only his impressive and pleasant voice.

4

"Yes, sir, only after suffering what I've suffered, only thanks to that did I realize where the root of the whole matter lies; I understood what's supposed to be and therefore, I perceive all the horror of what really is.

"So, now hear how and when everything began that led to my 'episode.' It all started when I was not quite sixteen. I was still a student in secondary school, and my older brother was a university student in his first year. I'd not yet known any women, but like all unfortunate children of our circle, I'd already lost my innocence: other boys had corrupted me two years earlier. By that time women, not any one in particular, but women as something sweet, women, every woman, their nudity tormented me. My periods of solitude were impure. I was tormented just as ninety-nine percent of our boys are. I was horrified, I suffered, I prayed, and I fell. I was already corrupted in my imagination and in reality, but I still hadn't taken the last step. I was languishing alone, but had yet to lay hands on another human being. Then my brother's comrade, a student, a lively fellow, a so-called nice lad—that is, the worst sort of scoundrel—after teaching us how to drink and play cards, persuaded us after a binge to go there.[9] We went. My brother was also still innocent, and that night he, too, fell. And I, a fifteen-year-old boy, defiled myself and took part in defiling a woman, without really understanding what I was do-ing. I'd never heard from any of my elders that what I was doing was wrong. Nor will anyone hear that now. True, it's in the Commandments, but the Commandments are necessary only for answering the priest's examination, and even then, not really, not nearly as necessary as the commandment for using the Latin conjunction *ut* in conditional sentences.

"So I never heard from those elders whose opinions I respected that it was a bad thing. On the contrary, I heard from those I respected that it was a good thing. I heard that my struggles and suffering would be eased after-ward; I heard it and read it; I heard from older people that it would be good for my health; from my comrades I heard that there was some merit in it, some daring. So, in general, I could see nothing but good in it. The danger of diseases? Even that was foreseen. The solicitous government was taking care of that. It oversees the correct operation of houses of ill repute and ensures depravity for its schoolboys. And doctors receive a salary to supervise it. It's all just as it should be. They maintain that depravity is good for one's health, so they organize proper, efficient depravity. I know mothers who worry about their son's health on this count. Medical science also sends them to brothels."

"Why science?" I asked.

"Well, what are doctors? They're the high priests of science. Who is it that depraves young men by telling them it's necessary for their health? They do. And then they treat syphilis with tremendous self-importance."

"Why shouldn't they treat syphilis?"

"Because if only one percent of the efforts directed at curing syphilis were directed at the eradication of debauchery, there would long since have been no trace of the disease left. Yet those efforts are directed not at the eradica-tion of syphilis but at encouraging it and guaranteeing the safety of debauch-ery. Still, that's not the point. The point is that with me, as with ninety percent, if not more, not only of our class but all classes, even the peasants, the terrible thing is that I fell not because I succumbed to the natural tempta-tion of a particular woman's charms. No, no single woman tempted me; I fell because people in my milieu regarded a fall as a most legitimate and salutary act for the sake of one's health, while others saw it as a most natural, not only excusable, but even innocent amusement for a young man. I didn't even under-stand that it was a fall; I simply began to indulge in those half-pleasures and

9. That is, to a brothel.

half-needs suggested to me as appropriate for my age. I indulged in debauchery just as I began to drink and smoke. Still there was something particular
and poignant in my first fall. I remember how at that moment, in that very
place, before I'd even left the room, I felt sad, so sad that I wanted to cry, to
cry about the loss of my innocence, about my relationship to women that had
been destroyed forever. Yes, sir, a natural, simple relationship to women had
been destroyed forever. Since then I've not had and could never have a pure
relationship with a woman. I became what's known as a fornicator. To be a
fornicator is a physical condition, similar to that of a morphine addict, a
drunkard, or a smoker. Just as a morphine addict, a drunkard, or a smoker is
no longer a normal person, a man who's known several women for his own
pleasure is also not a normal man, but one who's been spoiled forever—
a fornicator. Just as one can recognize a drunkard or a drug addict immediately by his face or his manner, so it is with a fornicator. A fornicator can
restrain himself or he can struggle; but he'll never have simple, clear, pure relations with a woman, brotherly relations. You can recognize a fornicator at
once just by the way he observes and examines a young woman. And I became
a fornicator and have remained one, and that's what brought me to ruin."

5

"Yes, sir, that's how it was. And it got worse and worse. There were all sorts
of aberrations. My God! I'm horrified when I recall all my filthy acts in that
regard! That's how I remember myself, a person mocked by my comrades for
my so-called innocence. You hear so much about gilded youth, officers, or Parisians! When all these gentlemen, and me, too, we thirty-year-old debauchers, with hundreds of the most diverse and horrible crimes against women on
our souls, when we, we thirty-year-old debauchers, are scrubbed clean, closely
shaven, perfumed, when we enter a drawing room or go to a ball wearing
clean linen, evening dress, or a uniform—then we're seen as the emblem of
purity—how charming!

"Just think about how things should be and how they really are. It should
be that when such a gentleman approaches my sister or my daughter in society, I, knowing his life, should go up to him, call him aside, and say to
him quietly: 'My dear fellow, I know how you've been living, how you
spend your nights, and with whom. This is no place for you. These young
women are pure and innocent. Go away!' That's what should happen; but
what really happens is that when such a gentleman appears and dances with
my sister or my daughter, embracing her, we rejoice if he's wealthy and
well connected. Maybe after sleeping with Rigulboche, he'll honor my

daughter.[10] Even if he has symptoms or some disease—no matter. Nowadays there's a cure. Why, I know parents of several young women in high society who've enthusiastically given their daughters away in marriage to men suffering from syphilis. Oh, how disgusting! May there come a time when this outrage and deception will be exposed!"

He emitted his strange sound several times and drank some tea. The tea was terribly strong and there was no water to dilute it. I felt especially stimulated by the two glasses I'd had. The tea must also have had an effect on him because he'd become more and more excited. His voice became more melodious and expressive. He kept shifting his position, first taking off his hat, then putting it on again, and his face kept changing in the semidarkness in which we were sitting.

"Well, that's how I lived until I was thirty, never for a moment abandoning my intention to marry and establish the most sublime and pure family life. With that goal in mind I inspected every suitable young woman," he continued. "I wallowed in the filth of debauchery, while scrutinizing young women pure enough to be worthy of me. I rejected many of them precisely because they weren't pure enough; at last I found one I considered worthy. She was one of two daughters of a landowner from the Penza province who'd once been very wealthy, but who'd fallen on hard times.[11]

"One evening, after we'd gone for a boat ride and were returning late at night in the moonlight, I was sitting next to her, admiring her shapely figure, her tight-fitting sweater, and her curls; I suddenly decided that she was the one. That evening it seemed to me that she understood everything, everything that I was feeling and thinking, and that I was feeling and thinking the most sublime things. In fact, it was only that her sweater suited her so well, as did her curls, and after a day spent so close to her, I wanted to get even closer.

"The astonishing thing is how complete is the illusion that beauty equals goodness. A beautiful woman says stupid things: you listen and don't see the stupidity, only the cleverness. She says and does nasty things: you see only nice things. When she doesn't say anything stupid or nasty, and is a beautiful woman, you immediately convince yourself that she's a jewel of intelligence and virtue.

"I returned home in ecstasy and decided that she was the height of moral perfection and therefore worthy of being my wife; I proposed to her the next day.

10. Rigulboche was the stage name of Marguerite Bodel, a French dancer and cabaret singer who was popular in nineteenth-century Paris.

11. The Penza province is an area about four hundred miles southeast of Moscow.

"What a mess it is! Of a thousand married men not only in our class, but unfortunately, even among the peasants, there's hardly one who hasn't been 'married' ten times, even a hundred, or a thousand times before his marriage, like Don Juan. (True, I've heard and seen that now there are pure young people who feel and know that purity is no joke, but is a great accomplishment. God help them!) Everyone knows this, yet pretends not to know. In all novels the heroes' feelings are described in detail, as well as the ponds and bushes they stroll past; but in describing their great love for some young woman, no mention is ever made of what's happened to the interesting hero before: not a word about his visits to those houses, or about the maids, the cooks, and other men's wives.[12] If such indecent novels exist, they're never given to those who need them most, to young women. At first they pretend to those young women that the profligacy filling half our towns and even our villages doesn't really exist at all. Then they get so used to this pretense that like the English they finally come to believe sincerely that we're all moral people and that we live in a moral world. The young women, poor things, believe it in all seriousness. My unfortunate wife also believed this. I remember how, once we were already engaged, I showed her my diary in which she could find out a bit about my past life, primarily about the last liaison I'd had, about which she might hear from others, and about which for some reason I felt obliged to inform her.[13] I recall her horror, despair, and bewilderment when she learned and understood. I saw that she wanted to leave me then. Why didn't she?"

He emitted his sound, fell silent, and took another sip of tea.

6

"No, anyway, it's better like this!" he cried. "It serves me right! But that's not the point. I wanted to say that it's only unfortunate young women who're deceived here. Their mothers know this, especially those who've been schooled by their own husbands; mothers know it perfectly well. Pretending to believe in the purity of men, in fact they act quite differently. They know what bait to use to catch men for themselves and for their daughters.

"You see, it's only the men who don't know, and we don't because we don't want to know; women know very well that the most sublime, poetic love, as

12. The hero of Tolstoy's *War and Peace*, Pierre Bezukhov, exemplifies this behavior with his early visits to brothels and his later marriage to the virginal Natasha Rostova.

13. An autobiographical detail from Tolstoy's own courtship: he showed his diary to his fiancée, Sofiya Andreevna Behrs, who was horrified. A similar scene occurs in Tolstoy's novel *Anna Karenina* when Levin shows his diary to Kitty.

we call it, depends not on moral qualities, but on physical proximity, hairstyle, the color and cut of a dress. Ask any experienced coquette who's given herself the task of captivating a man which she would rather risk: to be convicted of lying, cruelty, even dissoluteness in the presence of the man she's trying to charm, or to appear before him in a poorly made, unattractive dress— she'll always prefer the former. She knows that we all lie constantly about our lofty feelings—we really need only her body; therefore we forgive all sorts of abominations, but we won't forgive an ugly, tasteless, or unfashionable dress. The coquette knows this consciously, but every innocent young woman knows it unconsciously, just as animals do.

"That's why those vile sweaters exist, those bustles worn on their behinds, those bare shoulders, arms, and almost bare breasts. Women, especially those schooled by men, know very well that talk about lofty matters—is just that, all talk, and that a man needs a woman's body and everything that shows it off in the most alluring light; that's precisely what happens. Why, if we could only discard this outrageous habit that's become second nature to us, and see the life of our upper classes as it really is, in all its shamelessness, it's simply one unceasing brothel. Don't you agree? Allow me and I'll prove it," he said, interrupting me. "You say that women in our society have interests in life unlike those who live in a brothel, but I say that isn't true and I'll prove it. If people differed in their aims, in the inner content of their lives, then this difference would undoubtedly be reflected in their external appearance, and that would be obvious. But just look at those unfortunate, despised creatures, and at women in highest society: they wear the same outfits, the same fashions, prefer the same perfumes, have the same bare arms, shoulders, breasts, and tight-fitting dresses covering their prominent behinds, the same passion for jewels, for expensive, glittering trinkets, the same amusements, dances, music, and songs. As the former use every means to entice men, so do the latter. There's no difference at all. To define it precisely, one need only say that short-term prostitutes are usually despised, whereas long-term prostitutes are well respected."

7

"Yes, so that's how these sweaters, curls, and bustles caught me. It was easy to do so because I was brought up under conditions where amorous young people are forced to grow like cucumbers in a greenhouse. And our stimulating, excessive food combined with our total physical idleness constitutes nothing other than a systematic excitement of lust. Whether this surprises you or not, it's true. Why, until recently I myself hadn't seen it at all. But now

I have. That's why it torments me that no one knows about it; people say such stupid things, like that lady.

"Yes, sir, just this spring some peasants were working near me on a railway embankment. The usual food for a young peasant lad is bread, kvass, and onion; he's lively, vigorous, healthy, and does light fieldwork.[14] When he goes to work on the railway, his food consists of kasha and one pound of meat.[15] But he works off that meat toiling sixteen hours, wheeling barrow-loads weighing thirty poods each.[16] So it's just right for him. Well, we each consume two pounds of meat, game, and all kinds of strong food and drink every day—and where does it go? Into excesses of sensuality. If it does go there and the safety valve's open, everything's all right; but close that valve, as I did temporarily, and at once it produces a stimulus that, passing through the prism of our artificial life, is expressed in infatuation of the purest kind, sometimes even platonic. So I fell in love, as everyone else does. And it was all there: raptures, tenderness, and poetry. In fact, on the one hand, this love of mine was the product of the activity of mothers and dressmakers, on the other, of the excess food I consumed leading my idle life. If it hadn't been for that boat ride, on the one hand, the dressmakers with their slender waists, and so forth, if my wife had been dressed in a shapeless housecoat and was sitting at home, and if I, on the other hand, had been living under normal human circumstances, consuming only as much food as I needed for my work, and if the safety valve had been open—since it happened to have been closed at the time—then I wouldn't have fallen in love and none of this would've happened."

8

"Well, this time it all worked out: my condition, her pretty dress, and the nice boat ride. Twenty times it hadn't worked, but this time it did. Just like a trap. I'm not laughing. Why, marriages are arranged that way now, just like traps. Isn't that natural? The young woman's matured, so she must be married off. It seems so simple when she's not ugly and there are men who want to get married. That's the way it was done in the old days. The young woman comes of age and the parents arrange a match. So it was done, and so it still is for all mankind—among the Chinese, Hindus, Moslems, and our own peasants;

14. Kvass is a traditional Russian beverage prepared from flour or dark rye bread soaked in water and malt.

15. Kasha is porridge or cooked cereal.

16. The pood is a Russian measure of weight equal to approximately 36 pounds, so thirty poods equals about 1,080 pounds.

that's how it's done among some ninety-nine percent of the human race. It's only among one percent, or even less, of us lechers that we decided this old way was no good and came up with something new. What was that? The new way is that young women sit around and men come in to choose, just like at a bazaar. The young women wait there and think, but dare not speak: 'Take me! No, me! Not her, take me: look at my shoulders and all the rest.' And we men, we stroll around, look them over, and feel very pleased. 'I know, but I won't get caught.' The men stroll around, look them over, and feel very pleased that all this has been arranged for them. Watch out, if you don't take care—bang, and that's that!"

"How should it be done?" I asked. "Should the women propose?"

"I don't really know; but if there's to be equality, then let there really be real equality. If they've decided that matchmaking is demeaning, this new way is a thousand times worse. Then the rights and chances were equal, but now a woman's either a slave at a bazaar or she's bait in a trap. Try telling the truth to some mother or young woman, that all she's doing is trying to snare a husband. My God, what an insult! But that's really what they're all about; they have nothing else to do. And what's so awful is sometimes to see completely innocent, poor young women engaged in this activity. Again, if it were done openly, but it's all deception. 'Ah, the origin of species, how fascinating! Ah, Liza's very interested in painting! Will you be at the exhibit? How instructive! And the troika rides, the play, the symphony? Ah, how splendid! My Liza's mad about music! Why don't you share these convictions? Ah, a boat ride!' But the idea's one and the same: 'Take me, take me, my Liza! No, me! Well, just try!' What an outrage! What lies!" he concluded and, finishing the rest of his tea, began clearing away the cups and dishes.

9

"You know," he began again, packing the tea and sugar away in his bag, "the domination of women from which the world suffers, all stems from this."

"What domination of women?" I asked. "The truth is that advantages in rights are all on the side of men."

"Yes, yes, that's just it," he interrupted me. "That's just what I want to tell you: that's what explains the unusual phenomenon that, on the one hand, it's completely fair that women are reduced to the lowest level of humiliation, while on the other, they dominate. It's like the Jews, just as they pay us back for our oppression of them by their financial power, so it is with women. 'Ah, you allow us only to be merchants. Fine, then we merchants will own you,' say the Jews. 'Ah, you want us only to be objects of sensuality. Fine, then we objects will enslave you,' say the women. A woman's lack of rights arises not from the fact that she can't vote or become a judge—to be occupied with such matters constitutes no rights—but to be equal to a man in sexual intercourse, to have the right to use him or abstain as she desires, to choose a man she desires, and not be chosen. You say this is disgraceful. Fine. Then a man shouldn't have these rights either. But now women are deprived of rights that men have. And, to make up for this lack of rights, a woman acts on man's sensuality, and by so doing, subjugates him in such a way that he only chooses formally, while in fact she's the one who's making the choice. And once she possesses these means, she misuses them and acquires enormous power over people."

"But where is this special power?" I asked.

"Where? Why, it's everywhere, in everything. Stroll around the shops in any large town. There are millions, you can't even estimate the amount of human labor invested, but see if you can find anything in ninety percent of them for a man's use? All of life's luxuries are required and maintained by women. Consider all the factories. An enormous proportion of them produces useless adornments, carriages, furniture, and trinkets for women. Millions of people, generations of slaves perish doing this hard labor merely to satisfy women's whims. Like queens, they command ninety percent of humankind and keep them in bondage and hard labor. And all this because women have been humiliated, deprived of equal rights with men. And so, they take revenge by acting on our sensuality, by ensnaring us in their traps. Yes, it's all because of this. Women have made themselves such instruments for affecting our sensuality that men can't even treat them serenely. As soon as a man approaches a woman, he goes into a trance and loses his head. I used to feel awkward and uneasy when I saw a woman dressed up in a ball gown, but now I'm simply terrified; I see something dangerous to people, something illicit, and I want to call the police, to muster some protection against the peril, to demand that the dangerous object be taken away, removed forthwith.[17]

"Yes, you may laugh!" he shouted at me, "but this is no joke at all. I'm sure the time will come, perhaps very soon, when people will understand all this and will be surprised that any society could exist that tolerated such actions threatening social stability, such as the bodily adornments that openly arouse sensuality allowed women in our society. Why, it's like setting all sorts of

17. This passage was the subject of a famous cartoon; see Yu. Bitovt, *Count L. N. Tolstoy in Caricatures and Anecdotes* (Moscow: 1908).

traps along paths and promenades—it's even worse! Why is it that we forbid gambling, but allow women to dress like prostitutes to arouse sensuality? They're a thousand times more dangerous!"

10

"Well, that's how I was caught. I was 'in love,' as it's called. Not only did I imagine her as the peak of perfection, but during the period of our engagement I also imagined myself as the peak of perfection. There's no scoundrel who, if he searches, can't find other scoundrels even worse in some respect, and therefore can always find some reason to be satisfied with himself. So it was with me: I married not for money—profit was not an issue, the way it was for the majority of my acquaintances who married either for money or connections. I was rich and she was poor. That's the first thing. The second thing I was proud of was that others got married with the intention of continuing to live in the same polygamous manner as they did before their marriage; while I, on the other hand, had the firm intention of being monogamous after the wedding, and there was no limit to my pride regarding that fact. Yes, I was a terrible swine and imagined myself to be an angel.

"The time of our engagement didn't last long. I can't recall it without shame! What an abomination! It's supposed to be a period of spiritual, not sensual love. Well, if it's spiritual love, spiritual communion, then it should be expressed in words, conversation, and intimate chats. There was nothing of the sort. It was terribly difficult to talk when we were left alone. It was like the labor of Sisyphus. As soon as I thought of something and said it, we'd fall silent again and I'd have to think of something else to say. There was nothing to talk about. Everything that could be said about the life that awaited us, all the arrangements and plans, had already been said, so what else was there? Why, if we'd been animals, we'd have known that we weren't supposed to talk; with us, on the contrary, it was necessary to speak, but there was nothing to say because we were occupied by something that couldn't be resolved by talking. Besides, there was that hideous habit of eating candy, consuming a crude excess of sweets, and all those ghastly preparations for the wedding: talk about the apartment, the bedroom, linens, housecoats, bathrobes, underwear, clothes. You must understand that if people get married in accordance with the Domostroi, as that old man was saying, then featherbeds, dowry, linens—all this is merely detail necessary to accompany the sacrament. But among us, when only one out of ten men who marry not only doesn't believe in the sacrament but doesn't even believe that what he's doing constitutes some sort of obligation; and when out of a hundred men there's scarcely one who's not been 'married' before, and who hasn't prepared in advance to betray his wife at every convenient opportunity, and when the majority regard a visit to the church merely as the particular condition for possessing a certain woman—just think about the awful significance of all these details. That's what it's all about. It becomes like a sale. An innocent girl is sold off to a debauchee and the purchase is surrounded by certain formalities."

II

"That's how everyone marries and how I got married, and then the much praised honeymoon begins. Why, even its name is so vile!" he hissed spitefully. "Once when I was strolling around Paris seeing the sights, I dropped in to have a look at what was advertised as a bearded lady and a water-dog. It turned out to be nothing more than a man wearing a woman's low-cut dress and a dog stuffed into walrus skin swimming around in a tub of water. It was of very little interest; as I was leaving, the showman politely escorted me out; addressing the public standing at the entrance, he pointed at me and said: 'Ask this gent if it's worth seeing. Come in, do come in, only one franc per person!' I felt ashamed to say that it wasn't worth seeing, and the showman had obviously been counting on that. So, it's probably the same thing with those who've experienced the horror of a honeymoon and don't want to disillusion others. I didn't disillusion anyone either, but I don't see why I can't tell the truth now. I even consider it necessary to do so. It's awkward, shameful, vile, pitiful, and, the main thing, it's boring, unbelievably boring! It's something like what I experienced when I was learning how to smoke: I felt nauseous and my saliva was flowing, but I kept swallowing and pretending it was very nice. The pleasure from smoking comes later, if it comes at all, just as it does from that: the spouses must school themselves in vice in order to receive any pleasure from it."

"Why say vice?" I asked. "Aren't you talking about the most natural human function?"

"Natural?" he asked. "Natural? No, on the contrary I'd say that I've come to the conclusion that it isn't . . . natural at all. No, it's completely unnatural. Ask any child, any uncorrupted young woman. My sister married very young a man twice her age and a debauchee. I recall how surprised we were on her wedding night when, terribly pale and in tears, she ran away from him, her whole body shaking, claiming she could never tell us what he'd asked her to do.

"You say, it's natural! It's natural to eat. And it's enjoyable, easy, pleasant, and not at all shameful, from the very beginning; but this is vile, shameful, and painful. No, it's not natural! And, I'm convinced, an uncorrupted young woman always hates it."

"But how then," I asked, "would the human race continue?"

"Ah, yes, as long as the human race won't perish!" he said with malicious irony, as if anticipating this familiar and unprincipled objection. "Preach abstinence from childbearing in the name of allowing English lords to continue their gluttony as long as they wish—that's all right. Preach abstinence from childbearing in the name of greater pleasure—that's all right; but just breathe one word about abstinence from childbearing in the name of morality—good Lord, what an outcry! It's as if the human race might perish because a dozen or so people want to stop acting like swine. Forgive me, this light's annoying me; may I shade it?" he asked, pointing to the lamp.

I said that I didn't mind, and then, as he did everything, he hastily stood up on the seat and pulled a woolen shade over the lamp.

"Nevertheless," I said, "if everyone acknowledged this as their law, then the human race would come to an end."

He didn't reply at once.

"You ask how the human race would continue," he said, sitting down opposite me again, spreading his legs far apart, and resting his elbows on his knees. "Why should it continue, this human race of ours?" he asked.

"What do you mean, 'Why?' If not, we wouldn't exist."

"And why should we?"

"'Why?' In order to live."

"But why? If there's no goal, if life's given us merely to live, then there's no reason for it. And if that's so, then the Schopenhauers and Hartmanns, and all the Buddhists are absolutely correct.[18] Well, and if there's a goal to life, then it's clear that life must end when that goal's been achieved. That's how it turns out," he said with evident agitation, obviously valuing his own thought highly. "That's how it turns out. Just note: if the goal of humanity is happiness, goodness, love, just as you like; if the goal of humanity is what's written in the prophecies, that all people will join together as one in love, their spears will be beaten into pruning hooks, and so forth, then what is it that impedes the accomplishment of this goal? The passions impede it. Of the passions, the strongest, most evil, and most stubborn is

18. The German philosopher Arthur Schopenhauer (1788–1860) emphasizes the role of the will as a blind, irrational force, a stance that led him to a rejection of Enlightenment values and to pessimism. Eduard von Hartmann (1842–1906) was a German metaphysical philosopher, a follower of Schopenhauer, who sought to reconcile two conflicting schools of thought, rationalism and irrationalism, emphasizing the role of the unconscious mind.

sexual, physical love; therefore, if the passions were to be demolished, including the last and strongest of all, sexual, physical love, the prophecy would be fulfilled, people would join together as one, the goal of humanity will have been achieved, and there'd be no further reason to live. As long as humanity exists, an ideal stands before it, and that ideal, of course, is not the same as for rabbits or pigs, to multiply abundantly, and not the same as for monkeys or Parisians, to enjoy the pleasures of sexual passion in the most refined manner, but the ideal of goodness, attainable through abstinence and purity. People have always strived for it and will continue to do so. And look how it turns out.

"It turns out that physical love is a safety valve. If the current generation of humanity has not achieved its goal, then the sole reason it hasn't is because of its passions, and the strongest of those is sexual. But if there is sexual passion, and there is a new generation, then the possibility exists for reaching this goal in the next generation. And if the next one doesn't achieve it, then the one after that will, and so on and so forth, until the goal's been reached, until the prophecy's been fulfilled, until people come together as one. Or else, how would it turn out? If one acknowledges that God created people for the achievement of a certain goal, He would have created them either as mortal without sexual passion or as immortal. If they were mortal but without sexual passion, then how would it turn out? They would've lived and, without achieving their goal, would've died; but to achieve His goal, God would've had to create new people. If, however, they were immortal, then let's suppose (although it'd be more difficult for these same people to correct their mistakes and approach perfection than it would be for new generations), let's suppose they would've achieved their goal after many thousands of years; but what use would they be then? What could He do with them? So, things are best just as they are now. . . . You may not like this form of expression; perhaps you believe in evolution? Even then it turns out the same way. The highest order of animals, the human race, to survive in its struggle with other animals, should join together as one, like a swarm of bees, and not multiply endlessly; it should, also like the bees, produce sexless worker bees—that is, again it should strive for abstinence, rather than for inflaming lust, toward which our entire life is now directed." He fell silent. "Will the human race come to an end? Can anyone, however he regards the world, doubt that? Why, that's as indubitable as death itself. According to all church teaching the end of the world will come, and according to all scientific teaching, the same end is inevitable. What's so strange that according to moral teaching it turns out the same way?"

After he said this he remained silent for a long time, drank some more tea, and finished his cigarette; after taking out some others from his bag, he placed them in his old soiled cigarette case.

"I understand your thinking," I said. "The Shakers espouse something similar."[19]

"Yes, yes, and they're right," he said. "Sexual passion, no matter how it's arranged is evil, a terrible evil against which one must struggle, and it mustn't be encouraged as it is here with us. The words of the Gospel that whosoever looks at a woman to lust after her has already committed adultery relates not only to other men's wives, but precisely—and above all—to one's own wife."

12

"In our world everything seems to be the reverse: if a man thinks about abstinence while still a bachelor, then after he's married, everyone considers abstinence no longer necessary. These trips after a wedding, the seclusion to which a young couple repairs with their parents' permission—why, it's nothing more than for debauchery. But moral law avenges itself once it's been violated. No matter how I tried to arrange our honeymoon, nothing came of it. It was vile, shameful, and boring the entire time. But very soon it even became painfully difficult. That started very early. By the third or fourth day I found my wife bored and began asking her why; I started to embrace her, which, in my opinion, was all she could wish for, but she pushed my arms away and burst into tears. What about? She couldn't say. She felt sad and oppressed. Her nervous exhaustion had probably intimated the truth about the depravity of our relations; but she couldn't express it. I began interrogating her; she said something about feeling sad without her mother. I didn't think that was true. I began trying to reassure her, without saying a word about her mother. I didn't realize that she was merely feeling oppressed, and that her mother was only an excuse. But she was immediately offended that I hadn't even mentioned her mother, as if I hadn't believed her. She said that I didn't really love her. I reproached her for being capricious; all of a sudden her face changed completely. Instead of sadness, it expressed irritation, and she began reproaching me in the most venomous terms for my egoism and cruelty. I looked at her. Her face expressed utmost coldness and hostility, almost

19. A religious sect that developed in eighteenth-century England and became popular in nineteenth-century New England. The Shakers observed a doctrine of common property, communal living, and sexual abstinence. Tolstoy was in correspondence with several members of the group.

hatred of me. I recall how horrified I was when I saw it. 'How? What?' I wondered. 'Love—that union of souls, and this is what I get instead! This can't be! This isn't her!' I kept trying to soothe her, but encountered such an insurmountable wall of cold, venomous hostility that I hadn't even managed to look away before irritation seized me as well, and we said a great many unpleasant things to each other. The impression left by this first quarrel was awful. I call it a quarrel, but it wasn't really that: it was merely the uncovering of the abyss actually existing between us. Our amorousness had been exhausted by the satisfaction of our sensuality, and we were left confronting each other in our true relationship, that is, two totally alien egoists, each wishing to receive as much pleasure from the other as possible. I call what happened between us a quarrel, but it wasn't really a quarrel; it was merely the result of the cessation of sensuality revealing our true relationship to one another. I didn't understand that this cold, hostile relationship was our normal state, and I didn't understand it because at first this hostile relationship was once again concealed from us by the reappearance of concentrated sensuality, that is, lovemaking.

"I thought we'd quarreled and made up and that it wouldn't happen again. But during that first month of our honeymoon, a state of satiety soon returned; once again we ceased being needed by the other person and another quarrel ensued. The second one struck me even more painfully than the first. It must have been that the first one was not accidental, but how things were supposed to be and how they would continue, I thought. The second quarrel struck me more in that it arose from the most improbable pretext. Something having to do with money, which I'd never spared and would never spare with my wife. I remember only that she twisted the matter in such a way that some remark of mine turned out to be an expression of my desire to use money to dominate her, thus affirming my exclusive right—something inconceivable, stupid, vile, and unnatural both for me and for her. I grew angry, began reproaching her for insensitivity, as she did me, and off we went again. Both in her words and in the expression of her face and eyes I saw once more that same cold, cruel hostility that had struck me earlier. I recalled previous quarrels with my brother, my acquaintances, my father, but never did we feel that particular, noxious malice between us that was present here. But some time passed, and once again this mutual contempt was concealed beneath amorousness, that is, sensuality, and I was consoled by the thought that these quarrels were only mistakes that could be corrected. But then there was a third quarrel, and a fourth, and I came to realize that it was no accident; it was how things were supposed to be and how they would continue, and I was horrified by the prospect that faced me. In addition, I was tormented by the awful thought that I was the only one who got along so badly with his wife, so different from what I'd expected, while nothing of the sort was true in other people's marriages. I didn't know at that time that this was the general situation, and that everyone, just like me, imagines it to be their exclusive misfortune, and they conceal their exclusive, shameful misfortune not only from others, but even from themselves, and don't ever acknowledge it.

"It began during those first days and continued all the time, getting stronger and nastier. From those first weeks I felt in the depths of my soul that I'd been *caught,* that this wasn't at all what I'd expected, that marriage not only was not happiness but was something very onerous; but like everyone else, I didn't want to admit it (I wouldn't admit it to myself even now, if it weren't for how things turned out); I concealed it not only from others but from myself. Now I'm surprised that I didn't understand my situation as it really was. It could have been seen from the fact that our quarrels began with pretexts impossible to recall once the quarrel had ended. Our reason didn't have time to devise sufficient pretexts for the constant hostility that existed between us. But even more striking was the insufficiency of pretexts for our reconciliations. Sometimes there were words, explanations, even tears, but sometimes . . . oh! It's vile to recall even now—after the cruelest words exchanged, all of sudden—the silent glances, smiles, kisses, and embraces. . . . Ugh! Despicable! How is it that I didn't see all that vileness back then?"

13

Two new passengers entered and began to settle on the seats farthest from us. Pozdnyshev remained silent until after they were seated, but as soon as they had quieted down, he continued, obviously not losing his train of thought even for a moment.

"What is filthiest of all," he began, "is that in theory love's supposed to be something ideal, exalted; but in practice, love is something despicable, swinish, which it's even repulsive and shameful to mention or remember. It's not for nothing that nature made it that way. And if it's repulsive and shameful, then one must understand it as such. But here, on the contrary, people pretend that something repulsive and shameful is beautiful and exalted. What were the first signs of my love? I yielded to animal excesses, not only without feeling ashamed, but for some reason taking pride in the possibility of these physical excesses, without considering in the least either her spiritual life or even her physical life. I wondered where our mutual hostility had come from, but the matter was absolutely clear: this hostility was nothing other than the protest of our human nature against the animal nature that was overpowering it.

"I was surprised by our mutual hostility. But it couldn't be any other way. That hatred was nothing other than the mutual hatred of accomplices in crime—both for the instigation and participation in a criminal act. How could it not be a crime when she, poor thing, became pregnant during the first month, yet our swinish sexual contact continued? You think I'm digressing from my tale? Not in the least! I'm telling you the whole story of how I killed my wife. During the trial I was asked how and with what I killed her. Fools! They thought I'd killed my wife then, with a knife, on the fifth of October. I didn't kill her then, but much earlier. Just as they're all now killing, everyone, all of them . . ."

"But with what?" I asked.

"That's just what's so surprising: no one wants to know something that's so clear and obvious, what doctors should know and preach, yet they keep silent. Why, the matter's terribly simple. Man and woman are created like animals, so pregnancy begins after carnal love, then nursing—conditions during which carnal love is harmful both for the woman and for her child. There's an equal number of men and women. What follows from this? It seems clear. No great amount of wisdom is needed to arrive at the conclusion that animals reach, that is abstinence. But, no. Science has managed to discover some sort of leucocytes that course through the blood and all sorts of other stupidities, but this one fact it's been unable to understand.[20] At least one doesn't hear it said.

"So there are only two choices for a woman: one is to make a monster of herself, destroy in herself or, as need be, keep trying to destroy the capacity to be a woman, that is, a mother, in order that a man may calmly and continually enjoy himself; or, there's the other way out, not even a way out, but a simple, crude, outright violation of the laws of nature, practiced in all so-called respectable families. It's that the woman, contrary to her nature, must at the very same time be pregnant, and nursing, and a lover; she must be something that no animal stoops to. And she may not have enough strength. That's why in our family life we have hysterics and frayed nerves, and among peasants—shriekers.[21] Note that among young women, pure ones, there aren't

20. Leucocytes are white blood cells, small, colorless corpuscles in the blood, lymph, or tissues that destroy organisms that cause disease.

21. Women subject to so-called fits of hysterics, often thought, even as late as the nineteenth century, to be possessed by the devil.

any shriekers; it's only among peasant women, and only those who live to-gether with their husbands. So it is here with us. And it's exactly the same in Europe. All the hospitals for hysterics are filled with women who've been violating the laws of nature. But shriekers and Charcot's patients are com-pletely incapacitated, while the world is full of half-crippled women.[22] Why, just think what a great thing's being accomplished in a woman after she's conceived or when she's nursing a newborn infant. Someone that will continue on and replace us is growing inside her. And this sacred task is destroyed—by what? It's dreadful to contemplate! People talk about freedom, women's rights. It's as if cannibals fattened up their captives before eating them, all the while assuring them that they were concerned about their rights and their freedom."

All this was new to me and startling.

"Well then? If it's like that," I said, "a man can make love to his wife only once every two years; but for a man . . ."

"It's essential for a man," he interrupted me. "Once again our dear high priests of science have convinced us all. I'd order those magicians to meet the obligations of those women who, in their opinion, are so necessary to men. What would they say then? Convince a man that he needs vodka, tobacco, or opium, and then all that becomes necessary. It turns out that God didn't understand what was needed; therefore He didn't ask magicians and arranged things badly. Don't you see, it just doesn't add up. A man wants and needs to satisfy his lust, so they've concluded; therefore, childbearing and nursing in-terfere, hindering the satisfaction of that need. What's to be done? Turn to the magicians; they'll arrange it. And so they did. Oh, when will these magi-cians with their deceptions be dethroned? It's high time! It's already reached the point that men lose their minds and go off to shoot themselves, all be-cause of this. How can it be otherwise? Animals seem to know that their progeny continues their kind, and they adhere to a certain law in this respect. Only man doesn't know this and doesn't want to know it. He's concerned only with having as much pleasure as possible. And who is he? Man, lord of nature. Note that animals mate only when they can produce offspring, while that filthy lord of nature does it all the time, just for the sheer pleasure. And, what's more, he exalts this apelike pursuit into the pearl of creation—love. In the name of this love, that is, filth, he destroys—what? Half the human race. Of all women who should be helpmates in humanity's progress toward truth

---

22. Jean Martin Charcot (1825–93) was a French neurologist who founded a clinic for dis-eases of the nervous system, including "hysterics."

and goodness, man, for the sake of his own pleasure, makes of them not helpmates but enemies. Look, what is it that impedes the forward movement of mankind everywhere? Women. And why are they like that? Only because of this. Yes, sir; yes, sir," he repeated several times and began to stir, getting out his cigarettes and lighting up, obviously trying to calm down a bit.

14

"That's the sort of swine I was," he continued again, in his previous tone of voice. "And worst of all was that while I was living this swinish life, I imagined that because I wasn't seducing other women, I must therefore be living an honest family life, that I was a moral man, and not guilty in any respect, and that if we had any quarrels, my wife was to blame for them: it was a question of her character.

"Of course, she was not to blame. She was just like the rest of them, the majority of women. She was brought up in accordance with the demands of the position of women in our society, therefore as all women are brought up without exception in our well-off classes, and just as they have to be. They're talking now about some sort of new education for women. It's all empty words: the education of women is exactly as it should be, given the existence of our general view of women, our genuine view, not the one we fake.

"And the education of women will always correspond to men's view of them. Why, we all know how men regard women: '*Wein, Weiber und Gesang*,' and how the poets describe them.[23] Take all poetry, painting, sculpture, beginning with love poetry and naked Venuses and Phrynes, and you'll see that woman is an instrument for man's enjoyment; and so she is on the Truba or on Grachevka, and at a court ball.[24] Just note the devil's cunning: so, if she's there for enjoyment, pleasure, then let it be known as such, that woman is a tasty morsel. But no, at first the knights declare that they idolize women—idolize them, but still regard them as a means of enjoyment. And now they maintain they respect women. Some yield their places to them, pick up their handkerchiefs; others acknowledge their rights to occupy all positions and participate in government, and so on. They do all these things, but their view of women remains the same. Her body is an instrument of enjoyment. And she knows this. It's the same as slavery. Why, slavery's nothing other than the

23. The German phrase means "wine, women, and song."
24. Phryne was a famously beautiful courtesan in ancient Greece (fourth century B.C.) who served as the model for several statues. Truba and Grachevka were streets in Moscow where numerous brothels were located.

use by a few of the unwilling labor of the many. Therefore, so that slavery would cease, it's necessary for people to stop wanting to make use of the unwilling labor of others, and to consider it a sin or a shame. Meanwhile, people abolish the external forms of slavery, arrange it so that it's no longer possible to buy slaves, and imagine and convince themselves that slavery no longer exists; they don't see and don't want to see that slavery continues to exist because people still like to use the labor of others and still consider it right and proper. As long as they consider it a good thing, there'll always be people who're stronger and smarter than others and who know how to arrange things. It's the same with the emancipation of women. The slavery of women consists only in the fact that men wish to use them as instruments of enjoyment and consider that a very good thing. So they emancipate women, give them rights equal to men's, but continue to regard them as instruments of enjoyment; that's how they educate women in childhood and how they're regarded by social opinion. So there she is, the same humiliated, depraved slave, while man is the same depraved slaveowner.

"They emancipate women in schools and in courts of law, but regard her as if she were an object of enjoyment. If you teach a woman as she's taught here among us, to regard herself thus, she'll always remain an inferior being. Either she'll prevent the conception of offspring with the help of those scoundrel doctors—that is, she'll be an outright prostitute who's lowered herself not to the level of an animal but to the level of a thing—or else she'll become what she is in a majority of cases: mentally ill, hysterical, unhappy, just as they are now, lacking any possibility for spiritual development.

"Schools and women's colleges can't alter this. The only thing that can is a change in the way men view women and the way women view themselves. This will happen only when women regard the state of virginity as the highest state, and not as they do now, when the highest state of a human being is shame and disgrace. Until this occurs, the ideal of every young woman, no matter what her education, will still be to attract as many men as possible, as many males as she can, in order to have the possibility of choice.

"And the fact that one of them knows more mathematics, while another can play the harp—that won't change a thing. A woman's happy and attains everything she can wish for when she captivates a man. Therefore a woman's main task is to know how to captivate him. That's how it's been and how it will be. That's how it is during an unmarried girl's life in our society, and how it continues in her married life. During her unmarried life it's necessary so she can have choice; in her married life it's necessary so she can dominate her husband.

"One thing that curtails, or at least temporarily suppresses, this is children—and then, only if the woman's not a monster and nurses them herself. But here again, come the doctors.

"My wife, who wanted to nurse, and did in fact nurse her next five children, happened to fall ill after the birth of her first child. These doctors who cynically undressed her and palpated her everywhere, for which I had to thank them and pay them money—these nice doctors concluded that she shouldn't nurse; thus at first she was deprived of the only means that could've spared her from coquetry. A wet nurse fed the infant—that is, we took advantage of another woman's poverty, need, and ignorance, and lured her away from her own child to ours; in exchange, we gave her a fine headdress adorned with lace. But that's not the point. The point is that during the time my wife was free from pregnancy and nursing, this female coquetry that had previously been dormant in her arose with special force. Correspondingly, there arose in me with special force such pangs of jealousy that have continued to torment me throughout my married life, as they must torment all husbands who live with wives as I did, that is, immorally."

15

"During the entire course of my married life I never ceased being tormented by jealousy. But there were certain periods when I suffered from it especially severely. One of those was after the birth of our first child, when the doctors prohibited my wife from nursing. I was especially jealous at the time, in the first place, because my wife experienced a mother's typical restlessness that must be prompted by the groundless disruption in the normal course of life; in the second place, because, seeing how easily she'd shed a mother's moral obligation, I concluded, rightly although unconsciously, that it would be just as easy for her to shed her spousal obligation, all the more so since she was in perfect health and, in spite of the good doctors' prohibition, she managed to nurse her subsequent children herself and did a fine job of it."

"I see you really don't like doctors," I said, noting his particularly spiteful tone of voice every time he made mention of them.

"It's not a matter of likes or dislikes. They destroyed my life, just as they've destroyed and go on destroying the lives of thousands of people, hundreds of thousands, and I can't help connecting the effect with the cause. I understand that they want to earn money, just like lawyers and others, and I'd gladly give them half my income; everyone, if they understood what they're doing, would gladly give them half their property, as long as they'd refrain from interfering in our family life and would never come anywhere near us. I haven't assembled the evidence, but I know dozens of cases—there's no end to them—in which they've killed a baby in the mother's womb, insisting that she'd be unable to deliver, and later the woman gives birth perfectly well, or else they've killed a mother while performing some sort of operation. No one considers these murders, just as they didn't consider murders committed during the Inquisition, because they were supposed to be done for the benefit of mankind. It's impossible to count the crimes they've committed. But all these crimes are nothing in comparison to the moral corruption of materialism they introduce into the world, especially through women. I'm not even talking about the fact that in following their instructions, thanks to infections everywhere and in everything, people must be moving not toward unity but toward disunity: according to their teaching, everyone should sit apart and leave an atomizer with carbolic acid in their mouths (though they've discovered that does no good either).[25] But that's no matter. The main poison is the corruption of people, woman in particular.

"Today one can no longer say, 'You live badly: live better.' One can say this neither to oneself nor to others. If you're living badly, it's because of some abnormality in nervous functions, and so on. So you must go to doctors, and they'll prescribe some medicine for thirty-five kopecks at the pharmacy, and you take it. You get even worse; then there's more medicine and more doctors. A splendid trick!

"But that's not the point. I just told you that she nursed the children perfectly well herself, and that it was only her bearing and nursing the children that saved me from the torments of jealousy. If it hadn't been for that, everything would've happened earlier. The children saved both me and her. During those eight years, she gave birth to five children. And she nursed them all herself."

"Where are your children now?" I asked.

"My children?" he repeated anxiously.

"Excuse me, perhaps it's painful for you to be reminded of them."

"No, never mind. My sister-in-law and her brother took them. They wouldn't let me have them. I provided for them but they wouldn't let me have them. I'm something of a madman. I've just left them now. I've seen them, but they won't let me have them. Or else I'd raise them so they wouldn't be anything like their parents. But they're supposed to be like them. Well, what's to be done? It's clear they won't let me have them and they don't trust

25. Carbolic acid, distilled from coal or coal tar, was used in weak solution as an antiseptic or disinfectant.

me. I don't even know myself whether I'd be able to raise them. I think not, I'm a wreck, a cripple. I have only one thing. I know. Yes, it's true; I know something that everyone else won't discover for a while.

"Yes, my children are living and growing up to be the same savages as everyone else around them. I saw them, three times even. I can't do anything for them. Nothing. I'm going to my place in the south. I have a small house and a garden there.

"Yes, it'll be a while before people discover what I know. How much iron and what other sort of metals there are on the sun and stars—that may soon be found out; but anything that exposes our swinishness—that's difficult, terribly difficult . . .

"But at least you listen, and I'm grateful for that."

16

"You just mentioned children. Again what terrible lies are told about them. Children are a blessing from God. Children are a joy. It's all lies. It was all true at one time, but now it's nothing like that. Children are a torment and nothing more. The majority of mothers frankly feel this way, and sometimes they even say it openly. Ask the majority of mothers in our well-to-do circle and they'll tell you that they don't want to have any children out of fear that their children might fall ill and die; and if they have given birth, they don't want to nurse them because they don't want to become so attached and don't want to suffer. The enjoyment that a child provides by its charm, those little hands and feet, its whole little body, the enjoyment afforded by a child—is less than the suffering they experience—less than even the fear alone of the possibility of a child's illness or death, not to mention actual illness or the loss of a child. Weighing the advantages and disadvantages, it turns out that it's disadvantageous, and therefore undesirable to have children. The mothers say this openly, boldly, imagining that their feelings arise from love of their children, a good and praiseworthy feeling of which they're proud. They don't notice that by this reasoning they flatly reject love and only confirm their own egoism. They receive less pleasure from a child's charms than suffering from the fear it occasions, and therefore they don't want to bear a child they'd come to love. They won't sacrifice themselves for a beloved being; instead, they sacrifice a being they could love for their own sake.

It's clear this isn't love but egoism. But one can't condemn them, these mothers of well-to-do families, for their egoism; one can't raise a hand against them when you recall all that they suffer owing to their children's health, thanks again to those same doctors who meddle in our affluent life. When I remember, even now, my wife's life and her condition during the time we had three or four young children and she was so absorbed by them—it's awful. We had no life of our own. We were in a state of constant danger, escape from it, then imminent danger again, once more desperate efforts and escape again—such was our constant situation, as if we were on a sinking ship. Sometimes it seemed to me that all this was happening on purpose, that she was feigning concern for the children in order to subjugate me. It was all so enticing and very simply resolved all questions in her favor. It sometimes seemed that everything she said and did in these cases, she said and did intentionally. But no, she herself suffered terribly and blamed herself constantly for the children, their health or illnesses. It was a torment for her and for me, too. And she couldn't refrain from suffering. After all, attachment to one's children, the animal need to nurse them, cuddle them, protect them—was present, as it is with the majority of women, but that which animals possess— a lack of imagination and reason—was absent. A mother hen isn't afraid of what might happen to her chicks; she doesn't know all the illnesses that might befall them; she doesn't know all the remedies that people devise to save them from illness and death. And for a mother hen, her young aren't a source of torment. She does for her chicks what's appropriate and agreeable; her young are a joy for her. When a baby chick starts to fall ill, her anxieties are well defined: she warms it and feeds it. And, in so doing, she knows she's doing all that's necessary. If the chick dies, she doesn't ask herself why it's dead or where it's gone; she clucks a little, then stops and resumes her life as before. But for our unfortunate women and for my wife, this was not the case. Not to mention illnesses or how to cure them, she heard from all sides and read endlessly diverse and constantly changing rules about how to raise and educate children. This is how to feed them; no, not like that at all, but like this; how to dress them, what they should drink, how to bathe them, how to put them to bed, take them for walks, give them fresh air—about all this we, especially she, discovered new rules every week. It's as if we'd only begun having children only yesterday. And if a child hadn't been properly fed or bathed, or not at the right time, and that child fell ill, it turned out that my wife was to blame, and hadn't done what was really necessary.

"And that's when they're healthy. It was a torment even then. But if one fell ill, it was all over. Complete hell. It's supposed that illness can be cured and there's such a thing as science and people who're doctors, and that they know what to do. Not all of them, but the very best ones do. So a child falls ill and one must find the very best doctor, the one who can save them, and then the child is saved; but if you can't find that doctor, or if you don't live in the same place that he does, then the child is lost. And this is not only my wife's belief but that of all women in her circle, and she hears the same view repeated on all sides: Yekaterina Semenovna lost two of her children because she didn't summon Ivan Zakharych in time, but he managed to save Marya Ivanovna's elder daughter; the Petrovs followed the doctor's advice and dispersed their children to different hotels just in time and they all survived, but if they hadn't, the children would've died. And someone else who had a weak child followed the doctor's advice and moved to the south and thus saved her child. How can my wife keep from being tormented and agitated all the time when the lives of her children, with whom she has an animal attachment, depend on her finding what Ivan Zakharych will say. But no one knows what he'll say, least of all, Ivan Zakharych, because he himself knows all too well that he doesn't know anything and he can't help in any way, so he merely hedges his bets so people won't stop thinking that he knows something. Why, if she were really an animal, she wouldn't have suffered so much; and if she were really a human being, she would've had faith in God, and would've said and thought the same thing that believing peasant women do: 'God gives, God takes, there's no escaping God.' She'd have concluded that the matter of everyone's life and death, not only her children's, lies outside the power of people, and only in God's hands, and then she wouldn't have been so tormented, thinking it was within her own control to prevent the illness and death of her children, and she wouldn't have tried so hard. But for her the situation was this: she was given these very fragile, weak creatures, subject to countless calamities. She felt a passionate, animal attachment to them. Besides, these creatures were entrusted to her, while at the same time the means for preserving them were hidden from us and revealed only to total strangers, whose services and advice could be procured only by paying large sums of money, and even then, not always.

"Our whole life with children was not a joy but a torment, both for my wife and therefore for me, too. How could it be otherwise? She was constantly tormented. There were times when we'd just calmed down after a jealous scene or a simple quarrel and we thought we could live, read, and think; we'd start doing something, and suddenly we'd receive news that Vasya was throwing up, or Masha had blood in her stool, or Andryusha had a rash: well, then of course there was no peace. Where should we run? Summon which doctors? How isolate the child? So the enemas, temperatures, medicines, and doctors would start to appear. Before that episode was over, something else would happen. We had no regular, settled family life. There was only, as I've said, constant escape from imaginary and real dangers. This is how it is in a majority of families now. In my own family it was particularly intense. My wife loved her children and was very gullible.

"Thus the presence of children not only failed to improve our life but poisoned it. Besides that, children were another reason for discord. From the time we had children, and even more as they grew, they themselves became the means and object of discord. Not only the object, but the children were the instrument of our struggle; we used them to fight one another. Each of us had our favorite child—our chosen weapon for fighting. I used the eldest, Vasya, and she used Liza. Besides, when the children grew older and their characters became more defined, they became allies whom we enlisted on our own sides. They suffered terribly as a result, the poor things, but in our constant warfare, we didn't stop to think about them. The little girl was my supporter; the elder boy, who resembled my wife and was her favorite, was often hateful to me."

<h2 style="text-align:center">17</h2>

"Well, sir, that's how we lived. Our relationship grew more and more hostile. Things finally reached the point when it wasn't the discord that caused the hostility, but the hostility that caused the discord: whatever she said, I disagreed in advance, and it was the same with her.

"During the fourth year of our marriage it was somehow decided by both sides that we could neither understand each other nor agree. We ceased trying to reach any accord. We each stuck to our own opinions about the simplest things, especially regarding the children. As I recall now, the opinions I defended weren't so dear to me that I couldn't give them up; but she held the opposite opinion, so yielding meant yielding to her. I couldn't do that. Nor could she yield to me. She probably always considered herself completely in the right before me, and in my eyes I was always a saint before her. When we were together we were almost condemned to silence or to such conversations as, I'm sure, animals engage in among themselves: 'What time is it?' 'Time for bed.' 'What's for dinner today?' 'Where shall we go?' 'What's in the paper?' 'Send for the doctor.' 'Masha has a sore throat.' We needed only to take one or two steps outside this impossibly narrow circle of conversation topics for irritation to flare up. There were confrontations and expressions of contempt over coffee, the tablecloth, the carriage, or a lead in vint—all things that couldn't possibly be of any importance to either of us.[26] In me, at least, there often seethed a terrible hatred for her! Sometimes I'd watch how she'd

---

26. Lead in vint is a Russian card game similar to bridge and whist.

pour out the tea, swing her foot, or raise her spoon to her mouth, slurping, drawing in the liquid, and I hated her precisely for that, as if for the worst of deeds. At the time I didn't notice that these periods of anger in me corresponded quite correctly and regularly to those periods we called love. A period of love—then one of anger; an energetic period of love—then a longer period of anger; a weaker manifestation of love—then a shorter one of anger. At the time we didn't understand that our love and hatred were one and the same animal emotion, only from different ends. It would've been impossible to live that way if we'd understood our situation; but we didn't understand it and couldn't see it. Both the salvation of man and his punishment lie in the fact that when he isn't living in the right way, he can stupefy himself so as not to see the misery of his own situation. That's just what we did. My wife tried to lose herself in intense, always urgent household concerns, the furniture, her outfits, and the children's clothes, as well as their education and health. I had my own intoxication—the intoxication of work, hunting, and cards. We were both constantly busy. We both felt that the busier we kept, the angrier we could be toward each other. 'It's fine for you to make faces,' I thought about her, 'but you tormented me all night with your scenes, and I have a meeting today.' 'It's fine for you,' she not only thought, but even said, 'but I didn't get any sleep last night because of the baby.'

"That's how we lived, not seeing through our perpetual fog the actual situation. If the thing that happened had never happened, I'd have lived to a ripe old age that same way, and I'd have thought, as I lay dying, that I'd lived a good life, not an especially good one, but not a bad one either, a life just like everyone else; I'd never have understood the abyss of unhappiness and the foul lie in which I was wallowing.

"We were like two convicts, hating each other, but bound by a chain, poisoning each other's life and trying not to see it. I didn't know at the time that ninety-nine percent of married people live in the same hell as I did, and that it can't be otherwise. At the time I didn't know this about other people or about myself.

"It's astonishing what coincidences occur in a regular and even an irregular life! Just when the parents' life with each other becomes unbearable, it's necessary to provide the children with a city setting for their education. So the need arises to move to the city."

He fell silent and emitted his strange sounds a few times, which now sounded very much like suppressed sobs. We were approaching a station.

"What time is it?" he asked.

I glanced at my watch: it was two o'clock.

"Aren't you tired?" he asked.

"No, but you are."

"I'm suffocating. Excuse me, I'll take a little walk and get some water."

He made his way unsteadily through the carriage. I sat alone, mulling over all that he'd said, and was so deep in thought that I didn't notice his return from the other door.

18

"Yes, I keep getting carried away," he began. "I've thought about things a great deal; I regard them differently and want to talk about all of it. So, we started living in town. Unhappy people live better in town. A man can live there a hundred years and never realize that he died a long time ago and that he's rotting. In town there's no time to size things up: you're always busy. Business affairs, social relations, health matters, the arts, the children's health, and their education. One moment you have to receive this or that person, or call on these or those people; or, you have to go see something, hear someone, or do something. In town at any given moment there are always one, two, or even three luminaries that cannot possibly be missed. Or else one must undergo some treatment, or arrange for someone else's; then there are the teachers, tutors, and governesses; meanwhile one's own life is as empty as can be. Well, that's how we lived and didn't feel the pain of our living together nearly as much. Besides, at first we had a splendid pastime—getting settled in a new town, a new apartment, and then another pastime—moving from town to the country, and then from the country back to town.

"We spent one whole winter in town, and during the second there occurred an event, unnoticed by anyone at the time, seemingly insignificant, but one that caused all that subsequently transpired. She was unwell, and those scoundrel-doctors ordered her not to bear any more children and they taught her how to avoid giving birth. I found this disgusting. I struggled against it, but she insisted with frivolous obstinacy on having her own way, and I submitted; the last pretext for our swinish life—children—was removed, and life became even more despicable.

"A peasant or a worker needs children, even though it's hard for him to feed them; but he needs them, and therefore his marital relations are justified. But people like us who already have children don't need any more; children involve extra care and expense, and are co-heirs; they're a burden. So we have no justification whatsoever for our swinish life. Either we avoid having children by artificial means, or we regard them as a misfortune, the consequence of carelessness, which is even more despicable. There's no justification. But we've fallen so low morally, that we no longer see a need for justification. The majority of today's educated world engages in this depravity without the least remorse of conscience.

"There's no reason for remorse, because conscience doesn't exist in our way of life apart from, if one can call it that, the conscience of public opinion and criminal law. And here neither the one nor the other is violated: there's no reason to feel ashamed before society; *everyone* acts like that, both Marya Pavlovna and Ivan Zakharych.[27] So why breed paupers and deprive oneself of the possibility of social life? There's no reason to feel ashamed before criminal law or to be afraid of it. It's only outrageous hussies and soldiers' wives who toss their babies into ponds and wells; naturally, they have to be thrown into jail; but with us, it's all done in a neat and timely manner.

"Thus we lived for another two years. The means prescribed by those scoundrel-doctors, apparently, began to work; she put on weight and grew prettier, like the late beauty of summer. She herself felt this and paid more attention to her appearance. She developed a provocative sort of beauty, one that perturbed people. She was in the full vigor of a well-fed, stimulated woman of thirty, no longer bearing children. Her appearance disturbed people. When she passed among men, she attracted their glances. She was like a fresh, well-fed, harnessed filly whose bridle's been removed. There was no bridle whatsoever, as is the case with ninety-nine percent of our women. And I felt this and was afraid."

19

He suddenly stood up and moved closer to the window.

"Excuse me," he said and, staring at the window, fell silent for several minutes. Then he sighed deeply and sat down again opposite me. His face had become completely different, his eyes were sad, and some sort of strange expression, almost a smile, puckered his mouth. "I'm a little tired, but I'll keep talking. There's still plenty of time; it's not yet dawn. Yes, sir," he began again, after lighting a cigarette. "After she stopped having babies she put on weight; then this illness—endless suffering over the children—began to pass; it wasn't exactly that it passed, it was as if she'd recovered from a state of intoxication; she came to her senses and saw that there was an entire blessed world, with joys she'd forgotten all about, but a world in which she no longer knew how to live, an entire blessed world that she didn't understand at all. 'I mustn't miss it! Time's passing and it won't ever come back!' That's what I imagine she thought,

27. That is, both women and men.

or more likely, felt, and it was impossible for her to think or feel otherwise: she'd been brought up to think that there was only one thing worthy of attention in this world—love. She'd gotten married, received some of that love, but not only was it a long way from what she'd been promised, what she'd expected, she'd also undergone many disappointments and much suffering, and then, an unexpected torment—children! This torment had worn her out. At that point, thanks to the obliging doctors, she learned that she could avoid having children. She was delighted, tried it, and came back to life again for the one thing she knew—love. But love with a husband infected by jealousy and manifold anger wasn't the same thing. She began to imagine some other kind of love, pure and new, at least that's what I thought. So she began to look around her, as if expecting something. I saw this and couldn't help feeling alarmed. Time and again it would happen that while she was talking to me through other people as she always did, that is, speaking with outsiders, but addressing her words to me, she boldly declared, half-seriously, unaware that she'd expressed exactly the opposite view an hour before, that maternal care was a deception, and that it wasn't worth sacrificing one's life for one's children when one is young and can enjoy life. She spent less time with her children, with less anxiety than before, and she paid more and more attention to herself and to her appearance, though she concealed that fact, and to her own enjoyments, even her own self-improvement. She took up the piano again with enthusiasm, something she had completely abandoned before. And it all began with that."

He turned his weary gaze to the window again; evidently making a great effort, he continued immediately once more:

"Yes, sir, this man appeared." He hesitated and produced his peculiar sounds a few times through his nose.

I saw that it was terribly painful for him to name this man, to recall him, or talk about him. But he made an effort, and as if he'd shattered the obstacle hindering him, he continued decisively:

"He was a worthless little man in my view, in my estimation. And not because of the meaning he acquired in my life, but because he really was like that. However, the fact that he was so bad served as proof of how out of control she was. If it hadn't been him, it would've been someone else; it had to happen." He fell silent again. "Yes, sir; he was a musician, a violinist; not a professional, but semiprofessional, a semisociety man.

"His father was a landowner, my father's neighbor. He—the father—went broke, and the children—there were three boys—managed to get along somehow; only one, this youngest, was sent away to his godmother in Paris. There he was enrolled in the conservatory because he had a talent for music; he left there a violinist and began giving concerts. As a man, he was . . ." Obviously wishing to say something bad about him, he refrained and said quickly: "Well, I really don't know how he lived there; I only know that he returned to Russia later that year and appeared in my house.

"He had almond-shaped, damp eyes, reddish smiling lips, a little waxed mustache, the latest, fashionable hairstyle, and a commonly pretty face, one that women call 'not bad looking'; his build was weak, though not unsightly, and he had particularly developed buttocks, like a woman's, or as Hottentots are said to possess.[28] They're also said to be musical. Insinuating himself as much as possible to the point of familiarity, he was sensitive and always ready to yield at the slightest resistance with an observance of external propriety; he wore high-buttoned shoes of that particular Parisian flavor, bright-colored neckties, and other fads that foreigners adopt in Paris, which, by their novelty, always have an impact on women. In his manners, there was an affected display of gaiety. He had, you know, a way of speaking about everything in hints and fragments, as if you knew it all, remembered it, and could complete his thought yourself.

"So he and his music were the cause of everything. At the trial the case was presented as if all that happened was a result of jealousy. It was nothing of the sort—that is, it wasn't that nothing happened, but it wasn't that. At the trial it was determined that I was a deceived husband and that I killed to defend my outraged honor (that's what it's called in their language). I was acquitted as a result. At the trial I tried to clarify the meaning of the affair, but they thought I was trying to rehabilitate my wife's honor.

"Her relations with this musician, such as they were, meant nothing at all to me, nor to her. What does have meaning is what I've told you, that is, my swinishness. Everything occurred because of the terrible abyss that existed between us, the one I've told you about, the awful tension of our mutual contempt for one another, in the face of which the first occasion was sufficient for precipitating the crisis. Lately the quarrels between us had become simply appalling; they were especially startling because they alternated with equally intense animal passion.

"If he hadn't appeared, it would've been someone else. If there hadn't been a pretext of jealousy, it would've been something else. I insist on the fact that all husbands living as I was either must lead dissolute lives or must separate,

28. Hottentot is a derogatory term used by Europeans to describe native people of south-western Africa and to imitate the clicking sounds of their language.

kill themselves, or murder their wives, as I did. If this still hasn't happened to someone, it's a very rare exception. Before things ended as they did, I was on the verge of suicide several times, and she'd also tried to poison herself."

20

"Yes, that's how it was then, and not long before what happened.

"We were observing a sort of truce, and there was no reason to disrupt it; all of a sudden I began talking about some dog that received a medal at an exhibition. She says, 'Not a medal, but honorable mention.' An argument ensues. We begin jumping from one topic to another, with reproaches: 'Well, that's an old story, it's always like that: you said . . .' 'No, I didn't.' 'So, I must be lying!' You feel that any moment a dreadful quarrel will begin when you want either to kill yourself or murder her. You know it'll begin soon, and you fear it like fire; therefore, you'd like to restrain yourself, but wrath overtakes your entire being. She's in the same state, even worse, intentionally distorting your every word, giving it the wrong meaning; and her every word is loaded with venom; wherever she knows that I'm most vulnerable, that's where she attacks. The longer it goes on, the worse it gets. I shout: 'Shut up!' or something like that. She heads out of the room to run into the nursery. I try to restrain her so I can finish what I was saying and prove my point; I grab her arm. She pretends I've hurt her and yells, 'Children, your father's beating me!' I shout, 'Don't lie!' 'And it's not the first time!' she shouts, or something like that. The children rush to her. She calms them down. I say, 'Don't pretend!' She says, 'For you, it's all pretending; you'll kill someone and say he was pretending. Now I've understood you. That's what you want!' 'Oh, why don't you croak!' I shout. I recall how these terrible words horrified me. I never expected that I could utter such awful, crude words, and I'm astonished they could come out of my mouth. I shout these terrible words and run into my study, sit down, and smoke. I hear her go into the front hall and get ready to leave. I ask where she's going. She doesn't answer. 'Well, to hell with her.' I say to myself, returning to my study, lying down again, and smoking. Thousands of different plans enter my head about how to take vengeance, get rid of her, fix all this, and make it as if nothing had happened. I keep thinking and smoking, smoking, smoking. I think of running away from her, hiding, leaving for America. I reach the point when I start dreaming about how I'll get rid of her, and how splendid that will be; how I'll meet another woman, lovely, completely different. I'll get rid of her either by her dying or by getting a divorce, and I think about how to do it. I see that I'm getting confused and not thinking about what I should be thinking about; but, so as not to see that I'm not thinking clearly about what's needed, I go right on smoking.

"Life in the house continues. The governess arrives and asks, 'Where's *madame*? When will she return?' The footman asks whether tea should be served. I go into the dining room; the children, especially the eldest, Liza, who already understands, regard me with a questioning and disapproving look. We drink tea in silence. My wife's not back yet. The whole evening goes by, but she's not there; two feelings alternate in my heart: anger toward her for tormenting me and all the children with her absence that will end when she returns, and the fear that she won't come back and will do something to herself. I could go looking for her. But where to begin? At her sister's? It's ridiculous to go there and ask. Well, God be with her; if she wants to torment someone, let her torment herself. That's what she's been waiting for. And the next time it'll be even worse. What if she's not at her sister's, and is doing something to herself, or has already done it? Eleven o'clock, twelve midnight, one o'clock. I don't go into the bedroom; it's bizarre to lie there alone and wait; I'll lie down here. I want to do something, write letters, read; but I can't do anything. I sit in my study alone, tortured, furious, listening carefully. Three o'clock, four—she's still not back. Toward morning I doze off. When I wake up—she's still not there.

"Everything at home's proceeding normally, but everyone's perplexed and regards me with a questioning and reproachful look, assuming it's all my fault. The same struggle goes on inside me—anger at her tormenting me and anxiety over her well-being.

"Around eleven in the morning her sister arrives as her messenger. The usual business begins: 'She's in a terrible state. What's all this about?' 'But nothing happened.' I describe my wife's impossible character and say that I haven't done anything.

"'Things can't go on like this,' her sister says.

"'It's all her doing, not mine,' I say. 'I won't take the first step. If we separate, so be it.'

"My sister-in-law leaves with nothing. Talking to her, I'd boldly declared that I wouldn't take the first step, but as soon as she'd left and I came out and saw the children, so pitiful and frightened, I was already prepared to take the first step. I would've been glad to do it, but I didn't know how. Once more I walk around the house, smoke, drink some vodka and wine at breakfast, and achieve what I subconsciously desire: I no longer see the stupidity or vileness of my position.

"She arrives around three in the afternoon. When meeting me, she says nothing. I assume that she's given in and begin saying that I felt provoked by her reproaches. With the same stern and terribly tormented face she says that she hasn't come for explanations but to take the children away; she says we can't live together any longer. I begin to argue that I'm not to blame, that she's driven me out of my wits. She looks at me sternly, triumphantly, and then says:

"'Don't say another word; you'll regret it.'

"I tell her that I can't stand such comedies. Then she screams something I can't make out and runs into her room. I hear the key click behind her: she's locked herself in. I try the door; there's no answer, so I go away in a fury. Half an hour later Liza comes running in tears.

"'What is it? Has something happened?'

"'We can't hear mama.'

"We go. I tug at the door with all my strength. The double doors hadn't been well secured and the two sides separate. I go to the bed. She's lying there awkwardly in her petticoats and high boots, unconscious. There's an open bottle of opium on the nightstand. We bring her around. There are more tears and, finally, reconciliation. But not really reconciliation: there remains within the soul of each that old anger for the other with some added irritation for the pain caused by this quarrel, which each of us thinks is the other's fault. But we had to end it all somehow; life goes on as before. The same kind of quarrels occurred constantly, some even worse, once a week, once a month, once a day. It was always the same. One time I'd already acquired a passport to travel abroad—our quarrel had lasted for two days—but then there was a partial explanation, a partial reconciliation—and I didn't leave."

21

"So that was the state of our relations when this man first appeared. He arrived in Moscow—his surname was Trukhachevsky—and he came to my house. It was morning. I received him. At one time we'd been on familiar terms. He attempted to employ a tone somewhere between familiar and formal, tending toward the familiar, but I set a formal tone immediately, and he submitted at once. I didn't like him at all from the very first glance. But the curious thing is, some sort of strange, fateful force led me not to reject him or keep him at bay; on the contrary, I drew him closer to me. After all, what could be simpler than chatting with him coldly, then bidding him farewell, and not introducing him to my wife? But no, as if on purpose, I started talking about his playing and said that I'd heard he'd given up the violin. He replied that, no, on the contrary, he was now playing more than ever. He recalled that I, too, had played at one time. I said that I no longer did, but that my wife played the piano very well.

"What an astonishing thing! My relations to him that first day, at that first hour of our meeting, were such that could have been possible only after all that happened. There was something strained in my relations with him: I noticed every word and expression employed either by him or by me and ascribed significance to them all.

"I introduced him to my wife. The conversation turned to music immediately, and he offered his services to play with her. My wife, as always of late, was very elegant and charming, disturbingly beautiful. Obviously, she took a liking to him at first sight. In addition, she so enjoyed the pleasure of playing together with a violinist that she'd previously hired a musician from the theater to play with her, and her face expressed this delight. But, seeing me, she understood my feelings immediately and altered her expression; thus began a game of mutual deception. I smiled pleasantly and pretended that I found this idea very agreeable. Looking at my wife the way all fornicators regard beautiful women, he pretended to be interested only in the subject of their conversation, precisely the thing that no longer interested him. She tried to appear indifferent, but my own false smile of jealousy, so familiar to her, combined with his lustful gaze, apparently, excited her. From their first meeting I saw that her eyes glowed in a special way and, probably as a result of my jealousy, it seemed as if some electric current was immediately passed between them, evoking identical expressions, glances, and smiles. She blushed, and he blushed; she smiled, and he smiled. We talked about music, Paris, all sorts of trifles. He rose to leave and stood there smiling, his hat resting on his twitching thigh; he glanced first at her and then at me, as if waiting to see what we would do. I remember that moment because it was precisely then that I might not have invited him; nothing more would've happened. But I looked at him and then at her. 'Don't think I'm jealous of you,' I said to her mentally, 'or that I'm afraid of you,' I said to him mentally. I invited him to bring his violin one evening to play with my wife. She glanced at me in astonishment, blushed, and, as if afraid, began to decline, saying that she didn't play well enough. That refusal irritated me further, so I insisted even more on his coming. I recall the strange feeling with which I regarded the nape of his neck, his pale neck, in contrast to his black hair parted down the middle, as took his leave from us with his sprightly, birdlike movements. I couldn't keep from admitting that this man's presence tormented me. 'It all depends on me,' I thought, 'to arrange things so that I never see him again.' But to do that would mean admitting that I was afraid of him. No, I wasn't afraid of him! It would be too humiliating, I said to myself. And right there, in the front hall, knowing that my wife could hear me, I insisted that he come with his violin that very evening. He promised to do so and then left.

"That evening he arrived with his violin and they played together. It took a long time for them to begin playing; they didn't have the scores they needed, and what they did have, my wife was unable to play without practicing. I was very fond of music and supported their playing; I set up the music stand and turned pages. They managed to play something, some songs without words and a little sonata by Mozart.[29] He played magnificently and possessed in the highest degree what's called tone. Besides that, he had refined and elegant taste, not at all in keeping with his character.

"He was, naturally, a much stronger player than my wife and helped her, at the same time as he politely praised her playing. He was very well behaved. My wife seemed interested only in the music and was most unassuming and natural. Meanwhile I, although pretending to be interested in the music, was tormented by jealousy the entire evening.

"From the first moment he met my wife's eyes, I saw that the wild beast residing in both of them, in spite of all the conditions of their position and society, was asking, 'Is it possible?' and was replying, 'Oh, yes, certainly.' I saw that he'd never expected to find in my wife, a Moscow lady, such an attractive woman, and he was very glad of it. Therefore he had no doubt whatsoever that she was willing. The whole question was whether that unbearable husband of hers would hinder them. If I'd been pure, I wouldn't have understood this, but, like the majority of men, I regarded women in exactly this way before I was married, and therefore could read his soul like an open book. I was especially tormented by the fact that she had no other feelings for me except constant irritation, interrupted occasionally by habitual sensuality; and this man, both in his elegant appearance, his novelty, and mainly, his indubitably great talent for music, by the intimacy arising from their playing, by the influence produced by the music on their impressionable natures, especially the violin, this man was certain not merely to please her but to conquer her without the least hesitation, to crush her, twist her, wind her around his little finger, do exactly as he wished with her. I couldn't help seeing this,

29. The reference to "songs without words" may suggest the series of short, lyrical piano pieces by the German Romantic composer Felix Mendelssohn (1809–47). *Songs Without Words* (*Lieder ohne Worte*) comprises eight volumes, each consisting of six "songs" (*Lieder*), written at various points throughout the composer's life and published separately, two posthumously. That composition provided the inspiration and title of Sofiya Andreevna Tolstaya's second story included in this volume.

and I suffered terribly. But in spite of that, or perhaps, as a result of it, some sort of power forced me against my own will to be not merely polite but even affectionate with him. Whether I did it for my wife or for him, to show that I wasn't afraid of him, or for myself, to deceive myself, I don't know, but from the very first, I was unable to behave simply with him. In order not to yield to my initial desire to kill him at once, I had to be excessively nice to him. I treated him to expensive wines at supper, I praised his playing, I chatted with him wearing an especially affectionate smile; I invited him to dinner and to play again with my wife the following Sunday. I said that I would invite several of my acquaintances, music lovers, to hear him. And so it ended."

Pozdnyshev shifted his position in great agitation and emitted his peculiar sound.

"It's strange how that man's presence affected me," he began again, apparently making an effort to keep calm. "Returning home after seeing an exhibit on the second or third day, I entered the front hall and suddenly felt a heavy weight, like a stone, pressing down on my heart, and I couldn't explain to myself what it was. It was that passing through the front hall, I'd noticed something that reminded me of him. Only when I reached my study was I able to understand what it was; I returned to the front hall to check. Yes, I was not mistaken: it was his overcoat. You know, his fashionable overcoat. (Although I really wasn't aware of it, I paid unusual attention to everything that concerned him.) I ask: sure enough, he's there. I enter not through the drawing room, but through the schoolroom, into the hall.[30] My daughter Liza was sitting over a book, and nanny was at the table with the baby, making some sort of lid spin around. The door into the hall was closed, and from there I hear the even notes of an arpeggio and their two voices. I listen carefully, but can't make out what they're saying. Obviously the sounds of the piano were intended to drown out their words and maybe their kisses. My God! What I felt at that moment! I'm horrified when I merely recall the wild beast inside me at that time. My heart suddenly contracted, stopped, and then started thumping like a hammer. The main feeling, as always in any rage, was self-pity. 'In front of the children! And our nanny!' I thought. I must have appeared terrifying because Liza regarded me with a strange look. 'What shall I do?' I asked myself. 'Go in? I can't. God knows what I'd do.' But I couldn't leave. Nanny looks at me as if she understands my predicament. 'It's impossible not to go in,' I said to myself and quickly opened the door. He was sitting at the piano playing

30. This hall (zala), as distinct from the drawing room (gostinaya), was a more formal space where guests were received.

those arpeggios with his large white arched fingers. She was standing in the curve of the piano looking over some open scores. She was the first to see or hear me and looked up. I don't know whether she was frightened and pretended not to be, or she wasn't really frightened, but she didn't flinch or budge; she merely blushed, and not right away.

"'I'm so glad you're here; we can't decide what to play on Sunday,' she said in a tone she'd never use with me if we were alone. What annoyed me was that she said 'we' when talking about him and her. I greeted him in silence.

"He pressed my hand; with a smile that seemed to me purely mocking, he began explaining that he'd brought some music to prepare for Sunday and now they disagreed about what to play: something more difficult and classical, that is, a Beethoven sonata for the violin, or some shorter pieces. It was all so natural and simple: there was nothing to find fault with. Still, I was certain that it was all lies and they were conspiring to deceive me.

"Among the most tormenting conditions for jealous men (and in our social life all men are jealous)—are certain social conditions that permit the greatest and most dangerous closeness between a man and a woman. You'd be a laughingstock in other people's eyes if you prevented such closeness at a ball, or when a doctor examines his patient, or for those engaged in art, painting, and, primarily—music. Two people are occupied with the noblest art, that is, music; a certain intimacy is necessary and has nothing reprehensible about it; only a stupid, jealous husband can see anything undesirable in it. Meanwhile, everyone knows that it's precisely these pursuits, especially music, that account for the greatest number of adulteries in our society. Obviously, the embarrassment reflected on my face also embarrassed them: for a long time I stood there speechless. I was like a bottle turned upside down from which no water can flow because it's too full. I wanted to abuse him and throw him out, but felt that I had to be affectionate and polite to him again. And that's what I did. I pretended to approve of everything, and once more, with that same strange feeling that forced me to treat him with greater affection, the more I was tormented by his presence, I told him that I would rely on his taste and I gave her the same advice. I remained there as long as necessary to smooth over the unpleasant impression created when I'd first entered the room with my frightened expression and awkward silence; he soon left, pretending they'd decided on what piece to play the following day. I was absolutely certain that compared to what really occupied them, the question of what to play was of complete indifference to both of them.

"I escorted him into the front hall with particular politeness (how else could one escort a man who'd come to disturb the peace and destroy the happiness of an entire family?). I pressed his soft, white hand with special affection."

22

"I didn't speak to her that entire day: I couldn't. Her proximity aroused such hatred in me for her that I was afraid of myself. At dinner she asked in front of the children when I was leaving. I had to make a trip the following week to attend a session in the neighboring district. I said when I was going. She asked whether I needed anything for the journey. I didn't reply and sat at the table in silence; then I walked out in silence and into my study. Of late she never came into my room, especially at that time of day. I lay there in my study, furious. All of a sudden, I heard familiar steps. A terrible, hideous thought entered my mind: like Uriah's wife, she wanted to conceal the sin she'd already committed and that was why she was coming to see me at such an unusual hour.[31] 'Is she really coming in here?' I wondered, hearing her approaching footsteps. 'If she is, then it means, I'm right.' Inexpressible hatred for her arose in my soul. The footsteps drew closer and closer. 'Or could she be going past, into the hall? No, the door creaks open and there in the doorway stands her tall, beautiful figure; she has a timid and ingratiating look she's trying to hide, but I see it and understand its significance. I hold my breath for so long that I nearly choke; continuing to look at her, I grab my cigarette case and begin to smoke.

"'Well, what's this? I've come to be with you for a while, and you start smoking,' she said and then sat down next to me on the sofa, leaning up against me.

"I moved away so as not to be touching her.

"'I see you're displeased by my wanting to play on Sunday,' she said.

"'I'm not displeased at all,' I replied.

"'As if I don't see it?'

"'Well, I congratulate you for seeing it. I no longer see anything except for the fact that you're acting like a cocotte . . .'

"'If you want to swear like a cab driver, I'll leave.'

"'Then leave, but know that if you don't value the family honor, then I don't value you (to hell with you); but I value the family honor.'

"'What's this? What?'

"'Go away, for God's sake, go away!'

31. Uriah was a Hittite captain whose beautiful wife, Bathsheba, aroused King David's lust. He arranged for Uriah to die in battle so he could marry her (2 Samuel 11:1–27).

"Either she was pretending that she didn't know what it was all about or else she really didn't understand; in either case, she was offended and angry. She stood up, but didn't leave; instead, she remained standing in the middle of the room.

"'You've really become impossible,' she began. 'Your character is such that even an angel couldn't get along with you.' Since she always tried to wound me as deeply as possible, she reminded me of my treatment of my sister (it was the time I lost my temper and uttered rude words to her; she knew that the episode was still tormenting me, and this was the tender spot she pressed down on). 'After that incident, nothing from you would surprise me,' she said.

"'Yes, insult me, humiliate me, slander me, make me out as the one to blame,' I said to myself. Suddenly I was overcome with such anger toward her as I've never experienced before.

"It was the first time I felt like expressing that anger physically. I jumped up and ran toward her; but just as I was getting up, I recall that I became aware of my own anger and asked myself whether it was good to give way to this feeling; at once I told myself that it was, that it would frighten her, and then, instead of resisting the anger, I began inflaming it further and was glad that it flared up in me even stronger.

"'Get away, or I'll kill you!' I cried, going up to her and grabbing her arm; in saying this I consciously intensified the angry tone of my voice. I must have been terrifying because she grew so timid that she didn't even have the strength to leave; she merely said:

"'Vasya, what is it? What's the matter with you?'

"'Get out!' I roared even louder. 'Only you can drive me to such rage. I can't answer for myself!'

"Having given way to rage, I reveled in it and wanted to do something unusual to show the extreme degree of my fury. I felt a terrible desire to hit her, to kill her, but I knew that was impossible; therefore, to vent my rage anyway, I seized a paperweight from my desk; I shouted 'Get out!' again and hurled the paperweight past her and onto the floor. I aimed it very carefully past her. Then she started to leave the room, but first paused in the doorway. While she still was watching (I did it so she'd see), I began grabbing things from the desk, candlesticks, an inkwell, and throwing them onto the ground, continuing to shout:

"'Get out! Go away! I can't answer for myself!'

"She left—and I stopped immediately.

"An hour later our nanny came in and said that my wife was having hysterics. I went to see her; she was sobbing, laughing, unable to speak, and shaking all over. She wasn't pretending; she really was ill.

"Toward morning she calmed down and we were reconciled under the influence of the emotion we call love.

"In the morning, when I'd confessed after our reconciliation that I was feeling jealous of Trukhachevsky, she was not in the least embarrassed and began laughing in the most natural manner. She said that even the possibility of an infatuation for such a man seemed very strange to her.

"'Could a decent woman ever feel something other than pleasure afforded by his music? Yes, if you wish, I'm prepared never to see him again. Not even this Sunday, though all the guests have been invited. Write to him and tell him that I'm unwell, and that's that. What's most repulsive is that someone, especially he, might think he was dangerous. I'm too proud a person to allow anyone to think that.'

"And you know, she wasn't lying; she believed what she was saying. With these words she hoped to arouse her own contempt and thus defend herself from him, but she didn't succeed. Everything was pitted against her, especially that accursed music. And so it ended; on Sunday the guests assembled and they played together once again."

23

"I think it's unnecessary to point out that I'm a very vain person: if one isn't vain in our everyday social life, there's nothing else to live by. Well, on Sunday I'd organized the dinner and musical evening with great taste. I myself had purchased the ingredients for the meal and invited the guests.

"The guests gathered around six o'clock; he appeared wearing a tail coat with diamond studs in bad taste. He behaved informally, replied to everyone hurriedly, with a smile of agreement and understanding, you know, with that special expression indicating that everything you say or do is precisely what he was expecting. I noticed now with particular pleasure everything offensive in him; it was all supposed to appease me and prove that he stood on such a low level for my wife that she could never lower herself. I no longer let myself feel jealous now. In the first place, I'd already suffered this torment and needed some respite; in the second place, I wanted to believe my wife's assurances, and I did believe them. But in spite of the fact that I wasn't jealous, nevertheless, I behaved in an unnatural way with him and with her during dinner, and all during the first half of the evening, until the music began. I was still following all their movements and glances closely.

"The dinner was like every other one, boring and pretentious. The music began fairly early. Ah, I recall all the details of that evening; I recall how he brought his violin, unlocked the case, and removed the cover that had been embroidered for him by a certain lady, took the instrument out and began tuning it. I remember how my wife sat down at the piano and feigned an indifferent air, which I noticed was concealing her great nervousness—chiefly to do with her own ability—there followed the usual sound of an A on the piano, the pizzicato from the violin, and the arrangement of the score. I recall how they then glanced at each other, looked at those getting seated around them, then said something to each other, and it started. He played the first chord. He had a serious, stern, sympathetic expression; listening to his own sounds, he carefully plucked the strings and the piano answered him. And it began . . ."

He stopped speaking and emitted his sound several times in a row. He was about to speak, sniffed noisily, and stopped again.

"They played Beethoven's *Kreutzer Sonata*.[32] Do you know the first presto? Do you?" he cried. "Ugh! It's a dreadful thing, that sonata. Precisely that part. In general, music's a dreadful thing. What is it really? I don't understand. What is music? What does it do? And why does it do what it does? They say that music has a sublime impact on the soul—that's nonsense and not true! It does have an impact, a dreadful impact. I'm talking about myself: but it's not in any way a sublime impact on the soul. It affects the soul neither in an elevating nor a debasing way, but in an irritating way. How can I explain it? Music forces me to forget myself, my actual situation, and transports me to some other state, not my own; it seems to me that under the influence of music I feel something more than what I really feel, I understand more than I really understand, and I can do more than I can really do. I explain this by saying that music acts like yawning or like laughter: I don't feel sleepy, but when I look at someone yawning, I yawn; there's nothing to laugh about, but when I hear someone laughing, I laugh.

"It, music, immediately transports me directly into the spiritual state of the composer. My soul merges with his and I'm simultaneously transported to another state, yet I don't know why this happens. After all, the person who wrote the *Kreutzer Sonata*, let's say—Beethoven, knew why he was in such a state—and that resulted in his taking certain actions; therefore his state had

32. Sonata ("Kreutzer") for piano and violin, opus 47, composed in 1802.

meaning for him, but for me it has none whatsoever. Consequently, music merely arouses; it doesn't culminate. When they play a military march, the soldiers march and the music achieves its end; when they play a dance tune, I dance, and the music achieves its end; when they sing a mass, I take communion, and the music also achieves its end. Otherwise, it's only provocation, but what follows as a result of that provocation is lacking. That's why music is so dreadful and sometimes has such a terrible effect. In China music is a state affair. That's how it should be. Can we really permit anyone who wishes, to hypnotize another person or even many people, and then do with them as he wishes? Especially if this hypnotist is the first immoral man who just happens to turn up.

"Otherwise, it's a terrible instrument in the hands of someone who turns up. Take this *Kreutzer Sonata,* for example, the first presto. Is it really possible to play this movement in a drawing room in the presence of women wearing low-cut gowns? To play it and then applaud, to eat ice cream afterward, and gossip about the latest rumors? These pieces can be played only in certain important, significant circumstances, and then, only when certain important actions, corresponding to the music, are demanded. To play it and then act as the music directs. Otherwise the arousal of energy and emotion suited to neither the place nor the time, lacking an outlet, can't help but produce a harmful effect. At any rate, that piece had a terrible impact on me; I felt as if totally new feelings were revealed to me, new possibilities I'd never imagined before. It was as if something in my soul were saying, 'Yes, that's how it is, not at all as you thought and experienced previously, but like this.' I couldn't really explain what the new thing was that I'd discovered, but my awareness of this new state was very enjoyable. All those people, including my wife and him, appeared to me in a completely new light.

"After this presto they finished playing the superb, but ordinary, conventional andante with its vulgar variations and its utterly weak finale. Then they played Ernst's 'Elegy' at the request of the guests, and a few other short pieces.[33] All this was fine, but didn't produce even one hundredth of the impact that the first work did. All this occurred against the background of the impression of the initial presto. I felt lighthearted and cheerful. I'd never seen my wife behave the way she did that evening. Those sparkling eyes, the severity and significance of her expression as she was playing, and then the absolute melting quality of her weak, pitiful, blissful smile when they finished. I saw it all, but

33. Heinrich Wilhelm Ernst (1814–65) was a Moravian-Jewish virtuoso violinist and composer of salon pieces, fantasias, and musical variations.

didn't ascribe any meaning to it other than the fact that she felt the same as I did; that she felt some new feelings, never before experienced, now revealed or recalled, as it were. The evening ended agreeably and everyone left for home.

"Knowing that I had to leave to attend a session two days later, Trukhachevsky remarked, in parting, that he hoped to repeat the pleasure of the evening on another occasion. From that I could conclude that he didn't consider it possible to visit during my absence from home, and that pleased me. It turned out that since I wouldn't be returning before his departure, we wouldn't get to see each other again.

"I shook his hand with real delight for the first time and thanked him for the pleasure. He also said a final farewell to my wife. Their leave-taking seemed natural and proper to me. Everything was splendid. My wife and I were both very pleased with the evening."

24

"Two days later I left for the session, bidding farewell to my wife in the best, most serene mood. There was always an enormous amount of work to be done in the district and a very special life, a little world apart. I spent two days working ten hours a day at the session. On the second day a letter from my wife was delivered to my office. I read it at once. She wrote about the children, her uncle, the nanny, some purchases, and among other things, as if about a most ordinary event, she wrote that Trukhachevsky had dropped by, brought her some scores that he'd promised, and offered to play again, but she'd demurred. I didn't recall his promising to bring any scores: it seemed to me that he'd said his final farewell; therefore this news struck me unpleasantly. But I had so much work to do that I had no time to think about it; I reread her letter later that evening, when I returned to my rooms. In addition to the fact that Trukhachevsky had come again in my absence, I found the whole tone of her letter strained. The insane beast of jealousy began to growl in its kennel wanting to escape, but I feared that beast and quickly locked him in. 'What a vile feeling jealousy is!' I said to myself. 'What could be more natural than what she wrote?'

"I got into bed and began thinking about the matters I'd have to deal with the next day. It always took me a long time to fall asleep during these sessions, being in a new place, but on that occasion I dozed off very quickly. And, as sometimes happens, you know, all of a suddenly I felt an electric shock and woke up. I awoke thinking about her, my carnal love for her—and about Trukhachevsky and what had happened between them. Horror and rage gripped my heart. But I began reasoning with myself. 'What nonsense,' I said. 'You've got no grounds; there's nothing to it; nothing's happened. How can I demean her and myself, assuming such awful things? Some hired fiddler, known as a worthless type, suddenly takes up with an honorable woman, a respected mother of a family, *my* wife! Ridiculous!' So on the one hand it seemed to me. On the other hand, 'How else could it be?' How could it fail to be this simplest and most obvious thing, the reason I'd married her, the reason I stay with her, the one thing I need from her, and therefore what others must need from her, including this musician? He's an unmarried man, healthy (I remember how he crunched the gristle of that cutlet and how greedily he slurped that glass of wine through his red lips); he's well fed, suave, not only lacking in principles, but, obviously, having the goal of taking advantage of any pleasures that come his way. And between them, the bond of music, that most refined lust of the senses. What can restrain him? Nothing. On the contrary, everything attracts him. And she? But who is she? She's a mystery: as she was, so she still is. I don't know her. I know her only as an animal. And nothing can or should restrain an animal.

"Only then did I recall their faces that evening, when, after performing the *Kreutzer Sonata*, they played some passionate little piece, I don't remember by whom, a piece sensual to the point of obscenity. 'How could I leave?' I asked myself, recalling their faces. 'Wasn't it obvious that everything had happened between them that evening? And wasn't it clear then that no further barriers existed between them, and that they both, especially she, experienced some shame after what had transpired?' I remember her weak, pitiful, blissful smile, and then, as I approached the piano, how she was wiping the perspiration from her flushed face. Even then they'd avoided looking at each other; only during supper, as he was pouring her water, did they glance at each other and exchange a slight smile. Then I recalled with horror how I caught their glance and that barely noticeable smile. 'Yes, it's all over,' one voice said to me; then another said something entirely different. 'Something's come over you; it can't be,' said that other voice. I was terrified lying there in the dark; I lit a match and felt extremely afraid in that small room with the yellow wallpaper. I lit a cigarette; as always when you whirl around in one and the same circle of unresolved contradictions—you smoke; so I smoked one cigarette after another to enshroud myself and not to see all the contradictions.

"I didn't sleep the whole night; at five in the morning, having decided that I couldn't bear the tension any longer, I resolved to leave at once; I got up, woke the caretaker who was serving me, and sent him for horses. I posted a note to the council saying that I'd been called back to Moscow on urgent business; therefore I asked to be replaced by another member. At eight o'clock I got into my carriage and left for home."

25

The conductor entered; having noticed that our candle had almost burned down, he extinguished it without leaving a new one. It had begun to grow light outside. Pozdnyshev was silent, breathing heavily all the time the conductor was in our carriage. He continued his story after the conductor had left; the only sound in the semidarkness of the carriage was the rattle of the windows in the moving train and the clerk's rhythmic snoring. I couldn't see Pozdnyshev's face in the half-light of dawn. I could only hear his voice, more and more agitated, full of suffering.

"I had to travel thirty-five versts by horse-drawn carriage and eight hours by train.[34] The carriage ride was splendid. It was a frosty autumn day with bright sunshine. You know, it was the time when horseshoes leave their imprint on the oiled roadway. The roads were smooth, the light was bright, and the air was bracing. It was nice to ride in the carriage. After it had grown light and I was on my way home, I felt better. Looking at the horses, the fields, the passersby, I forgot where I was going. Sometimes it seemed that I was simply going for a drive, and the thing that had summoned me back had never happened. I found that kind of oblivion particularly pleasant. When I remembered where I was heading, I said to myself, 'It'll all become clear; don't think about it.' In addition, when we were about halfway home, an incident occurred that delayed me en route and served to distract me even further: the carriage broke down and had to be repaired. This event was very significant because it caused me to arrive in Moscow not at five o'clock in the afternoon, as I'd expected, but at midnight; I got home near one in the morning, since I wound up missing the express and had to take the local train. Getting a cart, the repair, payment, tea at the inn, a chat with the innkeeper—all this distracted me even more. By twilight everything was ready, and I was on my way again; it was even better to travel at night than by day. There was a new moon, a light frost, still a fine road, horses, and a cheerful driver; I drove on and enjoyed myself, hardly thinking about what was awaiting me; or I was so enjoying myself precisely because I knew what was waiting for me and I was bidding farewell to the joys of life. But my serene state and the possibility of suppressing my feelings ended with the carriage ride. As soon as I boarded the train, something altogether different began. That eight-hour journey in the railway carriage was something terrible for me, something I'll never forget for the rest of my life. Whether it was because once I'd settled in the car,

34. A verst equals about two-thirds of a mile.

I vividly imagined that I'd already arrived, or whether it was that railway travel has such a disquieting effect on people, but as soon as I sat down I could no longer control my imagination, and it began incessantly conceiving scenes with extraordinary clarity that inflamed my jealousy, one after another, each more salacious than the last, all on the same theme, about what was happening there, without me, and about how she was betraying me. I burned with indignation, rage, and some peculiar feeling of intoxication with my own humiliation, as I contemplated these images, and I couldn't tear myself away from them; I couldn't keep from seeing them, I couldn't erase them, I couldn't help evoking them. Not only that, but the more I contemplated these imagined scenes, the more I believed in their reality. It was as if the vividness with which these pictures appeared to me served as proof that what I was imagining was real. Some devil, as if against my own will, devised and proposed the most terrible ruminations. I recalled a previous conversation I'd had with Trukhachevsky's brother, and with some ecstasy, I rent my own heart with this conversation, relating it to Trukhachevsky and my wife.

"That had taken place a long time ago, but I remembered it. Trukhachevsky's brother, I recall, in reply to a question once about whether he frequented brothels, said that a respectable man wouldn't go to a place where he might get sick, where it was foul and dirty, if he could always find a respectable woman. And now he, his brother, had found my wife. 'True, she's no longer so young, she's missing a tooth on one side, and she's a little plump,' I imagine he was thinking. 'But what's to be done? One has to make the best of what is.' 'Yes, he's condescending to take her as his mistress,' I said to myself. 'But she's safe.' 'No, that's impossible! What am I thinking?' I said to myself in horror. 'There's nothing to it, nothing at all! There're no grounds for supposing anything like this. Didn't she tell me that even the idea that I might be jealous of him was degrading to her? Yes, but she's lying, it's all lies!' I cried, and began again. . . . There were only two passengers in our car—an old woman and her husband, neither very talkative; they got off at one of the stations and I was left all alone. I was like a wild beast in a cage: I jumped up, went to the car windows, then swaying, began to pace, trying to make the train go faster; but the car with all its seats and windows, kept on rattling, just as ours does now . . ."

Pozdnyshev jumped up and took several steps, then sat down again.

"Oh, I'm afraid, I'm afraid of railway carriages; terror overwhelms me. Yes, it's horrible!" he continued. "I said to myself, 'I'll think about something else. Let's say, the owner of the inn where I just had tea.' Well then, in my imagination I see the innkeeper with his long beard and his grandson—a boy the same age as my Vasya. My son Vasya! He'll see the musician kissing his mother. What will happen in his poor soul? She doesn't care! She's in love. . . . And once again the same thing enters my mind. No, no . . . I'll think about the hospital inspection. Yes, the patient who complained about the doctor yesterday. The doctor had a mustache, just like Trukhachevsky's. He so impudently . . . They were both deceiving me when he said he was leaving. And it started again. Everything I thought about had some connection to him. I was suffering terribly. My primary suffering was ignorance, doubt, the split within me, not knowing—whether I should love her or hate her. My sufferings were so strong that, I recall, an idea occurred to me that I liked very much: namely, to go outside, lie down on the rails underneath the train, and end it all. Then, at least, there'd be no more hesitation or doubt. The one thing that prevented me from doing this was the pity I felt for myself, and that immediately evoked hatred for her. I felt some strange emotion toward him and an awareness of my humiliation and his victory, but toward her, I felt terrible hatred. 'I can't put an end to myself and let her be; it's necessary for her to suffer, even a little, so she understands what I've gone through,' I said to myself. I got out at every station to distract myself. At one station I saw that people were drinking, and I drank some vodka myself. A Jew was standing next to me and also drinking. He began chatting, and I, so as not to remain alone in my train carriage, went with him back to his dirty, smoky third-class car, littered with the shells of sunflower seeds. I sat there next to him; he talked a great deal and told anecdotes. I listened to him, but was unable to understand what he was saying because I kept thinking about my own affairs. He noticed this and demanded my attention; then I stood up and returned to my own car. 'I have to consider,' I said to myself, 'whether what I think is true and whether there are any grounds to torment myself.' I sat down, wanting to reflect on the matter calmly, but right away, instead of calm consideration, the same thing began again: instead of reasoning—only scenes and imaginings. 'How many times have I tormented myself like this,' I said to myself (I remembered all my previous attacks of jealousy), 'and it turned out to be nothing. Just like now, perhaps even certainly, I'll find her sound asleep; she'll wake up, be glad to see me, and by her words and look, I'll know there was nothing to it and that it was all nonsense. Oh, that would be so nice!' 'But no, that's happened too often, and it won't happen again!' some voice said to me, and it all started again. Yes, that was my punishment! I wouldn't show a syphilis ward to a young man to rid him of his desire for women, but rather show my own soul, to see what devils were tearing it apart! Why, it was awful that I recognized my absolute, undisputed rights over her body, as if it were my own, and at the same time I felt that I couldn't own her body, that it wasn't mine, and that she could make use of it in any way she wished, and that she wished to use it not as I would like. There was nothing I could do to him or her. Just like Vanka the Steward standing before the gallows, he would sing a little song about how he'd kissed her sugary lips, and so on and so forth.[35] And he prevails. And I can do even less to her. If she hasn't yet done it, but wants to, and I know she wants to, then it's even worse: it'd be better if she's done it already, so that I knew, so there was no uncertainty. I couldn't really say what I wanted. I wanted for her not to desire what she must desire. That was complete and utter madness!"

26

"At the next-to-last station, when the conductor came in to collect the tickets, I gathered up my things and went out onto the brake-platform; the awareness of what was soon to follow was very close, that is, the resolution, and it increased my agitation. I felt cold and my jaw was trembling so much that my teeth began chattering. I exited the station automatically along with the crowd, hailed a horse-cab, got in, and set off. I rode along, glancing at the few passersby, the doormen, and the shadows cast by the streetlamps and my own cab, first in front, then behind, not thinking about anything in particular. After covering about a half a verst, my feet felt cold, and I thought about how I'd taken off my woolen socks in the train car and packed them away in my bag. Where was my bag? Was it here? Yes. And my wicker case? I recalled that I'd forgotten all about my baggage, but remembering it now and finding the ticket, I decided that it wasn't worth returning to get it, and continued my journey.

"As much as I try to remember now, I can't possibly recall my state of mind at the time. What was I thinking? What did I want? I don't know. I only recall that I was aware that something terrible and very significant in my life was about to happen. Whether that significant event occurred because I thought it would, or because I had a premonition of it—I don't know. Perhaps it's just that after what happened, all the preceding moments in my imagination acquired an ominous cast. I drove up to the front porch. It was after midnight. Several horse-cabs were waiting there, expecting to get passengers because there were still lights burning in the windows (those windows were in our apartment, the hall and drawing room). Without trying to

---

35. The hero of numerous folk songs, who boasts of his love for the master's wife or his daughter, and who pays for his bragging with his life.

account for why there were lights in our windows so late, I climbed the stairs in the same state of mind expecting something terrible, and I rang the bell. Our footman, the kind, hardworking, but very stupid Yegor, opened the door. The first thing that struck my eye was the fact that *his* overcoat was hanging on a hook in the front hall alongside other coats. I should have been surprised, but I wasn't; it was as if I'd expected it. 'That's how it is,' I said to myself. When I asked Yegor who was there, he said Trukhachevsky; I asked whether anyone else was there. He answered:

"'No one else, sir.'

"I remember that he replied with a tone as if he wished to bolster me and dispel any doubts that anyone else was present. 'No one else, sir. That's it,' he said, as if to himself.

"'And the children?'

"'Healthy, thank God. Asleep long ago, sir.'

"I couldn't breathe or keep my jaw from trembling. 'Yes, it must be different from what I thought: previously, when I thought something was a misfortune, it would turn out that everything was all right. But now it wasn't that way at all: everything was just as I imagined; I used to think it was only my imagination, yet here it all is in reality. It's all here . . .'

"I almost started sobbing, but just then the devil prompted me: 'Go on, cry, be sentimental, while they quietly say good night; they won't leave any clues, you'll have doubts and will torment yourself forever.' My sentimentality vanished immediately, and there appeared a strange feeling—you won't believe it—a feeling of joy that now my torment would end, that I could punish her now, be rid of her, and give free rein to my rage. And I did give free rein to it—I became a wild beast, mean and cunning.

"'No, don't, don't,' I said to Yegor, who wanted to enter the drawing room. 'Here's what you'll do: go find a horse-cab and drive to the station; here's my luggage ticket; fetch my belongings. Go on.'

"He walked through the corridor to get his coat. Afraid that he might alarm them, I accompanied him to his room and waited there while he got dressed. From the drawing room, through the room in between, I could hear the sound of their voices and of knives and plates. They were eating and hadn't heard the bell. 'If only they don't come out now,' I thought. Yegor put on his overcoat with an astrakhan collar and left. I let him out and locked the door behind him; I was terrified when I was left all alone and felt that I had to take action at once. What to do? I still didn't know. I only knew that now everything was finished: there could be no doubt as to her guilt; I would punish her instantly and end my relationship with her.

"Previously I'd entertained some hesitation and said to myself, 'Perhaps it's not true; maybe I'm mistaken.' Now there was nothing of the sort. Everything was resolved irrevocably. Hidden away from me, she was alone with him, at night! That showed a total disregard for everything. Or even worse: it was deliberate daring, audacity in crime, so that this audacity could serve as evidence of her innocence. It was all clear. There was no doubt. I was afraid of only one thing: they might run away, devise some new deception, deprive me of the evidence of their crime, and the possibility of punishment. And, so I could catch them more quickly, I tiptoed toward the hall where they were sitting, not through the drawing room, but through the corridor and the nursery.

"The boys were asleep in the first nursery. In the second, nanny was stirring, about to wake up; I imagined what she'd think after finding everything out. Such self-pity overcame me that I was unable to refrain from tears, and hastily tiptoed out of the room so as not to wake the children; I ran down the hallway and into my own study, where I collapsed on the sofa and burst into tears.

"'I'm an honest man, my parents' son; all my life I've dreamt of the happiness of family life; I'm a man who's never been unfaithful to her. . . . And now! Five children, and she's embracing a musician because he has such red lips! No, she's not a human being! She's a bitch, a filthy bitch! Right next to the room where the children are, those same children she's been pretending to love all her life. And writing to me as she did! Throwing herself on his neck so brazenly! What do I know? Perhaps she's been like this all the time. Perhaps she's been carrying on with the footmen and bearing their children who are considered mine. I'd have come home tomorrow and she'd have her hair all done up, with her narrow waist; she'd have greeted me with her indolent, graceful movements (I imagined her attractive, detestable face), and that wild beast of jealousy would have been lodged in my heart forever and would be tearing it to shreds. What will nanny think or Yegor? And poor Lizochka? She understands some things already. What insolence! Lies! And that animal sensuality I know so well,' I said to myself.

"I wanted to get up, but I couldn't. My heart was beating so fast that I could scarcely stand on my own two feet. Yes, I'll die of a stroke. She'll kill me. That's what she wants. Well, what would killing me mean to her? But no, that would be too advantageous for her, and I don't want to afford her that pleasure. Yes, I'm sitting here while they're eating and laughing and . . . Yes, in spite of the fact that she's no longer enjoying the bloom of youth, he didn't scorn her: she's still not bad looking, and the main thing is, at least she poses no risk to his precious health. 'And why didn't I strangle her then?' I asked myself, recalling the moment a week ago when I'd forced her out of my study and had begun throwing things. I vividly recalled my state of mind at that time; not only did I recall it, but now felt that same need to smash, and destroy as I'd felt then. I remember how I wanted to act; all other considerations except those needed for action, passed out of my head. I entered the state of a wild beast or a man under the influence of physical excitement at a time of great danger, when a man acts meticulously, deliberately, without losing a moment, with only one definite goal in mind."

27

"The first thing I did was remove my boots; I approached the wall above the sofa in stocking feet where my guns and daggers were hanging; I chose a curved Damascus dagger that had never been used and was extremely sharp. I removed it from its sheath. The sheath, I recall, dropped behind the sofa, and I remember saying to myself, 'Afterward I have to find it, or else it'll get lost.' Then I took off my coat, which I was still wearing; stepping quietly in just my socks, I headed in.

"I crept stealthily and all of a sudden, flung open the door. I recall the expression on their faces. I remember it because that expression afforded me agonizing delight. It was an expression of horror. That's just what I needed. I shall never forget the expression of desperate horror on both their faces at the moment they first saw me. He was sitting at the table, it seems, but having seen or heard me, he jumped to his feet and stood with his back to the cupboard. On his face was an expression of the most unquestionable terror. On hers was the same expression of terror, but also of something else. If it had been only terror, then perhaps what happened wouldn't have happened; but her expression also revealed distress and dissatisfaction that her amorous passion and happiness with him had been disrupted. It was as if she didn't require anything other than to be left alone with her present happiness. Both those expressions remained on their faces for one brief moment. The expression of terror on his face was immediately replaced by one of inquiry: could he start lying or not? If he could, he'd better begin. If not, then something else would happen. But what? He looked at her with a questioning glance. Her expression of annoyance and distress seemed to be replaced by one of concern for him when she glanced at him.

"I paused in the doorway for a moment, hiding the dagger behind my back. At that moment he smiled and in a ridiculously indifferent tone of voice, he began:

"'We've been concertizing . . .'

"'I didn't expect,' she began at the same time, falling in with his tone.

"But neither one nor the other finished speaking: the same fury I'd felt a week ago took possession of me. Once again I experienced that need for destruction and violence, that ecstasy of rage, and I yielded to it.

"Neither one finished speaking. . . . That other thing he'd feared happened, something that immediately obliterated everything they were saying. I rushed at her, still concealing the dagger so he wouldn't prevent me from stabbing her in the side just below her breast. I'd chosen that spot from the very first. Just as I was rushing at her, he saw me and did something I'd never expected: he grabbed my arm and shouted:

"'Come to your senses! What are you doing? Help!'

"I yanked my arm away and silently rushed at him. His eyes met mine and he suddenly turned as pale as a ghost, even his lips; his eyes shone in an unusual way, and he did something else I'd never expected, he darted under the piano and out through the door. I was about to chase after him, but some weight was hanging onto my left arm. It was she. I tried to free myself. She hung on even more tightly and wouldn't let go. This unexpected hindrance, the weight, and her repulsive touch aggravated me even further. I felt that I was in a total rage and must be terrifying, and I was glad of it. I shook my left arm with all my might and my elbow landed right in her face. She cried out and released my arm. I wanted to chase after him, but remembered that it would be absurd to go running after my wife's lover in my stocking feet, and I didn't want to be ridiculous, I wanted to be terrifying. In spite of my frightful rage, I was aware all the while of the impression I was making on others; it was even this impression that to some extent was guiding me. I turned to her. She fell onto the couch; clasping her hand to her bruised eyes, she looked at me. Her face reflected fear and hatred of me, her enemy, the way a rat does when you lift the trap in which it's been caught. At any rate, I saw nothing else in her besides fear and hatred for me. It was the same fear and hatred that would result from her love for another man. But I might still have refrained and not done it, if she'd remained silent. But she suddenly began speaking, trying to grab the hand in which I held the dagger.

"'Come to your senses! What are you doing? What's wrong with you? There's nothing to it, nothing, nothing . . . I swear!'

"I might still have hesitated, but these last words of hers, from which I concluded just the opposite—that is, that everything had already happened—demanded a reply. And the reply had to correspond to the mood I'd brought upon myself, which was rising in a crescendo, and had to continue growing. Rage also has its own laws.

"'Don't lie, you wretch!' I howled and seized her left arm, but she managed to pull away. Then, still clutching the dagger, I grabbed her by the throat, threw her back, and began strangling her. What a firm neck she had. . . . She grabbed my hand with both of hers, trying to pull it away from her throat; as if waiting for that, I plunged the dagger into her left side with all my might, just below her ribs.

"When people say that they don't remember what they did in a fit of rage—it's nonsense, not true. I remembered everything and didn't stop remembering even for one moment. The higher I turned up the steam of my rage, the brighter the light of consciousness burned within me, by which light I couldn't help but see everything I was doing. I can't say that I knew beforehand what I'd do, but at the time I was doing it, even, it seems, for a few moments before, I knew what I was doing, as if to make repentance possible, and so I could tell myself later that I could've stopped. I knew that I was stabbing her below the ribs and that the dagger would penetrate. At the moment I was doing it, I knew that I was doing something terrible, something I'd never done before, something that would have horrible consequences. But this awareness flashed like lightning, and the act followed immediately afterward. And the act became conscious with extraordinary clarity. I heard and recall the momentary resistance of her corset and of something else, then the penetration of the knife into something soft. She grabbed the dagger with her hands, cut them, but didn't let go. For a long time afterward, in prison, after my moral transformation had occurred, I thought about that moment, remembered what I could of it, and reflected on it. I recalled for one moment, only one, preceding the act, the terrible awareness that I was killing and had killed a woman, a defenseless woman, my wife. I remembered the horror of that awareness and therefore concluded, and even vaguely recall, that having inserted the dagger, I withdrew it at once, wishing to remedy what I'd done and to stop doing it. I stood there motionless for a second, waiting to see what would happen, whether it could be remedied. She jumped to her feet and screamed:

"'Nanny! He's killed me!'

"Having heard the commotion, nanny stood in the doorway. I was still standing there, waiting, not believing. But blood was gushing from under her corset. It was only then that I realized that it was impossible to remedy; I decided at once that it was unnecessary, that this was what I'd wanted, and was exactly what I should've done. I waited until she fell; nanny rushed to her shouting, 'Good Lord!' Only then did I toss away the dagger and run out of the room.

"'I must not get excited; I must know what I'm doing,' I said to myself, without looking at her or at nanny. Nanny was shouting, calling the maid. I walked down the corridor and, after sending in the maid, went to my room. 'What do I do now?' I asked myself and immediately realized what to do. Entering my study, I went up to the wall, removed a revolver, examined it—it was loaded—and placed it on the desk. Then I retrieved the sheath from behind the sofa and sat down.

"I sat there a long time. I wasn't thinking about anything in particular, and didn't remember anything. I heard the sounds of some commotion. I heard that someone arrived and then someone else came. Then I heard and saw how Yegor brought my wicker case into the study. As if anyone needed that!

"'Have you heard what happened?' I asked. 'Tell the doorman to summon the police.'

"He didn't say a word and left. I stood up, locked the door, took out my cigarettes and matches, and started smoking. I hadn't finished one cigarette before sleep arrived and overpowered me. I probably slept for two hours. I remember that I dreamt how she and I were friendly, then we quarreled, but made up, and that something was interfering, but we still were friendly. A knock at the door aroused me. 'It's the police,' I thought and woke up. 'I killed her, it seems. Perhaps it's she, and nothing happened.' There was another knock at the door. I made no reply, trying to resolve the question: had it happened or not? Yes, it had. I recalled the resistance of her corset and the penetration of the knife, and a chill ran up and down my spine. 'Yes, it happened. Yes, now I must do myself in, too,' I said to myself. But I said this and knew that I wouldn't kill myself. However, I stood up and took the revolver in my hands once again. But it's strange: I recall that previously I'd been close to suicide many times before, as I had earlier that day on the train; it seemed easy to me, easy because I thought that by doing so, I'd shock her. Now I was unable not only to kill myself but even to contemplate the act. 'Why would I do it?' I asked myself, and there was no reply. There was another knock at the door. 'Yes, first I have to find out who's knocking. I'll still have time.' I put the revolver down and covered it with a newspaper. I went to the door and unlocked it. It was my wife's sister, a kind, stupid widow.

"'Vasya! What's all this?' she said and began shedding tears, which she always had ready.

"'What do you want?' I asked rudely. I knew there was no need or reason to be rude to her, but I couldn't adopt any other tone.

"'Vasya, she's dying! Ivan Fyodorovich said so.' He was the doctor, her doctor and her adviser.

"'So he's here?' I asked, and all my anger at my wife welled up again. 'Well, what of it?'

"'Vasya, go in to her. Ah, this is awful,' she said.

"'To her?' I asked myself. And I replied at once that I had to go to her; that's probably what's done when a husband, like me, kills his wife, then he absolutely has to go to her. 'And if that's what's done, I must go,' I said to myself. 'If I need to, I'll still have time,' I thought about my intention to shoot myself and I went in. 'Now there'll be phrases and grimaces, but I won't give in to her,' I said to myself.

"'Wait,' I said to her sister. 'It's silly to go without boots. Let me put on my slippers.'"

28

"And, it was astonishing! Once again, as I left my study and passed through familiar rooms, the hope occurred to me that nothing had happened; but then the smell of the doctor's filth—iodoform and carbolic acid—struck me.[36] No, it had all happened. Walking down the corridor past the nursery, I saw Lizonka. She looked at me with her frightened eyes. It even seemed to me that all five of our children were there looking at me. I went to the door and the maid opened it for me from the inside and went out. The first thing that struck my sight was my wife's light gray dress lying on the chair, stained dark with blood. On our double bed, even on my side of it—it was easier to get to—she lay with her knees raised. She lay there, propped up by pillows, in her unbuttoned bed jacket. Something had been applied to the site of the wound. There was a strong smell of iodoform. What struck me first and most of all was her swollen face, with bluish bruises on part of her nose and under one eye. These were the result of the blow from my elbow when she'd tried to restrain me. She was lacking in all beauty, and there seemed to be something repulsive about her. I stopped in the doorway.

"'Go on, go up to her,' her sister said.

"'Yes, she probably wants to confess,' I thought. 'Forgive her? Yes, she's dying; I can forgive her,' I thought, trying to be generous. I went up to her. She raised her eyes to me with difficulty; one eye was black and blue. With difficulty she said, faltering:

"'You got what you wanted. You've killed me . . .' Amid the physical suffering and even the proximity of death, her face expressed that same old, famil-

---

36. Iodoform is a crystalline compound of iodine used as an antiseptic in surgical dressings.

iar, cold animal hatred for me. 'The children . . . I still won't . . . let you . . . have them. . . . My sister will take them. . . .'

"About what I considered the most important thing, her guilt, her betrayal, she seemed to think it not worth mentioning.

"'Yes, admire what you've done,' she said, glancing at the door, and sobbed. Her sister stood in the doorway with the children. 'Yes, see what you've done.'

"I glanced at the children and at her bruised, swollen face; for the first time I forgot all about myself, my rights, my pride, and for the first time I saw in her a human being. Everything that had offended me seemed so insignificant— all my jealousy; what I'd done seemed so significant that I wanted to press my face to her hand and say, 'Forgive me!' but I dared not.

"She closed her eyes and was silent, obviously lacking the strength to go on talking. Then her disfigured face trembled and grimaced. She pushed me away weakly.

"'Why did it all happen?'

"'Forgive me,' I said.

"'Forgive? That's nonsense! If only I don't die!' she screamed, raising herself up and directing her feverish flashing eyes at me. 'Yes, you got what you wanted! I hate you! Ah! Ay!' she cried evidently delirious, fearing something. 'Well, kill, kill, I'm not afraid. . . . Only all of them, all, and him, too. He's gone, gone!'

"Her delirium continued all the while. She didn't recognize anyone. That same day around noon, she died. Before that, at about eight o'clock, they took me to the police station and from there, to prison. While there, confined for eleven months awaiting trial, I reflected on myself and my past and came to understand it. I began to understand on the third day. The third day they took me there . . ."

He wanted to say something, but was unable to refrain from sobbing and stopped. After gathering his strength, he continued:

"I began to understand only then, when I saw her lying in her coffin . . ." He sobbed, but continued hastily without delay: "Only when I saw her dead face did I understand all that I'd done. I understood that I, I had killed her; it was my fault that she who was once alive, moving, and warm, was now motionless, waxen, and cold; and it would be absolutely impossible to remedy—never, nowhere, nohow . . . Oh! oh! oh!" he cried several times and fell silent.

We sat in silence for a long time. He kept sobbing and trembling silently in front of me.

"Well, forgive me . . ."

He turned away from me and lay down on the seat, covering himself with his blanket. At the station where I was supposed to get off—it was eight o'clock in the morning—I went up to him to say goodbye. Whether he was sleeping or pretending, he didn't stir. I touched him with my hand. He uncovered his face and it was clear that he wasn't asleep.

"Farewell," I said, holding out my hand.

He shook my hand and smiled slightly, but so pitifully that I felt like crying.

"Yes, forgive me," he said, repeating the same word with which he'd ended his story.[37]

37. The narrator's "farewell" and Pozdnyshev's "forgive" are related linguistically in Russian: the former (*proshchaite*) is the customary word used to take one's leave, but it is also the imperfective form of the verb (*prostit'*) meaning "to forgive."

Whose Fault?

SOFIYA ANDREEVNA TOLSTAYA

PART I

I

IT WAS A SPLENDID, CLEAR, MAGNIFICENT DAY. A real celebration of the peak of summer. The bright azure sky, the warm rays of the sun, and the many noisy colorful birds in lush trees and flowering bushes were all so dazzling and cheerful! In the distance the deep blue lake brilliantly reflected the sky as well as the bright, abundant, verdant vegetation along its shores.

The two young women running along the path from the lake to the large white stone house had the same festive, vigorous, radiant appearance. They were both barefoot, holding their shoes in their hands; wet towels were draped around their shoulders and their hair was unbraided. Their little feet, still pale and unused to the path, stepped timidly and lightly on the dewy trail, as if shuddering from contact with the ground, and the girls were laughing loudly.

"Be careful, someone might see us," said one.

"So what? Is it embarrassing?" the other asked, opening her eyes wide in surprise. "You know country women go barefoot."

"It's prickly and it hurts to walk."

"Never mind. It's easier if you run!"

The slim dark-eyed girl took off toward the house with such speed that when she found herself on the balcony, flushed, agitated, and gasping for breath, she suddenly looked around and came to her senses; feeling deeply self-conscious, she stood stock-still.

"What's wrong, Anna?" her mother asked sternly and in surprise, examining her flustered daughter from head to foot.

"Natasha and I were swimming and . . . and . . . we tried walking home barefoot. We didn't know," Anna said, hiding her feet.

Out of the corner of her eye she glanced at the outstretched hand of the male guest who had stood up from behind the tea table; then she looked directly into the eyes of the man who was offering his hand; smiling guiltily, she extended her own.

"I didn't know you'd come. Hello, Prince. . . . I'll be back in a moment."

The girl disappeared. The other one, without even pausing, darted after her.

The man who had extended his hand to Anna was their mother's old acquaintance Prince Prozorsky. He was about thirty-five years old and from time to time called on the Ilmenevs en route to or from his distant estate. He had known the children since their births; he loved the simple, delightful family ways of this entire household and often watched the growing girls with pleasure.

When both girls, one after the other, had vanished behind the doors, he continued smiling for quite a while. He hadn't visited the Ilmenevs for some time and, as often occurs, in the time he had spent abroad, something had happened to these girls. They had stopped being girls and suddenly had become young women.

Without completely realizing it, the prince felt this vaguely, and in his mind recalled again and again the image of Anna's graceful bare feet, her dark unfastened hair on her head tossed back, and her strong, agile figure beneath her loose white morning dress.

"My goodness. How nice it is here!" said the prince, glancing at the door where the girls had vanished; he experienced some youthful, invigorating surge of strength. "How pleasant, how cheerful! Ah, youth!" he added with a sigh. "Our youth has passed, Olga Pavlovna, but no one can keep us from admiring it."

"Well, if we remained young forever, then we we'd never appreciate it. . . . Do you think they notice it or value it? Not in the least," Olga Pavlovna said calmly.

After chatting a while longer, she excused herself, saying that she had to attend to some household chores, but that everyone would reconvene for breakfast.

"Meanwhile, Prince, you may read the newspapers; there's an interesting article about the unrest in France."

Olga Pavlovna left and both sisters soon returned. They had changed into dark, very conservative dresses, smoothed their hair, and had assumed an especially formal appearance.

"It's too bad you've changed your clothes," said the prince. "Now you've become proper young ladies; you were prettier and more natural before."

"This is more appropriate," said Natasha, pouring herself some coffee.

"That's all prejudice," Anna observed curtly. "Whatever people have grown accustomed to is appropriate," she added, nibbling some berries from a small plate, one at a time, just like a little bird.

"Are you feeling happy?" asked the prince.

"Terribly!" Anna replied. "Natasha and I are so very busy. Now I'm reading philosophy and writing a story. Natasha says it's good: every evening I read her what I wrote that morning."

"What kind of philosophy are you reading?"

"Dmitry Ivanych has lent me some Büchner and Feuerbach.[1] He says they're necessary for beginning my development. Now everything's become so clear to me. After seeing such clear proof I understand how one can become a materialist."

"How old are you?"

"I'll be eighteen soon."

"Toss away your Büchner and Feuerbach; don't ruin your innocent soul. You can't understand them and you'll only get confused."

"By reading philosophy? No, never! On the contrary, I'll come to understand myself and all my doubts. I've read your articles, too; but they're difficult. I really can't understand them very well yet."

"What's your story about?

"It's all about *how* one should love. You won't understand it. Natasha does perfectly."

"It's not hard to understand, but Anna's very sentimental. She dreams about a kind of love that should be pure and ideal, almost like a prayer," said Natasha.

"How does one reconcile that with materialism, Anna Aleksandrovna? Now you're caught . . ."

1. Friedrich Karl Christian Ludwig Büchner (1824–99) was a German philosopher, physiologist, and physician who became one of the principal exponents of scientific materialism. Ludwig Andreas von Feuerbach (1804–72) was a German philosopher and anthropologist. He was politically liberal, an atheist, and a materialist, and his book *The Essence of Christianity* (1841) initiated the quest for the historical Jesus.

"Oh, there's the butterfly Misha was hoping to add to his collection," Anna cried suddenly and unexpectedly; with her strong, nimble legs she hopped onto the balcony railing, trying to catch the large dark butterfly.

The prince blushed at the sight of Anna's graceful figure flashing in front of him as she jumped down from the balcony railing with the butterfly in her hand.

"Let's go for a walk," Natasha proposed, "a very long walk, and take Misha along."

Everyone agreed, went to fetch their hats, summoned little Misha, and set out for the neighboring village to visit Misha's former wet nurse.

The road led through the field; it was dusty and hot. Everyone ambled along lazily, and the conversation didn't go well. Anna led the way; the prince caught up to her, smiled, and said:

"Everything's so clear and simple in your life! No matter how hard you try to pose questions to yourself, there really aren't any and can't be any! You—your youth, your simplicity, and your faith in life, you yourself—you're the answer to all these doubts. God, how I envy you!"

"No, don't. I have so many doubts, and . . . I'm so immature," she replied gloomily. "When I understood that everything in the world is only movement and an association of atoms, I began to doubt whether God exists. Take Dmitry Ivanovich: you know him, he's a student who visits us from Sosnovka—he says that God's a fantasy, there's no such thing as the will of God, and that it's all the laws of nature. These are only the words of an unbeliever. He may even be right, but I don't understand. Sometimes I feel so much like praying—but to whom?"

"Don't listen to anyone. Dmitry Ivanovich confuses you, and that's not good," said the prince, scrutinizing the transparent skin on Anna's temples, beneath which her fine blue veins were pulsing.

Anna blushed.

"It's true he confuses me. But he's trying so hard to improve me. Misha, Misha, where are you going?" Anna cried suddenly.

But it was already too late. Misha, about whom they had forgotten entirely, wasn't walking along the bridge with everyone else, but was circling around, right through the marsh, and was stuck up to his knees. The prince extended his walking stick and pulled him out. But Misha was now soaking wet. Natasha, who had been off collecting flowers to dry, came running up and began to dry Misha off with grass and her scarves, scolding him in an angry voice. Anna laughed. But now it didn't make sense to continue their walk and they decided to return home.

Dmitry Ivanovich also arrived that evening from a neighboring estate; he was a pale, blond student with glasses and casual manners. Unembarrassed by anyone's presence, he never left Anna's side the entire evening. They sat together on the terrace stairs reading some book; Dmitry Ivanovich, constantly pausing, was enthusiastically explaining Darwin's system to Anna.

Since Natasha wasn't in a good mood either, and for some reason was reluctant to converse with the prince, he was left willy-nilly to have tea with Olga Pavlovna, who cast sidelong glances at Anna and her interlocutor.

The prince left late that evening, saying that he would definitely call on the Ilmenevs again on his way back to the country from Petersburg. As he said goodbye, he looked spitefully at Dmitry Ivanovich and, as if inadvertently, avoided shaking his hand.

"Yes, youth is to his advantage," thought the prince, after he had left the Ilmenevs and glanced at the starry sky, the darkened lake, and the mysterious distant woods lining its shores. It seemed to him that everything in the world had suddenly been extinguished, that all happiness resided somewhere out there, or behind him, or had drowned in this mysterious night, and he was filled with terror.

"This little girl, not long ago a mere child I carried in my arms, and I— no, it's impossible." He felt short of breath.

"It couldn't be! What? Is the same thing happening all over again? No, it's not the same: it's something new!" Once again he pictured Anna: in his imagination he mentally uncovered her graceful legs and her whole strong, supple girlish body.

"What eyes! Black as night, clear, truthful. . . . What sort of creature is she? Something very special. But when did all *this* happen? Why does it suddenly seem that I can't live without those clear eyes, that pure, sweet, cheerful look? Why, it wasn't all that long ago that I could regard these girls with serenity and delight. . . . And now? All of a sudden I've noticed that she's a woman, there's no one else but her, and that I must, yes, I can't do otherwise, I must possess this child . . ."

The blood rushed to the prince's head. He closed his eyes to call Anna to mind more vividly; his carriage raced on, swaying along the village road, lulling the prince to sleep, intensifying his feeling of voluptuousness and his need for experiencing pleasure that wonderful summer night . . .

2

The next day the two sisters were sitting at a table in a spacious, bright room on the upper floor. Natasha was sewing while Anna was reading her story aloud with emotion in her voice. The large Italian window stood wide open; the air was noisy and stirring: frogs were croaking in the lake, nightingales were singing in the garden, and the sound of men's singing was coming from the village. Anna's voice was trembling slightly while she was reading.

"In a small, poorly furnished little room sat a young woman zealously sewing something large and white. From time to time she glanced up at the window and sighed, listening through the birds' singing above for footsteps on the street. The young woman had recently married and was waiting for her husband to come home after teaching his lessons. They were both poor; both worked, but . . ."

"Is this your ideal, Anna? Oh, don't make a mistake! One can't live by flowers and birds alone, especially not in poverty! There's also the prose of life: sickness, the kitchen, faults, and quarrels. . . . But you seem to avoid these things on purpose both in life and in your story."

"None of this has to be: one doesn't have to dwell on it. One must live through spiritual life alone, while everything else is incidental. I feel that I can elevate myself to such a level of spiritual development that I'll never even want to eat. Isn't a crust of bread enough to sustain life? It is, isn't it? Well then, it will be provided. You know, Natasha, sometimes it seems to me that when I'm running, if I go on just a little bit further, if I dig my heels into the ground, then one, two three—I'll take off flying. That's just like one's soul, yes, even more so; it must always be ready to soar off into the infinite. . . . I know this well and feel it deeply! How come no one else understands it?"

"But how can you live on earth with such an unearthly view?" asked Natasha. "Yesterday you said that you absolutely had to get married. Well, in marriage, with children and everyday worries, you won't be able to live on just a crust of bread and you won't be able to soar anywhere."

Anna became pensive.

"Yes, if I regard marriage as you all do, then it would be better not to marry. First of all you need love, the kind that's higher than everything worldly, a more ideal love. . . . I can't explain it; I can only feel it . . ."

"Well, enough of this, Anna. Let's go downstairs now. Dmitry Ivanovich has come. Do you love him, Anna?"

"I don't know. I like talking with him, but in the evening when I shake his hand and he squeezes mine in a special way, and his hand is moist with perspiration—it suddenly feels so unpleasant! But I do think he understands things as they are; he's educated, clever, and he has his own ideals."

The sisters went downstairs. There was no one on the balcony except Dmitry Ivanovich and Misha's tutor. They were chatting about university matters and drinking tea. Anna asked Dmitry whether he had brought her anything good to read.

"What do you mean by good?" he asked, and took out of his pocket a collection of Tyutchev's poems.[2] "Here's what I happen to have in my pocket," he said.

Anna opened it and began leafing through it.

"I know this book. How I love his verse! 'Human tears,'" she read. "I know it by heart. 'Flow, you invisible, inexhaustible tears.'[3] Yes, those tears are the most agonizing; I'll have to shed many like that during my life."

"It always seems to me that you're someone who won't have to shed any tears. You're always so cheerful. But you're given to daydreaming, Anna Aleksandrovna. You can't live your whole life like that."

"How should I live it, then?"

"You should live more by social and earthly interests, live by participating in human affairs, and not bother about your inner frailties."

"What should I do?"

"Well, don't dwell way up in the clouds, but take action. Try to live more sensibly, Anna Aleksandrovna, without prejudices, and the main thing, without overly sentimental religious hypocrisy."

"I can try," Anna said gloomily. "But what do you mean by 'overly sentimental religious hypocrisy'? Don't you also have religion? Is it really possible to live without it? Tell me, do you believe in God?"

Dmitry Ivanovich smiled sarcastically and condescendingly.

"Why do you so like that word 'God'?"

"It's not the word, but the idea of a divine being that I find necessary. I won't surrender that, do you hear?" Anna said suddenly and with passion. "If there's no God, then I don't exist and there's nothing, nothing at all. . . . There's no life!"

Anna flared up, her eyes sparkled, and her voice trembled tearfully; she turned away and fell silent. Dmitry Ivanovich was about to smile again ironically, but, when he glanced up at Anna, he felt awkward and dropped his eyes.

Night fell. The moon had long since risen and had lit up a meadow near the lake that was not too far from the house. The contours of the dark greenery of the trees surrounding the meadow appeared even darker against the background of the bright sky. The light coming from behind the darkness was so enticing that after everyone had gone to bed, Anna stood on the terrace for a

2. Fyodor Ivanovich Tyutchev (1803–73), a Russian writer who was remarkable both as a highly original philosophical poet and as a passionate Slavophile.

3. A short lyric poem by Tyutchev composed in the autumn of 1849.

long time gazing at the meadow; the turmoil of thoughts that had occupied her of late as a result of her reading philosophy books and conversing with Dmitry Ivanovich, seemed to resolve quietly and fade away.

Some rustling from the garden caused her to shudder. Dmitry Ivanovich was emerging from it. He was coming from the wing of the house where Misha's tutor resided; he was planning to go home through the garden, but upon seeing Anna, he came up onto the terrace and drew near. She was annoyed that he had destroyed her mood; instead of glancing at him, she continued gazing at the bright meadow and farther into the depths of the lake.

"You had such an inspired look when you were talking about God, Anna Aleksandrovna!"

Anna stood in angry silence.

"You have so much fire and energy! You could be such a vigorous, splendid woman, if only you would believe in a more developed man, agree to accept his influence, and come to love him . . ."

Dmitry Ivanovich approached Anna quietly; taking her hand, he kissed it suddenly.

He never expected what happened next with Anna Aleksandrovna. This slim, tender girl turned into one of the Furies.[4] Her dark eyes hurled such a bolt of spiteful lightning at Dmitry Ivanovich that he stood rooted to the spot. She tore her hand away, turned up her palm in disgust, wiped it on her dress, and shouted:

"How dare you? Ugh, how disgusting! I detest you!"

Shame, despair, and spite at the destruction of her reverential, contemplative mood, squeamishness, and pride—all rose up in her. She ran straight into her mother's bedroom, threw herself down on the couch, and began sobbing loudly.

Olga Pavlovna, who was getting ready to go to bed, was terribly frightened.

"What happened? What's wrong?"

"Mama, how dare he? On the terrace just now, Dmitry Ivanovich kissed my hand. What filth!"

Anna seized a vial of cologne from her mother's dressing table and began washing away Dmitry Ivanovich's kiss, all the while continuing to sob.

"Where did you see him?"

"He . . . no, I was on the terrace, gazing at the moon; he came over to me; I was annoyed; he said something, but I wanted to be alone; and then, all of

---

4. Greek goddesses of vengeance usually characterized as three sisters: they are cruel but also known for being very fair.

a sudden, unexpectedly, he seized my hand and kissed it." Anna shuddered and wiped her slender hand on her dress once again.

"Well, it serves you right. What's a young girl doing out on the terrace all alone, when the whole house is asleep?" grumbled Olga Pavlovna. "Now, calm down," she continued in a gentler voice. "I'll write a note to Dmitry Ivanovich and ask him to cease his visits."

"Mama, please do!"

"Well now, go to bed. I really didn't care for your conversations even before this happened. Good night. Your sister went to bed a long time ago."

It took Anna a while to calm down. After going upstairs, she sat at the table in silence for a long time, trying to soothe her agitated heart; at last she picked up her diary and started writing:

"Yes, this love was a mistake, a trick of the imagination. What do I want? Why am I dissatisfied? Why is my heart aching so? Is it my youth begging for life, when there's no real life, or do I feel sorry for all those who are unhappy? But all egoists are happy. Where do people find happiness? From fate? But what is fate? The law of nature, the movement of the universe, the will of God. Yes, undoubtedly, it's the will of God. It's good to pray to God! But what if prayer is merely the plaything of bitter people? But I can't break it. I can't admit that everything on earth is just the movement of atoms, or that I'm good or evil just because the weather is fair or foul, or that people are moral just because their blood circulates more slowly and they're unemotional, or that a known combination of material particles produces upheavals in people and in their fates. . . . My God, there's such chaos in my head! Everything's so mysterious in this world; how pitiful I am, undeveloped, impotent, and perplexed. . . . My God, help me, enlighten me!"

Anna tossed her diary down on the table, fell to her knees, and prayed for a long time. She hadn't done so for a while. Such a state occurs in people during moments of severe grief or at times of great moral progress. Thus it was with Anna.

When she arose, exhausted and shattered, she felt that something had happened to her and that everything would be different from then on.

She lay down in bed; untying the pink ribbons of the white cotton bed curtain, she wrapped it around herself.

All was quiet; not a sound could be heard from the window. The pale summer sky looked sad, lit from one side by the moon that had just set, and from the other by the sun that had not yet risen.

Anna trembled in agitation, gazing out the window, and slipped into a troubled sleep.

3

An entirely new period in Anna's life as a young woman had begun imperceptibly. It was as if she had shaken off all searching, doubts, and those questions and mental worries that had been muddling her existence. Youth had triumphed. The carefree, cheerful Anna had begun to look God's world straight in the eye with such bold clarity, as if she had discovered joyful new aspects of it that had previously been concealed from her.

"Natasha, now I'm going to bring some order into my life," she said to her sister once, collecting her drawing instruments. "Before it starts getting too dark, I intend to paint with my oils absolutely every day this autumn. After dinner I plan to walk, read, and write in my diary. When you begin teaching in school, I'll help you."

"Well, I don't believe that. I know what your help is like: you'll run in for five minutes, chatter away, read something useless—and that's that."

"Ah, Natasha, you think all you need is arithmetic. In my opinion, moral development is even more essential."

"Well, the two of us won't really be able to accomplish that in only a few weeks. I won't be able to teach for more than two months before we leave for Moscow. If we're lucky, we'll just be able to start some reading and writing, but there's no way even to think about moral development."

"If only we could stay here all winter!"

"What does that matter? It's impossible. Mama's bored here and Misha's being sent to the gymnasium."

"When does school begin?" asked Anna.

"The older girls will come tomorrow evening. I promised to read to them. I'll open the school on Monday. I have to start it myself, get everything organized, and then hand it over to the teacher."

"Well I'm going, or else it'll be too late." Anna picked up a small canvas, a case with her oil paints, and an umbrella; she walked out into the garden and then headed toward the lake. After choosing a place that she had noted long ago as being particularly picturesque, she stuck the umbrella into the ground and set about work. She painted easily, cheerfully; a shaft of light in the blue sky in the overhanging tree branches came out so well that Anna admired her own work. She moved her hand quickly from the palette to the canvas and back again, so absorbed in her painting that she failed to notice the prince approaching from behind. Prozorsky, who was on his way back from Petersburg, had dropped in on the Ilmenevs once again.

"So, I find you out here," he said to Anna, greeting her. "You paint very well! I really didn't know how talented you are."

"Really? I plan to work a great deal. But if *you* say it, then I'll do even more. You understand everything," Anna added, looking into the prince's eyes trustfully and tenderly; since childhood she was used to regarding him in this way, though she herself never knew why. Probably it was because everyone in her house, including her old nurse, Olga Pavlovna, Misha—everyone had grown to love the prince, who was such a familiar and accustomed visitor in their household. He had been acquainted with Olga Pavlovna since childhood: they were neighbors. When Olga Pavlovna got married and received as her dowry the very same estate where she had lived since she was a child, the prince continued visiting her from time to time. Then she was widowed and for a long time didn't dare return to her estate. The prince had not seen her for several years and met her again only later, when the girls had grown up a bit and Olga Pavlovna had gotten old.

Prince Prozorsky was not as handsome as he was exquisitely elegant. A broad education and considerable means had opened doors for him everywhere. He had traveled widely and lived a stormy, carefree youth; now he was tired of everything, had settled in the country, and was busying himself with philosophy, imagining himself to be a great thinker. That was his weakness. He wrote articles, and many considered him very intelligent. Only sharp and very knowledgeable people realized that the prince's philosophy was in reality pathetic and ridiculous. He composed and published articles in journals without having anything original to say, merely regurgitating old, worn-out ideas from a whole range of thinkers, both ancient and modern. This rehashing was done so skillfully that the majority of the public read his articles even with considerable enjoyment; this limited success pleased the prince no end.

But this was not what compelled Anna to relate to the prince so trustfully and tenderly. She loved more his idiosyncratic, sympathetic congeniality in society, cultivated with great success, with which he related to all women and which attracted them to him. Natasha and Anna also succumbed to his charm, and the prince's visits were always a cause for celebration in the whole family. He knew, as they all said jokingly, how to *raise* interesting questions and conduct the most entertaining conversations. He knew how to assist Olga Pavlovna with her solitaire at just the right moment, to teach Misha how to make a collection of butterflies and beetles, to joke with the old nurse, and even to give generous tips to the servants.

"Have you been to our house already, Prince?" asked Anna.

"I was there just now, saw everyone, and came out to look for you; I was told to try here. Without you the house is like a lamp without light: it's dark and dreary."

"Do you really think so? What do you see in me?" she asked, blushing. It seemed such an unexpected happiness that this attractive prince, beloved by everyone, would talk about her in this way, an insignificant girl whom he had known as a child. She recalled how naughty she used to be, how mischievous, lazy, and irreverent. She also remembered how the prince used to interfere cautiously and gently in those cases when, with her usual liveliness and decisiveness, she would be saying or doing something extreme. Anna always thought that he despised her and approved of Natasha; yet now, all of a sudden, he had praised her picture and said it was dreary in the house without her. This unexpected happiness, completely unaccountable, engulfed her heart.

Anna continued to paint. She couldn't tear her eyes away from the wonderful weeping birch bent over the lake; its white trunk appeared unnatural on her canvas, but it was astonishingly beautiful against the background of variegated leaves that had already changed into their autumn colors. But she felt the prince's glance trained on her; her hand trembled and her heart was pounding.

"Enough, I can't go on," she said. "What's wrong with me? Why am I so agitated? Probably it's because of his praise," Anna thought. It began to grow dark and cool. She folded up her umbrella, gathered her things, which the prince immediately took from her hands, and they both headed back toward the house.

The prince walked behind and keenly admired, with the look of an authority on women, her easygoing, strong bearing, always indicative of a healthy inner organism; he admired the astonishing position of her dainty head on its delicate round neck, each curve of which was lovely and graceful; he admired her slender figure, her waist encircled with a ribbon. The wind blew her ribbons and dress back, which constantly revealed the shape of her legs; her fine, dark hair with a scarcely noticeable golden hue, imparted even more tenderness and paleness to her face and neck.

When they had approached the house, Anna glanced back at the prince and his gaze embarrassed her. "What's the matter with him?" she wondered. "He just praised me so politely, but now there's something strange in his eyes, something animal-like. . . . Why is that?"

Yes, why indeed? She was at fault only because her figure, her hair, her youth, her well-made dress, and her shapely legs—this whole temptation, unfamiliar to her childish innocence—had aroused this more experienced bachelor;[5] he had sensed in this girl that rare type of woman who, beneath her innocent, childlike image, hides within herself all the qualities of an ardent, intricate, artistic, passionate female personality. And although as a counterbalance to nature, the highest values of religiosity and chastity were firmly and unconsciously established in this young girl's soul, the prince failed to appreciate these latter ideals of hers and didn't even notice them; but he certainly sensed the former traits with all his being, and for that reason he devoured her with his almost animal-like gaze that had so embarrassed and frightened Anna.

4

Although the prince was supposed to be heading home to his own estate and had even said that he was eager to see his mother, he was unable to leave; instead, he began visiting the Ilmenevs every day. He pretended to have business in the nearest district town and asked Olga Pavlovna's permission to come after doing his business and to relax with her warm family. Everyone was delighted with the presence of this beloved guest, and he started showing up daily. He sensed without question that there was no turning back. His passion for Anna intensified with each passing day and so overwhelmed him that he was unable to sleep at night; he was tormented by doubt; most of all, he feared provoking confusion on her side instead of love when he proposed to her.

He rented a dirty room in the little provincial town. He was bored; he pined and wrote letters to Anna, which he carried in his pocket, but couldn't resolve to take action. He spent two weeks like that.

Meanwhile, Anna continued living her simple, cheerful life, busy in her own way. What could possibly be happier than the free, girlish leisure time that clever, vigorous young women know how to enjoy, which is spent irritating the nerves of abnormal ones?

Anna was occupied by her painting; with the gardener and peasant girls she planted specially ordered rare bushes and trees that she wanted to introduce into her garden; she wrote in her diary, taught music to Misha, and studied Bach's difficult fugues. In addition, with Florinsky's textbook in hand, she frequently went into the village to visit the sick, straining with all her

---

5. *"In fact, it was only that her sweater suited her so well, as did her curls . . ."* This and all subsequent notes in italics are quotations from *The Kreutzer Sonata*, which Sofiya Andreevna wrote in the margins of her manuscript of the present work.

attention and strength to offset her own ignorance and inexperience in the field of medicine.[6]

Days were spent in an entirely constructive and joyful manner, but the constant presence of the prince and the vague awareness that he was admiring her provided Anna with even more energy and heightened her greater interest in everything. A day when, embarrassed to be there all the time, the prince didn't visit the Ilmenevs, seemed incomplete and dreary; every one of her activities somehow seemed to lose its meaning. She waited for him to share everything that had transpired during his absence; she fervently involved him in all her pursuits; she was deceived by his approval that hid his simple delight with her, unaware that everything was directed only at her appearance and her youth.

Natasha opened the school and gave reading lessons to the peasant girls every evening. She dedicated herself entirely to this activity, suppressing some envy that the prince preferred her sister, since she too loved him, just as everyone else did. She was surprised by the prince's delight with Anna's life and pursuits; Natasha regarded those activities with a certain amount of contempt and considered them useless.

It was Sunday and a dozen peasant girls were seated around a simple wooden table in the small wing of the house that was devoted to the school. Several of them earnestly and attentively read haltingly, pointing their fingers at the words in the book, while others industriously and skillfully copied out letters and mouthed words. The tall, attractive Lyubasha sat next to Natasha and boldly read aloud a story about the daily life of peasants. It was very cozy and proper in this bright, little room, but everyone seemed to be exhausted and bored. Natasha was working conscientiously, but was unable to infuse any vitality into the endeavor.

The door opened quietly and Anna came in. She walked cautiously to the corner, sat down, and began listening. The prince hadn't been there all day, and although she had been missing him, she didn't want to admit it to herself. The Gospel lay on the table; she picked it up and started guessing her fortune with it, posing various questions to herself.

While perusing the imagined answers, she became distracted by reading that Holy Book which provides the solution to all of life's most complex uncertainties.

---

6. Vasilii Markovich Florinsky (1833–99), well-known obstetrician, professor, and writer in Saint Petersburg, was the author of numerous medical textbooks published in the 1870s and 1880s. Real doctors were rare (and expensive) in the countryside, so gentry with some knowledge of basic first aid often treated sick or injured peasants on their estates.

Abruptly she decided to ascertain these girls' level of spiritual development. She recalled the prince's story about the sort of answers that peasant
girls offer about the Holy Trinity and she asked them:

"Girls, what does the Holy Trinity consist of?"

"The Lord God, the Mother of God, and Saint Nicholas," Lyubasha
replied boldly.[7]

"What are you saying?" the quiet, serious Marfa interrupted her. "The
Trinity means: God the Father, God the Son, and the Virgin Mother."

"And the Holy Spirit," Natasha corrected her sternly.

"Have you read to the Gospel?" Anna asked.

"We've heard it read in church. Last year Natalya Aleksandrovna read to
us, during Holy Week, about Christ's passion."

"Well, I'll read to you about the teachings of Christ."

Anna found her favorite place and began reading the Beatitudes and the
Sermon on the Mount. Her clear, resonant voice with its natural sensitivity
lent particular expression to that which touches people, their hearts most of
all. When she had finished the chapter, she began explaining it. The girls
surrounded her; some didn't understand her very well, but Anna's religious
inspiration was communicated to these naïve listeners.

"More, more," they begged.

Then Anna read them about Peter's denial, the prayer in the Garden of
Gethsemane, and Judas's betrayal. She showed them pictures, interpreted
the words, and she herself became excited. Many of the girls wept. The
thoughtful Marfa took Anna's hand gently and held it in her own; the fervent Lyubasha encircled Anna's slim neck with her arm and kissed her on
the lips loudly.

At that moment the sound of an approaching carriage was heard at the
porch of the main house. Anna jumped up: her face glowed with joy.

"It's the prince," said Natasha. "Go on; you've just disturbed us here. I
thought he probably wouldn't come today. What's wrong with you?" asked
Natasha, glancing at her excited sister.

"Je crains d'àimer le prince," Anna muttered rapidly, pressing her hand to
her breast as if trying to stop her heart from beating so fast, and she ran out
of the room.[8]

---

7. Saint Nicholas (270–343) was a bishop of Myra, later canonized as a Christian saint.
Because of the many miracles attributed to his intercession, he is also known as Nikolai the
miracle worker.

8. The French sentence means "I'm afraid that I love the prince."

Flushed, agile, and swift, she ran into the spacious hall, where the prince was taking off his coat; when he glanced at her, he was struck by this blushing beauty, with her excited look, a result of the agitation she had just experienced, and her dark, fiery eyes regarding him cheerfully and tenderly. For the first time he felt that she was glad to see him and that love might indeed be possible on her side as well. But at the same time he wondered whether this magnificent creature whom he had grown to know so well of late, with her poetic, pure demands of life, her religious inclination, and her noble ideals, would collide against his egotistical, carnal love and his spent existence.

"It makes no difference; there's no other way; let it be like this," prompted the voice that was always ready to speak that way to people used to thinking only about themselves and valuing only their own happiness and pleasure. "Mine, all mine . . ." the prince rejoiced inwardly as he kissed Anna's hand.

That evening everything that he had so desired was meant to be accomplished. He himself felt that and so did Anna. There was some general awkward tension; the resolution of everything that had weighed upon them all was anticipated.

They had tea in the dining room; then they all went their separate ways. Misha went to bed early, Natasha set about correcting her pupils' notebooks, Olga Pavlovna sat down in her usual place on the sofa in a corner of the living room, laid out a game of solitaire, and took up knitting one of her numerous afghans intended for relatives and friends.

The prince asked Anna to play something and followed her into the hall.

"I don't feel like playing," she said. "I'm very tired today."

"Never mind, please, play something." The prince was agitated and wanted to win a little time. "Here's one of Chopin's Preludes; you play them so well.[9] No one could instill the subtlest human feelings into music as well as he did."

Anna began playing almost mechanically. The prince's agitation had been communicated to her. He stood against the wall and leaned back his handsome head. Apparently some intense internal process was transpiring within him; he finally worked up his courage and said quietly, pausing incessantly:

"Anna, I must speak with you. I've been meaning to do so for a long time, but it's so difficult!" The prince fell silent. "Has it ever occurred to you that this old family friend could regard you in a way other than as a sweet, lovable

---

9. Chopin's *24 Preludes*, opus 28, are a set of short solo pieces for piano, one in each of the twenty-four keys, originally published in 1839.

young girl?" The prince's voice broke off. Anna shuddered. "That he could feel," the prince continued after a pause, "that without this young girl no life was possible for him, no happiness—nothing at all."

Anna was trembling all over; her long, cold fingers stopped obeying, and Chopin's prelude was cut short.

"Go on, play," the prince implored her.

Anna continued softly and nervously running her fingers over the keys, and Chopin's poignant melody sounded again.

"Here's the thing, Anna. I'm not demanding anything of you yet. I merely love you in a way that no one has ever loved before. You may be amused to see your old friend lying at your childlike feet. But it's not at all amusing to me! I've been tormented all this time, and in spite of that, I ask you just one thing: if you think you won't be able to love me after you become my wife, don't say anything to me now; just reject me. It'd be better to endure that suffering now, rather than later, after you've become my wife."

The prince fell silent. He was pale and his lip was twitching slightly. Yes, this was love, totally unlike any of those casual affairs he was used to. In it he experienced that cleansing when he could forget all the impurity of his previous sins. The prince rejoiced, but at the same time was horrified by this idea.

Anna stopped playing, glanced up at him, and thought for a moment; then she suddenly rose resolutely, straightened up, and approached him.

"Yes, I will be able to love you after I become your wife," she replied simply and quickly, extending her hand to the prince, looking straight into his eyes naïvely and tenderly. He understood that she could not lie, she simply didn't know how to lie, and that this virtuous girl would keep her word as steadfastly and simply as she had given it at that moment.

The prince seized her hands and began kissing them.

"Is it true? Is it?" he repeated. She didn't pull her hands away and regarded his passionate kisses serenely and joyfully, but her face expressed not one trace of distress in response to his unbridled passion.

When later that evening after this important event she lay alone in her own bed, she imagined her entire future life. She neither feared nor worried that she might be unhappy for any reason with this familiar, kind, sympathetic family friend who loved her so much, and who was so clever, educated, handsome, and elegant. She rejoiced that she would be entering his life; she was eagerly prepared to offer her entire self to assist him in all his activities that were undoubtedly very distinguished, useful, and splendid in all regards; she fell asleep with a peaceful smile of happiness on her face.

5

The next morning Anna told her mother and sister about the prince's proposal. Everyone had been waiting for it and reacted as expected. Olga Pavlovna began fussing about the dowry and planned to leave for Moscow as soon as possible to assemble it. She announced to Anna that in about five days she would also take her to Moscow to try on everything that would be made for her. Anna tried to object and asked to be spared that torment. But Olga Pavlovna became so upset that Anna decided to yield and promised to submit.

The prince spent entire days alongside Anna. He was terribly agitated all the while and tried to advance the wedding date, saying that no dowry was really necessary. When he remained alone with Anna, his agitation grew to such an extent that he couldn't think of anything to talk about; he kissed her hands in silence and sometimes didn't even hear what she was saying.[10] As before, Anna tried several times to tell him about her personal interests, how hard it was to teach Misha music because he had no ear for it, how she had helped a deaf girl, or how she had suddenly understood Shakespeare and had fallen in love with his work—but he was indifferent to everything.[11] There was only one thing that preoccupied him: whether she loved him and how soon their wedding would be.[12]

Friends, relatives, and neighbors called to congratulate Anna; she proudly and happily accepted their congratulations, without doubting even for a moment that her happiness would know no limits.

But one day an inadvertent, but irreparable blow landed on her, one that poisoned her happy state.

A neighbor lady, an old landowner, who for some reason didn't much like the prince, had come to congratulate Anna. Chatting with Olga Pavlovna, she indicated somewhat mysteriously, in vulgar terms, and in Anna's presence that the prince was a womanizer; then she whispered something into Olga Pavlovna's ear. Olga Pavlovna was disturbed, but waved her away saying: "Well, all men are like that before they marry."

Anna had never considered the possibility that the prince, before he had reached his current age of thirty-five, could have loved anyone else; she was terribly embarrassed and sobs arose in her throat.[13] She went to her room and sat at the window in silence for a long time, trying to calm herself down.

---

10. *"I can't recall it without shame! What an abomination!"*
11. Tolstoy had an intense and notorious dislike for the works of Shakespeare.
12. *"It was terribly difficult to talk when we were left alone. It was like the labor of Sisyphus."*
13. *". . . and when out of a hundred men there's scarcely one who's not been 'married' before . . ."*

The prince entered and leaned over to her quietly. She turned to him; taking his hand, she sat him down next to her.

"Why are you so very serious today, Anna? What's wrong?" he asked.

"I must speak with you. Tell me the truth, Prince, the whole truth. Did you love many women before me? How many?"

Her voice sounded tearful.

"Why do you ask, Anna? You're tormenting yourself and me. Of course, I can't bring to our married life the sort of purity I'd like to. I'm already so old, Anna; I can't go back and correct the past," he added as if with regret. "I can only vouch for the future. What happened before, I can assure you, was not love. I have never loved *anyone* as I love you. This is something new, unexpected, and magnificent. It's what I never even thought of or dared dream about."

She looked at him very closely, wondering whether it was all true, and shuddered.

The prince perceived her shudder, understood it, and moved closer to her. She retreated a bit, but the prince took hold of her hands and began kissing them passionately.

"You do love me, Anna, don't you?" he asked.

"Yes, I do," she answered softly.

The prince cautiously leaned over even closer to her face and for the first time planted a kiss on her lips.

Anna didn't move; she grew numb. A wave of passion such as she had never experienced ran through her body and cast her into a fervor. A bevy of diverse women whom he had loved before rushed into her tormented imagination. She suddenly wanted to seize him in her embrace and shout: "Don't you dare love anyone except for me!" Her head was spinning; she shivered as if in a fever and didn't understand what was happening to her.

But the prince understood; smiling, he released her slender, trembling little hands and moved away.

Anna sat there a few seconds, her head lowered, and said sternly and serenely:

"Leave me now; I'll come out soon."

When she entered the dining room for dinner, she sat down at the table languidly and gloomily and didn't touch a thing. After dinner everyone went for a ride to the neighboring farmstead. Anna avoided speaking with the prince all evening. She ran off to a forest grove, gathered late flowers that had bloomed a second time, and breathed in the fresh air. "How nice and easy it is here!" she thought suddenly. "But there's something heavy weighing down my heart! I must forget, forget!"

Two days later Anna's mother took her off to Moscow to be fitted for her trousseau. Apathetic toward everything, she let them do anything they wanted to her. Neither dresses, nor lovely items, nor her fiancé's presents interested her much. Her mother was genuinely concerned that her daughter was too serious and pale, refusing to eat. Anna felt ill at ease in Moscow and was in a great hurry to return home. The prince's presence had become a necessity for her; she would behave in a more animated fashion only if he were around. Now they had exchanged roles. He was very talkative, tender, and affectionate with her; it was as if he were protecting her, trying to soothe her nerves. She sat in silence next to him, listened to tales about his travels, his life in different countries where he had lived either for work or pleasure; his voice had a calming effect on her, subjecting her completely to her beloved's will. Sometimes, looking flushed and agitated, she demanded that he relate stories of his previous attachments. He avoided any direct answers, seeing how those questions upset her; he managed to escape with tender words and platitudes. But she always came back to the same thing. These conversations provoked in her the same feeling one gets when, at the first ache in a temple or a tooth, one presses hard on the sore spot and this new pain seems to relieve the old one, momentarily causing one to forget all about it.

This is how it was with Anna; she couldn't escape this pain all during her engagement.

6

At last they agreed on the date for the wedding. Anna recalled afterward that entire day as if it had been a dream. The prince's relatives gathered as did their own; various young women friends helped her dress; Natasha and Olga Pavlovna wept as they arranged her veil and flowers. The groomsmen flashed by sporting white flowers in their buttonholes. A large number of carriages arrived, drawn by three or four horses; the horses were decorated with colorful ribbons and the coachmen were formally attired. Anna's carriage arrived: Misha, who was wearing a white sailor shirt and carrying an icon, was seated with her; she climbed in together with her godmother, Olga Pavlovna's aunt, an elderly lady-in-waiting who had come from Petersburg for the occasion.

There was a large crowd in the church; Lyubasha and Marfa flitted past, as well as many familiar faces from the village. The wedding ceremony affected Anna only slightly; she felt too paralyzed, as if turned to stone.

At home the tables in the great hall were set, decorated with flowers and fruits; some unfamiliar servants were standing in attendance.

Just as her mother was giving her blessing before the ceremony, Anna suddenly came to for a moment and realized that something in her life was being torn asunder; something with which she had lived from the day of her birth was ending today, that very moment, and all of a sudden sobs arose in her throat and she threw herself on her mother's neck; sobbing, she cried, "Farewell, mama, farewell. It was so nice being at home! Mama, thank you for everything! Don't cry, oh, my God, please don't cry! You're happy, aren't you?"

At last everything was over. They brought around a large new coach and loaded her trunks; the prince's coachman jumped onto the box. Anna, newly attired in her traveling clothes and accompanied by her husband, was about to take her place in the carriage. Once more she heard her mother's grief-stricken cry and Misha's howl as he was led away. The carriage door was closed and off they went.

It was September. There was a light rain; the prince's team of six magnificent horses, which had been sent over from his estate, tramped loudly through the puddles on the broad country road; the carriage lamps were lit and their light was reflected in the muddy water; it was damp and dark. After the brightly illuminated house, so full of guests and pleasant familiar faces, this transition to the dark of night and the silence of melancholy rural nature was especially abrupt. Anna sat in a corner of the carriage and wept softly.

"I'm sorry, my dear, that our marriage has caused you such grief," said the prince, taking Anna by the hand and kissing it.

"Didn't it ever occur to you that I'd be sad to leave all those people?"

"Why are you addressing me *formally*? Don't you love me?[14] Do you still consider me a stranger, my dear?"

"I'll get used to addressing you *informally*, but for now it still doesn't seem natural."

"But say you love me," repeated the prince, leaning toward Anna in the darkness of the coach and kissing her chilled tender cheeks passionately.

"I think I love you," she replied meekly, recalling once more her mother, Misha's tears, the room she had shared with Natasha, along with all the poetry of her maidenly life; she also remembered that in several hours she would be at home in a new place and that would be forever.

All of a sudden she felt the prince cautiously embrace her and draw her near him; she saw his unnaturally excited face up close and felt his hot, irregular

14. Russian distinguishes between *vy* [you—polite] and *ty* [you—familiar]. Anna uses the former, while the prince uses the latter.

breath, with its odor of tobacco and cologne. A frightened and submissive Anna threw her head back and pressed herself into the farthest corner of the carriage. The prince embraced her and kissed her passionately.

"Yes, this is what's supposed to happen, just like this," she thought. "Mama said that I have to acquiesce and not be surprised by anything. . . . Well, so be it. . . . But . . . my God, how awful and . . . disgraceful, how disgraceful . . ."

The carriage continued on its way. It was about sixty versts to the prince's estate. A relay of horses had been dispatched about halfway, and they needed to make a prearranged stop at the empty wing of an uninhabited manor house. When the door of the coach opened, Anna hopped out quickly; wading through puddles, she ran up some unfamiliar stairs through an open door into a spacious well-lit room. Tossing off her cape, she sat down on a sofa, drawing her legs up under her and shuddering all over; she glanced at a table set with a samovar, the warming stove, and at all the strange surroundings.[15]

"Why are you so frightened? Make us tea, my dearest," said the prince, kissing her.

"Yes, right away," replied Anna, as if emerging from her torpor and raising her head, sunk in shame.

"Why do I suddenly feel so strange and uncomfortable with him?" Anna wondered.

"How dull and tedious that she's so afraid of everything," thought the prince. "What will happen in the future? And this is only the beginning of our much praised and extolled honeymoon! Could it be that besides trepidation and grim submission, I'll get nothing else from her?"[16]

And he didn't get anything else from her. It was committing violence to a child; this girl was not ready for marriage; the woman's passion that had suddenly been aroused in her out of jealousy subsided once again, suppressed by shame and her resistance to the prince's carnal love. All that remained was exhaustion, oppression, embarrassment, and fear. Anna noticed her husband's dissatisfaction but didn't know how to prevent it; she was subservient— but no more than that.

It was impossible to continue their journey that evening, and the prince couldn't bring himself to demand it. The pouring rain, the darkness, and the

---

15. A samovar is a heated metal container traditionally used to heat and boil water for making tea.

16. ". . . and then the much praised honeymoon begins. Why, even its name is so vile!" and ". . . it's awkward, shameful, vile, pitiful, and, the main thing, it's boring, unbelievably boring!"

poor road all delayed the newlyweds, so it was necessary to spend the night in this unfamiliar house.

7

The next morning the newlyweds arrived at the prince's affluent estate. The prince's mother, an old woman, greeted them with an icon, bread, and salt.[17] Anna immediately grew fond of the kindhearted, well-brought-up old princess. She sensed in her affectionate female support for her own future in this house, and she felt at ease.

Anna ran all around the luxurious, splendidly appointed, beautifully furnished old house; she got to know the servants, asked where her bedroom would be, and began unpacking her belongings and arranging her new residence. With her own artistic taste she decorated her room in such a lovely and original way with all the things she had brought and been given by the prince that he himself was struck by its new appearance. There were her childish playthings, books, portraits, sketches, an easel with an unfinished landscape, and vases with multicolored autumn flowers and leaves.

But the young woman now sitting in this elegant room was no longer her old self. Anna was unable to apply herself to anything: neither painting, nor books, nor even strolls through the wonderful gardens and woods of her new abode. She felt crushed, dejected, and unwell.

"Why do I seem to have fallen asleep?" she often asked herself. "I married for love; we used to chat a great deal and so agreeably; but now I'm afraid of him and don't even know what to talk about with him."

The prince noted Anna's condition with a lack of comprehension and a certain amount of irritation; he realized that of everything his depraved imagination had invented when he had dreamt about a honeymoon with his pretty eighteen-year-old bride, nothing had materialized but boredom—boredom, disenchantment, and the tormented state of his young wife. Not once did it ever occur to him that he had to cultivate that aspect of amorous life that he was so accustomed to finding in those hundreds of women of every sort whom he had encountered previously.[18]

He didn't understand that what distressed him so much now was in fact her main attraction and would guarantee his peace of mind with regard to her purity and fidelity in the future. Nor did he understand that the arousal

---

17. The traditional Russian welcoming ceremony: the icon, of course, is a religious image; bread and salt are symbols of hospitality.

18. "*. . . the spouses must school themselves in vice in order to receive any pleasure from it.*"

of her passion for him alone, even though it might come later, would always continue; that her shyness with her husband would develop into even greater shyness with others and would assure his honor and equanimity forever.

Meanwhile, Anna became more and more accustomed to her situation and grew more attached to her husband. She tried as much as possible to enter into his life and interests and to help him. She walked or rode around the estate with him, read his articles, and corrected any errors; in the evening the prince or Anna would read new books and journals aloud to the old princess in her room.

Sometimes Anna would get into a childish, playful mood, amuse the old princess, run around, jump, and, feeling a need for movement and youthful exuberance, search for some outlet, never finding it in her monotonous surroundings.

The prince was a good landowner and loved his work passionately. Marriage had distracted him for a while from the management of his estate; now, however, he hastened to make up for lost time. Work was going on everywhere. In the forest crowds of peasants were clearing dry places; all day long the sound of axes and the call of voices could be heard in the woods. The digging had all been done; trees and plants were being moved into the greenhouse. In the barn energetic threshing was taking place with a steam-powered machine. The prince himself spent the whole day planting a young forest, which was his favorite occupation. He oversaw the operation, measured the distance between holes, and hurried the day laborers.

"Look, put some sod at the bottom of the hole, like this, turn the dirt over and break it up," he said to one woman. "Wait, not like that," he said to another. "You're burying the roots too deep."

Forty women and girls were planting rows of young trees; the short day was already ending and it was time to release the workers.

Anna, who was waiting at home to have dinner with the prince, grew impatient and went to look for him. From afar he saw her slim figure wrapped in something white, and smiled happily.

"Have you come to fetch me, Anna? I'm sorry that I was late for dinner. We're just finishing. It's time to let the workers go home."

"Can't I help?" she asked, drawing nearer, trying to fathom what work was left to complete.

"Of course, you can. Look, we still have to plant those trees over there by the holes, or else by tomorrow the wind will have damaged them."

"I'll plant them myself," she said.

Anna took off her cloak, hung it up on a branch, tied her white woolen scarf across her chest, tossing back the ends, and began planting the trees.

The prince admired her lovely, agile movements; he sighed happily and crossed to the other side of the field.

Anna moved from hole to hole, working cheerfully and chatting with all the countrywomen with whom she was not yet acquainted. One of them, Arina, came up to Anna, looked her straight in the eye, and said boldly and impudently:

"Well, little Princess, your Excellency, they're no longer hiring me as a day laborer in the master's house. Yesterday Avdotya got to wash the windows, but she's no good at anything. I used to do everything myself. You've got to have the knack."

"I don't know anything about it," replied Anna. "It's not really my doing. The housekeeper, Pelageya Fyodorovna, takes care of all that. Talk to her."

"Such a young girl," continued Arina, folding her arms and scrutinizing Anna who was becoming uncomfortable.

"Go back to work; there's no time to chat," Anna said coldly.

The woman walked away and began planting again. Another one, working next to Anna, approached her and whispered:

"Ugh! What nerve to upset the little princess. She used to be the prince's lover. Now, most likely, she won't be coming around, the rascal."

Everything went dark before Anna's eyes.[19] Her hands dropped heavily, her heart started pounding so loudly that for a moment she thought she was dying. A spasm gripped her throat. "What? Right here, just now, was one of those women he'd made love to? And forever, she'll spend the rest of her life here, next to us, bumping into me, looking at me with that same insolent glance, and everyone will know that I, the prince's wife, was the successor to this Arina! And who'll swear that he won't go back to her?"[20]

All this flashed through Anna's head in a moment. She imagined Arina's rosy face with her dark temples showing under her red kerchief, her insolent brown eyes, and her small, bright, white, widely spaced teeth.

Anna stood up from the ground slowly, took her cape, and moved away from the women. She was reeling; as soon as she turned the corner of the old oak forest, she broke into a run. She wanted to get as far away as she could so that he, her husband, couldn't catch up with her, so that she would never have to see his face again, feel his touch, or hear his voice which at special moments

---

19. *"I recall her horror, despair, and bewilderment when she learned and understood. I saw that she wanted to leave me then."*

20. Sofiya Andreevna had a similar experience. Just before their marriage Tolstoy had had an extended affair with a peasant woman on his estate. His fiancée discovered this from his diary, which he forced her to read before their wedding.

had probably uttered the very same affectionate words to that Arina that he now said to her.

Her despair was overwhelming, beyond relief: that despair and horror couldn't fail to leave their mark on a very young soul for her entire life; they were the sort of wounds that a young child experiences the first time it sees a decomposing corpse.

With difficulty Anna had just become accustomed to having relations with her husband—and now, suddenly, those relations appeared to her in a new, hideous light. The idea of running away flashed through her head for a moment, to run away, to go home, back to her mother.

"Ah," she sobbed, "Aaahh!" Panting from her run, she yielded to wild despair.

She ran all through the forest and garden, to the pond, and finally sat down in exhaustion on a bench and continued weeping. It was already growing dark. After crying her heart out, until all her strained nerves were worn thin, as only children can cry, she lay down on the bench, folded her white woolen kerchief under her head, closed her swollen eyes, and lay still.

Meanwhile the prince, having finished his work at the other end of the field, went looking for her.

"Where's the princess?" he asked the women.

"She left a while ago," they replied.

"Did something happen?" he asked fearfully.

"She must have gotten tired."

The prince went back to the house hurriedly and anxiously. In the entry, he was met by the waiter, anxiously awaiting the master's return for dinner.

"Has the princess returned?" he asked, sensing that Anna was not yet back home.

"No, sir."

The prince ran back outside; almost at a gallop he returned to the forest next to the field where they were planting.

"Anna, Anna!" he called.

No one answered. The dry, but still firm leaves of age-old oak trees were rustling; the biting, piercing wind blew straight into his face. The prince ran into the garden.

"Anna, where are you? Answer me, for God's sake!" he shouted, now in despair, walking along the narrow road.

She heard his voice, but kept silent. Anna was glad that he was looking for her; she knew that he would come upon her soon, but her grief and agitation had yet to subside; something alien and horrible had combined in her imagination with the handsome face of her beloved husband.

He finally drew quite close to where she was lying; suddenly catching sight of her, he looked at her closely in astonishment.

"What's wrong with you? Why did you leave?"

Anna was silent.

"Anna, my dearest, what is it?" he asked, now with trepidation.

Instead of replying, Anna burst into sobs once again. Her entire frail body shuddered; she pushed her husband away with her hand and was unable to speak for a long time. At last she said:

"Nothing, it's nothing. Leave me alone! Ah, what torment! Ah, aaahh!" she wept. "I'm dying!"

Anna lay face down on the bench again, sobs rocking her entire childlike body.

"I can guess," said the prince guiltily and gloomily. "Calm down, my dear, I'll do everything I can to reassure you. I can't bear to see you suffering. Anna, must you really do this? I love you more than anything on earth. Poor girl! Say something."

The prince lifted his wife up and wanted to sit her on his lap, but she escaped his arms.

"No, don't, I can't. . . . Go away, please, go away. I'll come soon, honestly, I will," Anna said, wishing only one thing, that he would love her even more and never leave her.

He understood this and stroked her, murmuring the most affectionate words. She wept quietly, listening to him, and gradually calmed down. The prince took her by the arm; asking nothing further, he led her slowly back to the house. She walked submissively along the path strewn with dry leaves, but her entire being was exhausted from the new sensations she had experienced.

The concerned old princess met them in the dining room. She hadn't heard anything, but glancing at Anna, she stroked her head and said softly, "*Pauvre petite!*"[21]

8

From that day forward Anna locked herself in her house and didn't venture out anywhere, even to take a walk. From afar even the sight of a homespun peasant skirt would cause her to shudder. She began seeking amusement

21. The French phrase means "Poor child!"

and finding the meaning of life in that limited, enclosed family milieu into which fate had cast her. She took up her favorite occupation once again—painting. She found two children with whom she created a charming group and painted from her models every morning. So that the children wouldn't be bored while posing, she had toys and sweets brought for them from town, and she herself would tell them stories and play games.

The old princess would sometimes steal quietly into Anna's room, go up to her, kiss her on the forehead, and encourage her to go out for stroll. Sometimes she would sit in an armchair and, smiling, survey Anna's work with approval. The prince took no interest at all in her art, and that grieved her very much. He rarely came into her room and merely pretended to praise her sketches with insincere and hypocritical comments, the way one encourages children. Anna saw that he hardly glanced at them from a distance and really noticed nothing.

Nowadays the prince went about his estate always alone and Anna sometimes waited for him with anxiety. Jealous thoughts entered her head frequently; as a result her relations with her husband became completely unnatural.

One evening, when it had begun to grow very dark and the prince had not returned from the threshing barn, Anna began to worry; then her anxiety started to devise jealous scenes; she thought about Arisha. Unable to wait any longer, she suddenly jumped up, quickly dressed, and ran off to the barn, taking a roundabout way so as not to meet anyone. Everyone had already dispersed; Anna was making her way quietly between the haystacks, listening and looking. But everything was quiet. She grew frightened and went running home. After circling the house, she climbed up on the stone terrace and peered through the illuminated windows of the study. She spied the handsome figure of her husband, who had returned home by another road and was calmly dressing for dinner.

"No, he's still mine!" she thought passionately. Her heart pounded unbearably and she felt ashamed of herself; circling the house, she returned to her own room unnoticed, through the servant's entrance.

"My God! Could I ever have believed that I'd act like this?" she wondered. "My dream was that my husband and I would be united in our first pure love! But now? I've been contaminated by the poison of jealousy and have no salvation."

Anna began to mourn the passing of her ideals and for a long time was unable to calm herself down. She was disconsolate all evening; after she was left alone in her bedroom to which she had retired early, she felt like praying.

She took off her silk caftan, tossed it onto a chair and, remembering that her husband might come in at any moment, she hastened to kneel in prayer. She asked God for serenity of her soul and the courage to meet all kinds of adversity in life; she also asked Him to forgive her sins. Tears of emotional tenderness and compassion for herself flowed from her eyes. Her bare shoulders shivered, and she didn't see or hear the prince enter the room. At first he didn't realize she was praying; going up to her, he pressed his lips passionately to her bare shoulders.

Anna shuddered, grabbed her peignoir from the chair, quickly wrapped herself up in it, and sat down on the bed. Tears were still in her eyes. "Once again it's only that: it all leads to the same thing," the idea flashed dimly through her mind. But she didn't allow herself to dwell on this thought and immediately found a justification for her husband. "He didn't notice that I was praying; he loves me so much! It's a sign of his love," and so forth.

The next morning her models, the children, came again, but Anna didn't feel like painting. The bright sun was shining through the window; the first snow had fallen that night and she ran into the garden along with the children, rustling in the leaves mixed with frosty snow along the paths. She felt at ease, cheerful; she felt like a child with these children, carefree, pure, and beautiful, just like nature that surrounded her. For a minute she wanted to become just as she had been before: to forget her jealous worries, this latest episode of her husband's vulgar and fervent passion for her, and his indifferent attitude toward her afterward. She was lost in those reflections, even though that eternal, insoluble, and tormenting question continued stirring in her soul: "Why is he so tender today? Why does he see only the good in me, but tomorrow, after his importunate caresses, I'll suddenly be at fault for everything? He'll complain peevishly and wound me by saying something especially painful. How can I understand where I'm at fault? He's so clever, good, educated. . . . And I? Ah, I'm so undeveloped!"

Having run around to her heart's content, Anna was getting ready to go home, when her husband, cheerful, radiant, and elegant, appeared at the end of the lane. Anna was delighted to see him and ran to meet him.

"Where are you coming from?" she asked.

"I was at our neighbor's house; we talked about the factory we want to build together."

"Factory? What factory?"

"A distillery. It's very profitable."

"What? You want to make vodka?"

"Yes, indeed. Why are you so foolishly surprised?" asked the prince with the familiar tone of irritation he had adopted when speaking with his wife after the passionate episodes in his love for her.

"No, I'm not foolishly surprised; I simply don't understand how you can produce the one thing that so harms the common people."

"How many times have I asked you not to interfere in my business affairs," said the prince, hastening his step and moving away from his wife.

"Ah, excuse me, please. Don't hurry on ahead; let's walk together!"

Anna's lips were trembling and her eyes filled with tears. The prince looked at her in astonishment and noticed that she had grown less attractive lately.

"Are you feeling out of sorts today?" the prince asked.

"Me?" Anna replied with surprise, recalling her especially cheerful mood that morning.[22] She also remembered her husband's docile tenderness the previous evening and replied to him with a silent, puzzled look. She wondered, and it seemed strange to her, that this man whom she loved and whom she was prepared to help and support in any way, how this man could engage in the production of vodka for the intoxication of the common people! How on earth could she support that?[23] "And why is he so angry with me? What have I done?"

They didn't talk any more. A young countrywoman went past with healthy, brisk steps, gaily greeting the master and mistress, swinging her wide homespun skirt first to one side, then to the other, and disappeared from view. Anna shuddered. The prince followed the woman with his eyes; noticing his wife's curious and discontented glance, he smiled weakly and said guiltily:

"I can't get rid of the old habit of looking at every young woman from a man's point of view. It's only because of you that I'm becoming better and better."

"He even confesses this!" she thought in horror; flaring up in anger, she said:

"What? You can see a woman in that woman? Ugh, it's as if you had no other interests on earth."

"I tell you how things used to be; but all that's passed now."

22. ". . . but it wasn't really a quarrel; it was merely the result of the cessation of sensuality revealing our true relationship to one another."

23. Tolstoy wrote a passionate treatise against the use of alcohol, tobacco, and other stimulants, "Why Do Men Stupefy Themselves?" (1890) and a peasant play on this theme, *The First Distiller* (1886).

"I don't believe it, I don't!"

"What's this, Anna? What a nasty character you have! It's unbearable!"

"Perhaps. But I hate salaciousness and immorality; I love purity, while you love the opposite."

"You have no right to say that."

"I do: I'm your wife."

"Ah, my God! This is awful!" exclaimed the prince. "Awful!"

"It's not awful for you, but it is for me . . ."

Their first quarrel continued for rather a long time and was very painful. The couple didn't see each other all evening. Anna went to bed and the prince didn't come to her room. She found these relations with her husband appalling and heartrending; besides, the maddening passion of jealousy at the possibility of the prince's betrayal once again overwhelmed her. She lay there, her eyes wide open, trying to ascertain whether her husband would come to her. But he didn't. Gradually the jealousy faded and she wanted to remain simply, unquestioningly friendly with him, so there would be no further rifts to diminish their happiness. She jumped out of bed, threw on her dressing gown, put on her shoes, and ran into her husband's study.

The prince was sitting on the sofa, gazing ahead silently and severely. When the door opened and he first saw Anna, his face assumed a malicious expression. She hesitated for a moment in indecision and was about to leave, but she found it so hard to be in her husband's bad graces, that she decided to try to reconcile with him.

"Why haven't you come to bed?" she asked.

"Is it really possible to sleep? My heart's still pounding from all these scenes! You'll make me have a heart attack . . ."

Anna frowned, but managed to control herself.

"I'm very sorry I upset you. Please, don't be angry."

She went up to him and sat down next to him on the sofa. He looked at her with bewilderment, but with greater affection. That heartened her and she took him by the hand and smiled. The prince drew her to him and kissed her.

When Anna realized that the reconciliation was proceeding in a different way than the one she had been hoping for, that there would be no communion of their souls, pure and genuine, but that it would be a reconciliation of kisses, she was overcome by horror and despair.[24]

---

24. ". . . but sometimes . . . oh! It's vile to recall even now—after the cruelest words exchanged, all of a sudden—the silent glances, smiles, kisses . . ."

"Ah, my dear, don't kiss me, please! I'm numb as far as *that's* concerned; after such spiritual pain, I can't be reconciled like *that*. I beg you to leave me alone and forgive me . . ."[25]

She freed herself from the prince's embrace, jumped up, opened the door, and ran out. The prince listened for a long time to the sound of the retreating footsteps of her swift and agile gait.

"What a strange and incomprehensible woman!" thought the prince. "And how plain she's becoming; one of her side teeth has already begun to turn yellow."

With each passing day Anna faded a little more. The old princess said that her eyes had turned inside, that "*la pauvre petite est souffrante.*"[26] As a matter of fact, Anna's first pregnancy was very difficult for her. For the most part she lay ill in the old princess's room and felt oppressed, sick, and weak. The thought of her future child did little to cheer her up because she was so overcome by agonizing apathy.

The prince, who at first had spent almost all his time at home, now returned to his previous habit of constantly riding off into town, to neighbors, or on a hunt. Obviously he was bored and feeling burdened by his wife's condition.

Days followed one after another, as did winter and spring; summer was beginning. Anna never forgot this period in her life. Everything was beyond the strength of her young, undeveloped character: neither physically nor morally was she prepared for the difficult position of an expectant mother or for total loneliness. Demoralized by her constant state of ill health and her husband's indifference, she became impatient and irritable. If the prince was late returning, Anna was overcome by despair; she wept to the point of hysteria and reproached him for tormenting her. The thing that constituted her power over her husband—her physical beauty—had faded temporarily; since he, apparently, required nothing else from her, this too drove her to a state of impotent desperation. For his part, the prince felt oppressed by her erratic, excruciating moods; as a well-bred and self-possessed man, he was gentle with his wife, but the pretense and remoteness of his gentleness was obvious.

The presence of her mother and sister would have been a great consolation to Anna at this time! But they had gone abroad for a while after Misha's

25. "*. . . but in practice, love is something despicable, swinish . . .*"
26. The French sentence means "The poor child is suffering."

recovery from pneumonia, since he had been forbidden to spend the winter in Russia.

It was a hot July day. The gathering of the grain harvest was well under way in the fields; the yield was abundant, and the prince, who was bored at home, but was unable to leave his wife's side because she was expected to give birth soon, was busy with various domestic pursuits.

He spent whole days in the field or in the threshing barn; now, when the grain was being carted, he was present as the haystacks were being unloaded. He walked around the barn, thinking about his wife—so pale, thin, and disfigured, with her large, somber, dark eyes that often looked at him full of questions or reproaches; he couldn't help comparing her to the young, healthy country woman—ruddy and cheerful, standing in the cart that had just passed by. He knew that two weeks ago that woman had also given birth to a child; that the child had died, and that she, without shedding a tear, without any attack of nerves, regarded that event very simply; now she had cheerfully merged with nature and was back at work next to her young husband.

"And what about us?" wondered the prince. He frowned and lit a cigar. "Yes, I forbid them to smoke in the barn," he thought and turned down the path into the woods. From behind he heard hurried steps trying to catch up with him. He turned around to look.

"Please come now, the princess is unwell," said the maid, short of breath, and turned at once to return to the house. She knew that the prince would understand what was really happening. He thought for a moment, like a person who has to undergo an operation and who thinks, "Isn't it possible that it might not happen?" But gathering his strength, and feeling that there was nowhere else to go and that escape was impossible, the prince hastened his step and returned home.

The house was already in a commotion. Beds were being rearranged, something was being carried out, and an elegant baby carriage was brought in with a bed curtain of white muslin. A strange lady who had so irritated the prince of late by her presence, young and well dressed, but now with her sleeves rolled up and wearing a white apron, was giving orders. The housekeeper Pelegeya Fyodorovna was bustling about most of all. The old princess was worrying in silence; she kept going in to Anna, making the sign of the cross over her, and kissing her forehead. Anna herself, unaware of everything around her, was sitting in an armchair at the window, waiting for her husband, and harkening to what was transpiring inside her. Her flushed face was solemn and serious; wisps of wayward hair surrounded her face and, lit by a golden hue, curled on her forehead and her temples; her large dark eyes looked without seeing, full of anxiety and fear.

When the prince entered, Anna rushed to meet him.

"You know it'll be soon, perhaps today. How strange and joyful it all is; *my own child*! What happiness! I'll endure it all; I feel very brave . . ."

She hastened to speak, but moaned again: "There it is, once again . . ."

She squeezed the prince's hand, her face distorted; she couldn't see anything, and her suffering became worse and worse. A few seconds later her face resumed its previous serene expression.

"It's passed," she said with a sigh.

"It's time to lie down, Princess," said the lady with the apron, whose presence had so unpleasantly grated upon the prince.

"You're not leaving? For God's sake, darling, stay with me," Anna implored her husband.

"Of course, I'm not leaving," said the prince. "Calm down. You're so agitated, my dearest," he added politely, pushing back the hair that was stuck to her temples.

Anna pressed her husband's hand to her warm cheek and thought with joy that perhaps the child she was expecting would draw her husband closer and eliminate the distance that had so tormented her of late.

Gradually Anna lost all ability to think or feel anything. The suffering became intolerable. It went on for a day and a night, and there was no end in sight. The doctor had been sent for from town some time ago; everyone was terribly worn out; the old princess lit votive candles in front of all the icons and prayed tearfully in her own room. The prince kept running out of his wife's room and throwing himself onto the sofa in the drawing room in exhaustion, feeling that his tiredness had driven him to the end of his rope.

Anna's terrible, savage cries hounded him everywhere. He couldn't get far enough away from her; she refused to release him for anything on earth; yet it was unbearable for him to be near her.

The second bright summer night arrived: after something savage and terrible in the confusion and in an effort of utmost exertion, there occurred the event for which everyone was waiting with such impatience. From Anna's room first came the sound of the inhuman, horrifying shriek of childbirth; afterward, as if unexpected and from another world, the unfamiliar, but somehow always delightful cry of the infant, this mysterious being from an unknown realm.

The prince sobbed and leaned over his wife. She crossed herself and said: "Praise be to Thee, O Lord!" She looked at her husband, extended her forehead to him, which he kissed, then let her head sink back onto the pillow in exhaustion.

When they handed Anna her washed and diapered son, she gazed for a long time at his wrinkled reddish little face, and bending over, kissed him. She didn't experience the joy she had expected, but it was something much more significant. It was pure happiness, the purpose of life, its true meaning; it was a justification of her love for her husband; it was her future responsibility; this would not be a plaything, as had seemed to her earlier, but once again a source of suffering and work.

Taking the child in her arms, Anna felt that she would be unwaveringly faithful to the obligations of motherhood, just as she had promised the prince when he proposed to her, that she would be faithful to the obligations of a wife.

When the prince looked at his son for the first time, he winced. He turned away squeamishly and said:

"Well, this is outside our sphere. When he grows up, it'll be different."

That was painful for Anna to hear. In no way had she expected such an attitude from a father toward his first son. "Is it really possible that he won't love him?" she wondered in horror, recalling her recent hopes that the child might eliminate the distance between them and reunite her with her husband through their love for him. She sighed and shed a tear.

PART II

I

Ten years passed. Anna continued living as before with her family in the country. The only change in her life was that the old princess had died three years ago, leaving only the very best memories in Anna's soul: she mourned her passing profoundly.

Anna herself had changed a great deal. From a slender girl she had developed into a strikingly beautiful, healthy, and energetic woman. Always confident, active, and surrounded by four charming, healthy children, she seemed happy and completely satisfied with her life. The prince had grown slightly gray, but remained the same elegant, handsome, well-mannered man and, apparently, still treated his wife well. But in the spiritual depths of these two spouses, also reflected in their external life, there was no longer anything much in common. The prince's love, which had led to his marriage, couldn't endure very long. It wasn't of that nature. He was a successful man; he needed a variety of sensations; that's what he had grown accustomed to. He found quiet family life in the country simply boring, and Anna felt that he was not to blame for that. But his boredom frightened her. She loved her husband and was jealous, afraid of losing the love that he had yet to withdraw thanks to her beauty, cheerful character, and flourishing health. Anna felt that this love was not the kind she desired; she suffered frequently from that fact. To fill that empty place in her heart, she dedicated herself passionately to her children and their care. Her husband related to the children coolly; it was hard for Anna to get used to his indifference concerning that, which constituted the center of her life, both internal and external.[27] She had to endure everything alone: illnesses, doubts about her children's qualities and flaws, decisions regarding their treatment, upbringing, nurses, and governesses. She had to provide lessons herself; she considered it essential to spend more time with them so she could get to know them better. In conversations about the children's successes, character, and illnesses, the prince either remained silent or pretended to smile, replying as usual with his gentle, polite phrases, such as, he was very glad his son was such a good student, or he was sorry that little Yusha had been born weaker than the others, or that Manya looked so very sweet in her new fur coat. This Manya, an eight-year-old little girl, was the prince's favorite: she was very pretty and spoke French fluently, having acquired a genuine Parisian accent from her governess, and this amused him.

The prince's life hadn't changed much at all: he continued to manage the estate, go hunting, and write articles. But Anna noticed that he related to everything with languor and without energy. He was bored, unbearably bored. Family life oppressed him. No matter how much she tried to find amusements for her husband, no matter how often she accompanied him on visits to the neighbors, or rides into town, to the local elections, or to meetings of the zemstvo, and the like—none of these diversions lasted for very long.[28] Besides, the children distracted her so much; she was always busy with them, nursing one, pregnant with another, or giving lessons to a third. In the midst of her household chores and domestic affairs, Anna rarely found time simply to go for a stroll or a ride with her husband.

As always happens in such situations, people invent some need to change their circumstances to disguise their true feelings.[29] The prince began saying that he wished to collect all his articles scattered about in various periodicals and publish them in one volume. This project would require his presence in

27. *"Children are a torment and nothing more."*

28. The zemstvo was an elected district council, organ of rural self-government in the Russian Empire established in 1864 to provide social and economic services.

29. *"Just when the parents' life with each other becomes unbearable, it's necessary to provide the children with a city setting for their education. So the need arises to move to the city."*

town; he proposed to Anna that they spend several months in Moscow. She agreed immediately, seeing it as the only way to distract him. Of late she had noticed that he had begun to seek out and enjoy the society of young women. He began to take greater interest in his looks and became more concerned about his hair that was once so attractive and curly; now it was turning gray and growing thin. She was afraid that their home's external appearance of domestic propriety would be damaged; she decided to fight energetically to preserve it—primarily so as not to spoil the family status of her children.

It was decided that they would go to Moscow at the end of October. The prince said that he first wanted to go hunting for a while in a distant field, and then would turn his attention to his book.

On the first of September the prince's modest but splendid hunt was being organized in the courtyard. The children accompanied their father, admiring the horses and especially the dogs. Manya shoved a lump of sugar into Nochka's mouth, a handsome, lean English borzoi. Drakon, a piebald dog, brown as if marbled, strained on his leash and whined with impatience. White Milka was off leash and free to run, waiting for the prince.

At last the prince emerged, bade farewell to Anna and the children, mounted his own Kabardinian, and, saying that he would return in no sooner than three days, galloped quickly away from the porch.[30]

He rode across fields leading to the distant estate of some acquaintances; Anna knew that among the hunters there would be a neighbor lady who had lately been flirting aggressively with the prince. She was much talked about; it was even said that before his marriage he had been in love with her. All of this greatly disturbed Anna; she would have gone on the hunt with the prince herself, but was still nursing little Yusha; real life, serious life asserted its rights, and Anna dismissed these foolish thoughts, directing herself instead to the children's world, full of concerns, pursuits, and love.

Just after escorting her husband, she summoned her children to begin their lessons. Manya and her elder brother, the handsome Pavlik, were in the garden. They brought in a basket full of acorns and energetically recounted how they had found some baby squirrels in a hollow of a tree trunk. But looking at their mother, they were struck by her sad appearance and dutifully prepared their books and notebooks. The lesson lasted an hour; Anna still hadn't finished correcting their notebooks when the nanny's assistant came in to call her to the nursery to feed the baby.

---

30. The Kabardinian were one of the old saddle and packhorse breeds first produced in the mountains of the northern Caucasus by the Kabardin people.

The children, left alone, began running around the table. Anna went off to the nursery and, passing by the large mirror in the drawing room, glanced at herself. "Oh, my God, what do I look like? This baggy old jacket and my disheveled hair! I have to think more seriously about my apparel and order something nicer from Moscow! Yesterday my husband said so disdainfully that I was paying too little attention to myself and was 'letting myself go.' For what reason should I dress up here? It's tedious and I have no time. But apparently, I need to!" she thought, sighing.

The baby's impatient cry was already audible from the nursery. Anna hastened her step and began unbuttoning her jacket.

"Well, well, little one, you're all worked up. . . . I'm coming, I'm coming," she said, taking the child from the nanny's arms. The child fell silent and soon the even sounds of impatient sucking and the hurried swallowing of ample milk could be heard. Anna gazed around the nursery silently and languidly, this familiar, serene refuge, where all her children had grown up and where she had experienced so many joys and worries; here, sitting with a child in her arms, she had often wept, thinking about how unexpectedly indifferent her husband was toward their children.

She also recalled those nights when, having spent several hours in a row in the nursery, ministering to a sick child, exhausted, she had returned to her bedroom to rest, and how her husband, without even noticing her fatigue and chagrin, opened his arms to her to embrace her and, like a beast, demanded her passionate response to his advances; worn out both physically and morally, offended by his indifference, she wept unnoticed by her husband, yet yielded to him, afraid of losing the love of the man to whom she had pledged her life once and for all.

"Does a woman's calling really consist only in this," Anna wondered, "to go from serving the physical needs of a nursing infant to meeting those of a husband? Taking turns—always! But where is *my* life? Where am I? That genuine self which at one time aspired to the sublime, to serve God and my ideals?"[31]

"I'm tired and worn out, languishing. I have no life of my *own*—neither earthly, nor spiritual. But God has given me everything: health, strength, ability . . . even happiness. Then why am I so unhappy?"

Anna raised the tiny closed fist of her sleeping infant to her lips and kissed it. The startled child began to search for the breast with his little mouth, but

---

31. *"It's that the woman, contrary to her nature, must at the very same time be pregnant, and nursing, and a lover."*

Anna stood up, rocked the child gently in her arms, placed him back in his bed, and went in to see her older children. They were both sitting under the desk; having tossed all the papers out of the wastebasket onto the floor, they were looking for envelopes and tearing off the stamps.

"I'm making a collection of only foreign stamps," said Pavlik.

"I have an Egyptian stamp: papá gave it to me."[32]

"What's this? What a mess you've made here!" Anna said as she entered. "Have you reread what you've written?"

"Not yet."

"Then what are you doing? You still have to practice your music. Clean this up quickly."

The children made haste. The sound of a thump was heard in the hall, followed by a child's terrible howl. Anna ran out into the hall. The five-year-old Anya was in the arms of the English governess and crying desperately.

"Where does it hurt?" asked Anna.

"It's nothing," replied the governess in English.

Anna grabbed the little girl and went to fetch a cold compress to apply to the bump on her forehead that was turning red and quickly swelling. When she came back to the other children, they had already left; Manya was diligently practicing her scales in the corner room.

"Ah, she's not playing the flat!" Anna cried and went to correct Manya's error.

Then the maid came in and asked how to sew the little anchors onto Pavlik's sailor suit. Anna carefully pinned the anchors on, showed the maid where her mistake was; after sending her away, she sat down next to the window to read an old book taken from the library: Lamartine's *Méditations*.[33] Gradually she forgot about everything that had occupied her in the preceding moments and delighted in the elegant Frenchman's subtle poetry. But her enjoyable rest didn't last long.

"The teacher's arrived," announced the lackey.

"Ask her in," Anna replied wearily.

The schoolteacher entered, a quiet, agreeable girl with a surprisingly nice-looking, childlike face.

"Have you come about the books, Lidia Vasilievna? Have you made a list? Thank you. I'll order them at once."

---

32. When characters use the French "papá" or "mamá," it has been retained in the translation.

33. Alphonse de Lamartine (1790–1869), French poet, statesman, and historian, best known for his first volume of lyrical poems, *Méditations poétiques* (Poetic meditations, 1820).

"Here's the section for reading, and here's the one for instruction. I think, Princess, that I'll read these books to them myself, since I'll have to explain them as I'm reading. It's good that you've purchased a globe and some relief maps. They're very interested in those, and our geography lessons are going well."

"Well, then, I'm very glad."

"After you leave for Moscow, Princess, who will I have to turn to?"

Anna invited the teacher to stay for dinner, and by five o'clock the children, as well as the governesses and the steward, were gradually gathering in the dining room. Anna conversed amicably with all of them. The steward, much like the teacher, voiced his regrets that the entire family was about to leave for town; he had talked to the princess about the peasants' situation for the current year. Anna was not fond of business matters, but followed with interest his general account of the economic situation in the region and the condition of the common people.

When her busy day had finally ended and she remained alone in her own room, she felt depressed and lonely. "Well, even though I'm married, I have no soul mate. Even as a husband and lover he's drawing away from me. Why? What have I done?"

Anna approached the mirror and slowly began undressing. After taking off her dress and baring her lovely arms and neck, she glanced attentively at herself in the mirror. Then she lowered her cheek onto her shoulder and looked at her unusually beautiful breasts, so full of milk, and she sank into thought.

"Yes, *this* is what he needs . . ."

She recalled her husband's passionate kisses; turning away, she resolved that if her power resided in her beauty, then she knew how to use it. Having shattered at once all her ideals of chastity, having relegated to lesser importance her ideas of spiritual communion with her beloved, she resolved that not only would her husband never leave her, but that he would have to become her slave.[34]

She loosened her dark golden hair, curling on her temples and the nape of her neck, lifted it up, turned her head, and examined her own face for a long time. Then from the armchair she picked up a cloak trimmed with feathers that she had dropped there and held it up to her breast. The contrast of the whiteness of her breast and the dark feathers was striking.[35]

---

34. *"Therefore a woman's main task is to know how to captivate him."*
35. *"Her body is an instrument of enjoyment. And she knows this."*

Anna remembered the lady who at the present moment was out hunting with her husband, and her customary feeling of jealousy arose with unbearable pain.

From the nursery she heard a child's cry. Anna tossed aside the cloak, gathered her hair, threw her lovely Persian dressing gown over her shoulders, and ran into the nursery.

Taking the child in her arms, she pressed her lips warmly to his cheek; without thinking about what she was doing, she whispered passionately: "Forgive me, my little one, forgive me!"

2

About two days after the prince's departure Anna went for a walk with the children; along the road to town she saw a carriage heading toward her.

"Who could that be?" she wondered. The carriage came closer and drew even with her; the children became excited, started shouting, and admired the sound of the carriage bells.

When Anna peered inside the carriage, she saw a man's unfamiliar face; at her glance, he greeted her in a very polite, but formal way.

"I don't know who this could be," she thought.

The carriage climbed the hill, went down, then up again along a broad regular alley of old birch trees, and finally drove directly up to their house at a rapid pace.

The man got out and asked the servant who met him whether the prince was at home. He was very embarrassed when he found out that the prince was not expected until the next day; he paused in thought in the front hall. At that moment the entire noisy family returned from their walk and was approaching the house. Anna hurried to enter first and asked the stranger with whom she had the pleasure of speaking.

The embarrassed guest hesitated a few seconds, and replied with a barely noticeable foreign accent:

"I'm very embarrassed, Princess, that I so unexpectedly burst into your house; I'm an old friend of your husband. My name is Dmitry Bekhmetev. I haven't seen my good friend in some twelve years and I'm very sorry not to find him at home."

"So, you're Dmitry Alekseevich Bekhmetev? I've heard so much about you! I feel as if we've been acquainted a very long time. Come in, please, come in. My husband will be back tomorrow; today you can be bored together with us."

"I'd be glad to, Princess, if I won't bore you," said Bekhmetev in a very unnatural voice that Anna didn't like at all.

"He seems so artificial," she thought.

Entering her own room, Anna changed her dress, carefully straightened her hair, and went to join her guest in the drawing room, surprising him with her budding beauty and her particularly lithe step. He also noticed her small head, thrown somewhat back and framed by the dark trim of her mantilla, the light pink color of her face flushed from the fresh air, and her splendid, large dark eyes regarding him so affably and attentively.

"So that's the kind of wife my friend has," he thought with a slight feeling of envy.

Soon Anna found out from her conversation with Bekhmetev that for reasons of ill health he had been compelled soon after his own marriage to go abroad in search of a milder climate. He had been living with his wife in Algiers, but she grew bored there and moved to Paris. They didn't have any children, but he had grown to miss Russia and his relatives, and had decided to return to his homeland for an unspecified period. From his hints Anna understood very well that there was some discord with his wife, and she refrained from asking him any further questions about it.

Now Bekhmetev was intending to settle in the country with his sister, Varvara Alekseevna, whom he hadn't seen for more than ten years. His sister, now a middle-aged widow, had an estate about twelve versts from the prince's, and Anna used to visit her on occasion. She was a well-educated woman of subtle intellect, who had lost both her husband and her child in her youth and since then had devoted her whole life to the well-being of peasant children. She had educated almost three generations in her own model school; she had built a library, a children's hospital, and a shelter. She couldn't stand seeing any child sick, cold, or hungry; besides children, nothing else in the world mattered to her or interested her. In appearance she was stern, cold, and aloof.

Anna insisted that Bekhmetev stay for dinner. But dinner that day was stressful. The governesses, the steward, and the children all felt awkward in the presence of the new guest. Manya and Pavlik came down with a bad case of the giggles and were even threatened with having to skip dessert.

After dinner Anna invited Bekhmetev into the drawing room but didn't neglect her custom of gathering the children around her and playing with them before they went to bed. They brought in several albums, illustrated books, games, and work. Each became busy with his or her own pursuits. Manya was meticulously knitting a scarf for the old gardener; the little girl was busy with her alphabet blocks looking for familiar letters; Pavlik sat down to draw. Anna also picked up an album and began sketching a likeness of the English governess who was sitting in the room with them.

Bekhmetev called Pavlik over and seating him alongside, began to draw in his book, telling him about Algiers and the dark-skinned people who wore large turbans; as he proceeded, he illustrated his tales in the album: Pavlik was thrilled. He seized the book and ran to show the drawings to his mother.

"Look, mamá, how Dmitry Alekseevich draws!"

"So you're an artist?" asked Anna, recognizing the technique of a skilled and experienced master.

"Yes, Princess, if you can call a man that who's spent his whole life painting, but who's yet to produce a single genuine work of art."

"At one time that was also my dream—to be an artist; but you see where my time and strength go these days."

She motioned with her hand around the table, indicating her children.

"Mamá knows how to draw, too," Manya cried. Taking hold of Dmitry Alekseevich's sleeve, she dragged him over to look at the landscape hanging on the wall.

Bekhmetev began to praise the painting in very sophisticated terms.

"He's behaving in an affected manner again," Anna thought.

"Why do you have such an accent? You sound like a foreigner," she observed.

"I spent my childhood in England, and then lived abroad for a long time. Is it really so noticeable?"

"I could even take you for a foreigner."

After the children had gone to bed and the others had dispersed, Bekhmetev was preparing to take his leave, but Anna insisted that he stay over until the following day, since the prince had promised to return home around noon.

In the morning Bekhmetev remained for a long time in the wing where he had spent the night, and Anna understood his tact. But the prince didn't return as promised, and as soon as it started to grow dark, Anna began to become agitated and planned to go meet her husband. She invited Bekhmetev to accompany her; first she went to nurse her child and then she got dressed.

Although worried, she paid careful attention to her apparel; she knew how much her external appearance mattered to her husband, especially in the presence of outsiders. Besides, the thought of that attractive, audacious lady who had gone on the hunt oppressed her and tormented her distraught imagination.

Two fine English saddle horses were brought around. Anna and Bekhmetev mounted and rode in silence along the lane up to the large road. The conversation that both of them tried to initiate simply didn't go well. Anna was too worried about her husband, and Bekhmetev realized that.

It was now completely dark. Anna was already intending to return home, fearing that her nursing child would soon begin fussing without her, when suddenly the clatter of horses' hooves, voices, and laughter could be heard.

Anna and Bekhmetev rode along the edge of the forest; a large party, headed by the prince and the lovely lady, was coming down the middle of the large road. Anna clearly heard the lady's laughter and then her words:

"Non, jamais je ne me dèciderai d'entrer à cette heure et dans ce costume chez vous."[36]

"Vous voulez mon dèsespoir!"[37] the prince replied, half joking, but with real feeling.

"Et que penserait votre vertueuse femme?"[38]

Anna called loudly to the prince. He wasn't expecting to meet his wife there and was annoyed.

"I was so worried about you, my dear; you promised to be home this morning," Anna began.

"Who are you with?" asked the prince, glancing at his wife's escort who was riding toward him.

"It's your old friend, Dmitry Alekseevich. He arrived yesterday."

"Dmitry! Where from? What a surprise!"

"Direct from Algiers. I'm so glad to see you! And with a family, so happy . . ."

"Well, wait, this is all so unexpected; I'm delighted to see you, but first I must make my excuses to the party."

The prince turned his horse around and rode up to the other hunters; addressing a few polite words to them, and tossing off some elegant pleasantries to the lady, and saying his goodbyes, he went to catch up with his wife and his old friend.

Drawing even with his wife, he rode a few steps alongside her, then whispered spitefully:

"I'm very glad to see Dmitry, but it's most improper for you to be out riding around at night in a tête-à-tête with a man you've just met."

36. "No, I would never dare appear in your house at this hour and in these clothes."
37. "You cause me to despair."
38. "And what would your virtuous wife think?"

He turned to look at Bekhmetev, who was unable to cope with his horse that had veered to one side.

"And do you think it's proper to invite as guests, without your wife's permission, ladies who can't even be admitted to our house?"

Anna bit her lips and fell silent. Tears filled her eyes; she had been waiting in such agitation all day, worrying about him, and this was their meeting! In spite of the darkness and dampness, she struck her horse with her whip and galloped away from her husband. The prince and Bekhmetev galloped after her, calling loudly for her to stop.

"Anna, slow down! The horse will trip. Don't be insane!" the prince shouted after her in despair.

But Anna didn't heed anyone or anything. Arriving home, she hurried into the nursery and didn't emerge from her room all evening.

3

The prince spent the whole next day at home with his old friend, showing him the estate and recalling old times, those youthful years when they had become friends and lived the same kind of life. Bekhmetev left toward evening, and the prince, after bidding a cold farewell to his wife, went to catch up with the hunt. They had sent word to him that the whole group, hunters and dogs, would be spending the night at a neighbor's house, an old bachelor landowner, and they would expect him there.

Bekhmetev came back two days later. The prince was still away on the hunt, while Anna, in low spirits, was home alone.

She was very pleased to see her guest; she blushed and was somewhat surprised that she found Bekhmetev's presence so pleasant.

"Excuse me, Princess, for coming to see you again. Your cheerful family nook attracts a lonely man like me."

"We're very glad to see you, Dmitry Alekseevich," said Anna, "but we're occupied with things that must be so uninteresting for you."

"Very interesting," Pavlik intervened. "Look how splendid. Mama, show him."

Anna opened the album in which an impressive variety of dried flowers was beautifully arranged. There were bouquets, wreaths, and figures of the most unusual shapes and combinations.

"Incredibly lovely! It's obvious that you're an artist, Princess. Well, Pavlik, let's you and I make something amazing."

Everyone began working again, and the evening passed quickly and merrily.

When the children went off to bed, Bekhmetev picked up a book from the table and was surprised to see that Anna was reading such a classic author, Lamartine.

"Princess, why exactly did you decide to read his work?"

"By chance. I'd never read him before, and now I'm taking great pleasure in it. If you don't mind, read some aloud to me."

"Gladly, Princess. I've forgotten him altogether."

Anna took up her work and sat down next to a lamp, experiencing a strange feeling of happiness and serenity. She really didn't appreciate loneliness! On occasion she glanced up at the lean, earnest, beleaguered face of her guest, at the tightly stretched skin on his high forehead, and the sparse black hair on his temples, and she thought:

"No, he's not putting on airs, as it seemed to me earlier. He's unhappy and must be a very fine man."

Bekhmetev read: *"La nuit est le livre mysterieux des contemplations des amants et des poètes. Eux seuls savent y lire, eux seuls en ont la clev. Cette clev—c'est l'infini."*[39]

"That's just where I stopped. It's in the commentary. I like it very much."

"And the relationship of night to the infinite, to *l'infini*—is astonishingly poetic. If one doesn't believe in this *l'infini*, it's terrifying to die."

"Why did you mention death?" Anna asked, and was surprised that her heart felt a sudden pang.

"Because for the last twelve years I've had to endure its threat, forced to live in foreign countries where it's warm; but now I've decided not to go anywhere else, to stay here, in Russia, in the country."

"We're going to Moscow for the winter. My husband wants to publish his articles."

"I've heard that, Princess, and I very much regret that this winter, when I'll be living here in your neighborhood, you'll be away in town. I'm always unlucky in all regards. Have you spent the entire year here before?"

"Yes, many years; in fact, even now I don't especially feel like going to Moscow. But it's time for supper; you had dinner early, and I won't let you go home without eating."

Anna rang for the servants and ordered that supper be served.

It was cozy in the dining room, bright and pleasant, as it was throughout the house. Anna sat at a small table with Bekhmetev, on which vases of flow-

39. "Night is the mysterious book of meditations for lovers and poets. Only they know how to read it, only they possess the key to it. This key is the infinite."

ers were placed alongside a cold supper. They chatted about what they had just read; Bekhmetev's carriage stood next to the porch and its bells were jingling.

The sound of an approaching carriage could be heard: one bell interrupted the other and someone entered the house. Anna and her conversation partner paid no attention to all these sounds and didn't even notice the prince enter the room. Anna was startled, jumped up, and asked:

"What happened?"

"Nothing, I simply reconsidered whether to continue the hunt," he said. "Hello, Dmitry, and good night. Excuse me, but I'm exhausted," he added, glancing unkindly at his wife and extending his fingertips to his friend.

"Aren't you going to have some supper?" Anna asked.

"No, I'm falling off my feet."

The prince left, and Bekhmetev, saying farewell to Anna, departed.

She ran in to her husband, seeing that he was upset. He was sitting on the sofa in his study, smoking. Suspecting the truth and knowing her husband's jealous nature, Anna sat down next to him and, in an unnatural voice, began inquiring what had made him come home so early.

"What made me return was that I knew you'd arrange this tête-à-tête. You still don't understand how inappropriate this is?"

"I didn't invite him, but I couldn't send him away."

"You didn't have to flirt with him. Don't you think I could see?"

"Flirt? Me? Enough of that, my dear. Aren't you ashamed to say that? If you only knew how bored I am without you, how glad I am that you've come back. Let's not quarrel, please!"

"She's certainly feeling guilty," the prince decided.

"Why did you look so startled when I came in?" asked the prince. "What was he saying to you?" He was becoming more and more agitated.

"I really don't remember," said Anna, fearing her husband's tone. She looked at his annoyed face: it was now distorted in anger. "We were reading Lamartine, and talking about his work . . ."

"No doubt taken with poetic feelings," said the prince ironically. "I don't believe a word of it. You won't tell me what you were doing or what you were talking about," shouted the prince.

He grabbed his wife's arm and squeezed it hard, just as the nanny suddenly knocked at the door and summoned Anna into the nursery.

Agitated and offended, she tore her arm away and ran to her infant. The child was screaming in impatience.

"These men: they are such egotists," she thought angrily. He's tormented by jealousy, while I sit here all alone and bored; now the baby will gulp down my soured milk and won't sleep a wink! And again it's me who'll have to pay the price!"[40]

Anna couldn't calm down. A feeling of irritation, contempt for the man whom she had tried so hard to love and with whom she had bound her life, failed to subside in any way.

"He doesn't need anyone or anything: neither the children, nor me. He's not interested in our lives in the least. He wants me only as an object, so that his vanity won't be offended. Yes, *his* wife! Nobody can dare speak a word to her . . ."

Anna became more and more upset. "But if he decides to pursue someone else, then that's all right. My God, my God!"

A feeling of self-pity gave rise to tears in her eyes.

At that moment her child choked and began crying. Anna was frightened, and turned the little boy over onto his side; kissing him affectionately, she whispered to him:

"Calm down, precious, calm down."

She looked at the sleepy boy's little face and said to him softly: "It's not for your father who has insulted me, but for you, my dearest; I'd never do anything that would make you ashamed of your mother . . ."

After feeding the infant, Anna made the rounds of the beds of all her children sleeping in their rooms. She made the sign of the cross over each one in turn, and pausing at the last, began to pray. Everyone around her was asleep. She stood there a long time, her head bowed over the child, absorbed and solemn.

If in our everyday, humble lives there weren't these moments of profound, stern reckoning with conscience, of severe and concentrated attention paid to our inner lives, of this intimate scrutiny of one's own "I" in relation to God, then how would our existence be possible?

Anna valued these moments; now, feeling calmer, she went to her own room.

When her husband came in, he assumed a conciliatory tone. He approached her, smiled, and embraced her in silence. Anna regarded this truce serenely and unresponsively; at that moment she felt so spiritually alone, so remote from that which interested him, that when he extended his arms to embrace her, she didn't understand at first what he wanted. Only when it became clear why the prince sought to make peace so quickly, she suddenly found him repugnant. She quickly withdrew from his arms and cried:

---

40. "*It's fine for you,*' she not only thought, but even said, '*but I didn't get any sleep last night because of the baby.*'"

"No, I can't, not for anything!"

Everything about the prince seemed unpleasant to her: his handsome face seemed coarse and stupid; his yellowing teeth, graying hair, and passionate eyes—had all become loathsome.

She lay down, blew out the candles, turned her face to the wall, and pretended to be asleep. Having recited the "Our Father" quickly and inattentively, repeating it over and over to make it more conscious, she crossed herself and, with a tormented soul, fell into a troubled sleep.

The prince's jealous outburst soon passed. He wrote a note to his friend inviting him to dinner, and by the time Bekhmetev began visiting them once again, the prince had calmed down completely with regard to his wife. His friend's tranquil, noble behavior could in no way give rise to any suspicions. His chivalrous politeness, propriety, and respectful admiration of Anna lacked any traits that could arouse the prince's vicious feelings of jealousy.

Meanwhile, Bekhmetev completely yet imperceptibly entered Anna's familial and personal life. He took walks with her and the children, played with them, and spent time with them, recounting interesting stories or drawing. Sometimes he had them sing or dance; they became so attached to him that they were bored when he didn't visit often enough.

As for Anna, she had never felt so happy and her life had never been so full. An atmosphere of love indiscernibly enveloped her on all sides. There were no tender words, no crude caresses, nothing that usually accompanies love, but everything around her breathed tenderness and everything in her life was filled with affection and happiness. She constantly felt that a sympathetic eye was following her through life, approving everything, admiring everything.

In the evening, when everyone was gathered around the large round table as usual, Bekhmetev and Anna took turns sketching portraits of those present in the same album. They alternated reading aloud the books of Jules Verne and others, modifying or explaining those parts that were difficult or unclear to the children.[41] Once it happened that instead of an illustrated copy of *Around the World in Eighty Days* they had received a plain edition.[42] Bekhmetev took it upon himself to illustrate the most important episodes, and this produced such excitement in the children's world that they could hardly wait for him to return to continue reading and drawing.

41. Jules Verne (1828–1905) was a French author of numerous popular books of science fiction.

42. The classic adventure novel *Around the World in Eighty Days* (1873) was one of Verne's most acclaimed works.

Bekhmetev's concern and attention to Anna's entire life were manifested in everything. She loved flowers—he filled the house with the nicest blooms. She loved reading aloud—he sought out the most interesting articles and books and spent whole evenings reading to her. Anna loved her school; as if to please the sweet, innocent teacher, he sent books, drawings, and various supplies.

Only such a caring and disinterested attitude to a woman could bring complete happiness to her life. Anna never gave herself a clear account of why everything that had seemed so difficult before, now seemed so easy. Why had everything that had previously angered or upset her now ceased to do so? All the trifles and disappointments of daily life became so unimportant; everyone seemed so kind. And what was most astonishing of all—but which undoubtedly also happened—was that she found her husband more pleasant. She was tender and affectionate to him, and that completely appeased his feeling of jealousy.

Thus passed autumn and when, at the beginning of November, the entire family was preparing to move to Moscow, no one wanted to part with this happy, quiet life in the country.

Only the prince was in a hurry to leave. Apparently, he was bored at home and was looking for excuses to escape to town and visit neighbors; he was always seeking diversions. This truly perturbed Anna. She saw that he was retreating farther and farther from the family, from her influence, and was showing his love less and less. She was afraid that he would leave altogether, and that the family she had tried to safeguard during these eleven years of married life would be destroyed. She resolved to use all her powers to retain her husband, to find ways and means by which she could attract him once again and keep him within the family. She vaguely knew what those means were; they were repugnant to her, but what else would work as well?

"If little by little I've lost my previous innocence and my maidenly ideals—then at least I can preserve the purity of the family ideal. I mustn't allow my husband, the father of my children, to abandon the family and find impure joys outside it."[43]

With these thoughts Anna gathered her strength and left for Moscow with the others.

---

43. *"Women, especially those schooled by men, know very well that talk about lofty matters—is just that, all talk, and that a man needs a woman's body and everything that shows it off . . ."*

4

On the evening of December 2 several carriages were pulling up to a large, well-lit, wealthy house on one of the cleanest streets of Moscow. Princess and Prince Prozorsky received guests every Sunday, and their living room was always filled with the most diverse visitors. Nowhere else was it as informal, cheerful, elegant, and stimulating as it was at Princess Prozorskaya's.[44] Always welcoming, smiling, and lovely, Anna knew how to bring together the kind of people who mingled easily; she always devoted herself completely to making sure that everyone around her was comfortable, happy, and attractive; the result was that in a very short time a pleasant and large society group had gathered around her.

The prince could not help but admire her: what had become of his previously retiring wife who so disliked society? It was as if she had been reborn: she received visitors, paid calls, dressed to the nines, and conceived the most entertaining amusements and activities in which she always involved her husband. "I feel bored or ill at ease when left alone," she would say, and the prince was always with her. He followed her with vigilance, observing the change that had made her so appealing, distinctive, and well loved in society. She startled him, having revealed this unexpected, completely novel side of her character and her charm.

That evening a well-known writer was supposed to read his new story; he had recently arrived from the provinces to publish his book. A large crowd had gathered. A lively conversation was in progress around Anna in the living room. An argument had arisen between two young women discussing the upbringing of children. One of them, Countess Velskaya, insisted that upbringing consisted entirely of exerting personal influence on one's children: the main thing, she said, was spending time with them, following the development of their characters and souls, and assisting them in their growth. The other party, the jovial and frivolous Baroness Innsbruck, maintained that the best thing would be to allow them to pursue what is innate in all children; upbringing does nothing for them, she argued; besides, it was best not to ruin one's own personal life. Everyone was quite animated, interrupting one another. One older general turned toward Anna and said:

"One should learn how to raise children from the princess. I've never seen more natural, healthy, and clever children than hers."

44. The feminine form of Anna's married surname.

"I think that one can bring up children only if you yourself know what's good and bad," said Anna. "You must develop the good and restrain the bad. For that reason I can only repeat Seneca's words: '*Les facultès les plut fortes de chaque homme sont celles qu'il a exercé.*'"[45]

"Where does all this come from?" wondered the prince. "What serene confidence! And those diamonds in her ears, how beautifully they sparkle, competing with the brilliance of her lovely, lively eyes!"

The prince knew that later that same evening his wife would let her dark golden hair down onto her bare shoulders, undress in front of the mirror, and turn to look at him as he entered the bedroom; recalling that such a moment was near at hand, he gladly stood to greet the famous author, who assumed that the prince's display of joy was due to his own arrival.

Anna also rose from the sofa to meet the celebrated guest. Rustling the silk-lined train of her gray dress trimmed with fluffy fur, she approached the writer and greeted him warmly:

"I know that this is hard for you—you don't like to read in public; therefore, I'm especially grateful to you," she said, seating the illustrious guest next to her.

The reading soon began. The story by the celebrated guest made a strong impression on everyone; a few praised his work timidly, others thanked him. But no one could convey the impression he had made more eloquently than Anna. She extended one hand to the writer and, with the other, wiped away her tears. He understood how deeply she had felt that which he had written while shedding his own tears, and he responded sincerely to her handshake.

When the guests had begun to depart, feeling that the evening spent in Princess Prozorskaya's home had been filled with interest and energy, Anna stopped a young man with sharply etched Armenian features and said:

"You promised to pose for me. Come tomorrow to sit and then we'll take the children skating. Agreed?"

"I'm delighted, Princess, and at your service."

"Don't worry: the sittings will be short and we can chat in the meantime. I really do need your type of face for the picture I'm planning. Well, good night."

When Anna was left alone with her husband, he asked sarcastically:

---

45. Seneca (c. 5 B.C.–A.D. 65) was a Roman Stoic philosopher, statesman, and dramatist. He served as tutor and adviser to Emperor Nero, who eventually obliged him to commit suicide. This quotation is from a French translation of his essay, *On Providence*, IV, 13: *id in quoque soldissimum est quod exercuit*, "The strongest faculties of each are those that he has developed."

"Where did you get the idea of painting that pup?"

Anna burst into loud laughter.

"A pup with a very typical face, precisely the kind I need; I'll definitely sketch him."

"But why go skating with him afterward?"

"Because out of his devotion to me he'll push the children around the ice on chairs, and I can skate alone."

What was it that was so sinister and strange in Anna's playful, cheerful tone? The prince couldn't identify it. He had never seen her before in high society, and her success and vivacity frightened him. Of late he had been entirely consumed by his wife. But she seemed to be slipping away from him; at the same time she had managed to arrange their life in town so that he was never bored and never sought out other pastimes.[46]

The next morning Anna received a note from an old acquaintance with the pressing request to escort her daughter to a ball. The event promised to be most enjoyable; the old friend was indisposed, but didn't want her daughter to be deprived of the pleasure. Anna had also been invited to the ball, but wasn't planning to attend. Now she reconsidered and wrote to express her agreement.

Until the last moment she hadn't told her husband about her intention to go; she knew he would be displeased, but she didn't want to disappoint her friend's daughter.

That evening the prince had invited guests to whom he was planning to read his articles. Anna already knew all these boring arguments, which she had copied so many times; there were so many incomprehensible, convoluted technical terms and expressions she had tried hard to fathom. She didn't attend the reading and spent time with her children. She involuntarily recalled Bekhmetev and the evenings spent with him in the country; she felt unbearably lonely and gloomy. After putting the children to bed, she began preparing for the ball. At about midnight, she stood in front of the pier glass dressed in something silvery with antique white silk lace and bright roses, her face made up and dazzling in her beauty. The maid, circling her carefully, blowing into a thin glass tube, sprayed her with perfume. The door opened and Anna shuddered. The prince came in; seeing his wife dressed to the nines, he stood there astonished and displeased.

"Where are you off to?" he asked.

"I'm taking Marusya Pavlovich to the ball at her mother's request, because she's ill," Anna replied serenely.

---

46. *"And she? But who is she? She's a mystery: as she was, so she still is."*

"Why on earth? And why didn't you tell me? A mother of a family—traipsing around at balls . . ."

"What a word! Traipsing! I wanted to do something nice for Marusya and her mother. Besides, I like going to balls. I love the radiance, beauty, and the delight of our young people. You know very well that I always sit with the older women at balls as if watching a performance.

"How should I know what you do there?" the prince replied petulantly, without taking his eyes off his wife. "I can't hide the fact that you look very lovely this evening," he added and left the room, slamming the door.

Anna followed him with her eyes full of contempt, and for some reason thought again about Bekhmetev, together with the endless expanse of melancholy, rural nature, autumnal haze, and her quiet, calm happiness.

Her arrival at the ball that evening produced a particularly strong impression. A small group of men was standing at the door of the large ballroom. One adjutant remarked: "Here's the royal entrance at the ball." Anna turned around. Always friendly and composed, the lovely Princess Prozorskaya showed no preference to anyone, as if promising it to everyone. As with almost all very beautiful women, she also had a kind, loving look that seemed to be a reflection of that expression with which people regard beautiful women, admiring them.

But that evening Anna's thoughtful and affectionate eyes, regarding this joyful, interesting crowd, imagined more and more often Bekhmetev's head bent over a book or a sketch, surrounded by her own beloved children; and she suddenly wanted to escape from the ball, away from the hustle and bustle of Moscow, and return to the familiar, simple, gentle peace and quiet of country life, the only place where she could really be happy.

The cheerful, sparkling Baroness Innsbruck came up to her and asked whether she was having a good time.

Anna laughed in surprise and asked what a ball could possibly do to make her happy.

"*Mais il y a dans cette toujours quelqu'un qui vous intèresse?*"[47]

"*Qui, il y a foule, mais pour moi il n'y a personne,*"[48]

"*Un seul être vous manqué, et tout est dépeuplé,*" the baroness declaimed a verse from Lamartine; then with a chuckle, she disappeared into the crowd,

47. "Isn't there always someone in the crowd who interests you?"
48. "Yes, there's a crowd indeed, but there's no one for me."

marveling at what it was that made Anna so happy, cheerful, and radiant.[49] She never danced or flirted with anyone—wasn't she bored?

But Anna wasn't bored because somewhere deep inside her burned a spark of genuine happiness, the ember of Bekhmetev's love for her, which fact she knew and which illuminated her entire life from within. She would never have acknowledged this to herself, but could not help feeling it. When she was admired, she saw at once how he admired her. Whether she was fulfilling her obligations or busy with some task, reading or drawing—she always thought about whether he would approve and how he would relate to her actions. If someone could have explained to her this condition of her soul, she would have replied with indignation and horror, considering it slanderous and an accusation of dishonesty. But this was indeed the case.

5

Life in town from day to day with the strain of attending to the tasks of keeping her husband from being bored and keeping him near her at home, combined with the effort of maintaining social relations, and the major responsibility for the children's upbringing—all this exhausted Anna to such an extent that she decided to leave for the country and spend a few days "collecting herself," as she put it. She was drawn to the peace and quiet, to nature, to recollections of her youth, and to the pure impressions of country life, while down deep in her soul, there stirred a vague desire to see Bekhmetev. She didn't let herself acknowledge that fact, but the image of this beloved man involuntarily merged with everything that drew her to the countryside.

Anna told her husband that she needed to return home to attend to some household matters; she said there were several problems in the school and she wanted to support and encourage the young teacher, who had been frightened by the inspector; last of all, she said that she was so tired of their city life in Moscow that she wanted to go to the country to gaze at the open sky, unimpeded by any houses, at the fresh snow, the forest covered in hoarfrost, and that if she didn't go, she would certainly fall ill.

All this seemed extremely bizarre to the prince, but he saw that it was useless to argue, that women make decisions that no one can possibly contradict,

---

49. Baroness Innsbruck's apt quotation is from a love lyric entitled "L'isolement" (Isolation) from Lamartine's *Méditations poétiques:* "Only one person is missing and besides him no one else exists."

and that if he were to try, he might come to grief, but she would never change her mind.

Anna packed a small suitcase with the help of a maid and, so as not to lose a whole day in transit, she left at night. As she said goodbye to the children, she was reluctant to leave them. She spent a long time making the sign of the cross and kissing little Yusha, who had recently been weaned, kissed her sleepy older children, and started to suffer pangs of conscience. But she couldn't remain at home—that would've been beyond her. The prince bade her farewell indulgently, but especially tenderly. For a long time afterward she felt the moist kisses of his lips and recalled his affectionate look, which of late had so often been fixed on her.

Anna had accomplished her goal: her husband had not left her. But at what cost? She recalled all that she had done to keep him: she felt repelled and disgusted with herself. And as for Anna herself? What had become of her? She had retreated farther and farther from the man who had destroyed the best side of her own "self," and she was horrified at that thought.

6

Anna sent word ahead that she should be picked up at the station. The old coachman greeted her especially warmly, bringing the familiar bay troika to the station platform.[50]

When she passed the gates, an unexpected feeling of ecstasy burst forth from Anna's breast. The morning was magnificent. The bright sun flooded the blindingly white, level fields with light. "Yes, this is the boundless, the infinite, *l'infini*—just what I've yearned for!" she thought. "I've been oppressed by walls, fences, and houses in that awful urban setting! Real life is out here, freedom, wide-open space, and God! Yes, I feel free as a bird; I'm my own mistress; I was born and grew up in the country; I can't live in town," she reflected. The troika raced along merrily over the snowy road, the carriage bells tinkling continuously; the sleigh, occasionally going over a pothole, tossed Anna from side to side, disrupting her joyful, thoughtful mood.

At last they entered the old birch-lined lane. The hoarfrost hung heavily on the branches of the age-old gnarled birches; sparkling with hundreds of little fires in the sunshine, it endowed all of nature with an especially triumphant and celebratory appearance.

"Ah, how fine, familiar, peaceful, lovely, and solemn it all is!" thought Anna, approaching the steward's cottage and glancing around at the large manor house.

50. A troika is a Russian cart or sleigh drawn by a team of three horses.

The steward was waiting with the samovar and tea that had been brewed with special effort. As Anna sat drinking her tea, served by an old woman, the steward's aunt, he delivered in an imposing voice a report obviously prepared in advance about the household affairs, the threshing, the livestock, and the tree-felling in the forest. He asked when she would like to examine the books.

"This evening; now I'll visit the threshing barn, the school, and the cattle yard."

"Shall I accompany you, Princess?"

"Yes, indeed."

Anna carefully made the rounds of the entire estate. Household affairs had served as the underlying justification for her journey home. She tried to be conscientious, but such matters interested her very little. She was simply happy, and everything seemed so novel to her in this old setting. She paid attention to the new calves and their mothers, and to the young horses in training. She saw how much grain was yet to be threshed, and insisted that it all be finished soon. She even inquired about the turkeys and geese, which had been of no interest to her before. But at least all this seemed natural and simple; it was nature itself, uncontrived and everlasting!

After releasing the steward, she went to visit the school. The young teacher, now thinner and paler, stood at the blackboard and was eagerly explaining a problem to a small lad who was looking at her with inquisitive, frightened eyes.

"Lidia Vasilievna!" Anna called to her.

"Ah, my dear princess! What brings you here? I didn't expect you. What joy!"

"Why have you grown so thin?" asked Anna, kissing the young woman.

"It's a very hard job, Princess. Then there was the unpleasant business with the inspector. I devote myself entirely to the work, but there's only carping: I'm not reading the right things or the textbooks aren't the best ones. The officials seem to want to keep the people stupid, instead of educating them."

Anna looked intently into the kind, pale face of the teacher, and it suddenly became clear to her how much better and nobler this unnoticed, unappreciated, self-sacrificing, and uncorrupted creature was than she herself; the teacher was devoting her entire young life to serving a cause in which she believed and which she loved more than anything, more than herself. While she? Never satisfied, wealthy, living in luxury, surrounded by her children—what was she doing that would be of some use to anyone else?

Anna felt disgusted with herself and wondered how this sweet young woman could be living her lackluster life without reward, while she was living her glittering life without punishment.

After surveying the school, Anna said a tender goodbye to the young teacher and went to call on the elderly former maid of the late princess; she was still living in retirement and now afflicted with paralysis.

The old woman was very glad to see Anna and began telling her endless tales, heard so many times before, of bygone days, of dogs the old woman had loved more than anything else on earth, the cow that had given birth at night, and how they had had to carry the frozen calf into the barn; how yesterday the Muscovy hen had laid her first egg and cackled about it all night; and many other things from the world of birds and animals. It was clear that her own lifeless existence was so filled with other lives, even though they were animals, that she was content.

"And so, my dear little Princess, I ask to buy some tea and so forth and a wax candle for Saint Nikola's day.[51] I light the candle to the saint and pray for the prince's good health, for his spouse, and for their offspring. As soon as I light it—I hear the steward, he's searching for the prince's hunting dogs. They've run off, those bandits, into the forest. I think: goodness gracious, they'll get lost, alas for the prince. So I start praying to the saint: Father, Saint Nikola, let my candle make up for the loss. Sinner that I am, little Princess! And then, all the dogs came back, damn them, real fast, too."

It was only with difficulty that Anna got away from the old woman; she returned home, had dinner with the steward and his aunt, and went off to wander all alone around her favorite, familiar places. It was frosty and astonishingly beautiful. Heavy hoarfrost hung everywhere on the trees, bushes, thatch roofs, and on all the grasses. Anna walked along the road to her favorite grove; to the left the sun was setting behind the young trees; on the right, above the old oak forest the moon was already rising. The white tops of the trees and all of winter nature were illuminated from both sides, mingling and combining the two reflections: the soft, pale light of the moon and the light pink glow of the evening sun. The sky was blue, and further off on the meadow, the white, white snow was shining brilliantly.

"Here's where purity lies! How beautiful it all is, this whiteness in nature, in the soul, in life, in morals, and in conscience! It's so beautiful everywhere! How I love it and how I've tried to maintain it in all places and at all times.

---

51. Saint Nicholas is honored twice in the Russian Orthodox Church calendar: December 19 and again in the spring, on May 22.

But for what? Who needs it? Wouldn't it be better to have memories of some passionate love, even if illicit, but real and full? Wouldn't it be better than this present emptiness and immaculateness of my conscience?" Anna shuddered. "Of course not! A thousand times no! Never!" she almost exclaimed. And suddenly, as if her soul were cleansed by this pure nature, she felt a surge of spiritual strength, such as she hadn't experienced in a long time. She returned to the house when it was already dark and distractedly set about inspecting the steward's account books. She made several remarks, dealt with the distribution of land to the peasants, and then, asking that the house be unlocked, went into her husband's study to fetch some books he had asked for. Entering his cold room, she shuddered and cast a glance all around. How many memories! So many experiences here, joy and grief and disillusionment! Anna sat down and began to finger her husband's things, his letters, papers, and diaries. Her cold, stiff fingers leafed through the pages of this familiar book, searching in vain for some trace of herself. Living in the country, the prince had related to his wife as if to a nonentity; she didn't interest him in any way whatsoever. But she came across her name: "Yes, he describes how I rode out to meet him—but there's only anger." There followed a description of the hunt and the attractive lady who participated. Anna's heart skipped a beat. She read it and was horrified at the salaciousness of her husband's language.

"Oh, how awful! How I've loved him and for so long!" Anna thought with a strange rush of tenderness, and tossed the diary onto the desk. The idea vaguely occurred to her that it was a good thing she had loved her husband according to the demands of her own pure, loving nature, and not for what he had given in return.

Anna went to bed still not knowing whether she would leave for Moscow the next morning, or visit Varvara Alekseevna's house in order to see her brother. She hardly slept at all that night. The bed was unfamiliar, and the steward's aunt who had ceded her featherbed to Anna and who slept nearby on the trunk, sighed and snored all night. At last the long December night came to an end. As soon as Anna had drawn back the curtain on the window and looked out at the brilliant frosty morning, she decided at once to visit Varvara Alekseevna. She gathered her things and had the horse harnessed. In her imagination she invented various pretexts for going to see Varvara Alekseevna. She had to inspect the school, to confer, or to find something out, and finally it would have been simply impolite not to call on her. But Anna's heart was pounding as she drove up to Varvara Alekseevna's estate. What would she say? There had never been any special intimacy between them. What excuse would she invent? And why exactly had she, whose place was in Moscow with her husband and children, come here, to visit this woman who was not even a close friend? And what about Anna's children? What were they doing now? Manya and Anna's favorite, little Yusha?

But it was already too late to reason thus. The sleigh approached the porch and Anna walked into the front hall of Varvara Alekseevna's small country house anxiously and timidly.

There was an ominous silence in the house, as if no one lived there. Everything was still, neat, and clean in the entrance and the hall where Anna glanced. She already felt like leaving when the old servant appeared, stepping quietly; he took Anna's fur coat and invited her in. He reported that the lady of the house was at home and he would announce her.

Anna had to wait rather a long time. She heard footsteps; then an austere, solemn, and courteous Varvara Alekseevna entered the room. She was clearly surprised by Anna's arrival; she listened with suspicion to her words about wanting to confer with her about some school affairs and the peasant children's education, and then invited her to stay for lunch. She didn't say a word about her brother; when Anna asked how his health was, Varvara Alekseevna frowned and said:

"He's not well. He has a terrible cough. I tried to send him to the doctor in Moscow, but he laughed and said: 'I've been in treatment for over twelve years. It makes no difference—sooner or later—the end is the same.' He went out for a walk," she added.

Anna's heart constricted painfully. "'Sooner or later, the end . . .' Yes, that's how it must be," she thought. "Nothing was ever supposed to come to an end on the journey of my life or my conscience. Everything's for the best. . . . But how will I remain alive? What will I live by?" Anna's inner voice cried out in horror; no consideration of her obligation, her husband, or her children could divert her from the horror of Bekhmetev's death.

Just at that moment his voice could be heard in the front hall, asking who had arrived.

"Some lady, the princess; I've forgotten her name."

Bekhmetev didn't wait to hear the reply and hastened into the drawing room. He blanched when he saw Anna and hesitated for a moment; then the blood rushed back to his face and he regained control of himself.

Struck by the change that had taken place in him, Anna stared Bekhmetev gravely in the eye; in this silent exchange of glances was their first, earnest confession.

"Least of all did I expect to see you, Princess," Bekhmetev spoke first, greeting her. He didn't ask why she had come to the country; he understood everything from the first moment, understood by the ardent, distressed, grim expression of her lovely dark eyes fixed intently on him; both joy and pain overwhelmed him together.

Their conversation was wide-ranging. Anna talked about Moscow, her exhaustion from city life, and continually shuddered at the abrupt, harsh sound of Bekhmetev's coughing.

When Varvara Alekseevna went to fetch something, Anna suddenly changed her tone and asked in an anxious voice:

"You're ill?"

"Yes, something in my chest isn't right. It'll pass when summer comes."

"We're coming back in March," Anna blurted out involuntarily.

"That'll be very nice! I've heard rumors about you, Princess, that you're enjoying unprecedented success in society," said Bekhmetev.

"Who told you? If you only knew that I have no one there at all!" she said.

"While no one interests you, everyone admires you. You know that if anyone falls in love with a woman like you, it's dangerous; it's impossible to stop halfway on the road to love; it consumes you entirely . . ."

Bekhmetev turned pale; he gasped for breath and his face even became unpleasant as a result of the impassioned severity of his expression. Anna looked at him with apprehension. She found these unwonted words from such an ideal person extremely confusing. She was silent. Bekhmetev's pained face continued looking gloomy, and his restrained passion seemed to distort it even more painfully. Anna regarded him with a look full of suffering.

"So, that's what you think? But such demands of love kill it, just as every day people kill it . . ."

"How then, Princess, can love survive, that is, live for a long time?"

"Oh, of course, only by a spiritual connection. Such love is eternal: death does not exist for it."

"You think, a spiritual connection *exclusively*?"

"I don't know whether exclusively or not, but in any case it's *first and foremost*, and it's undisputed happiness."

Bekhmetev grew thoughtful.

"Perhaps you're right, Princess," he said softly. "It's better that way and let it be so," he added, coming up to her and moving a chair so he could sit closer to her.

He began to inquire sympathetically and tenderly about her children, her painting, and her life in general. She described everything in great detail, as one does to someone who's certain to be interested in absolutely everything.

Varvara Alekseevna returned and invited Anna to inspect her school. Anna tried to pay the greatest attention, but this proved to be difficult. After dinner she began to hurry, so as not to be late for her train.

"I'll accompany you, Princess. May I?" asked Bekhmetev. "I have to be in town tomorrow, and I'll take advantage of the opportunity to go to the station with you."

Anna made no reply, but when they brought the sleigh around, she said in parting:

"Dmitry Alekseevich, you wanted me to drop you off at the station?"

"I'm ready now, Princess."

They didn't talk along the way. It was overcast, and a damp warm wind was blowing; the dim sky hung low; it seemed as if it would snow, and there might even be a real blizzard.

"We seem to be heading into a storm."

"Be quiet, please; you mustn't speak when it's so windy," said Anna.

He fell silent, but his eyes, facing forward but seeing nothing outside, saw only his own inner happiness, the happiness of being next to the woman he loved more than anyone else on earth, without daring to tell her that or about the love he was feeling at that moment. Anna noticed his expression of happiness; for a long time, a very long time afterward, his glance at such a painful time glowed inside her.

They went farther and farther, both thinking about the same thing, without demanding from fate or from each other anything more, and experiencing amid this snowy, pure, limitless nature their own relationship to it, to God, and to the eternity in which one must live one's own life now, and afterward, and forever, in which it is possible to be happy and pure, and to love unselfishly and perpetually.

"There are the station lights," said Anna.

"Well, Dmitry Alekseevich, you'll have to spend the night here at the station," said the coachman. "The snowstorm's really picked up."

"We can do that. We've arrived, Princess."

They bade farewell at the station, simply shaking each other's hands.

Bekhmetev waited for her train's departure and stood for a long time watching the line of cars disappear, winding like a snake around the bend of the road, and vanishing under the arc of the bridge.

7

As always when Anna was approaching home, she grew more and more agitated wondering what she might find when she got there: were the children in good health? Her anxiety grew with every minute.

"Is everyone well at home?" she asked the coachman who came out to greet her.

"I don't know, Your Excellency, I haven't heard anything."

Her impatience and anxiety reached a painful level as she approached the house and the servant opened the door for her.

"Is everyone well?" she repeated her question.

"Yes, thank God. The nurse says only that the little one has a slight fever."

Anna's heart sank. "I knew it," she thought.

After warming herself by the stove in the hallway, she ran straight into the nursery. The older children welcomed her: "Mama's home, mama's home!" they cried as she entered.

"Yusha has a fever," Manya announced triumphantly, hurrying, like all children, to be the first to convey important news.

Anna ran to the infant's crib and picked little Yusha up in her arms; when he saw his mother, he began crying in distress.

Horror and despair seized Anna's heart and she was tormented by pangs of conscience. Her entire trip had been egotistical; her uncharacteristic weakness now seemed loathsome to her. She looked at the feverish, fussing child, and dared not even kiss him.

"Has the doctor been sent for?"

"No," the nurse replied. "The prince said to wait for your return."

Anna hastened to write a note to the doctor and then asked where the prince was.

"He's in his study, working."

"It's all the same to him whether Yusha's ill," she thought with bitterness.

The prince still hadn't emerged from his study when the doctor arrived. Anna inquisitively observed the expressions and movements of the professor, a well-known specialist on children's diseases; she realized that Yusha's condition was serious.

"It's too early to say anything definite, Princess. Tomorrow we'll know for sure. His temperature's very high. I think it may be the measles, and there may be complications," said the doctor.

The infant was having trouble breathing and was coughing hoarsely. The prince came in. He greeted his wife and the doctor, and then asked:

"Have you been home long?"

"I arrived about two hours ago."

The prince spoke with the doctor, contemptuously displaying his lack of confidence in medicine, and then bade him a cool goodbye.

"I'll look in on him tomorrow morning, Princess," said the doctor, addressing Anna.

"Please do," she said, returning the sleeping infant to his crib. "You have dinner, nanny; I'll stay here with him."

The prince also remained in the nursery and began asking Anna about her trip.

"Where did you spend the night?" he asked casually.

"In the steward's house, of course; our house isn't heated."

"How inappropriate and foolish."

"What?" she asked in surprise.

"*C'est un jeune homme, et je vous dis que ce n'est pas convenable; vous manquez toujours de tact.*"[52]

"I slept in the room with his aunt," Anna managed to say with some difficulty; then she fell silent and gazed gloomily into her sleeping son's crib.

"Were you anywhere else?" the prince continued his interrogation.

"Yes, I went to visit Varvara Alekseevna to see her school and I met Dmitry Alekseevich there. He escorted me to the station. He's not well and coughs persistently."

"What? That, too? You rode with him at night?"

"Not at night, in the evening."

The prince jumped up and paced the nursery.

"God only knows how you behave!" he cried.

"Quiet. You'll wake the child!"

"We can't live like this! It's outrageous!" cried the prince. "You have children, yet you're ready to throw yourself on the neck of anyone who flirts with you."

Anna remained silent, but tears flowed from her eyes. Overwhelmed by pangs of conscience and anxiety over her child, and offended by her husband's suspicions, she could find no way to justify herself; she merely looked at him unkindly from the side, then at her child, and whispered softly:

"Please, be quiet."

The prince fell silent. For a minute he doubted the fairness of his reproaches and realized that if his wife was in fact innocent of any wrongdoing,

---

52. "He's a young man, and I tell you that it's not proper; you always lack discretion."

it was not because of him, who had offended her so frequently by his jealousy, but rather it was thanks to this feverish, much-loved little boy.

He left. He paced his study for some time. Of late jealousy had been tormenting him more and more. His imagination pictured the most salacious and indecent scenes. First he saw the steward entering his sleeping wife's room at night; then he imagined Bekhmetev, his old friend, embracing her in the sleigh. And she? He didn't know her; he had never made the effort to understand the sort of woman she really was. He knew her shoulders, her lovely eyes, her passionate temperament (he was so happy when he had finally managed to awaken it); but was she happy with him, was she completely honest, did she love him or not?—he didn't know any of that and was unable to resolve it. True, she submitted to his periodic demands, but he could never fathom what was behind that.

Pacing the length of his study for the tenth time, he recalled his own amorous intrigues before marriage. How cleverly and subtly he had deceived those trusting husbands, as he stole their wives away from them! How natural and even cheerful was this endless courting, these clever devices for arranging trysts and troika rides; when unnoticed by other people, especially the husbands, he would squeeze those ladies' warm hands under their fluffy cloaks and, sliding his arm around their slender waists, he would draw them toward him. "Why wouldn't other men do the same with my wife? Why wouldn't Bekhmetev take advantage and flirt with such a beautiful woman who's practically thrown herself at him?"

The prince was more and more tormented by jealousy, while hatred of the woman whom he wished to possess alone increased with terrible force. Along with this hatred grew his passion, his unrestrained, animal passion, whose strength he felt, and as a result of which his anger grew even stronger.

The children really had come down with the measles. All four of them caught it. With little Yusha, his measles were complicated by pneumonia. Anna moved into the nursery and monitored her children's condition with painful anxiety. She kept vigil for whole nights or paced up and down the nursery with little Yusha in her arms. Bending over his little face that had turned blue, she was in agony over his labored breathing, blew into his little mouth, kissing him, as if wanting to transfer her life and health to him. Sometimes she stood over his crib and prayed as only a mother can. Her prayer was not an entreaty of God to save her infant; rather it was an acknowledgement of her powerlessness before Him and her entrusting herself to His power.

"Here I am, Lord, suffering, weak, and submissive. Have mercy on me, if it be Thy will, and save my Yusha!"

Her husband, evidently, was oppressed by this period of the children's illness. He said that she was exaggerating the danger and causing misery for everyone in the house. He avoided meeting the doctor, who came to call every day, and was angry with his wife for her complete confidence in his advice. But Anna paid no attention to her husband; she always anticipated this kind, clever man's arrival with impatience. He related to the children and to her own anguish attentively and sympathetically. With such kindness in his eyes he looked at this passionate young mother who was wasting away from grief.

"There's no need to despair, Princess," he said, placing a compress on the little boy's chest. "Look at how much life there is in him; he's feeling a little better and is already playing."

Anna, worn down with suffering to the last extreme, was grateful with all her heart to this man who, in addition to his medical assistance, supported and consoled her during this most difficult time of her life.[53]

Little Yusha and the other children recovered. Once again Anna grew lively for a while and her soul was at ease. The prince also cheered up. He was glad that life had returned to normal, that his wife had moved back from the nursery to the bedroom, and that the doctor had ceased his house calls. Anna understood all this; as a result, one more crack appeared in her love for her husband. She never forgot it and never forgave his indifference to the children's illness and his lack of sympathy for her anxiety.[54]

While everyone else was feeling better, Anna's own weakened and exhausted organism broke down and she fell ill. The excessive efforts of caring for the children, the sleepless nights spent carrying a heavy infant in her arms for hours at a time, her emotional anxiety—all this caused her to give birth prematurely, followed by a serious woman's illness. She had to spend six weeks in bed.

At first the prince was terribly frightened; he summoned the doctors, couldn't sleep at night, and foresaw the possibility of losing the customary comfort of having such a beautiful, young, healthy wife. One minute he would behave tenderly toward her, and then the next he would become nervous and agitated, or would get angry with some of his wife's careless actions,

---

53. *"But no one knows what he'll say, least of all, Ivan Zakharych, because he himself knows all too well that he doesn't know anything and he can't help in any way, so he merely hedges his bets . . ."*
54. *"Thus the presence of children not only failed to improve our life but poisoned it."*

reproaching her for not taking good care of herself. But when the danger had passed and Anna, pale and serene, lay there with a book or some work in her hands, the prince began to feel terribly bored and found all sorts of pretexts to leave the house. He would even display a certain hostility, which caused Anna to recall the proverb: "A husband loves a healthy wife . . . and loves to make her feel bad about her illness."[55]

Gradually Anna grew used to her husband's salacious attitude toward her and to her own loneliness. She often thought of her mother and sister, who could have consoled her now; but they had gone abroad long ago for little Misha's well-being; it turned out that he had scoliosis, and for several years they moved him from place to place to preserve his fragile existence.

Anna surrounded herself with her children and her books. But her children exhausted her and were kept away on doctor's orders. However, no one took away her books. Rarely in her life had she been able to enjoy her leisure as she could now. It used to happen that browsing through some philosophical works in her husband's study, she would be able to read only a little; lacking time to read more, she had skimmed through some others. Now she took these beloved philosophical works and read them carefully, copying out those passages she liked most of all. After two months or so, Anna looked at her notebook and was astonished to see that the question of death was the one that interested her most of all, not in the sense of disappearance from life, but in that there was no such thing as death. A new religious feeling took possession of her soul. Everything was measured by her faith in immortality. She suddenly perceived that point which has no limit in all earthly things, through which her spiritual eye beheld infinity and immortality, and she felt both peace and joy.

"I have everything here from our church teachings that's been recorded about this question—where it also speaks of immortality. . . . Yet here's Epictetus, a philosopher, a pagan, and a slave: he understood there's no such thing as death, that death is the absorption of the human mind into the universal Mind," Anna reflected, turning the pages of her notebook.[56]

"Yes, this universal Mind absorbs us, this divinity which we know with all our being, which we love, from which we emerge, and into whose will we offer ourselves!"

In this new blissful frame of mind Anna left Moscow at the beginning of April and moved back to the country with her entire family.

---

55. *"In me, at least, there often seethed a terrible hatred for her!"*
56. Epictetus was a Roman Stoic philosopher (c. A.D. 50–c. 130), born a slave.

8

Anna's new mood bothered the prince. There was something unnatural, tranquil, enigmatic, combined with something self-assured in all her being, something that she was safeguarding from him and not granting him any involvement. He had never really understood his wife very well, and now, least of all.

In the country Anna began to recover rapidly from her illness. The doctor treating her warned the prince that in spite of the improvement in her strength, if the princess were to be careless, her ill health could return, and not just once. "Swimming in the river when the weather turns warmer, peace and quiet, and no further additions to the family," he added delicately with a smile.[57] The prince frowned upon hearing those words and made no reply.

Anna also conferred with a woman doctor with whom she was acquainted; in spite of the prince's dissatisfaction, she decided to follow their advice to remain healthy, strong, and attractive.

And this she managed to achieve. The doctors' counsel produced results; Anna blossomed along with the beauty of summer; she revived, grew lovelier, and all her dormant energy emerged with such force that often it seemed that she could do anything, that all human capabilities had materialized in her all at once.[58]

After the move, she settled into her familiar country setting, and at first devoted herself to the joys of springtime impressions, freedom, and nature. The prince also cheered up and began to treat his wife more calmly and with greater affection. He frequently invited her to accompany him on strolls, chatted with her about his ideas regarding various articles and his newly published books, and tried to interest her in household affairs.

"Is rapprochement still really possible?" Anna wondered with joy. She was attentive and gracious to her husband, fulfilled all his wishes, and tried to draw him closer to the children. As often happens during periods of complete family well-being, Anna surrendered entirely to her own happiness; she put aside all questions, doubts, and anything else that could damage this general positive mood. How simply and willingly she returned to her former love of her husband; once more she believed that she could be happy with him, that their disharmony was only temporary, accidental. She related to

57. "She was unwell, and those scoundrel-doctors ordered her not to bear any more children and they taught her how to avoid giving birth."

58. "The means prescribed by those scoundrel-doctors, apparently, began to work; she put on weight and grew prettier, like the late beauty of summer."

him so trustingly, sympathetically. She tried to expel all thoughts of Bekhmetev from that holy of holies in her soul, where he had imperceptibly come to occupy so large a place.

But, just as before, the prince's loving, peaceful mood didn't last very long. It always had its limits.

In the middle of May, on a hot day, rare during springtime, Anna awoke unusually early and went out onto the terrace. Everyone in the house was still asleep. She sent to find out if Manya and her governess were awake, and if so, asked for them to be summoned. But they still hadn't gotten up. Then Anna set off alone to the woods. The morning was unusually lovely, as happens only in May when nature has not yet produced everything, but promises more and more beauty and blossoming, when everything is still fresh, bright, new, and there's no fear, as in summer, that soon, all this mature beauty will begin to wither and fade.

As an artist, sensitive to all beauty, Anna was taking enormous delight in everything and didn't even notice that she had approached the river that flowed by about two versts from the house.

"It'd be nice to swim," she thought, and entered the newly constructed bathhouse. She was reluctant to disrobe and enter the water alone, but the bright, still river seemed to beckon her with its freshness. She quickly undressed and waded into the water. When she heard some footsteps and voices, she emerged from the river and hastily dressed. She felt relaxed and cheerful. Her spontaneous nature had given itself over completely, passionately to this simple familiar, rural life; nothing, it seemed, could destroy it. She ran swiftly and easily along the road home and met the steward. She asked where he was coming from and where was he going. He said that he was circling the fields on foot because his horse had gone lame and now he was heading back home.

"The morning's so splendid!" he added. "And Your Excellency woke up so early."

Conversations about the household, the sprouting wheat, or the new machines purchased by the prince and brought from Moscow, didn't interest her very much, but her happy mood rendered her so kind that Anna didn't want to offend anyone; she paid attention and even took an interest in the steward's concerns.

When the road came to a fork, one way leading to her house, the other to the steward's wing, Anna said, "Goodbye." Then all of a sudden she noticed her husband walking toward her. From a distance she called to him with a cheerful and tender voice, but when she got her first look at his face close up, her heart sank. It was distorted with malice.

"Where are you coming from so early?" he asked.

"I took a walk and went for a swim."

"*Et que veut dire cette intimitè avec l'intendant?*"[59]

"*L'intimitè?* Why? He was merely returning from the fields, and I was coming from the bathhouse; we met and walked home together—the road's the same, isn't it?" Anna explained in detail and simply, with a slight laugh.

"You've always lacked all discretion and always will; this tête-à-tête is inappropriate, *c'est presque un domestique,*" said the prince, choking with spite.[60]

"Oh, my God! Why do you always spoil our happiness?" said Anna.

"Now the sentimentality begins. *Je suis trop vieux pour cela, ma chère.*"[61]

"You're tormenting yourself and me for no reason," Anna continued. "I feel sorry for you. Look at me, look all around us, let's walk home together," she added tenderly. The prince was silent and rushed on ahead.

"Is it ever possible for you not to be angry? There's no cause for it! I may be indiscreet and foolish, but I feel sorry for you. I love you. I can't bear to witness this severity in you, this anxiety." She took her husband by the arm and pressed up against him, as if asking for his defense and affection. But the prince pushed her arm away and hurried home alone. Anna stopped; she looked at her husband with dry, despairing eyes, as if watching her last chance for happiness fade; sighing deeply, heavily, and loudly, she made her way home with quiet steps.

From that day forward the prince maliciously began to find fault with the steward and soon dismissed him without cause, depriving himself of an excellent manager.

Anna was neither capable nor did she wish to acknowledge her guilt in this humiliation of which her husband had accused her. She! It was she who placed her integrity above all else in the world; it was she, if required, who would sacrifice everything on earth for pure, happy family life!

And now, once more, her good relations with her husband were broken off. They became strained, distant, and unnatural.[62] Anna's heart ached severely; she hadn't been carefree and happy for very long. Her strength began

---

59. "And what's this intimacy with the steward all about?"

60. "... he's almost a servant."

61. "I'm too old for that, my dear."

62. *"At the time I didn't notice that these periods of anger in me corresponded quite correctly and regularly to those periods we called love. A period of love—then one of anger . . ."*

to fail again; trying to spare herself any anguish, she took up her old former pursuit—painting.

The next morning, packing a canvas, an umbrella, and her case, she left the house, planning to paint a landscape of the view on the edge of the pond. She was just ready to start when she suddenly heard the sound of a carriage. Glancing up at the road, she recognized Bekhmetev's coach and horses at once. He had been at their house only once since their arrival, when there had been a number of other people there, and she knew well why he had not come to visit more often. She had surmised that first and foremost his disinterested love didn't want to impinge on her family happiness or burden her honest soul; this noble trait elevated him even more in her eyes.

Bekhmetev recognized Anna from afar, stopped his horses, and climbed out of his carriage. After greeting her, he said:

"So you're here at work once again, Princess? I haven't painted anything for a long, long time."

"Let's paint something together and we'll see who's better. Shall we?" Anna proposed.

"I have nothing to paint with."

"I have enough materials for you. Go and greet my husband; then you'll find everything you need in the closet in the corner drawing room. There's the same kind of canvas, palette, and paints. I'll lend you brushes; I have lots of them here."

A half-hour later Bekhmetev returned with all the necessary items and began work.

"How's your health?" Anna asked, quickly and skillfully sketching the outline of the cottages.

"There's no change, Princess; it's not good. And you! How you've recovered, even blossomed."

"Yes, nothing seems to faze me. I'm too healthy."

"God's granted you everything: happiness, good health, family, and beauty."

"Do you think I'm *very* happy?"

"I can see it."

"Really?" Anna replied distractedly and despondently.

They continued to paint in silence.

"Working together motivates me," she said.

"And it draws us closer, connects us to each other—this mutual work," Bekhmetev replied softly.

"Let's translate something together. I'm reading Amiel's *Fragments d'un journal intime*.[63] It's remarkably good! I couldn't do it alone and you're so good at languages."

"That'd be wonderful, if you're in earnest, Princess."

"Me? Is there anything surprising about it? I love intellectual labor; you can help me."

They both fell silent. Anna suddenly recalled the evenings spent together last year, her happiness then, and her tranquility in this man's presence; joy, quiet, and good cheer suddenly lit up her entire being. She glanced at him and their eyes met inadvertently. In their exchange of glances there was no longer any harshness, or horror in the face of the possibility of a passionate, illicit outburst between them; there was only the acknowledged, joyful spiritual bond, which could injure no one, but would illuminate their lives with radiance, meaning, and endless bliss.

From that day on Anna became calm once again. Her vitality returned, as well as her faith in everything, and her gentleness. Everything that had seemed so urgent, all that had troubled her, now ceased to have any importance. She spent entire evenings occupied with translation; she was captivated by it. Bekhmetev visited almost every day; he helped her and, since even the prince was often drawn into this project, he too took an interest and related to his old friend amicably and trustingly.

Once after a prolonged session, Anna proposed as a form of recreation that they go for a horseback ride after dinner. She turned to her husband, asking him to accompany her. The prince willingly agreed; turning to Bekhmetev, he said:

"I hope that you, Dmitry, will also join us?"

"Very gladly."

Three splendid saddled horses were brought around. Anna looked astonishingly grand on her black horse with the bright color of her face and her black riding habit. The prince rode a pacer, and gave Bekhmetev an exceptionally valuable magnificent chestnut English mare.[64]

"I want to treat you to this horse; see what a beauty she is!"

"Yes, indeed, she's superb! And such a graceful gait."

They had ridden only a little way from home when they met a distant neighbor who was coming to see the prince on business.

---

63. *Fragments of an Intimate Diary* (pub. 1882–84), a masterpiece of self-analysis by the Swiss philosopher and writer Frédéric Henri Amiel (1821–81).

64. A pacer is a horse whose normal gait is a pace; an ambler.

"Oh, how annoying. I'll have to turn back," said the prince.

"What a pity!" Anna said with a sigh.

"Go on ahead with Dmitry; I'll catch up with you after I've spoken with my guest."

Anna showed a moment's hesitation and wondered whether to return home with her husband or to ride on with Bekhmetev. She suddenly felt afraid that the prince would notice her indecision; then she said with total simplicity and naturalness:

"Fine. We'll only circle the woods and you can meet us at the stream."

The road through the woods was very narrow. Bekhmetev and Anna rode along next to each other and kept silent. They couldn't speak about what concerned them both so deeply, and they didn't want to talk about anything else. The happiness of being together satisfied them completely. At last Bekhmetev spoke:

"What plans do you have for the coming winter, Princess?"

"I don't know yet. The printing of my husband's books is dragging out: he's upset and says that forwarding the proofs has delayed the whole affair. In the autumn it'll be necessary to move to Moscow again. He's bored here. But I can't even conceive of life in town. What are your plans?"

"I'll probably go abroad again. My health's really very poor. I have to seek a warmer climate."

"So you're leaving? For good or only a while?"

"I don't know, Princess. Besides, it's best for me to leave; you know that, as well . . . I don't dare seek happiness, and I'm losing my peace of mind."

"Have you tried seeking happiness?"

Bekhmetev didn't reply immediately; suddenly assuming a jocular, light-hearted tone, he began:

"Do you know your neighbor, Elena Mikhailovna? She's tried very hard to amuse me. She's so cheerful! Careful, Princess. You're not watching where your horse puts its hooves, and she may stumble."

"So, what about Elena Mikhailovna?" asked Anna.

"She used to host evening gatherings, large crowds; they were very lively, and she was most obliging. The time I spent with her was very nice . . ."

Anna remembered this presumptuous, brazen woman, Elena Mikhailovna, whom she had met with the prince on the evening of Bekhmetev's first visit, and of whom she had been so jealous over the prince's affections. This woman's house was the center of frivolous merrymaking for the entire neighborhood, but respectable women didn't associate with her.

"Do you like women such as Elena Mikhailovna?"

"I'm one of her great admirers," replied Bekhmetev with some malicious irony. "She's a cheerful and pleasant conversationalist . . ."

"What's happened to him?" wondered Anna. "He's teasing me."

But he wasn't. He could barely restrain from launching into the most desperate and passionate confession of love to this woman. He was choking with agitation; he felt weak and unhappy; he was muttering God knows what sort of inanities out of a feeling of self-preservation; he was ready to weep for having caused her pain, but he knew that he must not, dare not tell her that she was the only one on earth he loved; that he was here, amid this quiet, marvelous wooded nature, together with her, and had lost his head in happiness and despair; that he was unable to enjoy it and felt compelled to safeguard her peace of mind and her happiness with another man.

Anna stopped talking with Bekhmetev. She struck her horse hard with her riding crop and vanished into the forest grove. There was a stream along the road where the prince was supposed to meet them. Having spurred her horse on, she forgot all about the stream, and when she saw it, it was too late to stop her horse. But the quick English mare, coming to her senses, stopped suddenly. The horse's movement was so unexpected that Anna went flying over her saddle. Bekhmetev, who had caught up with her, saw it all and cried out. But Anna got up from the ground and recovered immediately.

"I took a little spill," she said, "but I don't even feel the impact."

"That's the way actors take falls on stage, Princess," said Bekhmetev, but his voice was shaking.

"Well, let's ride on," Anna said, trying to mount her horse.

"You won't be able to mount like that. I'll help you, if you'll allow me, Princess," said Bekhmetev, extending his hand so Anna could step on it.

She placed her small foot gently in Bekhmetev's hand. She felt his warm touch through her thin shoe and suddenly an unexpected tremor ran through her whole body. Her sight grew dim, and at the same time the image of her daughter Manya flashed through her mind. Several days ago, when Bekhmetev was spending an evening with her correcting her translation, the children came in to say good night. Manya glanced at Bekhmetev with angry eyes and absolutely refused to shake his hand. She never explained her behavior, and merely said, "I don't want to, I don't have to."

"My God!" thought Anna. "Poor, sweet Manya! Don't be afraid for me; I love you too much."

"No, you don't have to, you don't!" cried Anna. "I can't mount my horse that way, thank you. There's a tree stump over there; I can do it myself."

Bekhmetev led the horse to the stump, and just then the prince came riding up. Having dispatched the neighbor, the prince had caught up with his wife and friend. He was agitated all along the way. When he saw that Anna was not mounted, and that Bekhmetev was standing next to her, he experienced such terrible suspicion that he grew pale and couldn't think of anything to say. His lips trembled and he squeezed the reins tightly in his hand. His first impulse was to strike both of them with the riding crop in his hand. But he regained control of himself and listened calmly to the story of his wife's fall. He decided to take up the matter with her later and to put an end to Bekhmetev's visits.

After arriving home, Anna, without changing her clothes, threw herself on the bed and began sobbing.

"I'm a criminal, a miscreant, a pitiful, vile woman! I love him and I hate myself for it! Lord, help me! Children, my dear children, forgive me!"

Then she stood up, crossed herself as if disavowing this delusion, and began to change her clothes. As soon as she had taken off her riding habit, her husband came in. He had prepared his speech; he wanted to make a scene, but stopped, so struck was he by her beauty. The soft, dark folds of her riding habit spread around her; her lovely, strong arms were raised to twist her wavy, golden hair; her shoulders and neck, illuminated by the last rays of the pink sunset shining through the window, were radiant in their loveliness, just as her splendid dark eyes were flushed from tears and agitation.

The prince came up close to her and gazed into her eyes; noting her unusual expression, he asked:

"Do you feel all right?"

"Perfectly well," she said.

"Nothing hurts?" he asked, touching her back.

"No, no," she confirmed, freeing herself from his hands.

But the prince didn't leave. He walked away for a moment and locked the door to the room; coming up to his wife, he bent over and kissed her breast. Anna shuddered and retreated. But the prince pressed her to him and placed his lips passionately on her shoulder, her lips, and then embraced her. . . . She no longer resisted. Closing her eyes, thinking not about her husband, yet unaware of what she was doing, she trembled in his embrace. The prince was delighted by his wife's submissive, passionate response. She gave herself to him entirely . . . but her closed eyes saw only Bekhmetev; her imagination pictured him at the moment of his silent confessions and, together with him, she saw Manya's frightened, unfriendly little eyes, having understood in her innocent soul the grave danger her mother was in.

The next day the prince was very cheerful and inventive. His jealousy had abated for a time. He proposed various outings, drew up plans, joked, and was especially affectionate with his friend who came to inquire about any consequences of the princess' fall from her horse the day before.

9

For the first time in her life Anna's soul was experiencing inner turmoil. Steadfast, honest, and serene, she had always been self-confident and afraid of nothing. But now her strengths betrayed her. She knew that in August, Bekhmetev, already quite ill, would be leaving; she felt that the happiness that had sustained her all this time would soon come to an end. Then what? The house, her obligations, and her husband's apathetic egoism with his rude demands would remain, as well as her own inability to continue living the same way without the light of the love that had been nourishing her all this while.

"And the children? Have I really cooled toward them?" Anna asked herself with horror. "No, that's different; that love occupies an entirely different place in my heart. But I'm so tired! Awfully tired! And my husband? Where's my love for him? What's happened? Why can't I love both my husband and this other man who's loved me so unselfishly, so simply, so well, and for so long, without demanding anything for himself?"

In spite of all her thoughts of self-justification, Anna felt, and couldn't help feeling, that what had happened had to have happened in her life with her husband and her love for him, and not with any other man; and she felt that this must also happen in every good marriage.

Her soul had become attached to a man who had managed without any effort, without demands, without any rights, to illuminate her entire life with love; and when all this spiritual life had become full, the feeling of happiness and personal intimacy with this man awoke inside her. Why wasn't this man her husband? She had married with just such an ideal; she had idealized the first period of life with her husband; she had yielded to his influence for so long and so blindly, sensing only vaguely, though never admitting it to herself, that all this was not right, not right at all; she found painful his indifference to her whole inner life and to the children, and she considered degrading his interest only in the life of her flourishing beauty, her health, and her external success, all that which simultaneously gratified him and aroused his animal jealousy, as a result of which she had to suffer. "What will happen now? What sort of relationship will I have to my husband?" Anna wondered, like a drowning person grasping for a straw that could save her. And she was drowning, drowning, completely aware that this straw would bend in her weak hands and be unable to rescue her.

But for a while fate intervened and deceived her, promising an escape from her difficult spiritual dilemma.

The prince, who had been very busy of late with household improvements, left for town to take possession of a new steam-powered threshing machine. It was damp and cold; in spite of Anna's request that he travel in the carriage, he still decided to go on horseback. It was late in the evening and already dark, and the prince had yet to return. Anna had begun to worry when a carriage pulled up to the house and the prince was carried in by several people. When she saw him, she screamed in terror and rushed to him. He smiled painfully, moaned as they lifted him up, but hastened to say:

"I seem to have broken my leg; it's nothing, don't be afraid."

"Your leg! Thank God! I thought it was worse. We have to summon the doctor immediately." She ran out to send for the doctor, then back into the room where the prince was, helped him lie down, and arranged the position of his leg in the most comfortable way. Then she quickly and skillfully filled a rubber bag with ice and positioned it on his leg. After doing all this, she sat down firmly and calmly next to his bed. He moaned and tossed about, demanding her attention incessantly. No one else could please him. Shooing away the others, Anna looked after her husband tenderly and patiently. She was glad of this unquestionable fulfillment of her duty that fate had imposed upon her.

"Come here," he called constantly. "Arrange my pillow; ah, not like that. I've worn you out, my dear," he said, moaning again.

Toward morning the prince fell asleep. Anna approached him quietly and began examining his face carefully. Her husband's handsome, tormented features had a strange effect on her. She was transported to the distant past, to the time when she had loved this man trustingly, blindly, and simply, without analyzing or criticizing him.

"If only that could be possible again! Everything in him is good; he's loved only me and never betrayed me; I'm the one who's foolish, not he. What do I really want?"

She leaned over and gently kissed his forehead.

"Yes, I've loved only him, and he's dearer to me than anyone else on earth," Anna concluded, and suddenly cut off in her soul any further analysis of her inner, most confidential, intimate secrets. She wasn't lying as she resolved the question of her love for her husband. The strength of that love—young, passionate, idealized, that she had given her husband in those first years of their marriage—that strength was no longer there. How her husband responded to her love—that was a different matter, but that couldn't destroy it; her love surfaced at any convenient opportunity and grew fainter again whenever rebuffed.

Now the prince was asleep and Anna couldn't hear his voice that at times had offended her so rudely; she couldn't see his eyes that had regarded her—either angrily or tenderly—so unjustly; she saw only the man to whom she had pledged herself and her love entirely—and she loved him.

Every woman truly loves only once. She loves her love and safeguards it until the right moment. But, once she's bestowed her love, she protects it, preserves it, and closes her eyes to the faults of the one she loves. The recurrence of this feeling always develops on the basis of the past, the old ideals, and if it happens that a married woman comes to love another man, then her husband is almost always the one to blame; he has been unable to satisfy the poetic demands that a pure, young, female nature makes and dashes them, giving in exchange only the coarse side of marriage. Woe betide if another man manages to fill that empty place the husband's failed to occupy, and all that first, idealized love is transferred to another person.

The prince suffered terribly all that night: the doctor arrived only the next morning. He applied a bandage and prescribed complete bed rest for the patient.

Several terribly difficult days passed in the prince's illness. He was impatient, demanding, and impossibly suspicious. The fact that he couldn't move nearly drove him mad. He never let Anna leave his sight. The neighbors called in to inquire about his health. That distracted him for a time, but he was still terribly bored and pestered her constantly.

"Where were you?" he asked her after she had been away from his room for a little while. "What were you doing?"

"I went out for a walk with the children," she explained; or, "I wrote a letter"; or "I gave Manya and Pavlik their lesson."

The prince verified all these answers by interrogating the children and the servants, whom he asked unexpectedly leading questions about what their mamá was doing, or whether they knew where the princess was and what she was up to. He himself was unaware of what he suspected his wife was up to, or that it was something morbid, almost insane.

Bekhmetev called in only once to inquire about the prince's health. He himself was very ill and planning to go abroad. Anna didn't go out to meet him, pleading exhaustion. After the horseback ride with him, she harbored pangs of conscience, as if she had committed some unclean act. The feeling of self-preservation on the part of her conscience was so strong that with all her spiritual powers she forced herself to forget the sensation she had momentarily experienced.

Amid the obligations of being a wife and a mother she had managed to achieve that. Besides, the whole material side of her life as mistress of the household always disrupted any deviations.

"Your Excellency," the housekeeper said, calling Anna away from the prince's room. "Please come and look: the upholsterer's asking whether the furniture is as you ordered it."

Anna went into the servant's quarters to take a look and exclaimed in horror. The expensive upholstery had been sewn together inside out, and the bright cross-threads of the fabric on the reverse were an eyesore.

"What on earth have you done? How could you? It's inside out!" cried Anna.

They had to tear it all off; the fabric was ruined and Anna was upset for the whole day. A few days later the servants called her again.

"Be so kind, Your Excellency, the cook's unmanageable; he's dead drunk; he was supposed to serve the prince his soup and won't let anyone else do it. He keeps on yelling."

Anna went into the kitchen and walked right up to the cook; loudly, commandingly, unquestionably, she shouted at him, "Get out, this instant!" The cook went flying out of the kitchen immediately as if he had been shot, and handed the soup to the waiter. When Anna returned to her own room, she was shaking and had tears in her eyes. The entire material side of her life was hateful to her and her rage was unbearable.

10

It was the end of August. Autumn could already be sensed in the fresh evenings: the leaves turning yellow and red, the melancholy of the bare fields and meadows, and the shorter days.

The prince recovered, although he still used crutches to get around and constantly called for the doctor, complaining capriciously about his slow recovery. Anna grew noticeably thinner, but had regained complete control of herself and returned to her strict family routine, without regret, without hesitation, but with the joyful awareness of her fulfilled obligation and with increased, intensified energy.

It was some time since she had heard any news about Bekhmetev; in the depths of her soul she was worried and didn't know how to interpret his prolonged absence.

Once she was sitting in her husband's study reading the newspaper aloud to him. The prince lay on the sofa looking serenely out the window, awaiting the doctor's arrival.

"You probably forgot to send for him, didn't you?" he asked.

"I sent for him some time ago. Why do you need him? He can't help you; everything takes time. And since when do you believe in doctors so much?"

"The bandage is too tight. I know that all doctors are charlatans, but this is a mechanical thing; it's what they've learned to do."

"Someone's just arrived."

In fact, a light carriage had driven up to the porch; it was a messenger from Varvara Alekseevna with a note.

When Anna took the envelope, she froze. The prince carefully scrutinized his wife and waited to see what she would say. In order to hide her face, Anna turned away from him, as if seeking better light. She skimmed the note quickly and then managed to say calmly:

"Varvara Alekseevna's invited me to call on her this evening. Dmitry Alekseevich is leaving and they're holding a farewell gathering for him; apparently there'll be festivities and guests."

"Show me the note."

Anna smiled contemptuously and handed the prince the note.

"Well then, will you go?"

"No, I don't want to leave you alone. Here's the doctor."

A man about thirty years old entered; he was of average height, ruddy, handsome, with a definite German, self-satisfied character, kind and calm.

"The bandage is bothering you; we'll fix that immediately," he said, after greeting the prince and princess rather informally.

He rolled up his sleeves, washed his hands, and set to work, while Anna attentively and skillfully assisted him.

"Your Excellency," the nurse called Anna softly. "Be so good as to come here for a moment."

After finishing her work with the doctor for her husband, Anna left the room.

The nanny had called her to ask the doctor to examine a little peasant boy whose face had been cut by a horse. It was terrible to see this little four-year-old lad, who had bits of skin and flesh hanging from his face, covered in dark spots of blood, some already clotted and others still oozing. The pale, frightened mother looked with imploring eyes, waiting for Anna to help her son. First she sobbed, then rapidly narrated some of her dreams:

"I dreamt of a red rooster, that's what! Then I saw some old man go into the hut; well, then, deary, he was calling me, and I felt stuffy and sick. Ohhh!"

"Call Aleksandr Karlovich right away," said Anna to the nanny, and ran to fetch all the necessary items from her domestic remedies for applying stitches.

They washed the boy's face, calmed him down, gave him some sweets, and Anna took him onto her lap, while the doctor set about conscientiously sewing stitches, carefully joining the skin together. The lad was remarkably patient; the procedure went well and was nearing its end. The prince, whose wife had absented herself for some time, grabbed his crutch and went out to see what she was doing. He pushed the door open hard. Anna shuddered and glanced up at her husband with fear.

"Ah, Princess: hold his head still, for God's sake," said the doctor in annoyance. "I almost tore a stitch." The doctor grabbed Anna's hand and showed her how to hold the boy's head.

The prince's face was livid.

"Hand the boy over to his mother and come to me. I need you now," he commanded sharply, imperiously, and maliciously.

"But we must finish what we're doing with this poor child," Anna said timidly.

"I beg you. . . . *Vous m'entendiez!*"[65] the prince shrieked suddenly, thumping his crutch on the floor.

But Anna ignored him and held the child, while the doctor continued his work diligently and conscientiously; his hands, adjusting the position of the boy's head, constantly and inadvertently touched Anna's hands and even brushed across her breasts, where the child's head was resting. The doctor didn't notice and didn't even hear the prince's words; he was totally absorbed by his work.

Suddenly the prince approached, seized the injured child in his arms—his crutch fell loudly—and thrusting the lad into the peasant woman's arms, pulled Anna away and dragged her into his study. The astonished doctor watched as they left and muttered, "He's mad!" He then set about his work once again, asking the nanny to assist.

Meanwhile the prince, still holding Anna by the arm, flung her down on the sofa, knocked over the armchair with a clumsy gesture, slammed the door, and began pacing the room, thumping his crutch, and muttering in his fury:

65. "You hear me!"

"When I ask you something . . . you humiliate me by your behavior with this German whippersnapper! That intimacy . . . It's intentional!" he shouted, beside himself with rage.

But this time even Anna got angry.

"You've completely lost your mind! Just listen to what you're saying! There's no place for such thoughts when faced with a suffering child!"

"Silence! Your excuses are even worse than your vile behavior! It's better for you to leave! Yes, go now!" shouted the prince, and pushing her out the door, he threw himself down on the sofa.

Anna left, still reeling. When she reached the living room, she grabbed her chest and merely whispered:

"There's a limit to everything! My God!"

She didn't cry. Her eyes stayed dry and her stare became blank and harsh. Entering the bedroom, she sat down in the armchair opposite the mirror and inadvertently glanced at her own face. She was ravishing in her rage: her pleasing, pale face breathed energy and purity, while her dark eyes seemed even darker and deeper from their embittered expression.

She didn't see her husband for the rest of the day. He didn't emerge from his study for dinner, and she remained alone with the children and the usual domestic servants. The children were talking about the kite they planned to fly after dinner, while Anna suddenly made up her mind to pay a visit to Varvara Alekseevna.

"Have the carriage harnessed with the team of four horses," she ordered loudly, so that her husband would hear. "And tell Dunyasha to get my white woolen dress ready."

"Mama, where are you going? Don't go!" the children protested.

"Where are you going?" Pavlik repeated. "Bring Dmitry Alekseevich back to us. He hasn't been here for such a long time."

Anna was glum all during dinner and scarcely answered their questions.

Afterward, without going in to see her husband, she went into the bedroom, changed her clothes, and left for Varvara Alekseevna's.

Her heart was pounding in excitement at the thought of seeing Bekhmetev again; she was angry at her own excitement, but the desire to see the man whose intimacy had touched her life so tenderly and which was so opposite to her husband's attitude grew so intense after the rude scene staged by her husband that she resolved to visit Varvara Alekseevna and see Bekhmetev, most likely for the last time—come what may.

II

By the time Anna entered the low but rather large hall in Varvara Alekseevna's house, a large group had already gathered. There were neighbors, old friends and relatives, two or three young women standing near the piano with a young man, and even the brash Elena Mikhailovna, who had been the cause of so much grief in Anna's life. Bekhmetev, who had grown astonishingly thin, wasted, and gloomy, sat alone; when he noticed Anna's entrance, he made his way over to her without pretending or concealing his joy.

"You declined, but then you came. What a wonderful surprise. I couldn't think of leaving without seeing you."

"Why didn't you come visit us?" asked Anna, extending her hand to him, which he kissed.

"Yes, of course, I'd have come to see you tomorrow, and I will drop in to say goodbye to my sick friend. But you see how weak I am; I don't know if I'll make it as far as the Aeolian Islands," he added with a gentle smile.[66]

Anna sighed heavily and went to greet Varvara Alekseevna in the living room. Bekhmetev followed her.

Varvara Alekseevna hastily exchanged greetings with Anna, thanked her for coming, and then returned anxiously to the task of making arrangements for the picnic that was scheduled for later that evening.

"Dmitry, do you still insist on going to the lake for tea?" she asked her brother. "You know, it's too damp for you there."

"No, now more than ever. I want to show the princess those wonderful places that I'll probably never get to see again." He smiled once more.

"It's as if the idea of inevitable and imminent death cheers him up," thought Anna.

They sat down near the window in the living room, and Bekhmetev, pointing to his chest, quietly and earnestly said to Anna:

"Something's gone very wrong in here, Princess; I feel ill."

"You'll recover again after you've gone abroad."

"What for? Better to go away completely, into eternity! It's become too cramped for me here."

It seemed to Anna that while saying this Bekhmetev didn't see her at all; rather, his eyes were gazing far off into limitlessness, and she felt like going there, too.

---

66. The Aeolian Islands make up a volcanic archipelago north of Sicily.

Many carriages were drawn up to the house. Varvara Alekseevna decided who should sit with whom, and left herself room in the coach with her brother, to protect him and shield him from the damp.

But Bekhmetev went up to his sister and said softly, but firmly:

"Varenka, I shall ask the princess to do me the honor of accompanying me."[67]

Anna wanted to object, but Bekhmetev looked at her so sternly, imploringly, and decisively, that the words died on her lips and she fell silent.

Bekhmetev chivalrously offered Anna his arm and, after seating her in the coach, sat down next to her, wrapping himself in his coat and draping his legs with a blanket.

All the carriages started off.

"Turn right," Bekhmetev ordered suddenly, and his coach proceeded along a narrow, shady road into an old pine forest.

"We'll take a different route," he said. "It's so beautiful!"

When they were left alone, Anna felt pangs of conscience at this intimacy. Bekhmetev's proximity upset her terribly; his failing appearance drove her to such despair that she was afraid she might not be able to restrain herself and would burst into tears at any moment, begin screaming, or do something extreme. She tried closing her eyes or looking to the side silently, pressing her hands to her breast and heart, as if trying to stifle the life within her.

Is death—that destroys the everyday aspects of life—ever magnificent, beautiful, and significant? That day, August 22, was for her the time of the solemn, splendid, and silent death of everything—around her and inside her. The harsh, transparent, autumnal air reminded her of the imminence of fall— the death of nature. Her dejected, emaciated companion on this excursion reminded her of the proximity of death. Her aching heart had lost its life force. Death, death was everywhere, right here, nearby—it was horrible; Anna felt afraid, as if it would also grab hold of her . . .

They entered the old pine forest. The age-old trees, immobile and dark, scarcely admitted the rays of the bright red setting sun, casting special light on the meadows where they sometimes used to ride.

"This is our *last* excursion together ever," thought Anna, looking at Bekhmetev. He sensed her glance and said:

"It's lovely here, isn't it?"

"Yes, astonishingly beautiful. But why did you come here? It's so damp and cold today."

67. Varenka is a diminutive form of the name Varvara.

"No, it's nothing, let's go on farther. Ah, how nice it is! It's never been so delightful," he affirmed. "Look at the forest above the lake; we'll *never* be here again. Take a good look. I love these places so much: forests and lakes. What could be lovelier?"

"Yes," Anna thought, "soon you'll be *nowhere;* you'll never be anywhere again!" She grabbed Bekhmetev's hand with an involuntary gesture.[68]

"Are you cold? What cold hands you have!"

"Is he really dying? We'll never be able to say another word to one another; thus, loving each other with this pure, innocent love, both of us—he, dying, while I—alas—continue living—we must both sacrifice our happiness, even though it's only by means of it that we have been able to say how dear we've been to each other these last few years; how we mutually consoled each other and how each forced the other to forget his own unhappiness in the atmosphere of love in which we've spent every moment of our constant spiritual communion."

Was it worthwhile sacrificing that questionable coldness, that egotistical, sensual attitude she constantly encountered in her respectable, handsome husband? "Should I preserve my chastity for *anyone?*" Anna continued to wonder. "No, not for anyone in the world; it's false. . . . I've preserved it because I've *loved* it; I've valued it more than anything else; if this man is so dear to me, it's only because he's also like that."

As if answering her own thoughts, Bekhmetev suddenly said:

"This outing, Princess, is our final farewell. I'm leaving tomorrow, and in all likelihood, we'll never see each other again." He fell silent.

"I wanted to tell you," he began again, haltingly, "that in my entire life, the brightest spots were my visits . . . no, I must tell the truth . . . my friendship with you."

Anna wanted to say something, but she couldn't. A spasm gripped her throat.

Bekhmetev continued:

"I've never met a woman with such an aura of purity, lucidity, and love for everything sublime as yours. Come what may, Princess, may God grant you one thing: to remain just as you are."

The coach rolled gently along the forest road; it grew dark and Bekhmetev looked so serene, so happy, just as he had a year ago when he and Anna were returning from town in a carriage full of children whom they had taken to

---

68. In her thoughts Anna switches from referring to him with the formal pronoun *vy* to the informal *ty.* When she speaks again, she reverts to the formal.

the photographer, and when both of them understood it was possible to be happy, to love, and also to love and rejoice over a clear sky, splendid summer nature, and the happiness of being together; but then it was impossible to say all this, impossible to do anything that would awaken even the least pangs of conscience in the presence of those innocent, sweet, loving children; it was even impossible to confess to *themselves* the joy of love, pure love, chaste, never expressed, love that now, on this magnificent August evening, was dying together with him, together with these ideal relations with a person who had aroused the noblest and best parts in Anna's soul.

"Now I'll return home and my husband will look at me distrustfully, suspecting the most despicable and immoral things, while at the same time he'll be kissing my bare shoulders and arms. And all day, like two criminals who commit their crimes at night, we'll be silent with each other, he with his haughty contempt and indifference to my life, and I with my fear in the face of his suspicions and my lonely world of the children, my cares, and my struggle with the fading feeling of love for my husband and the burning feeling of love for another man . . ."

They continued their drive. Bekhmetev wrapped himself up and kept coughing; the evening chill was penetrating with its unpleasant dampness. This ride through unfamiliar places seemed to Anna to be leading them together to an unknown eternity, to a place that would never part them again . . .

The sun had set. "It, too, has died!" she thought. The last rays of the sun suddenly lit up the tops of all the trees in the garden they had approached. "Soon all nature will die," she thought again. "And so will he. No, it's impossible! How on earth will I go on living? Where will that pure happiness be from which I can draw my strength, become better, cleverer, and kinder. . . . No, it's not possible!" Anna almost exclaimed.

"We've arrived," Bekhmetev said softly, taking Anna's hand in silence, giving it a prolonged and tender kiss. In an even softer voice he said: "Farewell, dear Princess."

Anna leaned forward and kissed his forehead. The spasm, suffocating her all the while, seemed to resolve into a soft, painful moan. Tears flowed from her eyes; something had burst in her heart and died—forever. Yet another side, *this* side of her life, was cut off forever. *It* was over.

But she had to live, and had to live well . . .

A large, noisy crowd had already gathered in the spacious, round gazebo lit by colorful lanterns. The servants were busy with refreshments, tea, and

fruit; they were arranging wooden boards as benches, hanging the last lanterns in the garden, building a bonfire, and seeing to the other pointless, but
inevitable appurtenances of a picnic.

Bekhmetev was afraid to stay late and went home alone, after bidding
farewell to everyone there. Anna was planning to stay until the end; when
the evening drew to a close and she was sitting all alone in her carriage under
the steel-blue cold moonlight of a bright August night, her spiritual solitude
became particularly distressing, and sobs suddenly burst from her chest. She
wept long and hard, as if mourning the loss of someone else's life as well as
her own life that had ended. It was a wail of wild desperation; with such tears
her grief had to pass, and so it did, receding further and further. By the time
she approached her own house, she had regained complete control of herself;
her courage and energy for life had returned.

The pain of a broken heart at her parting with Bekhmetev swiftly receded
into the distance; it was as if, after crying herself out, she had dispensed with
it forever; it was not characteristic of her energetic nature to pine for a long
time. She felt dishonest in front of her children and her husband at this pain
of separation from another man. She felt guilty for going, having left her husband disgruntled and indisposed at that. She recalled how Pavlik had asked
her to stay—the whole world of her family surrounded her on all sides. Little
Yusha seemed especially active with his tender, clever little face; lively Manya
had her quick, categorical, and unexpected pronouncements about everything.
Anna remembered her children's lessons, and all her ideas about the importance of education for the next generation; by the time she had reached her
house, her spirits had already lifted; she entered with an awareness of her
obligations, and felt as if renewed.

She took off her cloak and went first into the nursery; then she quietly approached the door of her husband's study, where he was still awake.

12

Meanwhile the prince, as soon as he was sure that Anna had left the
house, without even stopping by his room, became terribly agitated; the wildest ideas entered his head. "Perhaps she's gone forever and will never return,"
he thought.

He shrank from the spiritual pain at the recollection of having shoved his
wife. He had never done anything like that before. "Ah, ah!" he moaned
to himself; but suddenly he recalled how, with his very own eyes, he had
watched that greasy German doctor, with his white hands, while repairing
the skin on the little peasant boy's forehead, pass his hands over Anna's

breasts. "Over *her* breasts! Probably on purpose! What was she feeling at that moment?"

Before his eyes the prince pictured clearly that splendid, full bosom—the one that had made him so often forget the whole world and become a slave to that woman!

In the depths of his soul he was aware that perhaps he was mistaken; that Anna's truthful eyes, her pure, almost childlike look, in spite of her thirty years of age, could never tell a lie; but pangs of jealousy tormented him all the more. "And now, why did she go over there?" he wondered. "Bekhmetev's there. . . . Who knows, if it's not the doctor, then perhaps my so-called friend is embracing her this very minute somewhere in the woods. I don't really know her; she's a mystery and more incomprehensible to me now than anyone. There's something she's hiding and it always escapes me."[69]

The prince tried to read, went in to see the children, looked at his watch, but could find no peace.

The nanny brought in his two youngest children—the little girl and tiny Yusha to say good night. He looked at the little girl as if she were a stranger; he reached for her little hands and began inspecting them.

"Who knows, perhaps this child isn't even *my* own daughter! Ugh! Yes, people say she has my hands, my way of holding a fork, of wiping her hands with a towel. . . . That's all true."[70]

He looked at the little boy; drawing him near, he gave him a kiss. He never had any doubts about that spit and image of himself.

Manya and Pavlik came in a little while later, also to say good night. He cut out some paper dolls for them and showed them how to blow on them and make it look as if they were fighting. The children laughed, but their laughter only annoyed him.

"Well, go on, off to bed. Is Yusha asleep?"

"He fell asleep a long time ago. He cried and asked for his mama to say his prayers."

"Good night, good night," said the prince, growing more and more annoyed.

"He called for his mama to say his prayers, while she's off wearing her white dress and flirting with that evil Koshchei."[71]

---

69. *"I don't know her. I know her only as an animal."*

70. *"Perhaps she's been carrying on with the footmen and bearing their children who are considered mine."*

71. In Russian folklore, a bony emaciated old man, rich and wicked, who knows the secret of eternal life.

The prince lay down on the sofa, lit a cigar, and began thinking about his relations with his wife: "How nicely and patiently she looks after me! Surely it's because she's feeling guilty. And what if she really is guilty?" he wondered with terrible clarity and certainty regarding his wife's guilt over her illicit love for Bekhmetev.

He jumped up, opened the window, glanced out at the round, bright moon that seemed so impudent, and began listening to the night sounds. He heard the gallop of horses and the sound of an approaching carriage. It was getting closer and closer.

"That's her," he thought. But it was the doctor heading home from the picnic; seeing the prince standing by the window, he stopped his horse.

"You're still awake, Prince? That's not good for a patient."

"Drop in for a minute. Tell me about Varvara Alekseevna's ball."

"Forgive me, Prince. I can't. I have to perform an operation in the village early tomorrow morning; I need to get up early and feel fresh."

"Is the princess on her way home? Did you see her there?"

"Yes, of course! Well, I don't envy her. They sat her in the carriage with that consumptive Bekhmetev. He took her off to show her some picturesque spots; he wouldn't listen when I said it was too cold and damp. Picturesque spots, indeed! That fellow's a goner. He's got about three months to live."

"Well, good night, doctor. It's chilly. Thank you," the prince said suddenly in an irritated tone and slammed the window shut. His face assumed a terrible expression. He had no further doubts: Anna was in love with Bekhmetev and having an affair with him! The prince began gasping for air. He stood there at his desk, nervously shifting objects around, moving his books and papers from one place to another, listening to the sounds.

Soon he heard Anna's coach approaching on its soft, rubber tires; it stopped at the front porch. The prince heard his wife enter the house, take off her cloak, go in to see the children, and then approach his study door with light, almost inaudible steps. The prince stood there stock still.

"Are you still awake?" Anna asked softly.

"The foul deceiver! She's still pretending!" thought the prince; he fingered the small, spherical handle of the heavy white marble paperweight lying on his desk.

Anna opened the door and went up to her husband.

"What's wrong? Are you feeling worse?"

"Not only am I feeling worse, but either my heart's about to burst or I shall have a stroke. I can't tolerate your behavior any longer."

"My behavior? What have I done?"

"You dare tell me that you're not in love with Bekhmetev?"

Anna flushed and said:

"I love Dmitry Alekseevich very much and . . ."

She fell silent.

"Perhaps you'll deny that you went for a ride with him, just the two of you, all evening, in front of everyone, to God knows where!"

"He's leaving tomorrow, and I feel very sorry for him . . ."

"You love him, and you've been his lover for a long time!"

"Be quiet, for God's sake!"

"I'll kill you . . . you vile slut. . . . I've had all I can take; I won't let you . . . My honor and my family's honor . . ."

The prince was choking with malice and distress.

"Your honor! Oh, you can rest assured about your honor," Anna said in her own defense. "Calm down, for heaven's sake, it's not good for you."

She came close to her husband and took him by the hand, but her touch maddened him even more. He grabbed the heavy paperweight off his desk, raised it up, and shouted:

"Get out of here! Or I'll kill you!"

"But for what? Could it be that you still don't know me? Calm down, for heaven's sake. Could there really be anything to it?"

"You lie all the time. . . . Be quiet! I can't vouch for myself. Get out!"

He was shaking all over; he lowered the paperweight, then he raised it again.

Anna tried once more to take the prince by the hand, but he turned away and shoved her aside; just after she ran behind the desk, he hurled the heavy paperweight at her. It sailed across the top of the desk, struck Anna's temple dully and harshly, and then fell to the floor heavily and loudly.

Like a wounded bird lowering its white wings and somehow folding clumsily in half, Anna collapsed behind the large desk into the soft white folds of her dress. A brief muffled moan emerged from her chest and she lost consciousness.

The prince rushed to her. A thin stream of blood was flowing from her blue temple, staining her white dress with little red spots. Her face was deathly pale, her lips open, her eyes rolled back, her arms bent in an awkward position.

"Anna! Anna!" cried the prince, trying to lift her up. But the crutch and his painful leg hindered his every movement.

He opened the door and called for the servants. The nanny and lackey came running in.

"The princess has fainted. Send for the doctor at once."

The nanny ran to Anna and screamed:

"Oh, my God, she hurt herself and fell! Good Lord!"

"No, she didn't hurt herself. I killed her," said the prince.

The shocked nanny looked at him, crossed herself, ran up to Anna, and cried:

"He's completely out of his mind and doesn't even know what he's saying."

She took some water from the prince's washbasin and began to wipe Anna's temple and sprinkle water in her face. She tried to lift her up, but couldn't. She called for the footman and the two of them somehow managed to drag Anna over to the sofa and lay her down there. Then the nanny called for some ice.

The maids, housekeeper, and English governess all came running—wearing the most amusing and varied sleepwear. The frightened Manya, roused by the noise, scampered in barefoot wearing only a nightshirt; she stood at a distance and screamed:

"Nanny, did mamá hurt herself? Will she die? Nanny, dear, where's papá? Is the doctor coming? There's a hole in her temple. It's bleeding! Ah! Ah!" Manya cried.

The poor little girl was trembling so much that her little body was bobbing up and down.

"Go and lie down, Manichka; the doctor's coming soon; it'll pass.[72] Mama stumbled and fell; it's nothing at all," said the nanny to console her. But Manya could see from the nanny's face that it wasn't "nothing at all." Nanny pressed the ice to her mother's temple and looked at her mistress's pale, lifeless face with a hopeless expression.

"I won't leave, nanny. I'm afraid. I'll stay here," said the little girl and jumped onto a large armchair. Folding her legs under her, she squatted and stared at her mother and her nanny. She was still shaking and her teeth were chattering.

All the while the prince was out of the room. He was sitting in the living room, waiting for the doctor.

"It's a fainting spell," he kept trying to console himself. "She'll probably come to in a minute. I hear someone talking about it in there. . . . So this is what her behavior's led to!" he said, trying to justify himself. "I can't risk any stain to my honor, can I? Yes, to the honor of my ancestors! We've never had any immoral women in our family! I'm a man and my behavior's always been beyond reproach. . . . It's a disgrace to the children that their mother's a debauched woman! And the possibility of having a child who's not mine?"

---

72. Manichka is an affectionate diminutive of the name Manya.

The prince was convulsed with pain, his face distorted by horror; he tried to stand up, but after making weak fists, he slumped back into his armchair.

"Well, fine. That's the way it had to be," he decided.

A bowl of plums stood on the table; he took one and began eating it. The old English clock slowly and deliberately sounded the hour with its resonant chime: two in the morning. The roosters started crowing in the village. The prince looked out the window. Bright stars were twinkling somewhere high in the dark sky; the moon had set; it was cold and he suddenly wanted to go to sleep.

"What was it all about?" he wondered all of a sudden. "Has she really not recovered yet?"

The prince ran into his study; the doctor arrived at almost the same moment. He went right up to Anna, removed the bag of ice, listened to her heart, felt for her pulse, and his face became darker and darker.

"What happened?" he asked.

"A blow was inflicted with this paperweight," said the prince, picking up from the floor the heavy object that hadn't been noticed by anyone up to this point.

"The blow was well aimed. Her pulse is very weak, as is her heartbeat."

The doctor reached for his medical bag and took out various bottles and medical instruments; after asking the nanny for assistance, he went back to Anna.

Her beautiful, pale head rested high on the leather pillow of the sofa. Her black hair with its golden sheen and its fine curls framed her face like a halo. The expression on her face was frightened and stern. Blood was still oozing from the deep, dark wound to her temple, dripping down her pale cheek onto her white dress.

The doctor tried to revive her, but none of his efforts could bring her out of her deep faint. The nanny led away Manya, who had begun to sob loudly.

The prince went up to his wife and glanced at the doctor with an inquisitive look. The doctor didn't say a word and continued his work.

Around ten o'clock Anna began to come to. The doctor sent everyone away, fearing too great a shock for the patient. A bandage was applied to the wound and it gave Anna a strange, pitiful appearance. At last she opened her eyes and looked around wildly.

"Call the prince," she said softly and closed her eyes again.

The prince came in and bent over her. Anna opened her large black eyes; as if exerting great effort, she began speaking in a weak, muffled voice:

"It had to be. . . . Forgive me. . . . You're not to blame. . . . But if I die, I have to tell you. . . ."

She hesitated and closed her eyes.

"What? What? Say it, for God's sake! Hurry up and tell me now," the prince implored, expecting a confession of her guilt.

"I was never unfaithful to you; I loved you as much as I could, and I will die chaste before you and the children. . . . But it's better this way! Oh, I feel so tired!" she sighed and fell silent.

"Anna, I'm guilty before you. Anna, my dear, forgive me . . ."

The prince began to sob, took her hand, and placed it against his cheek. Her hand was growing cold.

"Where are the children?" she asked suddenly and raised herself up slightly. "Quickly, quickly, call the children!"

Anna slumped in exhaustion and closed her eyes. She opened them a few moments later but by that time they weren't looking at anyone. Her eyes were serious, her gaze directed far away, beyond anything earthly.

"I wanted a different kind of love. One like . . ." Anna raised her eyes to her husband and, as if recognizing him with effort, added, "You're not to blame. . . . You couldn't understand that . . ." She hesitated and added with difficulty: "What's *important* in love . . ."

They brought in the children, frightened and weeping; Anna kissed them and wanted to make the sign of the cross over them as she did every evening when saying good night, but her arm drooped.

They took away the children; something ominous, quiet, and terrible floated into the room in their wake and hung there like a heavy cloud.

"It's finished," she muttered softly. "*Cette clef—c'est l'infini . . .*" she muttered even more softly, as if delirious, for some reason recalling Lamartine's words that Bekhmetev had read aloud to her a long time ago.[73]

The doctor drew near. He nodded his head slightly and signaled to the prince. The prince sobbed softly. Anna never recovered consciousness again. She died at exactly noon; by 7 P.M. that evening she lay on a table in the large hall attired in an elegant light-colored dress, so unpleasantly striking because of the contrast between the frivolous apparel and the seriousness and gloom of the pale, stony, deathly face with its pierced temple.

There was something terrible in the prince's despair. It was the feeble hysteria of a child lost in the woods. He slammed into walls, shouted, moaned, and threw himself down on sofas and armchairs, asking everyone to kill him, to send him to jail, to shoot him. He didn't eat, didn't drink, and didn't sleep.

73. The French sentence means "This key—is the infinite."

His friends and relatives shook their heads and said that he was losing his mind. Seeing his appalling condition, no one raised the question of how her death had occurred, and no one listened to the prince.

"She fell and seriously injured herself," they all said.

The despondent children grew thin and wandered miserably through the rooms, as if searching for something. The older ones wept to the point of exhaustion, so that people started to worry about them. On the table in the living room stood a sewing box and there lay—with a carefully inserted needle—Anna's work. On the windowsill stood roses that she had watered with the children just yesterday from her small watering can. On the floor lay some cardboard soldiers with which she had been playing with little Yusha, making him knock them down. They had both laughed when the prince came in. . . . On the desk was an unfinished letter to her sister Natasha; on the armchair lay her white cloth wrap, bordered with dark feathers, as if it had just been tossed off her shoulders. It seemed as if she might return at any moment . . .

But not only did she not come back, but, on the third day, amid great weeping, they carried her out of the house and lowered her into that terrible, deep hole that would forever instill horror, and from which one always hopes to retrieve, even if only for a moment, the beloved creature who's been lowered into it on long canvas strips, and then sprinkled with clumps of dirt landing on the coffin lid.

Now she had merged with nature that she had loved so much and passed into eternity with it . . .

The prince finally understood that she was no longer alive, that he not only had killed her with that piece of white marble but had murdered her long, long before by not knowing her and not appreciating her. He understood that the love he had given her was the kind of love that had killed her, and that it was not the way he should have loved her. . . .[74] And now, only after her body had disappeared, had he begun to understand her soul. . . . More and more he came to value the pure, tender, loving soul that had left him, and that had for so many years enlivened his life and that of his children so cheerfully and colorfully; all the more did he want to join his soul with hers . . .

The prince's friends and relatives said that he had become a desperate spirit and they feared for his mental faculties.

A month after Anna's death came news of Bekhmetev's death abroad.

---

74. *"During the trial I was asked how and with what I killed her. Fools! They thought I'd killed my wife then, with a knife, on the fifth of October. I didn't kill her then, but much earlier. Just as they're all now killing, everyone, all of them . . ."*

Song Without Words

SOFIYA ANDREEVNA TOLSTAYA

PART I

I

"WHY ARE YOU CRYING, MAMÁ? Tell me, tell me," insisted the six-year-old boy, prying his mother's hands away from her moist face, and looking at her from under the long eyelashes of his shining dark blue eyes. He was also ready to start crying; his eyes were filled with tears.

"My mamá, your grandmother, is dying; I feel sorry for her and want to go see her. Alyosha, darling, be well while I'm away; don't be naughty and do what your nanny says . . ."[1]

The boy threw himself around his mother's neck and burst into tears.

The bell distracted him and he shouted, "Papá's home," and ran to greet him.

Aleksandra Alekseevna also rose and greeted her husband with the telegram in her hands.

"Well, is she worse?" he asked.

"It's very bad. I'm packing my things and am about to leave. . . . I can't wait any longer; my heart's breaking."

And she started crying again.

A frightened and suffering Alyosha looked at his mother, went up to her, and quietly took her by the hand; but, noticing something in his father's hands, he rushed over to him and started laughing.

"What do you have there, papá? Where did you get that?"

---

1. Alyosha is a diminutive form of the name Aleksei.

Petr Afanasevich was holding two huge Spanish onions in his hands.[2] He was trying to hide them, considering their presence inappropriate at such a sad moment for his wife. But Alyosha grabbed hold of them and showed them to his mother.

"They're astonishing onions," an embarrassed Petr Afanasevich began explaining. "My friend the gardener, a German, gave them to me, and I'll definitely plant ones like these. . . . They're from Japan. . . . Look, Sashenka, they must weigh a pound and a half each . . ."[3]

But Sasha could take no interest in the size of the onions. Her heart was breaking from grief. Her mother, whom she loved dearly, was dying in the Crimea; her mother was her only friend in the world, who always understood her completely. Even when Sasha got married, they tried not to part, and spent every summer together. But this year her mother had fallen ill, was on a regimen of fermented mare's milk during the summer, and in the autumn had gone to the Crimea with her younger son. But neither the mare's milk, nor the warm climate—nothing helped, and Sasha kept getting worse and worse news; today she resolved to leave for the Crimea.

She had to pack and leave her only beloved son; she herself had weak nerves and suffered so badly from neuralgia every night that she couldn't sleep, and regarded with annoyance the sound sleep of her imperturbable, rosy-cheeked husband, who, after spending all morning in the office of an insurance company, arrived home at four in the afternoon, and immediately headed out into his garden, relatively large for being in town, and would dig around in the flower beds with pleasure, forgetting the entire world.[4]

Petr Afanasevich was a gardener by calling. He loved nothing in the world as much as the soil, its cultivation, and everything that grew in it. He was drawn to it even now, although it was autumn: the flowers had been nipped by the frost, the vegetables had all been dug up, and the spent soil had been removed from the seedbeds.

But it would be heartless to leave his wife now; besides, he felt sorry for her. He was a good, kind husband, simple, unassuming, and affectionate.

"Can I help you, Sasha?"

---

2. A type of onion that is typically fairly large, yellow or white in color, and fairly mild and sweet in flavor.

3. Sashenka is an affectionate diminutive form of the name Aleksandra. Sasha is another diminutive of the same name.

4. Neuralgia is intense burning or stabbing pain caused by irritation of or damage to a nerve.

"No, it's not necessary; you don't know at all what I need. . . . Even I can't figure it out myself! My God! Mamá, my dear, poor mamá! She's probably waiting for me. . . . Parasha, come here. Gather my things quickly . . ."

"Shall I pack your black mantilla?"

"Yes, of course, there's no way to know; it may be needed. . . . Bring me some writing paper and my travel inkwell. . . . Give me some cologne. . . . Petya, I have to get a permit. Sit right down now, write it out, and go have it certified. . . . Go on."

"Don't get so agitated, Sashenka; just look at you with your neuralgia . . ."

"Such grief, and I have to remember everything myself. Alyosha, call nanny."

A relatively young, very attractive, tall woman entered carrying Alyosha in her arms.

"Carrying such a big boy! Ay-ay-ay!" said Petr Afanasevich, taking the boy from his nanny's arms.

"Nanny, you may take Alyosha outside without me only if it's no less than three degrees below zero and there's no wind: that's if I return later than I expect."

"Yes, ma'am."

"And please feed him well, since Petr Afanasevich will ruin his stomach with his vegetarianism."

"So you think it's better to eat decomposing corpses?"

"Well, well, never mind, let him talk, so long as you buy a chicken for Alyosha for two days. Nanny, here's money for the household expenses."

A suitcase, a lap robe and pillow, a hat in a wooden box—everything was ready. Her travel documents were delivered from the police. Sasha got dressed, picked up her travel bag, stashed her book and purse in it. A chill ran up and down her spine from head to foot. She had never traveled such a long distance on her own; she had never been apart from her young son and her husband. In leaving them she felt that something was breaking in her heart. Petr Afanasevich tried to reassure her, but he was very worried about both her and the terrible emptiness and loneliness he would experience without his cheerful, clever Sasha, who always brought such rich substance, so much care, and such order into his life.

But time was rushing on; only three quarters of an hour were left until the train, and it was a long way to the station. Sasha kissed nanny and Parasha goodbye, then her husband, and finally, as if gathering her last strength, took Alyosha into her arms and tearfully kissed his little eyes, soft golden hair, the palms of his little hands, and his little lips. Then she made the sign of the cross over him and rushed toward the door.

"Mamá, mamá, goodbye, let me make the cross over you, too," cried the lad.

Sasha came back and Alyosha solemnly and clumsily made the sign of the cross over his mother and then felt relieved.

Petr Afanasevich suddenly remembered that he should escort his wife and went to get ready. But Sasha wanted to be alone and tried heatedly to dissuade him from coming; Petr Afanasevich, recalling that he had wanted to peruse a brochure he had just received about the raising of houseplants, was really very glad to stay home.

"You can entertain Alyosha and console him," Sasha added.

Dusk was falling when Sasha drove away from her house. She glanced at her things in the open carriage, counted them, and closed her eyes. She could no longer cry, nor recall those she had left at home, nor think about what awaited her in the Crimea.

She was too tired from the agitation and worry she had experienced these last few days up to the present moment; the gentle shaking of her carriage on its rubber tires uneasily lulled her to sleep.

2

"Am I late?" asked Sasha, driving along the paved road up to the large, new railway station brightly lit with electric lights.

"The Kursk train? No. There's still twenty minutes left before it leaves," said the porter, removing her things from the carriage. "Where are you heading?"

"To the Crimea, the through connection."

"What number seat?"

"Eighty-six."

"Which class?"

"Second."

Even under the weight of her luggage, the porter moved so quickly that Sasha could scarcely keep up with him. He stowed the pieces intended for baggage, and went to fetch her ticket.

"Kursk, 7 poods 16, Tula, 4 poods 24, Yalta, 3 poods 8—the weigher announced in a particularly raucous voice as he checked in the baggage.[5]

Here finally was seat number eighty-six. The porter brought both her ticket and the receipt for her baggage; the bell rang and Sasha once more

5. The pood is a Russian measure of weight (each consisting of forty *funty,* the second number mentioned in each example here), approximately thirty-six pounds.

rushed along the platform, catching up with the porter and overtaking the hurrying passengers.

"Second class, ladies' car . . ."

"If you please, one lady only . . ."

"That's splendid. Thank you," said Sasha, thrusting thirty kopecks into the porter's hand, and entering the half-lit women's compartment. The porter distributed her things on the racks and, bidding her farewell, said:

"Safe journey."

"Thank you; but where are my lap robe and pillow?"

"Over here."

"Could you get them, please?"

The porter took her lap robe out of its bag; the third bell rang and he jumped from the train car; then the whistle sounded, the locomotive puffed, and the train, which lurched backward as if to gather its strength, slowly began to move forward.

Sasha looked out the window. Those who had come to see off passengers were walking slowly along the platform. Then Sasha looked at the other woman in the compartment. She was middle-aged and her appearance had a calming effect. Sasha took out her book, searched for something in it, and, after hanging the traveling candlestick on the wall, began reading. It was *Consolation de Marcia,* from Seneca's philosophical writings.[6]

"*Quelle folie en effet de se punir de ses misères, de les aggraver par un mal nouveau,*" Sasha read Seneca's advice to Marcia to console her in her grief—over the death of her son.[7] Yes, Seneca says one should not surrender to grief. He gives an example of two women from the ancient world: Octavia and Livia, each of whom was grieving over the death of her son. The former devoted her entire life to solemn grief and ordered that her son's name never be mentioned in her presence. The latter, Livia, after losing her son, continued to live cheerfully, constantly recalling and praising her son's name, making him a part of her own life through memory.

"Can a person be consoled one way or another? Is it really possible, after losing a loved one, as I am losing my mother, to think about consolation? It's impossible to go on living, simply impossible," Sasha thought; tears clouded her eyes and prevented her from reading.

6. Seneca's *De Consolatione ad Marciam* (On consolation to Marcia), written around A.D. 40, concerns Stoic precepts of life and death. Sasha is reading the book in French translation, which is more like an adaptation of the original Latin. The first passage she reads is from section III.

7. "What madness this is, to punish oneself for one's misfortunes, and to increase them with new grief."

"*Mais si nul sanglots ne rappellent à la vie ce qui n'est plus,*" she read further, "*si le destin est immutable, à jamais fixé dans ses lois, que les plus touchantes misères ne sauraient changer; si enfin la mort ne lâche point sa proie, cessons une douleur qui serait sans fruit. Soyons donc maître et pas jouet de sa violence . . .*"[8]

"Ticket, please," the ticket collector said in a deep bass voice. Sasha shuddered and at first didn't understand a word. Then hurrying, she dug into her handbag and handed over her ticket. The ticket collector announced: "Moscow to Yalta"; the conductor wrote it down in his notebook; the pleasant odor of fresh air wafted in from the open door; then silence settled in again.

"Clickety-clack, clickety-clack"—the wheels of the train car rumbled along the rails with their monotonous metallic din. Sasha closed the book; after reading those words, there now transpired in her soul a painful struggle between her grief, despairing at the imminent death of her mother, and a desire not to suffer, a desire for permission to continue living her own young, energetic life.

"Clickety-clack, clickety-clack"—the wheels rumbled laboriously. Sasha had yet to grow used to this unbearable sound. She started paying attention to it; then her thoughts began to wander and she dozed off. Suddenly from this monotonous sound a melody arose in her head imperceptibly, and it took the form of a whole musical phrase that emerged in Sasha's head, combining with the soft sounds of full orchestral accompaniment. The melody was solemn, sorrowful, and magnificent.

Sasha was very musical. She played the piano well, sang suitably with her not powerful, but pleasant, soft, and energetic voice; in her childhood, they had wanted to send her to a conservatory. But Sasha married early; her husband, although he tried to indulge her musical interests, disliked music intensely, and was unable to conceal it. Sasha played and sang only when he was not there, and lately she had stopped altogether, as a result of her nervousness and insomnia.

A bell—the finale of the melody, and the train stopped. The woman in Sasha's compartment started putting on her coat and hat.

"What's this?" asked Sasha.

"It's a large buffet and you must get something to eat," she replied. "Come along."

---

8. "But if no sobs can summon back to life the one who is no more, if fate is immutable, forever fixed in its laws, than the most poignant sorrows will not change; if death never releases its prey, then let us end our sadness which will bear no fruit. Let us then be the master and not the plaything of death's violence"; from section VI.

"Yes, right away," Sasha said hastily, and they both ran to the door of the brightly lit station, along with a large crowd of other passengers, bustling and rushing unpleasantly toward the food, lackeys in frock coats, chefs in white hats standing behind tables with their dishes, and porters in white aprons. Lacking any desire to eat, Sasha swallowed her hot, fatty cabbage soup, paid, looked for her traveling companion, and was glad to return to her own compartment once again.

3

But now, at last, after an exhausting two-day journey, the train arrived in Simferopol.[9] It was already night; the cab proceeded quietly through the unfamiliar town, which, in the moonlight, seemed to be made entirely of white stone. It was impossible to make anything out; besides, Sasha was so tired that she was delighted to find a spacious hotel room, where the bed with its wooden screen, washstand, symmetrically arranged sofa, and armchairs were exactly the same as they are in all provincial Russian hotels.

When the door closed behind Sasha and she was left alone, she felt so terrified that she began calling loudly for the bellboy.

"Bring me some tea and the schedule for carriages to Yalta."

"The carriage leaves tomorrow morning at 7 o'clock," the footman reported, as he wiped the litter from the table with a dirty cloth.

Sasha took out her book and began reading, but couldn't understand a thing. Clickety-clack, clickety-clack—once again the sound echoed in her head, and once again the melody, unfamiliar but magnificent, began to emerge.

"Perhaps, mamá's already gone! My God: I want to look into her big, earnest eyes one more time, those affectionate, all-forgiving eyes that only mothers have, those eyes that used to look at me like that!"

Sasha hardly slept a wink that whole night, afraid she had missed the carriage to Yalta. A little past six in the morning, after packing her things, she came out onto the hotel porch. The day was fresh and clear. The harnessed carriage was already standing ready at the entrance. A German in his broken Russian was directing the conductor to do something and was asking about his things. A young cadet was smoking a cigarette self-importantly, and was shivering from the morning chill and the early hour.[10] Two more men arrived; there were no women, and that bothered Sasha. The German helped Sasha into the carriage and sat down next to her; he observed her with curiosity; she

9. The capital city of the Crimea.
10. A cadet is a student at a military school.

squeezed herself into the corner and snoozed. All of sudden her face grew animated.

"Ah, how nice!" she cried involuntarily. "The mountains with clouds beneath."

"*Die Dame reist zum ersten Mal?*" the German asked with a smile.[11]

"*Ja*," Sasha replied tersely, unable to tear her eyes away from the sunlit mountaintops, and astounded at the scattered downy clouds, floating gracefully just below the peaks. The German looked at Sasha again affectionately and indulgently, as at a child. They soon began to converse; the German was a druggist; the cadet was going up to Yalta to stay with his mother because diphtheria was spreading through his school and all the pupils had been sent home. Sasha no longer felt so lonely; people helped her, and the cadet began rattling on in such an amusing fashion that his merriment infected even Sasha.

"Stop!" The carriage suddenly halted and the conductor jumped down from his coachbox.

"A wheel has broken and it's impossible to go on. Alushta is about one verst from here."[12]

"What's to be done?"

"We'll have to fix it."

"How long will it take?"

"About three hours."

"I won't arrive in time and won't get to see my mother," was the first thought that came into Sasha's head. The feeling for self-preservation is strong in everyone, and she tried to overcome her grief-stricken impatience. Sasha managed to reach the station on foot with all the other passengers and there had some borscht for dinner; after inviting the cheerful cadet, she went out for a walk with him to pass the time. They walked along a rocky road; suddenly some unfamiliar, unknown sound struck her hearing and forced her to stop.

Sasha had never traveled and had never seen anything except for Moscow and the village where she had been born. She looked around her with curiosity, listened intently, and suddenly cried out in a loud voice:

"The sea!"

... Yes, the sea, noisy, agitated, powerfully raising and lowering its gray-blue waves; it was the mysterious, terrible, and at the same time, attractive sea with its majesty and its bottomless depth.

---

11. To the German question "Is the lady traveling for the first time?" Sasha answers in the same language, "Yes."

12. Alushta is a resort town on the Crimean coast.

"So that's what the sea looks like!" Sasha cried and ran down to the shore; the water receded and then advanced toward her with the eternal, uniform movement of its waves, forward and backward, tormenting and disturbing her. Sasha was stunned.

"The sea, the sea!" she repeated, and her heart was torn by some unknown agitation.

She looked at the sea for a long time; the young cadet, collecting pebbles and shells, pressed her to return to the station.

"The carriage will leave, Aleksandra Alekseevna," he called to her.

When Sasha got back to the station with her comrade, they had to wait for another hour, but at last everything was ready and they continued their journey.

The closer they got to Yalta, the more terrified Sasha felt. Finally they saw the lights of the town, closer and closer. . . . Now Sasha didn't want to arrive, but the carriage stopped, and someone's familiar voice called to her:

"Sasha, you've come!"

"Yes. How's mamá?" What will he say? Oh!

"Alive, but very weak."

"Thank God! Where is she?"

"In the Rossiya Hotel."

"Who's with her?"

"Imagine our luck: we came across Varvara Ivanovna down here, and mamá was very glad to see her; now she won't leave mamá."

When Sasha got to the hotel, she decided not to go in to see her mother immediately. The patient had to be forewarned, and Sasha had to prepare herself for the painful sight of her dying mother.

4

Sasha was shown into a large cold room: there was none other available, since all other rooms were occupied. A candle was lit that dimly illuminated the small surface of the table on which it stood and cast only a mysterious gloomy light into the remaining space of the enormous room. They brought in her things; Sasha still stood there, rooted to the spot, in the middle of the room, without taking off her coat, and trembling slightly.

Her brother, who was with their mother in Yalta, went to inform mamá of Sasha's arrival, and sent Varvara Ivanovna, their distant relative and friend of their mother, to fetch Sasha. She had always lived in convents and now had come to Yalta to take the waters.

"Greetings, Sashenka. What's wrong? Take your coat off."

"Hello, my dear Varvara Ivanovna. It's so nice that you're here. I'm afraid to see mamá. How is she? Very bad?"

"It's the absolute end; she'll be very glad to see you. Come, Sashenka; be brave. It's all the will of God; we must be humble and pray for His help."

In the corridor Sasha's brother was already on his way to meet her. Sasha stopped in front of the door of her mother's room and crossed herself. The elderly maid Nastasya, hearing footsteps, opened the door quietly; seeing Sasha, she immediately burst into tears.

"Who's there?" the patient asked in a fading voice.

Sasha went up to her mother's bed with a decisive and light step; without looking at her, she bent over swiftly, kissed her on the cheek and the hand, and then stood still.

"It's a pity you've come here in the autumn, Sashenka; it's nicer here in the spring," her mother said.

"Why talk about me, mamá, my dear? How are you?"[13]

"Not well. The doctor says I should eat calf's-foot jelly, but I can't; I choke on it. There's no need to do so, is there?" the patient asked Sasha.

Sasha suddenly felt some estrangement from her sick mother, who had started talking about calf's-foot jelly right when she arrived. With pain in her heart she realized that death had almost come, and that mamá's suffering body had released her soul.

"Of course, mamá, don't torture yourself. What hurts you?"

"Everything. And it's hard to breathe. Turn me over," she said, addressing her son and Nastasya.

They turned the patient over on her other side.

"Not like that. Sashenka, come here and rub my side."

With trembling hands Sasha rubbed her mother's side; after she had calmed down, Sasha ran out of the room in despair, sat down next to a small table, and burst into tears.

The dark, gray hall was empty. In the middle of the space a stream of water from a fountain was flowing monotonously into a marble pool. Sasha surrendered completely to her grief and cursed fate, the cruel fortune that was taking her beloved mother away from her.

Varvara Ivanovna approached her softly.

"Sashenka, submit to the will of God. Can you really grieve like this? It's sinful."

"What sin? What kind of God sends such suffering?"

13. Sasha addresses her mother with the formal *vy*, while her mother uses the informal *ty*.

"Oh, you unfortunate, unbelieving woman; believe, my friend, that death is better than life. Why, the soul still lives, and without the burden of our sinful body."

Sasha listened to Varvara Ivanovna's efforts to console her; she wanted to be consoled, but it was impossible.

The next morning Sasha's mother seemed to revive somewhat. She asked for her beautiful red dressing gown and some black lace for her head; she managed to sit up and ordered tea served in her room.

"We're going to celebrate Sasha's arrival," she said. "Open the window; that's right. The sea is so nice; I don't feel like dying here."

The fresh sea air rushed into the room. Bright autumn flowers were still in bloom in front of the hotel windows, chrysanthemums: their small, motionless, frost-covered heads sparkled in the rays of the November sun. This sun, even though it was shining and casting its rays on the pale face of the dying woman, was no longer a spring sun promoting growth and life. It was cold and hopeless. Its rays were reflected in the shallow rippling of the serene sea. It was as if golden threads in the shape of waves trembled on its surface.

Sadly and without moving the patient looked at the sea in the distance.

"Dmitry, come over here," she said to her son. "I will die soon; take care of Sasha. She'll do something to herself. . . . Do you hear, Dmitry. I'm entrusting her to you. I know her; we loved each other too much . . ."

The earlier light in her eyes seemed to flare up for the last time and her sincere worries about her beloved daughter invigorated her once more.

The sick woman stopped, gasped for breath, and at once tears flowed from her eyes that had once again grown dark.

"Perhaps, you'll recover," began Dmitry, but he couldn't lie. "You know how I love Sasha; I won't desert her and will try to comfort her, as best I can. Don't be concerned about that."

They lit candles and gathered in the patient's room; Varvara Ivanovna poured tea; there was nothing gloomy in the setting, but everyone felt that death was already present, nearby, and therefore no one could speak, or eat, or drink.

The next day, in the evening, the sick woman began to toss about, complained about a pain in her side, and asked to have the doctor called. He arrived and said that the patient would die before the end of the day. They sent for a priest. The sick woman made her confession in a loud voice, received communion, and dismissed the priest. Then she asked the doctor to relieve her suffering. The doctor brought some morphine, began to inject it, and suddenly gave a shout. The needle had broken. He quickly pulled it out of the patient's side, and hurriedly administered a second injection.

"What have you done to me?" asked the patient.

"What do you feel?"

"I've turned to stone . . . I don't feel . . . anything at all. . . . What's this?" she cried suddenly.

Sasha and her brother ran up to the sick woman, and pressed their lips to her hands; she could scarcely utter, "Farewell," before she lost consciousness. Varvara Ivanovna was praying softly in the corner. Nastasya cried, muttering something. Death throes began. Everyone fell silent in anticipation of the great, terrible event—death. Sasha's mother died four hours later.

Supported by her brother, Sasha rushed out into the stone hall with cries and shrieks of loud despair. During the time her mother's body remained in the hotel, then at the funeral, and even afterward—Sasha was in such a state that people feared for her life. She talked about suicide, forgetting all about her husband and son; it was only after her brother said that they were about to leave for home that she came to her senses and calmed down.

Three days later Sasha arrived home; only when she took her little Alyosha into her arms did she come back to life for the first time and return to something that would bind her to it.

5

Her grief had affected Sasha so profoundly that she suffered all winter; by springtime, she wandered like a shadow, capricious, gloomy, and frail. All of a sudden, for no apparent reason, she would burst into tears and run off to her room, where she would remain all day without food and doing nothing, not wishing to see anybody, merely repeating, "Mamá, where are you? Where are you?" Her husband annoyed her with his good-natured, natural sympathy; noise her son made frequently drove her to tears. The doctors said that Sasha's grief had affected her already irritated nerves and that she was suffering from neurasthenia.[14] One doctor recommended sending her abroad, another advised electric therapy—but Sasha wouldn't listen; she grew angry and remained ill.

Spring came early, a season that had once filled Sasha with new hopes, plans, and a surge of energy and unconscious ecstasy. But the birds of spring arrived, streams of water coursed through the streets of Moscow, carriages rumbled by, the church bells of Easter rang out—yet Sasha remained unmoved by any of it. Her husband proposed that she go to her mother's village,

14. Weakness or exhaustion of the nervous system, usually the result of emotional trauma.

to visit her brother Dmitry, and to make arrangements to spend the summer there. At first Sasha was afraid of gloomy memories, but she felt just as miserable in Moscow as she did anywhere else, and she agreed to go to the country with her husband, as if she wanted to test her strength, to see whether it would be possible to live there, where she had spent every summer of her life with her mother.

At the beginning of April, Sasha and Petr Afanasevich were approaching the long-familiar little station two miles from her late mother's estate. It was early morning. The train stopped; the sleepy passengers woke up, glanced through the window, and, seeing only forest, immediately went back to sleep, assured that it was too early for them to get off the train. Petr Afanasevich carried the luggage out onto the platform. The train stood there for a minute; Sasha quickly jumped down and accepted the sacks, lap robes, and baskets her husband handed her. Then he jumped down onto the frost-covered tracks, and the train left the station with a loud whistle.

"Have horses come for us?" asked Petr Afanasevich.

"They have," replied the familiar stationmaster, raising his hand to his red cap in salute. "But the road's a disaster! You can't go in a sleigh or a carriage. They've come to pick you up in two sledges."

"Splendid. Sasha, what air! The seedbeds have probably been filled, and Timofeevich has planted everything."

Sasha was silent. She looked around her: it was as if she didn't recognize anything. She had changed so much during this time! Her grief was reflected in everything. Nevertheless, the morning sun shining in the clear bright blue sky was so lovely, so dazzling, and those transparent brown tips of the young birch trees were so delicate, they seemed to dissolve unnoticed into thin air, merging with the pink sky of the morning dawn. The oaks of the old state-owned forest still retained their dry, brown autumn leaves that for some reason they had not managed to shed in the autumn or winter. Buds, now ready to burst, were swelling on the ivy and aspen, and birds were making their exuberant noises in the forest.

They arrived at the manor house. "Is this really our home, our lane, everything as it was when we lived here?" wondered Sasha, as they drove past the pond.

Peasant women they knew waved in greeting from the raft with their red hands, cold from doing laundry. . . . Two sleighs were delivering manure to the seedbeds. Male peasants were coming out of the forest carrying brushwood. Everything was so orderly, serene, beyond question, necessary, and important—like everything that was done in the countryside.

Petr Afanasevich was in ecstasy.

"Why are they bringing manure this late? It's probably for the new seedbeds we added for late plantings. . . . The snow's holding fast in some places. . . . Look, Sashenka, what kind of bird is that, I can't make it out. . . . It's so nice, so very nice! The only real life is in the country!"

"Petka, Petka," he cried to a lad who was running past.

Petr Afanasevich couldn't restrain himself; he jumped down from the sledge and ran ahead. He loved the country and nature; he loved it simply, like a child, and he loved working to obtain from the soil everything that could be taken from it.

Sasha's brother met her on the porch; he was agitated and delighted at the same time. He himself had returned not long ago to the country house that seemed so empty without his mother, and he was suffering acutely from loneliness. He had done everything so that Sasha's first impression of the house would be welcoming, and not melancholy at all. A samovar was boiling on the table; coffee was ready; radishes and flowers, which Sasha so loved were also there; a bright sun cast its slanting rays on the parquet floor in the hall; and Dmitry himself had such an affectionate look. But as soon as Sasha entered the house, she was overcome by such an attack of despair that just glancing at her, it was impossible not to weep . . .

"And mamá, where is she? Where?" she repeated in horror and anguish.

This question haunted her painfully; it was the main thing that she wanted to clarify for herself, but couldn't. Her wild, muffled shouts along with this question, "Where? Where is she?" rang throughout the entire house as Sasha began to run through all the rooms: her mother's bedroom, her own room next door, the living room, the terrace—the nest of her childhood that she had loved her whole life and that had now lost all its charm without her beloved mother.

"No, I can't, I can't live here. I will leave today! My God, my God!"

That very evening, to Petr Afanasevich's chagrin, Sasha decided to return back to Moscow, but not from the local station, rather from the provincial town where she had spent the night, and to leave the next morning on the express train. It was dangerous to travel to the station at night: the stream had recently overflowed near the bridge, and the horse might begin to sink and wind up stuck in the water.

Petr Afanasevich was sad. Working with Timofeevich, he transplanted into the seedbeds the young shoots of flowers that had just sprouted their two tender little leaves, and with pleasure they harvested radishes and admired the young ovaries of the cucumbers. The luxurious, bright pink color of the peaches in the conservatory also transported him into ecstasy; tearing himself away from all this entailed suffering for Petr Afanasevich.

The hotel in the provincial town where Sasha stayed overnight was located on a large square. Worn to a frazzle, exhausted, she immediately got undressed and went to bed.

When she awoke the next morning, Petr Afanasevich was already absent: he had gone off at her brother Dmitry's request to find out the price of oats.

Sasha got up, went to the window, and felt afraid of being alone. The windows opened onto the square where there was no one at all. Pigeons were sitting on the windowsills; Sasha took the remains of the white bread from the table where last night's tea had been served; crumbling it up, she stuck her hand out of the little window vent and sprinkled the crumbs on the windowsill. The pigeons, billing and cooing, were frightened at first, and flew off, but then set about the bread, snatching pieces from one another's beaks. Sasha watched them for a long time and felt less lonely. She recalled seeing the wonderful painting by Yaroshenko in the Tretyakov Gallery in Moscow, and uttered quietly, "Yes, life is everywhere!"[15] She began to straighten up the room and to collect her things. Petr Afanasevich was still not back. Sasha waited for him with impatience, glancing out the window. Two cows were walking through the square, picking through some scattered hay.

"Why have they let these cows loose on the street?" Sasha asked the servant who was preparing tea.

"An old woman lives here on the square and she keeps cows; and it hardly costs her anything to feed them."

"How can that be?"

"Three days a week there's a market here; people come with straw, hay, and oats. Here and there they drop some of it; she lets out her cows and they nibble on it; they're content all day long. . . . She also picks some up herself. That's how she lives: she keeps cows and sells the milk."

"That's amazing!" thought Sasha. "That would never have occurred to me! How little we know of real life! Yet life is everywhere," she repeated.

Petr Afanasevich finally returned and brought something in a small sack.

"What's that you have?" Sasha asked.

He opened the sack with a sly smile and sprinkled some seeds into the palm of his hand.

---

15. This work, by the Ukrainian-born painter Nikolai Yaroshenko (1846–98), a member of the Russian group of artists "The Wanderers," is called *Life Is Everywhere* (1888) and shows a young child taking delight in feeding some pigeons through an open window.

"This is what the Shatilovs' steward gave me. They're fantastic seeds . . . and he's taught me how to cultivate roses. If you want your roses to be black, you have to graft them onto a plum tree or even an oak. . . . I'll certainly experiment. . . . It's extremely interesting!"

Petr Afanasevich spoke, drank his tea, and smacked his lips loudly, munching on his roll.

Sasha didn't like it when he smacked his lips; she looked at her good-natured, self-satisfied husband disapprovingly, and for the first time in her life it suddenly occurred to her with particular clarity that there was very little in common between them. True, he loved her, and he was a kind man, even gentle. . . . But did he understand her? Did he ever penetrate her internal life; did he ever see that his interests in the Insurance Company or in the cultivation of the largest possible onions, in both of which she had always shown interest, couldn't really absorb her completely? And now, in her grief, when with all her spiritual strength she was seeking something to hold onto in life, when her soul was so highly strung, trying passionately to penetrate the mystery of life and death, had he helped her, had he looked deep into her soul, was he capable of rousing her interest, giving her something, explaining to her the whole horror of death or the entire meaning of life that lay ahead? No, she knew that he couldn't help her; and she herself was so weak, nervous, and unhappy . . .

"The train will be leaving very soon. . . . Is everything ready? Good work, Sashenka, you're all packed," Petr Afanasevich added, trying to say something affectionate.

Half an hour later the express train was already carrying Sasha and Petr Afanasevich back to Moscow.

6

Genuine springtime arrived unnoticed. Window frames were removed and the dusty streets of Moscow were cleaned; fluffy down on trees in the gardens and along the boulevards was beginning to turn green; residents were already carrying tea tables out into their gardens, or sitting on balconies and porches in anticipation of moving to the country or the dacha.

University and high school students, and all the other young people engaged in study, were suffering in their hot uniforms and at the prospect of their imminent exams. Conscientious ones were cramming; the indolent ones were complaining and sitting by open windows with books in their hands, envying the lucky ones riding by on bicycles, in carriages, or in landaus on their way out of town for a spin.

Carts loaded with furniture, straw mattresses, children's wagons, plants, trunks, and cows with their horns tethered to the carts stretched along Moscow streets all the way to the town gates, leading to the residents' dachas.

Doormen wearing vests over red shirts who had seen their masters off to the country stood casually and cheerfully at the house gates, enjoying their new freedom and leisure.

Life in Moscow during the winter season was ending; an entirely new summer season was beginning.

Petr Afanasevich was tired of waiting for their move to the country; little Alyosha, pale from his enclosed, winter life, should have been in the country long ago, but Sasha insisted on staying in Moscow, showing no desire whatever to relocate; she remained silent on the subject or else complained about her lack of will. Finally, one fine day in May, she announced decisively to her husband that she would not move to the country for any reason; everything there reminded her too much of her grief. She added that if Petr Afanasevich wished it, she was willing to spend this summer at a dacha near Moscow and nowhere else.

This was a blow to Petr Afanasevich, but he knew that it couldn't be otherwise; besides, his kind nature was unable to oppose his wife's strong will, and he diligently started looking for a dacha in the outskirts of Moscow.

At last he found something that he thought would be suitable and asked Sasha to go and see it. She agreed reluctantly; taking Alyosha along with his nanny, she left after the heat of the day to inspect the dacha that her husband had found.

"Is it really late spring already?" Sasha wondered, turning into a country road, trembling with the same joyful feelings the season used to arouse in her. "Where was I? Oh, why do I feel all this anxiety? Is it really possible for me ever to rejoice again?"

Turning off the main road, they entered a forest. It was peaceful and solemn. Birds were busy in the bushes. In the distant marsh, over which a mist hovered, corncrakes were calling to each other with their harsh voices. Frogs were croaking loudly, making a racket as they do in spring, bringing back memories of Sasha's family's estate and the old pond they would drive around on their way to the house as they moved into it every spring. "I don't need these memories; I don't want to, I can't suffer and cry any longer. . . . I have to look ahead and live, not look back," Sasha thought, glancing at the lovely scene where the quiet carriage was carrying her. "I want life, life. . . . 'Life is everywhere!'"

"Mamá, let me get out and run," Alyosha begged excitedly.

"In a minute, as soon as we get closer."

And in fact, the coachman, who had been at this dacha once before with his master, soon deposited Sasha there as well. The watchman led her up to it, describing it, and displaying all its conveniences.

The dacha stood on a high spot; a little river flowed below. Farther on it was dammed up and two new wooden bathhouses could be seen.

"Whose house is that next door?"

"Nothing special, a small dacha, rented by a single gentleman."

"Oh, it's unpleasant to have neighbors. Are there any other dachas nearby?"

"No, nothing else. About a verst from here, near the main road, there are a few more, but here there's only one. No need to worry: you have a garden, and so does he, and you can't see or hear anything beyond the trees. We know the gentleman: he's a quiet man."

Alyosha chased after June bugs, picked early wild flowers from the field with pleasure, and drank tea in the little garden. He was ecstatic and didn't want to go back to Moscow. But it was getting cooler. Sasha liked the dacha; she handed over a deposit and they left for home.

It was a splendid May evening: the sun was setting with a glow in the sky; there was a quiet stillness in the air, and only when the roar of Moscow cabs on the road once again began to impinge on Sasha's hearing did she fall back into her previous anxious mood. But upon nearing their house, she could see a bright greenish star beautifully pouring its mysterious light above the garden through transparent green branches. "That's Venus! Venus—the star of love! What a beauty she is; what hope is she promising me with her greenish light?" wondered Sasha sentimentally, and she couldn't tear herself away from this star; once again she thirsted for some new life.

Alyosha fell asleep; they carried him in from the carriage, and put him to bed, sleepy, flushed, and intoxicated from all the fresh air.

The next day they speedily packed up their belongings and one day later a more cheerful Sasha moved to the dacha.

7

"I planted seeds here; they'll produce some wonderful Romaine lettuce," said Petr Afanasevich, wearing an apron while digging in freshly dug beds with his sleeves rolled up. He was completely happy in his sphere of gardening work.

"And here are my radishes—eighteen varieties."

"Who's going to eat them all, such a huge quantity?" asked Sasha, sitting on the balcony in her white dress, pressing the first flowers of spring into a large red album to dry.

"If we plant seed, we'll find mouths to feed," Petr Afanasevich muttered, laughing foolishly. Sasha was irked and smiled scornfully.

"You'd be better off planting flowers; we can buy all this produce for a few kopecks."

"I've planted masses of flowers; I have to go water them now."

"I'm going with you, papá," cried Alyosha, carrying a small watering can in one hand and a hunk of bread in the other.

"Come on, come on, let's go water mama's flowers," Petr Afanasevich said graciously.

"What are they carrying?" asked Sasha, pointing at some approaching carts.

"It's our neighbor moving into the yellow dacha," said nanny.

A few minutes later an old footman from the neighboring dacha arrived, and asked whether Petr Afanasevich's doorman and footman could help him for a few minutes to move a piano.

With a shout, special care, and great effort they lifted the heavy instrument from the cart by means of long strips of cloth and carried it into the dacha. Then from the other cart they removed the modest belongings of the resident of the yellow cottage, and carried in his trunks, chairs, bed, baskets, and so forth. The old footman thanked them for their help, gave each a small tip, and everything quieted down. It remained quiet for several days. No one could be seen on the terrace or through the windows of the neighboring dacha. The newly arrived old footman, Aleksei Tikhonych, whose name soon became known among the servants at Sasha's dacha, sometimes sat on a bench and out of boredom followed the goings-on at the dacha next door, concluding that they were good people, but that the husband was an eccentric who spent his entire day digging around in the dirt, which would produce flowers, lettuce—which is to say, grass—and even tomatoes that were of no use to anyone and that he, Tikhonych, would never dream of eating.

Little Alyosha would sometimes walk past Aleksei Tikhonych with his nanny; once Alyosha asked him what his name was and rejoiced that he had found a namesake. Another time the lad, who felt great sympathy for Tikhonych and decided that he must be very bored, invited him to gather morels with him.

"Right away, my good sir, as soon as I lock up the dacha."

From that day forward a warm friendship was forged between Tikhonych and Alyosha and his nanny. They often took tea together in the front garden; Tikhonych knew how to fashion flutes out of sticks and roosters out of paper;

he told Alyosha folk tales and taught him songs that he had learned from his master's pupils.

During the early days following their move to the dacha, Sasha had begun to feel stronger; rejoicing in springtime, nature, the forest, and the nightingales, she felt that she had begun to be consoled. But at times the morbid anguish would return to her; she wouldn't eat, couldn't sleep, and would sit limply in the corner, doing nothing.

It was a bright summer evening. After a splendid, serene day in May during which Sasha wept disconsolately, she was sitting alone on the balcony, listening to the slightest noise, and expecting the arrival of Petr Afanasevich who had been away in Moscow on business. Little Alyosha had approached her several times; either with unhappy curiosity or egotistical childish annoyance that his cheerful life had been troubled, he had asked his mother: "Mamá, when will you stop crying?" Finally he went off to bed. Sasha walked out to the road; once again, the first thing that struck her sight was that greenish star—Venus, shining with challenging brightness in the clear spring sky. Once more a desire for happiness, consolation, and joy awoke in her heart for a moment. She turned back, and without entering the house, lay down on a bench, remembering her late mother, recalling all that she had read by various wise men about death, and all that she had copied down from selected works into her red album while pondering the eternal, unsolved problem of death. She wanted to discover some sort of escape, some solace.

"*La mort c'est l'absorption des eléménts de l'intelligence humaine dans l'intelligence universelle*"; she recalled the words of Epictetus, trying to be consoled in that the *intelligence universelle*—was God, and that her mother was now with God.[16] Furthermore, to the question where does man go after death, the answer was: "*Vers des choses amies et du meme genre que toi—vers les eléménts.*"[17] In other words, her mother had merged with nature, and that was a good thing.

Lev Tolstoy writes somewhere: "Death is only the annihilation of temporary form; but this annihilation never ceases . . ."

Further, he says: "The best proof of immortality is that no one is able to conceive of the end of his own existence, and the very impossibility of imagining one's *death* is proof that it really doesn't exist . . ."[18]

16. "Death is the incorporation of the elements of human intelligence into the universal intelligence."

17. "Into amicable spheres and of the same kind as you—into the [natural] elements."

18. I have been unable to identify the source of Sofiya Andreevna's citation of her husband's work.

But mama's no longer here, that's *for certain* . . . even though it's said that the soul is immortal, that the body is its burden—"*tu es une âme, qui porte un cadavre*," Sasha remembered.[19] But it would be better if that body bearing her mother's soul were still alive and sitting here with her, as she did before, in the empty house of their estate, and they would all be so happy. . . . But now she was alone, all alone. . . . Sasha started to feel sorry for herself, and a simple physical, almost childlike despair overcame all her arguments; her head drooped onto her arms and she wept, her bosom heaving . . .

Suddenly in the gentle, quiet May night there rang out vibrant melodious sounds produced by expert hands, playing Mendelssohn's *Song Without Words* in G Major.[20] The first note of the right hand, hesitating for an almost imperceptible moment, groaned deeply, protractedly, and expressively. The left hand seemed to accompany the melody not with its fingers but with a breath of air; then it became impossible to hear the note A, either from the left hand or the right; everything merged and began to sing, as if the song at one and the same time was telling Sasha about her grief, but also consoling her and promising her happiness, life, and a new love . . .

Sasha didn't know this particular song and did not want to know anything else at that moment; she didn't even guess immediately that the sound of the *Song Without Words* was coming from the little yellow dacha next door. The performer played it as people do only when they think no one is listening. They feel no self-consciousness playing music when they are alone. There is no impact of the effect of the audience and the performer on each other, except something serene, reasoned, and profound, some sort of mysterious bond between the dead composer and the brilliant performer. Such was the performance of Mendelssohn's *Song Without Words* that she was hearing now.

When it was finished, the invisible inhabitant of the yellow dacha began to play it again, repeating certain musical phrases, trying to play them softer, then louder, sometimes holding one note to make it seem longer; first he emphasized, then understated, one or another note. He employed the musical instrument as if it were his own voice, and the piano obeyed his brilliant hands, as if it were alive and loved its master.

In every way possible it turned out splendidly, and the *Song Without Words* said something tender and affectionate to Sasha's ailing soul; it both consoled

19. "You are a soul carried by a dead body."

20. *Songs Without Words* (*Lieder ohne Worte*) is a series of short, lyrical piano pieces by the German Romantic composer Felix Mendelssohn (1809–47).

and gladdened her. But then the conclusion—pianissimo, one and the same phrase sounded imposingly and tenderly like three sighs, and then all was silent. Sasha also sighed, as if her overflowing bosom was relieved by the sounds conveyed to her heart by the piano.

It fell silent in the yellow dacha again. This May night was so very quiet and warm. The silence entered Sasha's soul, filling it with joy.

"Thank you, God!" she said softly. And for the first time since her mother's death, Sasha smiled and felt reconciled to life.

The invisible musician once again struck some chords and played something complex and tragic, from which there emerged a wonderful melody in a minor key, apparently something the musician was improvising. Clickety-clack, clickety-clack: Sasha recalled the sound of the rushing train cars when she was traveling to the Crimea to visit her dying mother; the melody that she had heard then through her dream was undoubtedly the very same one she was hearing now.

"Yes, it is!" Sasha cried suddenly, and she felt afraid. She rushed home, had tea served in her room, locked herself in, had the shutters closed and the lamps lit, and greeted her husband with exaggerated delight when he finally returned home in a carriage loaded with all possible provisions and purchases brought back from Moscow.

8

Sasha didn't say anything to her husband about the inhabitant of the yellow dacha or about the strong impression that his playing had made on her. She jealously guarded the secret of her consolation and waited with anguished impatience for the time when she would again hear sounds coming from the neighboring house. But all was quiet for a few days. The performer of the *Song Without Words* led an unusually proper life: he got up early, went for a swim, dined at 1 P.M., appeared again sometime after 5, and went off to stroll for the entire evening. No one visited him except for one young man, to whom he was, apparently, giving lessons.

A week passed. Sasha stopped going for walks in order not to miss any playing by the resident of the yellow dacha; she was interested in nothing else. Every day she went to sit on the bench opposite his house, waiting to hear the stranger's playing once more.

It was evening. The elderly footman on the small balcony of the neighboring dacha was gathering some cups; then he took away the samovar and locked the door behind him. But the windows were open and Sasha heard the lid of the piano being raised and several chords being struck. She recognized the beginning of a sonata by Chopin and held her breath.[21] Soon the expressive, tragic tale of the entirety of human life began to sound in this sonata. At first everything was serene and resonant, then forlorn and agonizing; next a pause—and then came the sound of a funeral march, rhythmic, performed with classical severity. Then a melody of tender, heartfelt reminiscences, just like those Sasha's soul had experienced so many times; and once more, the march, gloomy, inconsolable, and in it, a strictly enforced rhythm.

"Oh," moaned Sasha. In this highly artistic work she experienced emotionally and with terrible force all the episodes of a person's beloved and lost human life. Then, like a light breeze, like spirits floating above graves, the airy and tender finale arrived swiftly. Sasha rushed toward the yellow dacha and sat down on its balcony porch, listening to the pounding of her own heart reverberating under the bodice of her light, white dress. Then it was all over.

The performer of the sonata pushed the door open with his powerful arm and emerged onto the balcony. Sasha shuddered; still unable to sort out the feelings that were overpowering her, she didn't immediately understand what was happening. It was only when the broad figure of the musician was standing right over her, carefully examining her with his dazzled, somewhat excited, rapidly blinking eyes, that she grew frightened at what she had done. Taking flight like a bird, and mumbling in confusion, "Forgive me," she rushed home to her own dacha with terrible speed, light as air, with a flash of her delicate sleeves and the airy skirt of her white dress.

In great astonishment the inhabitant of the yellow dacha followed with his eyes the slender figure of this unknown woman who had disturbed his solitude and serenity. His aesthetic vision couldn't help but admire the grace and beauty he had observed at once in her nimble figure. He was annoyed by the intrusion into his life; he was irritated at having his peace and quiet disturbed, and also by the fact that this meeting had upset him inadvertently; and that now he was peering into the darkness, searching for this unexpected apparition.

He fell into glum thought, took off his glasses, and perched on the balcony railing. Completely unnoticed, the impression left by this unidentified woman and his annoyance over her appearance gradually faded from his memory; in their place there arose in his mind that rich melody he had just improvised. That splendid, tender, radiant, and luxuriant melody became clearer and clearer to him; it sang in his head, yielding effortlessly to the most unexpected, elegant variations, each one richer than the last. . . . It became more defined, more striking, and the image of the vanishing white figure of the

21. Frédéric Chopin's *Piano Sonata* no. 2 in B-flat Minor, opus 35, written mainly in 1839.

unidentified woman arose clearly before the composer, also elegant and nimble, as if an earthly embodiment of its artistic motifs. It would disappear, and then reappear again. . . . It was almost like a dream.

Ivan Ilych was no longer annoyed. Smiling joyfully, he hurried back into his room and at once began to jot down on music paper the splendid melody that in time must become the main theme of the symphony he had begun working on. He wrote for a long time, then sat down at his piano and played through what he had written. It was a while since he had experienced such ecstasy from his own composition. All the powers of his genius were concentrated that night on his work, and for the first time, breaking the routine of his life, he sat composing until dawn. He lay down to rest for a few hours only after the eastern sky had grown light with the rising sun, and the bright morning dawn had penetrated the small windows of his little dacha and entered his bedroom.

9

"Sashenka, this neighbor of ours is a splendid fellow. I went swimming with him this morning and promised to give him some radishes," Petr Afanasevich informed Sasha, as he came out onto the balcony with his damp towel and wet black hair sticking to the temples of his glowing face. "I'm so glad we've become acquainted. And he's a musician; perhaps he'll play for you someday. You love music."

Sasha remained quiet and blushed, as if her secret were incriminating. She was not pleased by her husband's acquaintance with this mysterious musician. Why was it necessary? Wouldn't it be better if her only impression of him was artistic, the one that had brought her so much happiness and solace, rather than the impression of his personality which might ruin everything? At that very moment their nanny came in with Alyosha and announced:

"Madam, your neighbor has asked to borrow a mill: he has no way to grind his coffee. Can we lend it to him?"

"Mamá, do lend it to him, Yesterday he gave me some chocolate. He's a nice man."

Sasha smiled. This magician of music drinks coffee and eats chocolate!

"Of course, nanny, give him anything he asks for; we always lend our things."

"By the way, nanny, I'll go cut some lettuce and pick some radishes for him; send them to him and find out his first name and patronymic.[22] Tell him that his neighbors send him greetings and invite him to dine with them tomorrow."

---

22. In formal address, Russians use a middle name derived from the father's first name.

"There's no need, no need for this friendship," Sasha hastened to say, impulsively and capriciously, almost in tears. "I'm not seeing anyone, let alone a total stranger."

"But at one time everyone was a stranger," Petr Afanasevich said, feeling offended; he was bored at the dacha and very much wanted to make the acquaintance of their neighbor. But he was not in the habit of contradicting his wife, and obediently declined to make the acquaintance of the inhabitant of the yellow dacha, adding that there was no reason to fear their neighbor: he was an absolutely decent and tactful man.

Petr Afanasevich went off to harvest his radishes, while Sasha, knowing that there would probably be no music played at that hour, since it was the time when their neighbor usually took his stroll, also went off alone to wander in the nearby grove. She walked for a long time and rejoiced when she arrived at a place she had never seen before. She began picking bright, fragrant violets, gathered a large bouquet, and then went running down to the spring to rinse the stems. Having descended into the ravine where a bright stream flowed, cutting through it in a straight line, Sasha washed the flowers and began scooping up some water to drink with the palm of her hand. She felt cool and comfortable here and was enjoying her solitude; she sat down and began sorting her violets one at a time, arranging them into a bouquet. Only the stream interrupted the silence with its monotonous, gentle gurgling. Then she heard some other sound, the pages of a book being turned, and someone's breathing. . . . There, on a stump, book in his hand, no hat on his head, Sasha recognized the inhabitant of the yellow dacha. He didn't hear her; his face was almost melancholy. Sasha didn't know what to do. Run away—but why? That would be awkward. Stay there—she'd have to start talking and she didn't want to make his acquaintance. What to do? But while she was thinking, the stranger stood up, bowed to Sasha, and said:

"So you like this spot, too? It's not too hot here."

"This is the first time I've come here; I don't know the local places at all," Sasha replied, feeling some sort of tremor in her body. "I'm going home now . . ."

"If you like, we can walk together," the stranger said simply and calmly.

"Yes. What's your name?"

"Ivan Ilych. And yours?"

"Aleksandra Alekseevna."

"Do you like music? You came to listen. If you do, I'll play for you sometime."

"No. . . . Yes, thank you, sometime . . ."

Sasha's heart was pounding from agitation. It was so simple, so easy to partake of this happiness, right away, yet it seemed beyond her reach . . .

They emerged at the top of the ravine, mounted a hillock, crossed over the gully on a sturdy little brushwood bridge, and then climbed onto a mound. A wonderful view of the river opened before them; in the distance they could see the bright sunset on the left and an old forest on the right.

"How lovely; I've never been here. And there's a boat on the riverbank: how pleasant!" Sasha cried. "Whose is it?"

"I don't know. If you'd like, we could go for an outing. I'll row."

"Thank you, I'd love to," Sasha agreed impulsively, hastening toward the river.

With strong, handsome, but clumsy hands unaccustomed to hard work, Ivan Ilych took hold of the chain; holding onto the boat, he jumped into it. He offered Sasha his hand and in a few minutes they were gently moving in the direction of the town.

The blazing column left by dusk was sinking and disappearing into the water. It was quiet and the evening mist was settling onto the river; the town could be seen along the shores, also through the mist, as they drifted along, almost without conversing.

A joyful serenity settled upon Sasha. The simplicity, the gentle tenderness of this man immediately eased her heart and her resolve; having surrendered her willpower, she felt only good as a consequence.

Sasha returned home with Ivan Ilych rather late that evening. Petr Afanasevich was very worried; he had gone off to look for her, and was overjoyed to see her coming back with their neighbor.

"You've become acquainted; I'm so pleased! Come and have some tea, warm yourselves up—it's damp outside."

"It's hot. There's no need to warm ourselves up; we've had such a nice boat ride together," Sasha said.

"Boat ride? Is that so!" Petr Afanasevich thought to himself.

Ivan Ilych ate some bread and butter and fresh cheese with quite an appetite. Pouring lots of cream into his tea, he was already drinking his third cup.

"Do you have a piano? What sort is it?" he asked.

"We do, and it's a very good one: a Bechstein.[23] I used to play a great deal at one time. But Petr Afanasevich doesn't like music and even suffers from the noise, as he says, so I've almost given up playing."

---

23. Carl Bechstein founded his piano factory in Berlin in October 1853. He soon became the official piano maker for the tsars of Russia.

"May I try your piano?"

Ivan Ilych played a piece, then became thoughtful, hung his head, and as if recalling something, moved away from the piano, sat on the very edge of the bench, and struck the opening chords of Beethoven's Sonata, opus 31.[24]

"What's that?" Sasha asked herself suddenly, blushing, as if hot steam enveloped her completely. "Yes, I know. But how he plays this sonata! It all sounds so new. It's so fine; no, it's not fine, it's wonderful, he's a nice man, very nice!"

Sasha was out of her mind with excitement; a slight tremor shook her entire body from her ecstasy. That first largo, pianissimo, and then the allegro, so expressive. And Beethoven—where had he overheard these feelings in Sasha's heart?[25] "He understood everything, and the performer understands Beethoven, and I understand them both, and I feel and I love . . ." Sasha looked at Ivan Ilych's face, at his serious, wandering eyes, at his tense expression, and at his exquisite hands. Suddenly everything started to vanish.

"My God! Where will it lead?" the question flashed into Sasha's mind, as if it was drawing her, blind and weak, into some unknown world . . .

The sonata resounded with unexpected beauty under the hands of the performer, all the more meaningful and magnificent.

"But all this is not unknown to me," Sasha kept thinking, "It's not unfamiliar. Once everything was just that happy and fine. But where? When? Isn't it from there that I came into this life, where everything is elusive, boundless, and timeless?"

Sasha tried to catch Ivan Ilych's glance, but his solemn eyes, significant in their expression, saw nothing and no one. "Where will it lead, where?" Sasha repeated mentally. Suddenly from the depths of her soul, a reverent disposition arose in her slowly and triumphantly. In accord with her childhood habit, she raised her eyes to the icon and her thoughts to God, to spiritual joy and eternity, to death and immortality, to everything that was outside space and time; to the death of her mother, who had passed into eternity. All of these thoughts were joyfully resolved by her: both the pain of loss and the chaos of tormenting doubts about human life and death, with all the sufferings, temptations, and evil—all this became clear like the bright sky after a storm, illuminating nature refreshed by the rays of the sun.

24. The Piano Sonata no. 17 in D Minor, opus 31, no. 2, was composed in 1801–2, and is usually referred to as *The Tempest* (*Der Sturm*).

25. This probably refers to a lyric poem by the writer A. K. Tolstoy (1817–75), "You think in vain, oh, artist" (1856). Referring to Beethoven, he wrote: "While he, though deaf to the earth, could overhear unearthly sobbing."

The sounds coming from his brilliant hands sounded even better, more meaningful, and more powerful. Sasha felt that she was starting to choke on her tears; she jumped up from her place and ran into the next room, lowered her head to the dressing table under the mirror, and hid her face on her folded arms; her tremor resolved into quiet sobs.

Sasha wanted to fall on her knees before this man, and, like an ancient pagan before an idol depicting art in such perfection, she felt like bowing down to the earth and worshiping the force that had aroused such splendid emotions in her and summoned her back to life.

"So that's what music can do," Sasha thought with astonishment. "Why didn't I know about this sooner?"

Ivan Ilych finished playing, fell silent, looked at the clock, and said in an apathetic voice:

"It's time to sleep. Goodbye."

It was as if the flame suddenly went out of him; fire, energy, and strength, which were felt in his playing, all of that seemed spent and covered over by a lid behind which his treasures were stored. It was as if Ivan Ilych intentionally became prosaic, physical, and boring. But Sasha wasn't deceived by this. She understood that tone; she understood that he wanted to say to everyone: "Don't touch me when I don't want to be touched; don't peer into the holy of holies of my world of art which I love more than anything else on earth."

Sasha wanted to thank him, but couldn't. She extended her hand; her eyes, moist and shining from tears and agitation, expressed more than her words ever could do. Ivan Ilych seemed to keep Sasha's hand imperceptibly in his; standing there in some indecisiveness, he gazed closely and with curiosity and interest into her lovely, innocent eyes, and then went out onto the terrace, not understanding very well whether his new acquaintance was merely pretending to be such an ecstatic admirer of music or whether she really was so sensitive and receptive to it.

10

The next morning Ivan Ilych's pupil arrived and for two and half hours Sasha heard the sound of chromatic scales being practiced in the yellow dacha, interrupted by conversation and the young man's raucous laughter.

Sasha became cheerful, too. She also felt like laughing and moving. She played with Alyosha, ran out into the garden, and tackled various domestic chores. But how trivial all these everyday problems and worries seemed after yesterday's important event—Ivan Ilych's performance of the Beethoven sonata! Sasha regarded with such meek and indifferent simplicity the various muddles at home, her husband's exaggerated despair that some of his seeds had sprouted badly . . . "Oh, how lovely, what pleasure!" Sasha shivered with joy, recalling Ivan Ilych's playing yesterday. "Perhaps this happiness will be repeated again tomorrow, and all summer until we leave the dacha to return to Moscow! What a nice man!" Sasha thought tenderly, turning her affection to the indeterminate creature who had afforded her such enjoyment.

"Our windows are so dim and dirty in the sunlight. It's from the lamps and the dust!" Sasha recalled that her husband had complained about this yesterday. "I must scold Parasha. . . . No, it's not necessary to scold anyone about anything. Let *everyone* rejoice. How splendidly he began that largo yesterday! Yes, it was wonderful! Marvelous! What joy!"

Sasha picked up a towel and wiped the window glass, carefully shifting the almost transparent new growth of the feathery, tender fern on the windowsill, and moving her hand around the roses in full bloom in their pots on the sill delighting her sight. "There's no need to scold Parasha. Let her sleep. She was so tired yesterday. . . . And then there's the finale of the sonata. It's not only music, not merely notes on a page, it's a poem about passionate human life. . . . And the recitative? That tells me what a marvelous, all-comprehending, sensitive soul Beethoven was, as well as the man performing his music. How delightful! How nice it is to be alive!" Her heart jumped and pounded; it seemed as if she couldn't stand this musical abundance any longer.

Sasha sat down at the piano and played softly through the sonata she had heard yesterday, trying to phrase the music just as Ivan Ilych had. She wasn't listening to herself; she could only hear yesterday's performance. After playing it, she felt calmer.

"Sashenka, have a look at these imported tomatoes," said Petr Afanasevich upon entering. "Here, take them; I'll grow some, too."

"What? What tomatoes?"

At first Sasha didn't understand. But when she did, she took the slippery red vegetables into her hands with a smile.

Even this didn't annoy her now. Isn't everything lovely? Does anything on earth matter when the whole world's suddenly started singing those wonderful sounds that restored her to life and that would now fill her completely, tomorrow, a month from now, perhaps even forever?

Petr Afanasevich went out to his garden and began tying up his cauliflower leaves. Sasha, who had never taken any part in his affairs, suddenly felt cheerful and found it easy to help her husband. She did everything impulsively, as if not thinking about what she was doing. She was still listening, as if waiting for something.

Ivan Ilych walked past the vegetable garden with his pupil and paused near the fence for a minute, greeting Sasha and her husband.

"Permit me to introduce my pupil, Tsvetkov," said Ivan Ilych.

Tsvetkov smiled at once so gladly and boldly with both his mouth and his narrow, laughing eyes that everyone else did the same. Bowing from some distance, he kissed Sasha's hand and began praising the locality. Tsvetkov was so cheerful and robust, everything seemed so easy for him, he was capable in so many ways, that there was no time for him to be bashful. He seemed carried away, but devoured absolutely every vestige of existence with intense enthusiasm, turning them as much as possible to his own happiness and advantage.

"You must both come and dine with us," Petr Afanasevich invited them generously. "They've brought us a huge pike, and I've picked some asparagus as large as candles—you'll see."

"What are you doing here?"

"Sasha and I are tying up cauliflower leaves."

"Come with us for a swim."

"Right away, with pleasure. I'll go fetch a towel."

Petr Afanasevich went into the house, while Sasha, stopping her work, ruddy and happy, laughing, said to Ivan Ilych:

"You certainly played the scales very diligently."

"You heard?"

"Of course!"

"Well, as a reward, we'll play something nice for you this evening."

"Well, well, thank you. I look forward to it."

The men went off and Sasha went to arrange their dinner. She suddenly wanted everything to be elegant, especially fine and festive. She made large bouquets of wildflowers, roses, jasmine, yellow lilies, and fern fronds. She straightened up the room herself and even rearranged the furniture, trying to make it all attractive and comfortable. She very devotedly wiped down the white and black keys of the piano with her scented cambric handkerchief and then sat down to play. Little Alyosha came in.

"Mamá, come play with me," Alyosha begged.

"Wait a bit, my dear," implored Sasha, picking out the prelude that Ivan Ilych had sent her that morning.

"Come on, mamá . . ."

But Sasha was delving into a complicated part of the prelude with great enthusiasm, trying to hear one voice after another as they were introduced and juxtaposed. This process of trying to grasp the composer's thoughts afforded her enormous pleasure.

Alyosha started to cry. Sasha was appalled at her own preoccupation; she grabbed her son and ran out into the garden laughing, where she played with him in a particularly creative and animated way for a long time. But the prelude still rang in her ears, and her brain was working intensely, recalling the complex patterns of this composition.

Many guests gathered for dinner. Petr Afanasevich's friend Mukhatov had come: he was a wealthy landowner who visited them and harbored a secret love for Sasha. A student named Kurlinsky, who had just arrived at the dacha after finishing his law course and exams, was also there; exhausted and pale, he was Sasha's distant relative who was spending the summer at his aunt's dacha, where his pretty cousin Kate was also staying. Ivan Ilych was there with Tsvetkov. They had dinner in the garden; Sasha's bouquets were lovely; the bowls of fruit, the English china, the sparkling silver, the bright summer sun—everything was so festive, splendid, and celebratory.

Tsvetkov was seated next to Kate; Sasha invited Ivan Ilych to sit next to her. But he regarded his pupil and the young lady sitting next to him with envy, chatting so cheerfully and laughing together. Sasha was nervous and spoke in an affected manner with her neighbor, growing irritated at her husband, who was either dishing out food onto the guests' plates or filling their glasses with wine. Mukhatov, an opera lover, thought it necessary to talk with Ivan Ilych about music. Ivan Ilych, who ate everything with great delight that Petr Afanasevich served him, listened to Mukhatov's ecstatic praise for Wagner with noticeable mild irony.

"Of course, you love Wagner, Aleksandra Alekseevna?" Mukhatov asked Sasha.

"I don't know him at all," she replied.

"You don't? You must study him: an entire world of pleasure will be opened up to you. He's a genius! What astonishing thought in the leitmotifs contained in his music, and in the various musical phrases at every moment of an opera's performance."

"It's all a big muddle," Sasha observed timidly. "I find it boring."

"Good Lord! Boring! You must listen carefully: it's not that drip-drip of Verdi's Italian operas; this is something new and original: the human voice comprises something like a link in the chain of a graceful, unified entity; the voice enters into the whole orchestra, becoming one of its finest instruments. Oh, Wagner's harmonies—I know nothing better in the whole world! Next spring I'll certainly go on vacation to Bayreuth."[26]

26. The site of an annual music festival in Germany where Wagner's operas are performed.

"To me all this new music is pure suffering. It seems to me that people pretend to understand something in it. But it's only noise and it hurts my ears," Petr Afanasevich ventured his opinion.

"New music is the music of the future," Kurlinsky observed modestly.

"Especially the kind that Ivan Ilych writes," Tsvetkov declared enthusiastically.

"Would you like me to give you a plot for an opera?" Mukhatov asked, addressing Ivan Ilych. "It's a wonderful one!"

"I'd be very glad," said Ivan Ilych, once again with a light touch of irony.

"Can one really provide a plot?" Sasha suddenly flared up. "A plot can only be one's *own* personal inspiration, emerging from the particular character of the composer. If he's a genius, then he himself will experience not only the contemporary demands of his art, but also the progressive demands of all humanity, and he'll respond to them with his compositions."

"Yes, if they do respond, but often they have no success at all," Mukhatov objected caustically and with annoyance, distressed by Sasha's disgruntled protestation.

"Aleksandra Alekseevna's right," Kurlinsky observed with admiration to Sasha, who was blushing.

Ivan Ilych looked into Sasha's eyes once more with interest and, momentarily embarrassed, blinked and continued eating his strawberries. Dinner was over. Afterward everyone dispersed. Kate went back to her dacha to put on her riding habit, planning to go for a ride with Tsvetkov, to whom Petr Afanasevich had offered his horse.

Mukhatov chatted with Petr Afanasevich about whether the insurance claim of the owner of a factory that had been torched by the workers would be paid.

Ivan Ilych sat down to play chess with Kurlinsky. Sasha picked up her needlework and sat in silence sewing. She felt so good, so peaceful. She knew that today Ivan Ilych was sure to play, and this happiness of expectation provided her with serenity in her soul. From time to time she glanced at Ivan Ilych's beautiful hands as they moved the chess pieces in silence, and she thought about what sort of man he really was. She was unable to understand him.

It began to grow dark. Suddenly someone's voice spoke up behind her. Mukhatov, having finished his conversation with Petr Afanasevich, approached Sasha quietly and began chatting with her in an excited tone of voice:

"Have you been interested in music for a long time?"

"Not long; I've fallen in love with it again."

"And who or what caused you to fall in love again?"

"Why are you interrogating me?"

"Because your every disagreement with my opinions, your every dissatis-faction drives me to despair . . ."

"Really?" Sasha replied naïvely.

"I'd prefer that we were always united in all things, that we liked the same things, that . . ."

"You're saying all this to me?" Sasha asked distractedly, glancing at Ivan Ilych; she stood up and went out onto the terrace; after standing there a moment, she gazed up at the sky.

"Ah! There it is, my star. All spring it's been both delighting and annoying me. For some reason it's just as meaningful to me as the comet was for Pierre in *War and Peace*, when he looked at it with his moist eyes as he was riding along in his carriage, just as he was becoming aware of his love for Natasha the very first time. . . . [27] Could it be that I love someone? Pierre rejoiced, while I? Yes, in my own way I'm rejoicing at this new love for . . . music," Sasha said to herself. "Not for anything in the world would I give up this bright, new love, from which I've nothing special to expect in the future but which, among the minor stars of ordinary, everyday life, with its boredom, suffering, and emptiness, shines so brightly in my soul like this bright green-ish star amid the innumerable large and small stars disappearing into space, just like Pierre's dazzling comet."

Sasha came back to her senses as she heard the loud voices of Tsvetkov and Kate as they approached the terrace. Two saddled horses were being led behind them. Kate, flirtatiously, demanded that Ivan Ilych admire her horse and stroke it.

"Well, lend me your brilliant hands and help seat me on my horse," she said, laughing.

"I'm not very competent," Ivan Ilych replied, bustling about and drawing near Kate.

But she was so attractive and looked at him with such cheerful daring, that he made haste and began helping her mount her horse. He admired her graceful figure and her small foot, and he envied Tsvetkov.

27. The Great Comet of 1811 was visible for around 260 days. At the midpoint of the novel, Tolstoy describes his hero observing this "enormous and brilliant comet . . . that was said to portend all kinds of woes and the end of the world."

"My God, how naïve he is, and how vulgar in everyday life!" Sasha thought with annoyance. She met Ivan Ilych's eyes inadvertently, and with her calm, proud step, raising her head slightly, she swept right past him and vanished.

Ivan Ilych was about to leave, but Petr Afanasevich tried to detain him, inviting him to have some tea, and promising to treat him to some amazing melon. Ivan Ilych, who was in the habit of looking at his watch constantly, took it out, and announced:

"It's late," but he did stay.

Everyone gathered again on the terrace for tea, and Sasha, looking pale, wrapped in a white cape over her white dress, poured the tea in silence. Some sort of conflict was transpiring within her; the episode with Kate annoyed her, as well as the fact that there would be no music today, whereas she really wanted to hear some.

"Would you like me to play for you?" Ivan Ilych asked her suddenly. Sasha shuddered, as if fearing something terrible approaching her.

"Very much," she replied quickly.

Ivan Ilych went into the hall and began playing some Beethoven variations.[28] Suddenly everything in Sasha calmed down again and she felt pleased. The 18th variation seemed particularly fine to her—gentle, soft, and so expressive. The graceful variations ended; Ivan Ilych thought for a moment and then played an octave in the key of E-flat with a strong hand.

It was the opening of Chopin's polonaise in A Major.[29]

"Ah!" Sasha cried and fell silent. Once again some invisible gate opened, and the noble, majestic sounds, rending and thrilling Sasha's soul, overwhelmed her, giving her no chance to come to her senses, with all its splendid, secret musical ideas, which Ivan Ilych, understanding the composer so well, was able to communicate brilliantly to his audience. But the only real audience was Sasha: she unlocked her soul entirely to receive artistic impressions. She grasped and devoured everything that these two geniuses could convey to her: the composer and the performer. She had never experienced such bliss before in her entire life.

But in this perception of bliss so rarely encountered, there was something even criminal; the bond between listener and performer was so strong that

28. Beethoven wrote a total of twenty-one sets of variations, ranging from short and relatively simple sets, to massive and demanding compositions.

29. This polonaise, opus 40, no. 1, was composed by Frédéric Chopin in 1838. It opens with a strong A major chord.

she was no longer able to break it; it would last a long time, forever, no matter what happened to Sasha after this evening and no matter how her life developed. At that moment Ivan Ilych had conquered her completely; this domination of her soul was stronger, more significant than any over her body. Sasha felt terrified. She looked at Ivan Ilych submissively, passionately, and he, after finishing the polonaise and glancing up at her, suddenly understood his victory and power over this subjugated young woman.

"My God!" Sasha uttered softly. "What is this? Thank you," she said, "What a marvelous polonaise."

"Yes, my friend, it is powerful," said Petr Afanasevich.

Ivan Ilych, almost reeling, stood up, looked at Sasha with his wandering eyes, glanced at his watch, and then bade her farewell.

"You're a good listener," he said with a smile. Taking hold of her hand again, he held it affectionately for a long time.

There was something tender and intimate in this delay: Sasha wanted to keep her hand in his for a long, long time, to stare into his kind eyes, now completely lacking in fire.

"Farewell," he said, and the gate closed once again, that is, the treasury of artistic riches into which Sasha had just been able to peer.

"No, not farewell," thought Sasha, "only goodbye, until tomorrow." Everything in Sasha felt overjoyed, and everything was singing: the triumphant sounds of the polonaise, the complicated combinations of the voices in the prelude, Beethoven's variations, and Mendelssohn's *Song Without Words*.

That's how Sasha fell asleep, amid these sounds overpowering her completely. She dreamt of Ivan Ilych and in her dream felt his closeness, his warm breath. She saw his inspired face as it was transformed during his playing from apathetic serenity to something powerful, strong, and stirring.

II

"May I come in for a minute?" asked Kurlinsky, approaching the terrace where Sasha was sitting reading a biography of Beethoven lent her by Ivan Ilych.

"You may," Sasha agreed reluctantly. "Come in."

"I've come to thank you for yesterday—for the enjoyment your neighbor provided us."

"Then you must thank him; I had nothing to do with it."

"I've already been to see him, and read him my poem."

"Is it something decadent again?"[30]

"That's how you choose to characterize the new trend in poetry. You're very sensitive to all things, Aleksandra Alekseevna, but in this matter I see you have preconceived ideas and prejudiced opinions."

"Not at all. I don't like anything preconceived. It's just that I'm so stupid that I don't understand and can't appreciate the poetry of Balmont or Baudelaire, or the music of Wagner."[31]

"May I read you my verse?"

"All right, I'll listen out of my friendship for you."

Kurlinsky took from his pocket a rather large notebook and began to read a series of meaningless poems in a funereal voice. He read the last one, which was about her; he glanced at Sasha with loving eyes, but then immediately grew frightened and dropped his eyes. Ivan Ilych was standing on the balcony steps, listening to the last verses.

"Splendid," he said, with slight irony as always. "I'll compose the music for you, and your sister can sing it. Fetch me some music paper from my house."

Kurlinsky left, while Ivan Ilych asked Sasha whether he was bothering her.

"Oh, no; there's nothing I have to do. I just finished with some countrywomen who constantly come for medicines. It's terribly difficult to play doctor to the common people."

"I think, on the other hand, it's enjoyable."

"No, not always. I know that it's absolutely a good thing to clean a wound and rewrap it, but one's ineffectualness in those cases when you don't understand the illness and can't help—that weakness and doubt—all that's terribly painful."

"How enthusiastically you relate to everything. You should be more serene."

"Thank you for your advice. I will learn from you."

"Yes, I don't like to worry."

"But are you really at peace when you're playing or composing?"

"Completely."

"*How* do you compose?"

Ivan Ilych became thoughtful.

30. The literary movement called decadent was characterized by refined aestheticism, artifice, and the quest for new sensations.

31. Konstantin Dmitrievich Balmont (1867–1942) was a symbolist poet, translator, and a major figure in the Silver Age of Russian poetry. Charles Baudelaire (1821–67) was a French poet who also produced notable work as an essayist, art critic, and translator.

"It's hard to say. In small sections; I cogitate and then one idea emerges unnoticeably from another and blends with it. One must study a great deal and become musically educated in order to compose; it's no use waiting for inspiration."

"Yes, but this education of yours has eliminated melody. In new music all attention is focused on harmony. It would be good to have some lucid expression of simple feelings in the melody."

"No, it's not. It's boring!"

"Isn't it even more boring that romanticism has completely vanished from life and from music? Everything's become so rational."

"No, everything's become more spiritual, and that's better. Of course, the musical philosophy of untalented composers is uninteresting, but the spirituality of talented composers is demonstrated; therefore the musical impact of such new works is perceived not by the nerves but by the spiritual, rational side of the human soul."

"So that's how you explain new music. That's good. Well, play something spiritual for me . . ."

"It's too warm; maybe later. I'll think about it and select something appropriate."

Kurlinsky returned with the music paper, but Ivan Ilych didn't sit down to write; instead the three of them decided to go for a stroll and have a look at the hay gathering. They took along little Alyosha; Sasha put on her large straw hat and everyone set off down to the river where a whole colorful crowd of countrywomen was raking hay on a large green meadow. The wonderful smell of dry green grass wafted up to meet the strollers. Little Alyosha went charging into a mound of hay and began burrowing in it with merry laughter.

"But there are clouds gathering and the hay will turn black if it rains again," said Sasha.

"But this hay isn't yours, is it?" asked Ivan Ilych in surprise.

"So what? Does it matter? It's not important whether it's mine or yours: the fact itself is of interest. In the country my husband's always angry that there's so much stealing: the common people's attitude to everything is predatory. While I, for example, feel sorry for the apple tree's loss of beauty when the peasant children break its branches stealing apples; I feel sorry when the peasants' cows are on the loose and trample a wonderful thick field of rye; I feel sorry when they cut down an old oak or birch tree, or cut down young spruce to plant a crop, but not because we're poorer for it—let whoever needs it more take it. It's simply that I don't like any sort of destruction."

Ivan Ilych looked closely at Sasha again and blinked his eyes. "She's definitely not like other people," he thought. "But, what does that matter to me?" he continued his thought anxiously; suddenly, feeling happy about something, he added ironically:

"That means, that if I fell over now and broke my hand or even died, you'd feel sorry that I couldn't play Beethoven's sonata or Chopin's polonaise, but not sorry for me as a person, because you only love the 'fact.'"

Sasha was puzzled for a moment and sank into thought.

"I think you're right: I'd feel more regret for you as a musician than for you as a person, not because you've afforded *me* so much pleasure by your music, but because in general, something good and talented would disappear and be lost for no reason."

"In other words, you wouldn't feel sorry for anyone as a person?"

"I think only for Alyosha."

"That is, yourself," Ivan Ilych said sarcastically.

Sasha didn't say anything more and went up to the countrywomen who were working; she was thinking that if she came to love the person of Ivan Ilych, she would lose her pure attitude toward his art and would consider that a shame.

"How's your little Mishka?" Sasha asked the young woman with clear blue eyes who was taking a red kerchief from her sweaty forehead, revealing strands of blond hair on her temples.

"Thank heaven, with your drops he felt better very quickly. Thank you, dear lady."

"Well, well, I'm very glad. Give me a rake," Sasha moved together with the countrywomen, nimbly, skillfully raking the hay. How many times in her childhood had she worked in her mother's village with the women and the young girls she knew during the periods of happy summer mowing. Sasha suddenly recalled her childhood, her mother, and the loss of everything she loved so dearly: she tossed away the rake, took Alyosha by the hand, and walked quickly away from the other women.

"Shall we rest here? Would you like to?" she asked, turning to her companions, barely able to restrain her tears.

"Are you going home, Aleksandra Alekseevna? What's the matter?" Kurlinsky asked with sentimental tenderness.

"It's nothing. I was remembering the past in the village where I spent my childhood. Give me your arm, Ivan Ilych," said Sasha, for some unconscious reason seeking support from the arm that so powerfully allayed the grief in her soul and reconciled her to life.

Ivan Ilych took Sasha's arm under his own; his eyes stared vaguely into the distance, and he blushed. He was surprised at the decisiveness and simplicity with which Sasha had requested his arm.

Climbing the hill, Sasha suddenly felt calmer; after choosing a nice spot in the shade, she invited everyone to sit down. It was very hot; Alyosha picked and ate berries; after pulling a large clump of hay from the nearest pile, and putting it down under his head as a pillow, Ivan Ilych sprawled languidly on the grass, but with obvious physical pleasure.

Kurlinsky began declaiming some lines of Tyutchev:[32]

If God does not bless it,
No matter how the soul suffers while it loves,
Alas, it will not attain happiness,
Though by suffering it may attain itself.

Invisible in the distance the high-pitched sound of grasshoppers chirping was coming from all sides while insects were swarming in the direct rays of the sun.

"How lovely! What force of summer, at its height!" said Sasha.

"Mama, look at the circles made by the fish. Let's come back here to go fishing sometime," said Alyosha, staring at the cove of the river.

"Yes, all right," said Sasha distractedly. At that moment she was recalling and pondering her conversation with Ivan Ilych. The tormenting thought occurred to her that if human influence interfered even, for example, in the form of love, everything in life could fritter away her chaste purity. If you fall in love with a person, and he's not with you, will you love nature and rejoice in it as much? No, you won't; everything will be diminished, all beauty and joy will vanish if the beloved person is not with you in the midst of this splendid nature. And the purity of your relationship to nature will disappear.

What if you absolutely love music, and you come to love someone who doesn't share that love at all? No, then you won't hear it in the same way as you will with him and from him.

If you go alone to look at paintings, and you haven't seen your beloved for a long time, you see and understand everything with him with such great pleasure! But when this is absent from your life, when you're completely free

---

32. Fyodor Ivanovich Tyutchev (1803–73) is generally considered the last of three great Romantic poets of Russia, following Pushkin and Lermontov. This is the first stanza of a lyric poem written in 1865.

of human love, then nature, music, painting, and family afford such pure, chaste, complete enjoyment . . .

"Oh, God, save me from this poison on the path of my life!" Sasha prayed silently. "Preserve my purity and help me to love You in nature and in art, and in everything that comes from Your sacred font." Getting up from the ground, a thoughtful and serene Sasha walked home quietly, and there bade farewell to her friends.

PART II

I

Summer Is Passing

Sasha spent the whole summer as if in a dream. Time for her was divided into periods when Ivan Ilych was playing and the times until he would be playing again. In the intervals she tried anxiously to distract herself, to work, to forget; she became nervous, feverishly thinking up and then doing things that sometimes seemed unnecessary, but which forced her not to notice the hours. Strange to say, it was only in his presence, even when Ivan Ilych was not playing, that serenity settled on her and something rejoiced in her and calmed her inner life.

Often the whole company would go for long walks together: Sasha and Petr Afanasevich, Kurlinsky with his cousin Kate, Ivan Ilych, and little Alyosha— everyone would almost always take part; often Tsvetkov would join them.

Sometimes they would take lunch along; they would set off around noon for a neighboring village or nearby grove, and would spend the entire day in the woods, gathering mushrooms, discovering lovely new spots, and relaxing; they would return home in the evening, happy, cheerful, and ready to listen to Ivan Ilych's marvelous music.

Tsvetkov, who was in love with Kate, brought much joviality and his youthful joy of living. Petr Afanasevich, who loved nature, was in a state of bliss when he could tear himself away from Moscow and spend time at the dacha. He was the purveyor of refreshments on all their outings and excursions; he treated everyone generously, arranged places where the women could sit, brought along extra clothes and baskets of provisions, and even carried little Alyosha when he got tired; he took care of everything, lifting the ladies across ditches and ravines, and, upon their return home, sometimes hauling baskets loaded with mushrooms, he sorted them all himself. He would lovingly trim the thick stems from their firm little caps, then with Parasha he would salt or marinate them, and storing the jars all over the house, showing them to everyone, and giving them as gifts to all his friends and acquaintances.

The relations that developed between Sasha and Ivan Ilych were such that they left her with nothing but the most poetic and serious memories. Completely unnoticed, the two of them began to experience everything in the world together. Every strong impression of nature affected them similarly. Ivan Ilych finally came to believe in Sasha's genuine love of music and her sensitivity to it; he would play excerpts from his compositions for her.

"How do you compose?" Sasha posed the question to him again and again. "I've always been interested by the musical process of creation. I can understand verbal art more easily, but not musical art."

"Well, it's hard to say, Aleksandra Alekseevna. Each musical idea arises imperceptibly: a melody appears . . . you make a little effort to catch it, retain it in your memory, and . . ."

"Well, and then . . ."

"Then it's impossible to get rid of it; it becomes obsessive, and everything else is arranged around it; then come harmonic notions, and the further you go, the easier it all becomes . . ."

"But from where, for example, does the dramatic quality of the musical phrase arise, such as the one you played for me yesterday?"

Ivan Ilych smiled and did not answer right away.

"I read a story and was struck by the heroism of the Scythians who were obliged to perish rather than surrender. I felt heroically inclined and wrote this excerpt . . ."

"So you're inspired by something?"

"Sometimes."

"Looking at you, it always seems to me that you fabricate everything in your own mind. I want to provide you with stimulation, inspiration . . ."

"There's no need, Aleksandra Alekseevna. Serenity is better in all things."

"But it seems that in your everyday life everything appears to be so peaceful, but not in your music; in it you're someone else. You have an entirely different place for it. Everything in your music is so full of meaning—passion, in fact, at times."

Ivan Ilych suddenly became serious and fell silent.

They were approaching the house; turning to Ivan Ilych, Sasha asked:

"Are you coming in?"

"Of course. I wanted to play you the beginning of my symphony."

"Ah, what a delight!"

"Really?"

Sasha made no reply. The principal pleasure came in this constant exchange of ideas, in this interchange on purely abstract terms.

Summer wore on; the evenings grew longer and rainy days arrived. The intimate circle of people who had drawn close during the course of the season gathered in the evenings at Sasha's dacha for reading, chess, music, and intimate conversation about art, often introduced by Sasha.

Petr Afanasevich, who was deaf to all this, was delighted that Sashenka had cheered up and recovered. He revered Ivan Ilych for being able to console her with his music. After a few more days of summer heat, which the dacha residents took full and feverish advantage of, strolling and swimming, a spell of cold, nasty weather arrived.

Ivan Ilych began to prepare to leave for the Crimea, and Aleksei Tikhonych began packing. Carts arrived for the piano and his belongings, but for some reason he delayed his departure and continued on at the dacha without his things, dining every day with his neighbors at Petr Afanasevich's insistent request.

Sasha grew restless once more, nervous, and so miserable that she was unable to continue her everyday life.

2

A Gray Day

There are days in August when, after a spell of intense heat, you wake up in the morning and the sky is gray, a strong wind is blowing, and it's chilly and gloomy. You raise the blinds; you're surprised, and retreat to your still warm bed. You lie there, get warm, and daydream. What's this? The end of summer? Really? So soon! You close your eyes again, while thoughts and memories flood into your mind. Yesterday was such a clear, bright, hot day; in the evening, at twilight, you floated gently down the river, coolly dipping your hands into the soft, warm water, caressing all being. Where is all that? It's so far away. It was so long ago—and so very nice!

Your soul is adjusting to autumn; you begin thinking about how to spend the day; you try to go on as if it were still summer. But you lack the energy, the energy that only the sun can provide, when just yesterday morning you jumped out of bed and said with pleasure, "What heat!" You raced through the garden to the river. What vitality there was in everything. How splendidly the dew shone on every blade of grass and every leaf, glistening in the morning sun!

You don't really want this cold; you want that languor again, that heat, that torpor in which everyone spent those days and which you now sincerely regret losing.

But you have to get up. You have to adjust to the new situation, to a different mood; once again, although in a different way, you have to live life. How often as a result of the slightest change in one's surroundings there comes to mind the simple truth that you have to go on living. It's as if you make a discovery and take pride in this clarification of your thought: *you have to go on living.* Were you really not living just before you asked yourself this question? How does one capture what life really is and what futility is, mere vegetation, for the time being killing time . . .

The philosopher Seneca exclaims in his book with desperation: *"Hélas, la plus grande partie de notre vie n'est pas vie, mais durée . . ."*[33]

Ivan Ilych thought and experienced all this, having awakened on the morning of August 7 in his little yellow dacha. Aleksei Tikhonych brought his clothes and boots into the room and began complaining about the cold.

"These walls are thin as paper; our dacha can't be heated. You could die here from the cold. It's time to return to Moscow."

"No, it's still very early, Tikhonych. Light that large lamp and take it to your room."

"What? If I light the kerosene lamp, it costs us money. We have to leave. We're also paying for rooms in town."

Ivan Ilych always felt very restless when Tikhonych was dissatisfied with something. He hastened to get up, dress, and go out onto the balcony. With his usual meticulousness about his routine, he went off to take his summer walk. Beyond the garden, he stopped on the pasture and began peering into the distance at the nearest surroundings. It was cold and damp; the swallows were swooping low to the ground, flying past Ivan Ilych in such a way that he thought they might graze him. Huddling against the cold, and turning his face away from the piercing north wind, Ivan Ilych followed their swift flight. He did not feel like moving at all. Where to? What for? To do what? It was annoying . . . he lacked the energy for work that he had felt yesterday as well as yesterday's enjoyment of life—now there was nothing, simply nothing, and he did not desire anything.

---

33. "Alas, the greater part of our life is not life, but the passing of time." This is an inexact French quotation from Seneca's *De Brevitate Vitae* (On the shortness of life), 2, lines 22–23: "'It is a small part of life we really live.' Indeed, all the rest is not life but merely time [*tempus*]."

Whoo! The wind was hooting, followed by some rumbling; Ivan Ilych noticed a carriage coming up behind him. "Who could that be? So early!"

The carriage drew even with him and he saw Sasha sitting in it, wrapped in her white Orenburg shawl.[34] There was a suitcase under the coachman's legs and a lap robe strapped beneath it. Parasha sat next to Sasha.

"Where are you going, Aleksandra Alekseevna?" Ivan Ilych asked in surprise.

"Stop, Fillip," Sasha said to the coachman. "I'm going off to prepare for communion at the Trinity Church," she replied.[35]

"You weren't planning this. Why did it occur to you? Have you sinned a great deal?" Ivan Ilych asked with his usual irony.

"Yes, I have sinned, and suddenly decided to prepare myself."

"And Petr Afanasevich?"

"He's at home with Alyosha."

"Will you be gone long? Perhaps you'll find convent life to your liking and decide to stay there?"

"I don't know. Anything can happen."

"Will you come back here?"

"Yes, of course."

"When do you leave for Moscow?"

"I don't really know. I must remain in nature longer. Well, goodbye."

"Goodbye, Aleksandra Alekseevna. Godspeed."

Sasha pulled off her glove and extended her hand to Ivan Ilych. Once again he inadvertently held her hand in his handsome, warm hand, and Sasha did not withdraw hers; she did not experience any agitation, but once more felt a soft, serene sense of joy and serenity.

Ivan Ilych stared after her departing carriage and was surprised that the sky became even darker, the north wind more piercing, and the swallows fussier. He wanted to return home, warm himself in his cozy corner, and allow his soul to repair to his beloved art.

After reaching his dacha, he went up to his piano and began improvising. Ominous chords, one after another, formed strange harmonic progressions. Something was tragic in their moans, and Ivan Ilych was carried away, surrendering to his musical feeling that invariably, always faithfully and significantly, imbued his entire life.

---

34. A finely knit lace shawl made from a blend of silk and goat fiber, originating in the Orenburg area in the eighteenth century.

35. Preparation for receiving communion consists of a period of prayer and fasting.

3

Sasha's train arrived toward evening, just as the bells at the monastery were announcing vespers. On the large square opposite the old guesthouse, a great commotion was ensuing: a large crowd of pilgrims and others had gathered around the stalls selling toys, icons, dishware, and dried herrings. Coachmen, bringing and fetching passengers to and from the trains to the Khotkovsky Convent, the Chernigov Hermitage, the Retreat, the Theological Academy, and other environs of the convent, circled the entrance to the guesthouse, ringing their bells and negotiating with people trying to hire them.

Sasha entered the guesthouse with Parasha and ordered tea.

"Parasha, while we're waiting, I'll go to the convent."

"You should rest, Aleksandra Alekseevna."

"I'm not tired at all."

Sasha went out onto the square and headed for the gates of the convent. Suddenly an accented female voice speaking very quickly began speaking right behind her next to her ear. Sasha shuddered and wanted to flee, but a gypsy woman, dark-skinned, with very expressive dark eyes, disheveled, ruddy and withered, demanded her attention so insistently that Sasha stopped.

"You love a fair-haired man, you really do love him. . . . If you like, I can cast a spell on him. . . . Give me ten kopecks, so help me God I'll bewitch him. I can give you the root of an herb; you wrap it up in your kerchief, strike him on the shoulder—he'll waste away out of love for you."

"No need, no need," Sasha said, trying to get away, but the gypsy woman would not be put off.

"Come see me. Everyone knows the gypsy, Mariya Ivanovna. The horse dealer, Nikita, is my husband. Come. We have our own house. I know all the spells. . . . Well, give me ten kopecks. . . . He'll love you, that's right! Now he doesn't dare."

"Leave me alone, let me be," cried Sasha in despair, and rushed to the convent gates. People were going into the church, and Sasha blended with the crowd, entered through the low vaults of the Church of Saint Sergius.[36] People lined up to touch the relics. Sasha stood behind an old woman and mechanically, without thinking, frightened and upset, threw herself down in front of the icon of the saint, praying for salvation.

From what was she being saved—she did not know and did not dare admit to herself.

36. A spiritual leader and monastic reformer of medieval Russia, Sergius became one of the most highly venerated saints in the Russian Church.

A priest was performing the vesper service and reading the acathistus to the saint.[37] The choir was chanting the long monastic service in unison. The monks were moving like shadows with their unhurried steps, lighting candles, swinging censers, collecting money, and chatting with the worshipers. Sasha was glad to be one amid the crowd. There was some security in this, some independence, for which she felt a need in her spiritual state.

The next day, early in the morning, Sasha went to church again; once more the singing, the crowd, and the reverent mood affected her. She stayed for the entire service; only when children began to receive communion and there arose a cry and commotion did Sasha observe the preparations in the refectory on the occasion of the holiday. The novices routinely and skillfully arranged dishes, mugs, large platters with bread, kvas, and pitchers on long tables.[38] One of the monks began to describe with pleasure the kind of fish, home-brewed beer, and kisel there would be today because it was a holiday.[39] Sasha found this reminder of material objects unpleasant.

Stopping by her room for a few moments to fortify herself with some food, Sasha returned to the church once again.

"Where do they hear confession?" she asked the women pilgrim-worshipers who were making the rounds of all the holy places, and were preparing to take communion.

"Over there, from Father Fyodor, in the new church. Come along with us, dear lady, we'll go confess together."

Sasha joined the women, and for a long time they walked through some stone passages and corridors, until they reached the doors of Father Fyodor's cell.

As soon as Sasha would stop, the pilgrims would call to her and minister to her with some special tenderness.

"Sit down, madam. Over here, it's nice."

Father Fyodor's cell was located above; his door opened onto a large stone square with a balcony, beneath which stood a lovely new church. Vespers were in progress.

People making confession were entering and leaving Father Fyodor's cell. In the middle of the first small room one of the confessants sat reading a holy book.

---

37. Any of several Lenten hymns sung in honor of Christ, the Virgin Mary, or one of the saints.

38. Kvas is a slightly fermented beverage made from black or regular rye bread.

39. Kisel is a fruit soup, popular as a dessert, consisting of sweetened juice, thickened with cornstarch or potato starch.

"Go on, you can enter now," said a pilgrim, pushing Sasha. She had just talked with a young monk, her godson, whom she had not seen since childhood, and to whom she delivered a small package with sweets from his family.

"I'll speak with him some more. Lord, how you've changed! Tell me, Stepasha, has it been hard for you?"

"At first it seemed very hard, but now it's nothing; I've grown used to it. The worst thing is reading psalms over the dead. I feel afraid."

Sasha quietly opened the door to Father Fyodor's cell and entered a small dark room lit only by a wax candle.

A totally white, ancient elder sat at a lectern and barely raised his tired eyes at Sasha when she entered.[40] His eyes no longer expressed anything. He was a living corpse. Exhaustion after a long life, struggle, and deprivation had all left their traces in the wrinkles of his face. But he sat completely still, indifferent, and stern.

"What's your name?" he asked and began to hear Sasha's confession with his monotonous, customary cadences. "Married? How have you sinned? Have you been unfaithful to your husband? Do you believe in God, observe the fasts, harbor any doubts? Well, God will forgive you."

Father Fyodor raised his stole above Sasha's head and absolved her sins. But did Sasha absolve herself?

After confession, now feeling exhausted, she sat down on a bench and waited for her new friends; then they returned together. A monk was reading from the monastic rules, but Sasha was so tired that she could not listen and started to doze, swaying back and forth.

When she returned to her room, she reckoned that she had spent a total of nine hours in church. After getting undressed, she threw herself down on her bed; without letting herself think or recall anything, she fell fast asleep on a bad bed with springs sticking up and with her head resting on a small, hard pillow.

4

Dried Flowers

The trip to the Trinity Church calmed Sasha completely, although it was only a temporary distraction from the inner, agitated state of her heart. Nevertheless, when she returned to the dacha, her first thought was—had Ivan Ilych left and would she ever hear his music again? Approaching the dacha,

40. An elder (or *starets*) of a Russian Orthodox monastery functions as a venerated adviser and teacher.

she saw that the shutters at the yellow house next door were closed and it was enveloped in its customary silence.

"He's gone!" Her heart sank. She did not even know where in Moscow he lived, where he had gone, whether he had ever come to see them. "Why should I even care? Now I'll have Alyosha and Petr Afanasevich, and will devote myself to my son, my home, and my music . . . music without Ivan Ilych, without any outside influence, entirely and exclusively to music."

Sasha entered her room and shuddered upon seeing some music and a note on the small table. Ivan Ilych had left it all there on the day of his departure. In it he bade farewell in cool, awkward expressions, and asked Sasha's permission to dedicate to her this romance that he had composed in her absence and was now sending.[41]

"Mamá, what did you bring me? Show me," cried Alyosha as he came running in. "Did you bring a little icon for nanny?" the lad persisted.

Sasha hugged her son, handed him toys and small icons, and called her husband, who came running from the garden with his sleeves rolled up and his hands dirty from digging in the earth.

"Well, well, Sashenka. It's good that you've come home. Alyosha and I have missed you."

"What were you doing?"

"I've been digging up dahlias; I want to clip the last flowering one."

"We need to move back to town soon."

"The summer's passed quickly, and we've had a good time. It's too bad we have to leave: there'll still be some fine days."

Sasha suddenly agreed with him and they decided to stay until September.

Day followed day, monotonous, boring, but serene. Sasha felt so well disposed that she did not undertake anything new, did not hurry anywhere, and was afraid to upset the order of her life that provided such complete satisfaction of fulfilled duty and a tranquil conscience.

For several days Sasha did not even peek at the romance sent her by Ivan Ilych. But once, feeling completely calm, she decided to look at it and even to sing it. In all of his compositions it was always hard to fathom his musical ideas the first time through. But the longer you played or sang them, the more the charms of his music came to the fore, and the more you would discover its depths and his genuine magnificent talent. But this romance was not like any

41. During the eighteenth and nineteenth centuries Russian composers adapted the French romance, a short instrumental piece in ballad style, as a sentimental Russian art song.

of his previous compositions. Right from the first phrases and words there was so much passion in it, so much graceful elegance that Sasha understood it at once and became terribly agitated. Had he really written this? Whose passionate words were these? Was it possible that this self-possessed man had composed something like this? Where did it come from and who was it for? The stormy accompaniment went along with a lovely, impassioned melody, transitioning into the tender sounds of a soul in love.

Sasha sang this passionate summons to love over and over; her heart pounded faster and faster. She jumped up and shouted to someone or other: "I don't need it!" At that moment she remembered the gypsy at the Trinity Church who had offered her a spell; rushing all around, she became so frightened of her own thoughts that she cried out, "Lord, save me!" Moving away from the piano, she sank helplessly into an armchair. Gradually she managed to calm down. On the table lay the large red album in which all summer Sasha had been pressing and pasting flowers, together with Alyosha to entertain him.

Yes, the whole story of the summer was contained in this book. Here were the lilies of the valley, yellow and wrinkled. How strong they had been, so firm and fragrant when she picked them, out strolling with her husband through the small birch forest. How tender and attentive he had been to her then, when she was still suffering from her recent grief, and how nice it had been to experience his simple, natural kindness.

Then the forget-me-nots blossomed. Here they were! How well they have kept their tender blue color, and how well preserved in her memory was the day she had picked them. It was hot, the sky was the same color as the flowers; she had gone for a swim, but her husband and Ivan Ilych were in the bathhouse; she had to wait for them to come out. She had walked along the river and picked these magnificent dark blue forget-me-nots. Ivan Ilych came out of the bathhouse and asked Sasha for the flowers. He admired them, kept some for himself, and handed the rest back to her; she had noticed the beauty of his hands and for some reason suddenly found it pleasant to bury her face completely in these fresh flowers.

Here were some shorter herbs. . . . She and he had been sitting at the edge of the forest when Sasha found them and picked them; they had talked about how good it was to live as they did, day by day, without a care, almost exclusively in nature, doing unhurried, free and easy work, under a scorching sun that comforted both body and soul. . . . That was when Alyosha had eaten too many berries and had spilled red juice all over his chest; then he started putting berries into his mother's mouth and into Ivan Ilych's as well. For some reason Sasha found this combination enjoyable. She recalled how she had thought about the enormous number of insects on the ground that were going about their own business.

Sasha turned the page. Here were all the pansies, big and small, like an array of faces. . . . Her husband had planted and then picked this diverse collection. She had glued them in a circle in the shape of a wreath; now all these big-eyed flowers seemed to be looking at her ironically, the way Ivan Ilych sometimes did, and she turned the page quickly.

Cornflowers . . . a few had lost their petals and turned white, while others were still bright blue. Sasha remembered the endless field of rye, glistening and agitated. The heavy stalks were all bent over; the rye had already ripened and there was a feeling of tension in this matured flowering of summer.

They had had guests; how boldly and cheerfully Sasha had strolled with them along the narrow path through the field. She had sensed Ivan Ilych's presence behind her; that day he had commented on her summer attire and she sensed his admiration. Then he fell behind and began picking cornflowers.

"Look, how lovely. They're so big and bright this year," he said, handing her a bouquet.

Sasha reached out her hand and accepted the flowers; her heart was pounding joyfully. That evening she had dried them and wrote the date underneath.

"Enough of this. . . . Yes, and here were the ferns. . . . Alyosha brought them to her, saying they looked like green feathers. And here on the last page were some late, large sterile flowers she had picked recently from the strawberry patch. The leaves were lovely; the flowers had little mustaches, but would not produce any fruit. . . . Why had the strawberry bloomed again so close to autumn, out of season, and with no chance of fruiting?

And why in her own soul had this futile and unnecessary feeling of love for music and its agent blossomed? Why did her heart ache so when the lively music in the yellow dacha fell silent and the house became empty, and when only this morning they had removed Ivan Ilych's last belongings and his piano?

Was it true that *everything* had ended? The summer, the flowers, the music, as well as Mendelssohn's *Song Without Words* and her insane, brief, carefree happiness, brought on by those miraculous musical sounds that had healed her, that song in G major that resounded in all of her being, and some kind of poison that had entered her heart; feeling weak and upset, Sasha hung her head over her book and burst into tears.

5
Last Days at the Dacha

Sasha spent another two weeks at the dacha with her son. Sometimes Petr Afanasevich came to visit, but his business at the Insurance Society demanded his presence. There was a commotion following an enormous fire that had undermined the resources of the society; an investigation was under way regarding possible arson. The usually unruffled Petr Afanasevich was beside himself; he shouted when telling Sasha all about the swindle. He became totally engrossed in the business of the department where he had spent several years and to which he had devoted all his energy. Sasha was not burdened by loneliness in the least. She read a great deal, copying out from books those thoughts she especially liked. Besides that, she continued to occupy herself intensively with music. She spent long hours sitting at the piano with the greatest enjoyment. She learned several pieces, including one of Ivan Ilych's recent compositions, about which she was ecstatic. It was an astonishing work combining pagan beauty with spiritual awareness of Divinity. The accompaniment to the theme was so airily light, trembling so imperceptibly in its pianissimo, that one could hear the vacillations of a soul in prayer in the presence of a Divinity. Then triumphant chords would suddenly sound, as if constituting the Divinity's answer to the soul in prayer; the chords grew more majestic, fuller, stronger, more momentous, lifting the soul higher and higher; it reached the ultimate limits of spiritual tension and suddenly ceased. Then in some airy realm, diminishing to piano, the sounds subsided into tender pianissimo, as if someone's soul was being carried off into eternity and was fading away into nonbeing.

The piece was difficult; Sasha spent hours learning it, but the enjoyment she experienced rewarded her efforts.

If it had not been so chilly and she was not afraid that Alyosha might catch cold in that badly heated dacha, Sasha would have prolonged her quiet life there even longer. She was thinking neither about Ivan Ilych nor about what awaited her that winter in Moscow; she was living in nature and in music, and was enjoying them both in a pure, elevated manner. Once again she felt herself so independent, free of all vile human feelings that she did not want to destroy her good mood for anything in the world.

But autumn arrived and it was early, stormy, and cold. Alyosha fell ill with a head cold; it was impossible to go out for walks; the lad had begun to feel bored and kept asking to return home to Moscow, to see his papa. Sasha felt that it was really time to move back, and she began preparing for the journey.

She wanted to revisit all her favorite places in this beloved locale where she had spent such a momentous and even happy summer. After gathering her music and her favorite cherished belongings, portraits, and important papers, she left the packing to Parasha and went out for a walk. The short autumn day changed its mood capriciously several times, just as in summer. In the morning it was damp; then it drizzled, and the sun finally made its appearance. Sasha emerged from the forest and stopped on the slope of the hills. To the right was a low planting of spruces in which some young birches had taken root here and there. With their small, pale yellow, dry leaves they were especially noticeable against the background of thick green fir trees and the steely, dark gray sky in which the full arc of a bright rainbow was boldly projected with all its might. On the left one could see the reddish-yellow glow of the setting sun, especially bright, and joyful, as if pitting its cheerful summery beauty against the gloom of the dark autumnal sky with the rainbow spread across it. The sun, as if reassuring all expiring nature, suddenly and generously lit up the tips of the pale yellow birches and bright spruces; only the stubborn, leaden sky refused to submit to its warm caress and remained disconsolate.

Sasha was simply astonished at all the beauty and majesty of nature. "I'm leaving you," she thought, addressing nature, "and I will perish amid human passions and temptations . . ."

She hastened her step, fearing the approach of darkness in the forest. It was quiet and one could hear the rustling leaves were dropping from the trees with such speed, as if someone was constantly whispering above them. They fell in bunches; Sasha's feet sank into these dry, brown leaves, crunching under her steps and swirling to both sides with the movement of her dress.

Here was the old oak tree and its gnarled root protruding onto the path. She had stepped on it almost every day, going to swim and meeting Ivan Ilych there almost daily. . . . Where is he now? She suddenly remembered him, and a tormenting desire to see him and hear him arose so suddenly in her heart that she almost ran the rest of the way home, right into her own room. There she feverishly packed her remaining things, ordered a carriage and a cart, and resolved to leave for Moscow early the next morning.

Before her departure, under the false pretense of having forgotten some music in the yellow dacha next door, Sasha asked the doorman to open it and, walking excitedly through the small empty rooms, she stopped in a corner of the hall in the place where the piano had stood and Ivan Ilych had played. Recalling his playing, Sasha said with despair, submitting to her own feelings: "You restored me to life, but you'll also destroy it!!"

6

She's Crushed

After moving back to Moscow, Sasha immediately purchased a subscription to the symphony and busied herself with her apparel. She loved to wear nice clothes, but preferred primarily black and white dresses in the most varied combinations. She was in a lighthearted, carefree mood; she made the rounds of shops and fixed up her house; she did not read much, rarely stayed at home, and feared the piano, as if it were an enemy.

She spent a month like that. She heard that Ivan Ilych was in the Crimea and would be returning in a few days. His absence alarmed Sasha even more. Her desire to see him reached such a painful state that when, on one of the last evenings in October, he unexpectedly called on her, she almost felt ill. He paused at the door of her bedroom that was partitioned into two parts and inquired timidly:

"May I come in, Aleksandra Alekseevna?"

"Yes, yes," Sasha replied, turning so pale that Ivan Ilych was surprised when he saw her.

"What's wrong, Aleksandra Alekseevna? Are you ill?"

"No, I'm perfectly fine; I'm simply exhausted; I've been running errands and rearranging the house. Do come in."

"I've come to tell you some sad news. Do you know that Kurlinsky has refused to enter military service?"

"Really? The poor fellow. Where is he?"

"He's in a military hospital while they determine whether he's mentally or physically ill. You could exert some influence on him. He's very devoted to you."

"Yes, I'll try to bring him to his senses. He's spent too much time of late reading various prohibited books and this is the result. I feel sorry for him. He'd be better off if he kept writing his bad but innocent poems. Have you seen him?"

"No, but I plan to."

"How have you spent your autumn?"

"Splendidly. The weather in the Crimea was magnificent. I took many walks and composed music while listening to the sound of the waves."

"How lucky! I, too, have lived well. I'm content with how I spent my autumn."

Ivan Ilych examined the things Sasha had scattered on the table, and for some reason found the senseless chaos of this woman's everyday life very endearing. Right next to some fine old lacework lay a copy of Taine's *Philoso-phy of Art* in French; in a little wooden box there were some small foreign playing cards for solitaire.[42] There was also a bill from the dressmaker, together with one of Alyosha's clumsy sketches, and some scattered colored pencils. Here was a handwritten copy of a musical romance, a little piece of white voile on a plush tea rose, and a small red notebook . . .

Sasha's entire life.

"May I have a look at your notebook?" asked Ivan Ilych, taking the small volume into his hands and leafing through its pages with his handsome, slen-der fingers.

"You may, but it's not very interesting."

"I'll see for myself."

Ivan Ilych began to read aloud with irony: "Collect a lorgnette from Shvabe's shop. . . . Tsarskoe Selo, Konyushennaya Street, no. 18. . . . Length 2½, width 1½. Shoes for Alyosha. Tchaikovsky's Fifth Symphony. . . . 'It is not the strength, but the duration of great sentiments that makes great men . . .'"[43]

"Who said that?"

"Nietzsche, I believe."

"It's clever."

"'*Sache envisager sans frémir cette heure, qui juge la vie; elle n'est pas la dernière pour l'âme, si elle l'est pour le corps.*' Sénèque.[44]

"Do you think about death, Aleksandra Alekseevna?"

"Often. And how lovely and always consoling is the promise of eternity . . ."

"Well, and what else is here? 'Make efforts on behalf of Sem. Iv. in the almshouse. Learn: Chopin's Etude No. 9, Allegro assai. Papers, envelopes, gum Arabic, a spool of pink silk thread,'" Ivan Ilych read in a patter. "My God, what variety; wait, here's something from Cicero: 'Make use of what you have, and always act in accordance with your strengths—that is the rule of wisdom.'

---

42. Hippolyte Taine (1828–93) was a French critic, historian, and positivist philosopher, who attempted to explain moral qualities and artistic excellence in purely descriptive, quasi-scientific terms.

43. Tsarskoe Selo is a town some fifteen miles south of Saint Petersburg where a residence of the imperial family was located. The quotation is from Friedrich Nietzsche, *Beyond Good and Evil* (1886), chapter 4.

44. "Be able to look without fear at the hour when all life is judged; it is the final hour of the body, but not of the soul," a quotation from Seneca.

"It's good that you made a note of this, Aleksandra Alekseevna. You constantly do things beyond your strength, you're always upset, and you waste too much energy."

"That's why I constantly teach myself wisdom. I recently read somewhere that spiritual anxiety is a source of vital energy and that it's necessary to maintain the vigor of body and spirit."

Ivan Ilych put the notebook down; his hand brushed against a ball of wool and accidentally knocked it off. The ball rolled behind the partition and underneath the bed; try as she might to pull on the long red strand, Sasha was unable to retrieve it.

"Alyosha, come here, Alyosha."

"Don't worry, Aleksandra Alekseevna. I'll get it."

"No, why?" Sasha said, embarrassed that Ivan Ilych would see her bed on the other side of the partition.

But Ivan Ilych did not grasp that; he bent down clumsily, pulled out the ball of red wool, and suddenly, also feeling embarrassed, noticed something covered with lace—it was Sasha's white bed; there was her washbasin and her elegant toilette—everything so lovely, pure, and appealing. It had been a very long time, back in his distant youth, when the bachelor Ivan Ilych had last beheld a purely feminine setting, this *Ewig weibliche*, so attractive in the tender, mysterious elegance of its intimate female life.[45] He winced: his face became stern and something altered in his mood.

Embarrassed, Sasha stood up, took the ball of wool, thanked Ivan Ilych, and invited him to have tea in the dining room. Passing through the living room where their piano stood, Sasha paused and asked timidly:

"Would you play something?"

"I haven't played for a while; I really can't play anything," Ivan Ilych replied curtly.

"Well, well, just play a little something," Sasha said softly, her innocent, earnest eyes shining; she blushed, clasped her hands feverishly, brought them to her chest as if she wanted to hold something inside; then she sat down in a corner of the hall.

Ivan Ilych went over to the piano, struck several sonorous, resonant chords: all of a sudden Sasha felt that she was lost. The *Song Without Words* in G Major, which she had not heard since that evening back in May, resounded under Ivan Ilych's fingers; it sang out even more expressively and tenderly than ever

---

45. The German phrase meaning "eternal feminine" is from the final line of Goethe's *Faust, Part I* (1808–32): "The eternally feminine draws us on."

before. Sasha clasped her hands even tighter and sobbed inwardly. She suddenly realized that those sounds, which had first afforded her such serenity and joy, now occasioned only fear and painful, distressing anxiety. They beckoned her to the one who had already taken possession of her—art had emerged from abstraction and had moved into the realm of earthly feeling. It had lost its purity and its chastity.

It's all over! All her efforts to remain calm, to separate music from human passion—everything was demolished that evening. From now on Sasha's entire inner life would have to assume an entirely different form.

Ivan Ilych also played some variations from a sonata by Mozart; then Petr Afanasevich came in and the three of them had evening tea together. But it was as if Sasha were absent during the last part of that evening: she did not speak and turned serious, even somber.

Ivan Ilych returned home on foot; he felt a bit dislodged from his normal routine. But for him the entire evening with Sasha, during which he had felt a bit softened, was merely a brief episode that had no real impact on his work or the regularity of his everyday habits—whereas for Sasha, an entirely new era had begun.

7
She's Surrendered

When Ivan Ilych left, Sasha did not see him out as she usually did. Pressing one knee against the sofa where he had just been sitting, directing her dry, grave eyes at the wall, she remained motionless for a long time. The severe expression on her face was terrible. It was as if she was considering something important and consequential without a struggle, without hesitation. Everything that had recently seemed so distant to her, so impossible, so sinful and terrible—all this was now immediately clarified as something indubitable, completed, and irrevocably present. This man who appeared to be serene and indifferent, who related so ironically to her and her outbursts, this musical genius, this strange and alien Ivan Ilych, had suddenly turned out to be so dear to her, so necessary—no, more than that . . . he constituted the very center of her life; he alone occupied her entire world; he alone meant *everything* to her.

"And what about music? After all, I grew attached to him because he provided consolation, sublime artistic delight, because he summoned me back to life; through him I came to understand so many brilliant musical ideas of both living and dead composers that I became filled with that art than which there is nothing higher in the world.

"Could it really be that this Ivan Ilych, this tranquil Ivan Ilych who loves to eat grapes and dates, who blinks his eyes and keeps consulting his watch—could it really be that he's come to occupy a larger place than music?"

And now like an ancient vestal virgin who fell in love with a mortal and lost her life, Sasha, too, having fallen in love with the man Ivan Ilych, was losing her *real* life, her purity, her chaste relationship to art.

She was not a woman capable of compromises, obfuscation, or self-justification. Sasha clearly, simply, though painfully, surrendered and laid down her arms. She knew that from that day forward any struggle was completely useless, unnecessary, and she did not even want to try. Let her love be ridiculous, illicit, sinful, let the whole world point at her, laugh at her, and condemn her, let her husband weep—all this would be so insignificant to her, so much less tormenting than the aimless passion devouring and destroying her.

Her feeling of love for Ivan Ilych grew larger, and in accordance with the usual nature of passion, it consumed her completely. When did this happen? In real love it's never possible to trace the exact moment when it begins. Two people see each other today, they meet happily tomorrow, and a week later each feels bored without the beloved; a month later they spend a wonderful evening together and chat so warmly. . . . And in three or more months—there's no longer any life or happiness without the other person . . .

If Sasha had tried to track her feeling strictly, she would recall that like poison, it had first entered her heart that evening when the sounds of Mendelssohn's *Song Without Words* in G Major rang out from the yellow dacha amid the quiet May night.

But that was not yet love for Ivan Ilych. That was a summons to love by means of music. And Sasha had fallen in love with music in answer to that summons. She did not know, still did not see the person who had summoned her back to life. It was only much later, when she had gotten to know the talented musician better that she fell in love with him as a man. Fine, genuine, strong love is always conceived as an abstraction and only later moves into the realm of passion.

So, was she guilty in all this? Was it not fate with its inevitable destiny that blindly and by degrees led her to what at this moment she so sternly admitted to herself?

In the next instant her awareness that she was lost reduced her to wild despair. She rushed to get dressed, put on a warm blouse, and as if with someone else's will, raced to the door and wanted to run after Ivan Ilych.

Nanny called after her, saying that Alyosha had a fever.

"Alyosha? What?"

At first she did not understand, but when she did, she was horrified; she took off her coat and ran into the nursery. With repentance she placed her lips to the sleeping boy's forehead, and sat down quietly next to her son's bed. "This is in retribution for my sin," Sasha thought.

She sat up all night with her son. Petr Afanasevich crept cautiously into the nursery several times in a bathrobe and slippers, and begged Sasha to lie down and rest, but she found it unpleasant to enter the bedroom, as if, once having felt illicit love, she had already deceived her husband.

Toward morning Alyosha's fever broke and Sasha calmed down. But she still had not gone to bed. Her son's brief illness was for her something like a temporary distraction from the painful spiritual sufferings she had experienced after acknowledging to herself her love for Ivan Ilych.

When Alyosha woke up the next morning feeling better and more cheerful, and his illness turned out to be due to temporary gastric obstruction, Sasha's heart turned once again with terrible force to her insane love. She could not sit at home and could not do anything; after feeding Alyosha some bouillon with an egg, she began to get dressed, without knowing where to go. But she was interrupted once more. Someone called in and informed her that a lady visitor wished to see her for a few moments.

"Ask her in," Sasha said reluctantly. "But it's so early!"

A middle-aged woman came in wearing an old-fashioned dress; she was timid, serene, and melancholy.

"A petitioner," thought Sasha. But recognizing Nastasya Nikitichna right away, she rushed to kiss her.

"Sashenka, my dear, hello," the woman said. "You may have heard that my son refused to enter military service and that he's been sent to a hospital. You probably know the result of similar acts. Sasha, you must help me rescue him!" Her voice broke. "He loves you and will listen to you."

"I'd be very glad to help, my dear. . . . I feel so sorry for him. . . . But how do we save him?"

"Just go and see him; they'll let you in. Persuade him."

"Have you come here for long?"

"I don't know; I can't leave, but it's both expensive and dreary to live in furnished rented rooms."

"Well, well, never mind. You'll move in here. I'll go to see him today, but I don't know whether it will help!"

"You think when your children grow up your worries are over, but it turns out that when your children are little, they keep you awake, and then when they're bigger, you can never fall asleep . . ."

Nastasya Nikitichna burst into tears.

"Now, now, my dear, don't cry. God grant that we can bring him to his senses, my dear. Stop your crying."

Sasha embraced and soothed Nastasya Nikitichna; after she had managed to do that, she heard the whole story of the Kurlinsky family, just like all family histories—both touching and interesting. After serving her coffee, Sasha left with her. Nastasya Nikitichna hired a cab and returned to her furnished rooms, while Sasha proceeded on foot to calm her nerves that were agitated in every way possible.

8

On the Street

It was a clear day and a little frosty; light snow that had fallen during the night had powdered the streets and roofs here and there and shone in a thicker coat of white in the gardens and on the boulevards of Moscow. The horse-drawn tram proceeded, squeaking along cold rails and ringing its bell at intersections. Sasha jumped onto a tramcar as it moved past; standing on the platform, she rode it to the end of the line. Then she got off and waited for the return tram. The thought "I seem to be losing my mind" flashed through her head. A tram approached: Sasha got on and sat down. At the next stop a woman with a child whose eye was bandaged jumped on the tram hurriedly; she began looking for a place to sit. Sasha gave up her seat, feeling sorry for the sick child; standing on the platform once again, she began observing the passengers, trying to sort them by social class and character. The good ones and bad ones were especially noticeable when the conductor asked to see their tickets. Some intentionally crumpled them and thrust them at the conductor in annoyance. Others diligently straightened them and held them calmly in their hands, waiting until they were asked for. A third group, having misplaced their tickets, fussed and searched all their pockets and gloves looking for them. Sasha stood there, handed her ticket over, and a young man, cheerfully addressing her, offered her his seat.

"Tsvetkov, darling, is that you?" Sasha recognized Ivan Ilych's student, and suddenly the entire summer came flooding back into her memory and she became very agitated. "Where are you going?"

"To the conservatory. And you, Aleksandra Alekseevna? Why are you on the tram? You have your own horses."

"Sometimes I like to take the tram."

"Where to?"

"To see Kurlinsky; he's in the military hospital. Did you hear that he's refused to enter military service?"

"Yes, I heard. Quite an eccentric! But this isn't the right way. It's in the other direction."

Sasha was embarrassed and said:

"Ah, I'm so absentminded." Bidding goodbye to Tsvetkov, she jumped off the tram and started walking toward the house where Ivan Ilych lived. Her heart was torn with a desire to see him. Before she even reached the lane where he lived, she stopped in front of the gates of some house. A water carrier was blocking her way, making enormous efforts to move a large barrel into the courtyard. A small rise in the pavement leading to the gate was hindering him, and the barrel kept rolling backward.

With her strong, robust hands, Sasha leaned against the barrel and helped the water carrier.

"Come on, we'll push together," she said in her affectionate, bold voice.

The barrel promptly rolled into the courtyard; the astonished water carrier, the smiling passersby, and the doorman—all looked with curiosity at this well-dressed young woman calmly rearranging the dark golden curls of her hair that had escaped from under her hat, and who was flashing the usual smile that lit up her entire face, brightening the affectionate, welcoming sparkle of her large, innocent dark eyes.

"Is it really possible not to love me?" her eyes asked. "I so love you and everyone else . . ."

Everyone felt this, and everyone was ready to love Sasha.

"What are you doing?" said a familiar voice, at the sound of which Sasha's heart immediately skipped a beat.

"You saw it?"

"I did. Do you want to become a water carrier?" asked Ivan Ilych ironically. "You won't be able to play music: you'll harm and ruin your hands."

Sasha was silent, still trying to catch her breath from her recent exertion and agitation.

"Let's go," she said softly. "You must think I'm insane."

"I think that your character is full of contradictions and contrasts: you're like a Rembrandt painting—with much shadow and much light."

"And moving a water barrel—is that light or shadow?" Sasha said, smiling cunningly and matching Ivan Ilych's tone of voice.

"Light."

"And what's shadow?"

"The shadows are unsteadiness, thoughtlessness, illogical and swift conclusions, an inability to concentrate . . ."

"You don't say! There are so many shadows; I must ask you to illuminate me."

"I don't know how, Aleksandra Alekseevna; and I don't have time.
I'm lazy."

Sasha blushed. Ivan Ilych glanced at her and, turning away quickly,
blinked his eyes and speeded up his pace. His anxiety embarrassed him, as
did his desire to wound Sasha somehow and, at the same time, the pity, almost
tenderness that he felt for her, once he had wounded her.

"Where are we going?" Sasha asked suddenly, frightened by her own
mood.

"I'm going to find out about our quartet, when my musician friends will be
playing it. Where are you going? I'm afraid I don't know, and it seems that
you don't either."

"No, I do know. I'm going to the military hospital to see Kurlinsky and I
shall take a cab right now . . ."

At that moment a pregnant woman who was walking along the sidewalk,
and who with difficulty had picked up a rather big girl, was trying to carry her
across the busy street along which carriages, horse-drawn trams, and cabs
were constantly passing by. The girl was behaving capriciously, kicking her
mother in the stomach. Without hesitating even for a moment, Sasha took
the child in her arms and said:

"Now, now, little one, don't cry. Mama will catch up with us . . ." She carried the girl to the other side of the street easily, powerfully, and quickly. The
child, intrigued by this game of catch-up, with her mother chasing after
Sasha, who had run away with her, fell silent immediately; looking around
at Sasha, she started laughing.

"Now you've become a nanny," Ivan Ilych cried after her. But Sasha did
not return to him; handing the child over to her mother, she got in a cab and
headed for the hospital.

Ivan Ilych unconsciously darted after her, but stopped at once. His face
assumed a dissatisfied expression. He was annoyed at himself and at Sasha;
this disappearance of hers was not the first time he had felt a desire to rush after
her, not to be parted from her, to look into her innocent, earnest eyes, always
unexpectedly fiery or dark with passion, or with affectionate welcome and
childlike merriment.

"What spontaneity," Ivan Ilych thought, feeling moved as he thought
about Sasha. "And what energy, lucidity, and simplicity!"

9
The Military Hospital

Sasha's driver turned out to be a poor one; he drove slowly, but he loved to talk. He told her how his brother, who lived in the country, had separated from the peasant commune and married a young woman from another village. This woman was so awful that she had driven away the rest of the family.

"She's a witch, not a woman. . . . So now I have to drive the cab here all winter, but come spring, I'll go home to plow. Now that we've rented some land from a lady landowner, things have become better; last summer there was a time when we had to buy our wheat."

"Where are you from?"

"I'm from Kaluga.[46] Last summer we had such a terrible famine that we had to feed the cow all the straw from the roof; by summer she was barely alive. We tried to get her to stand up by pulling her up with a rope, but she couldn't. Come on, get moving," he shouted to his horse and shook the reins.

Sasha listened to the driver and was moved by this peasant who spent long winters in town all alone, remote from the thoughts and emotions of Moscow, and whose interests revolved around family, country, and that earnest, meaningful, simple life which, in spite of its severity and deprivation, still attracted him.

But now she saw a red building, gates, and a guard. This was the military hospital. Sasha felt a bit anxious: she was still young enough to fear sick, insane, and incarcerated people; besides, she was very much on edge after a sleepless night and all the agitation she had experienced. She felt uneasy in this place where everything was so strange, mysterious, and unfamiliar.

The soldier standing in front of the gate asked whom she wanted to see; after receiving a tip, he admitted her. He rang the bell. A few minutes later someone turned a key and opened the gate. Escorted by another soldier, Sasha entered through a large, heavy door leading into a garden, or, more accurately, a courtyard planted all around with trees. The door behind her was locked immediately.

"What's this? Is this where patients can stroll?" she asked.

"Yes, ma'am," replied the soldier in a non-Russian accent and led her to the door of the large red building. Once again a key turned with a click and a heavy door opened; they entered a dark hallway.

---

46. A region of central Russia on the Oka River about ninety miles south of Moscow.

"You certainly keep the doors well locked," Sasha observed with a smile, experiencing an unpleasant feeling as each and every door was locked after her.

"Yes, ma'am," the soldier repeated again, with a stupid grin.

Sasha took her coat off in the hallway and climbed the stairs. The first sight that greeted her was a group of people in gray dressing gowns seated on a bench along the wall directly opposite the staircase. They regarded this young woman dressed in unfamiliar clothes with curiosity but without understanding, and they continued sitting there motionless. There were about six men. They sat there idly, dully, merely for a change of setting, to avoid looking at the walls of their own rooms, which they were sick of.

An overfriendly soldier, obviously more civilized than those unlocking all the doors, approached Sasha and, after ascertaining whom she wished to see and receiving a few silver coins as a tip, politely escorted her to a long, narrow door that had also been locked.

Kurlinsky sat near a window. He rose to greet Sasha and went up to her, shuffling in his oversized hospital shoes. He was wearing a large gray dressing gown made of military cloth, obviously not his size, which he clumsily tried to wrap around himself, growing embarrassed and starting to blush. His face was pale and thin; a pitiful smile, as if taking shape with difficulty, appeared on his lips from time to time.

"Aleksandra Alekseevna, is it really you?" he asked ecstatically in a muffled voice. "This is my friend and comrade Petrovsky," he said, introducing the young man sitting next to him.

"Why on earth have you decided to ruin yourself, Kurlinsky?"

"How am I ruining myself? On the contrary, I feel fine, having followed the dictates of my conscience."

"I don't think it's the dictates of your conscience. Tell me, what's inspired you to do this?"

"I don't know. I simply couldn't behave otherwise when the question was posed to me directly: to go or not to go. I can't bear arms and will never kill anyone."

"It'll never come to that. But what will certainly happen is that now they'll draft someone else whom they wouldn't have chosen if you had gone."

"Oh, that's an old argument! I refuse to enter military service because I don't acknowledge the use of force against anyone."

"What childish reasoning. Let's talk in earnest: you don't acknowledge force, yet you're using it by your own action. You're committing violence against the person who'll be drafted instead of you; you're coercing those who have to keep you locked up here; you're committing violence against those who'll be compelled to punish you, torment you, and force you to bear arms," said Sasha, getting more and more upset.

"But they don't have to do this," Kurlinsky said timidly. "No, not everyone can do that. People all live in a state of inertia. Some chosen ones, progressives, show the true path and speak the truth. At first only a few people will follow them, but then more and more will join . . ."[47]

"Don't you see, my friend," said Sasha, recalling Kurlinsky's mother's tears and loading her words with even more energy and feeling, "isn't it clear that there's already been significant progress in this direction? Humanity protests against war; the old chivalrous attitude about defense of the fatherland and the honor of bearing arms has vanished. What's left is a crushing feeling of necessity. Try to bear this burden together with those who submit to it against their own will. That will also be a form of heroism . . ."

"Your reasoning is very paradoxical, Aleksandra Alekseevna, and you're being illogical."

"Well, let's not say terrible things. Let's not attempt to be logical," Sasha said, looking closely at her interlocutor with her large, affectionate eyes. "You must simply take up arms, submit to your commanding officer, join the military, and . . ." Sasha paused. "Believe me, every one of your actions, your words, even your breath—will express your protest against war, and by so doing you'll be spreading your views much more successfully than by your confinement here."

Kurlinsky became thoughtful.

"If I so much as breathe a word of protest, they'll kill me," he said. With a slight movement of his head he pulled the rough, gray collar of his dressing gown away from his tender young neck with its transparent, white skin and small veins.

"And this boy is voluntarily choosing torment!" Sasha thought sadly, desperately wanting to save him.

"Well, well . . . try to submit, merely try; submit patiently and quietly to necessity with your own inner protest against war. Look around you and strive to regard with affection, kindness, and goodwill those unfortunate soldiers who've been taken away from their families, the men with whom you'll be in close contact, and by so doing you'll already be a Christian, not a man of war. By your influence and attitude you'll demonstrate to them and to your

---

47. Kurlinsky is here echoing an argument made by the "new people" in N. G. Chernyshevsky's controversial and influential novel *What Is to Be Done?* (1863).

commanders that there's no place for killing where only love and humility exist. Then God Himself will help you and you'll escape the difficult situation you're in now . . ."

"But I harbor no doubts, Aleksandra Alekseevna. I'm prepared for anything," Kurlinsky said, admiring Sasha's animated and audacious expression. Kissing her hand as she was preparing to leave, he added:

"Your visit has made me very happy. Thank you."

Bidding him farewell, Sasha said a few touching words about his mother and her tears, and made her way out through all the heavy doors that were unlocked and then locked again behind her.

"Well then, are there healthy people here, too?" she asked the soldier who let her out.

"Yes, ma'am," he replied.

She got in a cab once again with a heavy heart. Her nerves were even more on edge; she felt depressed and kept hearing the sounds of locks and the repeated "Yes, ma'am. Yes, ma'am."

"Can it really be that all these people are so beaten down by military discipline and have grown so stupid from fear that they can't really speak and they dare not?" wondered Sasha, and she kept hearing his "Yes, ma'am. Yes, ma'am."

The driver suddenly pulled up his horse smartly and Sasha came to her senses. The whole street had been turned up: they were repairing the water mains; piles of dirt lay along both sides, and a deep trench was visible in which a man was working. Sasha wondered whether from this open hole damp mother earth had been given a chance to take even one breath, this earth that was covered with stones and asphalt, deprived of the possibility of bearing plants, trees, and anything else that this plot of urban ground might have nourished. A deep sigh escaped her breast. She sighed over her own soul, so beaten down by passion, for the driver, beaten down by privation and oppressed by the unkind, fettered life of Moscow, for the soldier, beaten down by discipline, for the earth, beaten down by stones and asphalt, and for her own living soul that could not bear chains and that longed for freedom, life, fresh air, and happiness . . .

10

The Husband

When Sasha returned home, she went into the nursery to see Alyosha, who was building houses of cards on his table. She wanted to spend some time with her son; taking a volume of Grimm's Fairy Tales, she began reading to him.[48] The boy was delighted that his mother had come to be with him, but her interest did not last long. Sasha's soul was suffering excruciating pain. She tossed the book aside and went into the hall where the piano stood. Alyosha ran after her, but she sent him out for a walk. She found the music for Beethoven's sonatas and began playing the one she liked best.

Her playing was not really playing, but a moan of suffering. She could not finish the piece; her head sank down onto her hands that had frozen on the keys, and she began sobbing fitfully.

"Sasha!" the desperate whisper of her husband could be heard suddenly just above her ear. "Sasha, my dear, what's the matter?"

"Nothing, nothing at all; my nerves are on edge," she replied quickly, wiping her eyes and recoiling from her husband. "I visited the military hospital and I feel so sorry for Kurlinsky."

"No, Sasha, that's not it. . . . You were just playing that sonata; you love it," Petr Afanasevich said, hesitating, timidly and sorrowfully. "And you're in love with Ivan Ilych . . ."

"That's not true, it's not. I'm not in love with him!" Sasha cried in a desperate voice, stretching her arms out, as if trying to defend herself. "I love music, I love this wonderful sonata, and nothing else . . ."

Her voice broke off; she folded her arms, exhausted, hushed, and submissive.

Her husband suddenly understood everything; shaking with agitation, his face became pale as if whitewashed with lime. He stared closely and protractedly at his wife's dejected face and suddenly dissolved in tears.

When a woman cries, especially if she's amiable and attractive, one feels sorry for her; but when a man cries, it's a terrible thing.

Petr Afanasevich cried as if everything by which he had lived had suddenly been ripped away from him forever. He had *never ever* been jealous of his wife: he simply did not know that feeling. Trusting, polite, and kind, all his life he had loved only Sasha in his childlike way; it could never even enter his mind that she or he could love someone else.

This was a misfortune, a genuine misfortune, not for him alone, but for both of them. When he regained control of himself, he stood up, went over to his wife, and quietly took hold of her hand.

"Sasha, don't say anything. I understand everything. We've been sent a test and must endure it as best we can . . ."

Sasha looked at him with her dry, lowered eyes and remained silent.

48. The brothers Jacob (1785–1863) and Wilhelm (1786–1859) Grimm were German folklorists and philologists who published three volumes of stories between 1812 and 1822.

"My dear, honest, virtuous, steadfast Sasha! Poor, poor you!"

He choked on his tears once again and fell silent.

"Sasha, you're a good person," he continued boldly. "You're energetic and strong. My dear friend, we'll get through this difficult situation together, but don't deprive me of your trust and friendship."

Sasha squeezed her husband's hand firmly, looked at his distressed face, and said softly:

"Yes, I promise you that; I won't leave you; I won't do anything foolish. . . . And he doesn't even love me," she added bitterly, wounding her husband even more with those words. "But if, in spite of all my efforts, my soul fractures, against my own will, forgive me, if I'm to blame. . . . You're right, this is a misfortune . . ."

Petr Afanasevich kissed his wife on the forehead and went into his own room.

From that day forward he monitored Sasha's condition very closely. He never said another word to her about her feelings for Ivan Ilych, but there was something strained and unspoken between the spouses; an oppressive atmosphere prevailed even among others in their household. Petr Afanasevich did not alter his attitude toward Ivan Ilych one bit, but clearly suffered in his presence.

II

The Convent

"Madam," nanny said to Sasha the next morning, "dinner's being prepared for the poor in our convent today. You ought to go have a look and let us go, too. They'll feed everyone and pray for the tsar. They'll serve more than six hundred people."

"Yes, I've heard about it; I must go and see," said Sasha, who was eager to do anything that would keep her from sitting at home, thinking, and seeing her husband.

From childhood Sasha had loved convents; during her youth even before she had tried to enter the conservatory, she had planned on entering a convent. She liked the poetry of monastic life, the idea of service and contemplation of the divine, renunciation of physical life, and the ideal of spiritual self-perfection. She particularly wanted to visit the convent in her current mood.

After seeing Petr Afanasevich off to his Insurance Society, she got dressed and headed for the closest convent located on the outskirts of Moscow. Sasha jumped onto a tramcar already full of people. When she had reached the last stop, the view of fields, woods beyond the river, and the prospect of endless space with no houses, fences, streets, or city crowds immediately sobered her and afforded her spiritual sustenance and serenity.

After standing for some time at the gates, Sasha entered the enclosed area around the convent and saw an enormous crowd of women of various ages, classes, and apparel: women with nursing infants and young children, old women, poor women, cheerful and depressed women, some even dressed up, peasant girls in red shawls, downtrodden women, some sick and wearing rags—all women, women . . .

The convent porter, keeping approximate count of those entering, allowed about two hundred people through the gates at one time, first onto the territory of the convent, then into a low stone church where dinner was being prepared; the rest waited in line.

In a low-ceilinged ancient church stood long, narrow tables covered with tablecloths; long, narrow benches stretched alongside. A large table was placed to one side on which stood great mounds of pies and breads, kettles of cabbage soup, and mugs of *kisel*.

Young novice nuns, pale and appealing, with a look of reverence and consequence for their work, distributed bountiful baskets containing chunks of rye bread and large wheat pies filled with cabbage.

After about two hundred women had entered and taken their places at the tables, the priest emerged and began reciting prayers for the repose of the dead; a wonderful choir of nuns accompanied him. While they were reciting these prayers, the women stood reverently, listening and crossing themselves. Then the nuns distributed spoons and began serving the cabbage soup, arranging it so that several women could eat out of the same bowl.

Sasha was surprised at the silence and decorum with which everything transpired. It was as if this large crowd was performing a religious rite. She went up to the table where the children were seated; she felt elated as a result of their happy mood, especially when they were served the dessert of *kisel* with milk.

All during the meal a young nun read loudly and clearly in a high thin voice the life of Saint Isidore.[49]

Dinner was nearing its end and mugs of beer and mead were being served; an older woman wearing a nun's habit, the bookkeeper, was distributing five kopecks to each woman as a gift from the abbess.

---

49. Isidore of Pelusium was a monk in the Egyptian desert who died in about 436. In one of his many letters, he wrote: "It is more important to teach by a life of doing good than to preach in eloquent terms."

After dinner the priest recited another prayer and the women began to file out of the church. First each of them approached two elderly nuns who were standing at the door and thanked them. The nuns kissed each woman on the lips and said, "Well, you've been well fed; now thank God, and go with God." The women crossed themselves and bowed.

While they were letting the first group out one door and allowing the next group in through the other, Sasha went up to the bookkeeper and asked how long she had been living in the convent and what had motivated her to join.

"Oh, my dear lady, since the age of fourteen I dreamt of entering a convent. My father was a poor civil servant from a provincial town," she said. "He didn't want to hear a word about it. I grieved and grieved, and then, at the age of seventeen, ran away from my parents' home and came straight to Moscow."

"Without any money and not knowing the city?"

"It's all in God's hands, my dear. I managed it all in Christ's name; kind people directed me to this convent. I went right to the abbess; she was so very nice to me."

"Really? She accepted you immediately?"

"She said, 'Stay here, God has sent you to us.' They assigned me the task of looking after the incurables and old people in the hospital. At first it was very hard work; never mind, I endured it. The abbess praised me and gave me an easier job. I've been living here for the last forty years, happy and content. I thank God for everything . . ."

The elderly nun's kind, generous smile on her humble, serene face covered in little wrinkles, shone so blissfully from her lips that Sasha felt envious of the spiritual peace radiating from this woman's whole being.

Another nun stood there, leaning her back against the nearest column; she was tall and plump, with a face completely unlike that of the nun with whom Sasha had just spoken. Her gloomy face expressed complete hopelessness, although her lips were whispering prayers. Sasha approached her cautiously and greeted her.

"Have you been a nun for long?"

"I've been praying for a long time, a very long time; my heart's turned to stone. I've committed many sins."

"Why are you in such despair, mother?"

"Ugh, my sins are heavy. I've been praying for thirty years and there's no way I can atone for them. My heart's turned to stone."

"Do you have a particular sin on your conscience?"

"My sin is such that it can never be expiated—it's forever unforgivable; my sin is heavy, ugh, ugh," she moaned in genuine distress, crossing herself hastily.

Her large figure, as stony as her heart, stood there firm and still, indestructible, so strong that it would force her to live forever and drain the cup of spiritual suffering.

Sasha moved away with a weighty feeling of her own sin; after crossing herself, she left the church.

In the door she once more encountered nuns carrying baskets of bread; in the courtyard crowds of women were still waiting in line. A few approached her and begged for alms; after distributing all the coins she had, Sasha managed to tear herself away, took a seat on the tramcar again, and left for home.

12

Devotee of Art

Upon arriving home, Sasha heard the sounds of her piano while still in the hallway.

"Who's here?" she asked, her heart pounding with unconstrained elation.

"Ivan Ilych came some time ago. I told him you weren't home. He said he would wait," explained the servant, taking Sasha's plush jacket from her.

Excited after her trip, thrilled at the prospect of seeing Ivan Ilych and by the fact that he had waited for her return, Sasha flew like a bird up the stairs with her light, swift steps, threw open the door with her strong hand, and stopped in front of the piano—beautiful, flushed, and passionate.

As if to respond to her emotion, Ivan Ilych, without exchanging a word of greeting, finished the loud, splendid, and meaningful musical phrase of his symphony and rose, extending his hand to Sasha.

"Our symphony!" Sasha cried, as if completely inadvertently.

"Ours?" Ivan Ilych repeated sarcastically. "I would've been very glad, Aleksandra Alekseevna, if you had helped me compose it, but now it's finished; in a few days I'll be conducting it at a symphony concert."

"Yes, what I said was foolish. But I so empathized with you while you were writing it, when you played parts of it for me during the course of the summer, that for some reason this symphony has also become mine . . . and my favorite," Sasha said softly, timidly, and blushed. "Is this unpleasant for you?"

"No, not at all . . ."

"It doesn't trouble you?" Sasha said, interrupting.

"Well, no, it doesn't."

"And that's all!" Sasha thought with despair in her heart. "That's how it has to be; it serves me right, and the worse he is to me, the harsher he is, the more justified I'll consider it for myself. But, my God, how painful, how unbearably painful!! How I need his love, how impossible my life has become without this man!"

Sasha looked closely at his face, lifeless after he had finished playing, no longer expressing anything special; she wanted to peer into the depths of his soul, to understand what this man was really all about—but not only did she not understand him now, she never had. Is it possible that this musician of genius, who had turned her life upside down, was really only a musician, and that nothing human or worldly affected him any longer? In fact, he behaved in such a way that nothing essential disturbed or troubled him, and in this way he was right. He maintained all the purity, the chastity of his precious art; he guarded the sacred flame of the temple and the divinity he served. He was so filled with music in all its manifestations that there was no room for anything else. Everything in his life—nature, people, their passions, and events—everything was supposed to serve music in one way or another; that was the point around which everything else centered.

And in Ivan Ilych's music, in his compositions as well as in his playing, one could sense that significance, that sublimity to which he had elevated music. It was impossible not to believe in it, impossible not to allow it that significant place he had afforded it.

"What have you been doing all this time, Ivan Ilych," asked Sasha.

"I've been finishing work, orchestrating part of my symphony. My pupils have also been coming to see me in the evenings, and I've been reading a great deal lately."

Ivan Ilych looked at his watch and was about to take his leave.

"Are you going already?" Sasha asked in horror, looking closely into his eyes.

He regarded her inquiringly from under his brow and hastened his preparations to leave.

"I must go; I've stayed too long waiting for you. I just dropped by to inquire about our friend Kurlinsky whom you visited, and I almost forgot to ask."

Sasha told him in detail about her visit and conversation. Ivan Ilych did not venture his own opinion about Sasha's action; he merely observed as he was leaving:

"As always, you aren't very logical; but you have a great deal of energy. If good deeds could be put at the service of this energy, you'd become a very valuable person indeed."

"You seem to compare me with mill water under which a millstone must be placed so that it can do its work."

"Perhaps that's true. . . . Work is a very good thing. Well, goodbye."

After Ivan Ilych had gone, Sasha experienced a feeling of dissatisfaction, an insane desire to keep him there or go after him; she always felt the aspiration to delve into his impenetrable, unfathomable soul, but never could. What did he think of her? Did he understand her torment? Perhaps in his own soul he was mocking her, despising her, condemning her for her love and everything she said and did. Oh, the tormenting secret of the workings of the human soul; it was even more tormenting in a person you love and whose thoughts you wish ineffectually to fathom, but cannot. "One, only one little indication of his approval, his love for me, just one moment of happiness, one instant of the kind of love I experience—that would be enough to guarantee my happiness for the rest of my life!" Sasha thought.

Meanwhile Ivan Ilych ambled home slowly thinking that he needed to walk more for exercise and still not be late for tea and the lesson he was giving two poor, but talented pupils.

Meanwhile, as he made his way along the boulevard, he thought about Sasha. "For what reason has this woman come to occupy such a large place in my life? In part it's curious and rather amusing. But I mustn't get distracted and lose my way. How exhausted and unappealing she seemed today! Still, she's unusual and receptive," he thought. "But she diverts me; I must go there less often . . ."

But Ivan Ilych did not like the idea of seeing less of Sasha. He unconsciously loved the poetic, affectionate atmosphere with which she and her setting surrounded him; before reaching any decision, he arrived home.

Tea, bread, and ham on a small plate were waiting for him in his small, comfortable apartment. Aleksei Tikhonych, in anticipation of seeing his beloved master, was chatting with two young men, Ivan Ilych's pupils. It was light, peaceful, and pleasant in the great musician's simple abode. Large shelves with musical scores and books lined the walls of his room; two pianos stood in the middle; scores and music paper were laid out on a large table, portraits of Tchaikovsky and Rubenstein hung on the walls.[50]

"Ivan Ilych, my romance is being published," his favorite pupil Tsvetkov shouted as he came in. "I just found out about it today."

"I'm delighted, my boy. I liked your piece very much. Greetings," he said, turning to the other young man, an awkward and unattractive fellow, the

---

50. Nikolai Rubenstein (1835–81) was a pianist and composer who founded the Moscow Conservatory. His brother Anton (1829–94) helped to establish the Saint Petersburg Conservatory.

complete opposite of Tsvetkov. "Why haven't you been to see me? You're busy with your Wagner. Have you had tea? Well, show me your assignments."

The pupils handed over their music notebooks, and Ivan Ilych, sitting down at the table, began correcting and explaining the mistakes in the pupils' assignments. He was an excellent teacher. Together with his extensive musical education, he possessed pedagogical talent and was very patient, logical, and serious. In addition, he was unusually kind to young people and had earned such deep respect and affection among them, that it was considered a great blessing to be one of his pupils.

"Well, now let's have some tea," said Ivan Ilych, after finishing his corrections and interrupting the lesson temporarily.

Aleksei Tikhonych was present almost all the time; it was clear that after a whole day of solitude he was glad that the house had livened up from the presence of its master and his admirers. The unattractive pupil of Wagner's music left soon after tea, while Tsvetkov stayed on to spend the night at Ivan Ilych's house.

13

The Symphony

The painful period of suffering as a result of Sasha's unexpected and undesired love for Ivan Ilych had begun to pass and was gradually being replaced by the opposite sensation, when love becomes a heartfelt celebration, a radiant, joyful affection for the entire world and all humanity. Everything became important and interesting, everything sparkled and was straightforward; Sasha had sufficient energy and strength to do everything. She had enough love for her own happiness, even though it was not reciprocated. With all her being she strove toward this reciprocity and believed in it, but for the present, it was not necessary. Only in her imagination did she devise the most insane scenes of mutual love between herself and Ivan Ilych. She dreamt that she would inspire him and together with him would serve that art they both loved so much. Never once did the possibility enter her head that she would betray her husband—she did not consider this love a betrayal; her husband remained her husband and she remained his honest wife who loved him after a fashion—but her relationship to Ivan Ilych was something special, poetically artistic, a spiritual celebration, a gift from on high . . .

Petr Afanasevich noted that Sasha had stopped grieving and had become cheerful, even peaceful; he thought she would overcome her unfortunate passion and had calmed down. This also calmed him down. He was not jealous by nature, only distressed that his tranquility had been destroyed, as well as his trusting relationship with his wife; he desperately wanted to restore his previous attitude to her and his serene life. He believed that Sasha was especially passionate about music; he even encouraged her to attend concerts, operas, and other musical events. Sasha met frequently with Ivan Ilych; sometimes she invited him into her box or took a seat next to him. It made her sublimely happy to experience together with him those aesthetic pleasures that musical impressions would afford both of them. Sometimes, without previous discussion, their eyes would seek each other out at a moment of brilliant musical performance or upon hearing some splendid musical composition; they both rejoiced and lived by the spirit of their beloved music.

Returning home after a concert, Ivan Ilych would sometimes escort Sasha to her house; in his soft, even voice he would explain some harmonically complicated musical piece or would tell her something about the life of the composers. Strolling together, feeling neither tired nor cold, Sasha would experience the ecstasy of someone in love, when there was nothing more to be wished for, everything was granted by God, everything—when there was nowhere else to go and nothing else to desire.

At last the day arrived, January 26, when Ivan Ilych was to conduct his own symphony. This was quite an event in the musical world. Professors came from the conservatory in Petersburg to hear the symphony. For several days before the concert Sasha did not see Ivan Ilych and sensed that he was busy preparing for that evening and afraid to be distracted from his task.

Sometime after 8 P.M. carriages with lanterns, sleighs, drivers, and cabs, all driving past mounted gendarmes, converged from various directions, while very chilly pedestrians hastily arrived at the doors of the concert hall; special solemnity surrounded the evening's event; the public seemed nervous, excited, and prepared to experience the enthusiasm communicated both by composers and performers.

Along the walls lining the staircase of the small entrance where Sasha always went in, women, caretakers, and footmen were standing with bundles chatting merrily. Sitting behind a table covered by a green cloth near the entrance were two women students from the conservatory; they were handing out concert programs to the public. The audience was filing in, tossing jingling coins onto a large plate. In side sections a crowd of people was promenading back and forth, waiting for the bell.

Sasha had ordered a white dress for the occasion. It suited her flushed, excited face so well, her brightly shining eyes, and the diamonds in her hair and ears; by her appearance alone she expressed the solemnity and significance of this evening's great event. Greeting her acquaintances who admired her dazzling beauty and apparel, and trembling with anticipation, Sasha took her reserved seat. Ivan Ilych's symphony was the first piece on the program. The musicians began entering and taking their places. On the left sat two sisters, brunettes, both violinists; then came the first violinist, a gray-haired, esteemed professor at the conservatory. The discordant tuning of instruments commenced. Finally, silence reigned. Ivan Ilych emerged with awkward steps, but in a dignified and composed manner, and walked slowly across the stage. Applause rang out; Ivan Ilych bowed slightly and looked in the direction where Sasha was sitting. She caught his glance; unnoticed by others, she nodded and smiled. He recalled for one instant Sasha's white, fluttering figure on the porch of his little yellow house, when he first found her listening to his playing, that evening when for the very first time that magnificent theme had arisen in his head, the one on which today's symphony was based. This moment was fleetingly brief, and Ivan Ilych, wholly consumed by his task, higher than which nothing could exist for him, pale, but serene, glanced at the orchestra, and with a precise, energetic gesture of his hand, began conducting his own symphony.

"My God! It's outstanding! How profound!" Sasha thought in excitement.

Applause burst out after the first part. Then came the powerful andante; how much strength of feeling, expressed more and more intensely by harmonically complicated but rich sounds! The theme stood out beautifully, appearing first in one, then another variation. The richness of voices, interrupted by original and unexpected transitions, was astounding. Suddenly, like an inexhaustible stream of the most passionate feelings, this magnificent andante emerged from some deep place filled with new energy, brimming over with solemn phrases. Ivan Ilych's face had changed completely. His restrained excitement and seriousness, and the weight of his expression, rendered him almost handsome. He conducted the entire orchestra with strong and precise movements of his fine hands; one could sense the unity of the conductor with his musicians performing this splendid composition under the composer's direction.

His success was enormous. The audience called for the composer many times. And his success was not artificial, but sincere, indubitable, fervent from a public so affected by the brilliance of the composer's work.

Sasha felt jubilant. During the intermission she made her way to the greenroom and there found Ivan Ilych. He looked at her questioningly with his wandering eyes, this time filled with excitement.

"Amazing!" said Sasha in a husky voice, filled with tears. "I congratulate you on your success. I never doubted it, even for a moment."

"I doubted it all the time and still have my doubts. There are so many of my friends in the hall that they made it the success you've just described."

Various musicians began coming up to Ivan Ilych and congratulating him. He was surrounded on all sides and carried off. Sasha did not see him again for the rest of the evening.

"Why am I not his wife? Why don't I dare follow him everywhere, share his triumph, take pride in his success before the whole world?" Sasha wondered in despair, standing at the doors awaiting her sleigh that the doorman had gone to fetch. "And why don't I dare seat him in my sleigh, go to where he just went, express all my sympathy, my joy at his success, my admiration for his brilliant composition? Where is he? Where?" Sasha tormented herself, and suddenly jealousy arose in her soul toward those people with whom he was spending this triumphant evening.

Trembling under the impact of these vivid impressions, Sasha went to meet her sleigh, harnessed with her favorite pair of grays, and left for home.

"What use is this joy at Ivan Ilych's triumph?" Sasha suddenly came to her senses. "Where is music itself, where are those pure joys of consolation and enjoyment of art that I lived by previously? I don't need this dependence; I don't want this love! Let art remain independent, untainted by anything personal; it's better and higher and must remain on a summit. Why did I bind it to my feelings? Why didn't I remain just as independent as Ivan Ilych himself? He's right, a thousand times right, while I . . . I'm lost," Sasha thought in despair. The cold was severe. Hoarfrost covered everything with a thick layer of fluffy, silvery ice. It hung on trees, lay on rooftops, fences, curbstones, cornices, people, and horses, as if trying to conceal everything grimy, rough, coarse, and unattractive—with its even, sparkling, beautiful, white coating. It hung there, turning the air silvery, shining, while way off in the distance, its dazzling whiteness competed serenely with the yellow light of the lanterns and the red light of the small fires built at the intersections of Moscow, surrounded by cheerful lads or disconsolate tramps in torn trousers and unfastened old shoes, all of whom were trying to keep themselves warm.

In the air, also filled with hoarfrost, broad white lines of telegraph wires led in various directions, the herald of the most critical events that upset humanity—deaths, births, marriages, victories, fires, all the misfortunes and joys of human life. These lightly powdered lines leading in different directions abruptly intersected the dark, distant sky with its frosty stars, also darkened by the hoarfrost, and sprinkled widely in the endless expanse.

It seemed to Sasha that the beauty of this wintery night was sharing the success of her beloved musician's genius with her. But it was not a feeling of earthly love for him; rather it was the triumph of musical art that now shone in all the dazzling silver of this celebratory hoarfrost spread around the whole world that was as pure, majestic, and beautiful, as nature itself.

14
Jealousy

Ivan Ilych's musical friends persuaded him to go to Petersburg and conduct his symphony there. Sasha found this out and felt out of sorts when she did not get to see him anywhere. As she did with everything in her life, she now devoted herself passionately to music; she practiced six hours a day and made great progress, but hopeless inner anguish overwhelmed her. She grew so noticeably thin and sickly that Petr Afanasevich became alarmed in earnest; he summoned doctors, who were extremely puzzled. Everything in Sasha's strong, lovely organism was in good working order and healthy; it was only her emaciation, her nerves, and the ominous expression of her large, serious, dark eyes. The doctors prescribed peace and quiet, bromides, daily walks, baths, and diversions. If things didn't improve, then a trip to the Crimea would be needed, or even abroad.

"Mamá, where's that nice old Tikhonych, the man who lived at the dacha with Ivan Ilych?" Alyosha asked his mother once.

"He's here, in Moscow, still living with Ivan Ilych."

"Oh, mama, my dear, let's go visit him," Alyosha implored. "I so love that nice old man with his split yellow beard."

"Fine, Alyosha, we'll go," Sasha agreed, thinking that Ivan Ilych was still in Petersburg and unconsciously wanting to have a look at the place where this man, so beloved by her, lived and created his work.

Sasha felt a little anxious and guilty bursting into the apartment of a bachelor in this way, but she justified herself by the fact that she had a child with her and that Ivan Ilych was not at home. Alyosha brought some tobacco along as a present and was ecstatic that when they rang the bell, the first person he saw was Aleksei Tikhonych.

"Alyoshenka, my dear boy, it's you.[51] It's so nice of you to remember an old man," Tikhonych said, greeting the lad.

"Here, Tikhonych, this is for you," Alyosha said, solemnly handing over the gift.

"Thank you, Alyoshenka. Come on in. I'll tell Ivan Ilych you're here."

---

51. Alyoshenka is an affectionate diminutive form of the name Aleksei.

"Ivan Ilych? Has he returned?" Sasha asked with horror. "There's no need, no need. We have to go right home, and Alyosha would be too warm here in his fur coat."

Sasha made haste to leave, but at that very moment Ivan Ilych poked his head in from the door; seeing Sasha, he blushed deeply. They were both awkwardly silent for some time. At that moment Tikhonych, who had taken off Alyosha's coat, led him away into the apartment, promising him some chocolate.

"I didn't know you were back, Ivan Ilych," Sasha spoke first, extending her hand.

"Hello, Aleksandra Alekseevna. I'm very glad to see you," Ivan Ilych said in his self-possessed voice.

"Alyosha kept asking to come see Tikhonych, and I agreed, but I . . ."

"I understand that you thought I was still in Petersburg and came to see Tikhonych. Of course, I dared not expect such an honor for myself," Ivan Ilych said with certain irony once again.

"Honor's not the word, but . . ."

"But what?"

Ivan Ilych took Sasha's hand and for a long time held it in his own warm, handsome hand.

"Are you coming in, Aleksandra Alekseevna?"

"Yes, I have no choice now. Since I'm here, I'll come in," said Sasha, taking off her jacket and entering Ivan Ilych's rooms. "I haven't seen you since that evening when you enjoyed such great success, Ivan Ilych. How did things go in Petersburg?"

"Thank you. I didn't receive such ovations in Petersburg. In Moscow my friends inflated my success."

"Your symphony is really very fine . . ."

Sasha was unnatural and timid. She felt that as a young woman, it was not entirely appropriate for her to be visiting Ivan Ilych; but the joyful intoxication of seeing him again was so strong that she was unable to leave. In the next room Alyosha's and Tikhonych's animated voices could be heard.

"A meeting of old and young," said Ivan Ilych. "They're enjoying themselves."

"I wanted to ask you, Ivan Ilych, where you spent that evening after you performed your symphony here in Moscow?" Sasha inquired with unexpected suddenness. "You probably had supper with your musician friends?"

"No, I don't like that and avoid it; I wanted to go home earlier and go to bed, but at the entrance I was met by Anna Nikolaevna who took charge and whisked me off to her house. I don't like going with women . . . but I had to accompany her."

Sasha knew that Anna Nikolaevna was a visiting singer from the provincial opera who at one time had flirted with Ivan Ilych. It was rumored that he had been attracted by her in his early youth. Insane jealousy and vexation that precisely on the evening of his great triumph, when she had experienced all the anxieties and joys of success together with him in her soul, suddenly overcame Sasha with such strength that she could scarcely breathe. She would have exchanged half her life to have been with him that evening; meanwhile, he had sat next to that young imposter, gone home with her, and listened to her intimate and indecent prattle.

"You don't like going with women? Is that a hint, Ivan Ilych, that you've sometimes escorted me from concerts and found it tedious and unbearable?" Sasha asked tactlessly and too frankly all of a sudden.

"No, Aleksandra Alekseevna, I wasn't thinking . . ."

"You weren't thinking, but you offended me," Sasha said with tears in her voice, losing control of herself. "I don't need escorts; I could have a lot of them, if that's what I wanted," Sasha continued proudly. "I considered you a friend, a close friend; I loved conversing with you; I held you higher than anyone else on earth . . . but you're dropping such hints that . . ." Sasha said in a constricted voice, growing more upset, her wide-open eyes now flashing, no longer innocent, but insanely passionate and full of tears.

"Aleksandra Alekseevna, forgive me if I've offended you," Ivan Ilych said serenely. "I didn't want that. I've always found it very pleasant to be with you, and what you just said to me . . ."

"I don't remember what I just said to you," Sasha suddenly recovered, and justified herself tersely and abruptly. "It's time for me to go home. Call Alyosha."

Ivan Ilych stood up; casting a fleeting glance at Sasha, he wanted to say something more to her, but hesitated.

Alyosha, lips covered in chocolate, holding a package in his hands, beaming with delight, and exchanging kisses with Tikhonych, said goodbye to Ivan Ilych and emerged into the entryway with his mother.

Ivan Ilych removed Sasha's jacket from the hanger and clumsily helped her on with it. For a moment his hands suddenly came to rest on Sasha's shoulders; she did not understand whether it was intentional or accidental, this strange gesture, and she turned her face toward him; their eyes met and Sasha's face expressed frightened astonishment. "Could it really be?" she wondered. Sasha's fingers were trembling such that she could not fasten the clips of her jacket.

"Let me do it," said Ivan Ilych.

Sasha, once again submissive, affectionate, and tender, leaned her whole slender body toward Ivan Ilych, whose hands fidgeted clumsily under her chin; he finally managed to fasten her jacket clips. It was as if an electric shock ran through Sasha's body from Ivan Ilych's touch. She turned bright red, threw him another glance, and fell silent.

"Goodbye," said Ivan Ilych. "May I come to see you?"

"Farewell," Sasha said softly.

Sasha took Alyosha by the hand; no longer capable of going on foot, she summoned a cab and headed for home.

"Perhaps he really does love me," the thought flashed through her mind for an instant. "But I wouldn't be glad. Why don't I experience that happiness now that I dreamt about, if I were to believe in the reciprocity of his feelings? No, I don't want it, I don't dare; I can't become involved in an unhappy affair with this man. More than anything else I love my own integrity. Let him remain a virtuous priest of his art, let him serve it, preserve the chastity and serenity of his own soul, filled by that sublime art he serves. And let my life end, but let it do so unblemished by any illicit love or by the sin of his love that could spoil or destroy this brilliant composer's life. Perhaps he's also frightened by the possibility of loving me. . . . Enough, enough of this tormenting desire for his love. I don't need it; it's time to come to my senses; it's time to realize that it's both impossible and detrimental to us both . . ."

15

More than a month passed. March arrived with Lenten services conducted in all the churches of Moscow, with a lull in the exciting and endless urban festivities, with the poetry of anticipated spring, with the nervousness of impending student examinations, and with all that is repeated in each given month of every given year.

But for Sasha the world did not exist. After resolving to overcome her love for Ivan Ilych and to separate it at all costs from her love for music, she began to avoid seeing him. She played the piano for entire days, studying difficult pieces; she found a teacher for herself from the conservatory and made striking progress.

Concerts began again during Lent, and Sasha frequented them assiduously. She saw Ivan Ilych from a distance, but no longer asked him to accompany her home, to ride with her, or to come and play for her. Between them cooler, distant relations were established; the previous simplicity, trust, and intimacy had all vanished, when they had felt so confident of one another, feared nothing, and revealed their souls to the very depths. Ivan Ilych rarely visited Sasha and was puzzled, or perhaps he guessed, why she had so suddenly altered her behavior toward him. He did not suffer as a result; he was too busy and valued peace and quiet for his musical activity. Sometimes he felt a certain lack: he missed that affectionate, lovely atmosphere of poetic love with which Sasha had surrounded him and which he had come to enjoy almost unconsciously.

For Sasha life without the anticipation that Ivan Ilych might soon be coming to visit her, sit down with her, or play for her—became completely unbearable and lost all its meaning. She wandered around the house exhausted and distressed; she wept, sometimes shouting the words of his romance in a distraught voice: "Come, oh come to me . . ." She would sit at the piano and converse with his compositions, "Here's where you suffered and here's a plea; when you wrote this wonderful work, you were praying for something. . . . And here's your love. . . . But for whom? And this serene, rational contemplation of some inner spiritual process . . . or nature, perhaps. . . . Music is splendid in that its dream lives for each one of us. I've studied your entire musical soul, all of it; I know it very well and love it dearly . . ."

Sasha would jump up; she would recall his strange look and her arms would seek in vain the embrace she desired so insanely with all her young, passionate being.

"Here's a letter for you, Sashenka," said Petr Afanasevich, coming in from the front hall where he had just received an envelope from the mail carrier.

"Ah, my God, it's from Kurlinsky. Where could he be, the poor man?"

Sasha began reading the letter:

You recall, Aleksandra Alekseevna, that day when you appeared as an angel-comforter in my jail cell and tried to persuade me not to oppose the general trend and to enter military service voluntarily? I have thought a great deal since that time. I know that you wanted to visit me again, but they wouldn't admit you. It was better that way. In my solitude I weighed all the bad things that would arise in both cases: if I refused to serve completely and if I went to serve voluntarily. I realized that you were right and there was more evil in my refusal and that I must yield and submit to necessity, even though it is evil. I've been wearing a soldier's uniform for a month now; in a few days they're sending us to the Persian border. Before our departure I want to bid you farewell, even if only in writing, and to thank you and tell you that as I leave, I bear in my memory your radiant image. I thank fate for the happiness it sent me in the form of my getting to know you.

And may the same fate send you happiness that must always safeguard your clear, pure path in life.

Your Kurlinsky

"Happiness—me? The path of my life is no longer so clear and pure!" Sasha thought.

"Well, thank God!" she said aloud.

"For what?" asked Petr Afanasevich.

"Kurlinsky joined up as a solider at last and he's leaving with his regiment for Persia. He'll see much of interest there and will come to his senses."

"I don't see anything wonderful about his decision," said Petr Afanasevich gloomily. "His heroic refusal would've been better."

"Would his mother's grief, torment, and suffering have been better?" Sasha objected in irritation. "You men are all alike. The more violence and evil, the happier you are . . ."

Lately there had been established a tone of irritation and unspoken, concealed sorrow between Sasha and her husband. Both suffered and awaited some resolution; but it did not occur, and their life together was getting more and more intolerable.

Petr Afanasevich went over to the window and began transplanting from one box to another the young plants that had just sent out their first tender leaves. His face was thoughtful; it no longer expressed any cheerful lightheartedness; Sasha had begun to feel sorry for him. She stood up and approached her husband.

"What is it, Sasha?"

"Nothing, I want to be with you."

"I'm very glad, my dear. Look at how the verbena's sprouted. It's a rare variety. Wait until you see it this summer!"

Sasha silently began to help her husband with his work; several large tears dropped onto the young plants.

"What a fortunate, nice, naïve man he is!" she thought. "And I? I will pick these verbenas, admire them, decorate my hair, and employ them to please another man who doesn't even want to know me."

Sasha could not restrain herself any longer; she retired to her own room. After getting dressed, she went out without saying a word to anyone.

It was the holiday of the Annunciation.[52] Spring had arrived early, and the ice on the Moscow River had just broken up. Porters swept water from the streets, and broad streams ran along the edges of sidewalks and disappeared underground. Sasha went to the bridge to have a look at the river. Leaning over the railing of Kamennyi Bridge, she watched as blocks of ice floated past. Standing on end, they slammed against the sides of the bridge. The mass of workers, now become festive, holiday spectators, making comments and spitting out the hulls of sunflower seeds, crowded her. A thick layer of these hulls on the bridge railings and on the stone ledge danced before her eyes.

She spent a long time looking at the passing blocks of ice. Her head was spinning: the bridge seemed to be floating as well; when she came to, she saw the ice moving by. But then something different began: now it was not the blocks of ice floating past, but the whole bridge, and she herself, and the crowd of gawking factory workers, and everything else being carried along swiftly in this bright spring sunshine. The blue sky was reflected in the seething, turbid water, muddied by the city, and Sasha's head began to spin.

"I'm floating . . . I'm going . . . where? Yes, where indeed? A long time ago, very long ago, when Ivan Ilych was playing the sonata, that same question of purpose arose. Isn't it that same aspiration that carries us off to eternity, resolving the question of 'Where' once and for all? If that question is real, then it has to be the same mysterious place to which we're all going, and which we love because that question 'Where' always undoubtedly makes us happy."

The thought of death suddenly occurred to Sasha so lucidly and blissfully that she almost threw herself into the water. But the muddy Moscow River seemed horrible to her. Sasha's love of cleanliness stopped her even here. "There's still time!" she thought, just the way everyone thinks who's not yet ready to die or commit suicide.

Sasha did not know how long she stood there. It was already growing dark when she came to her senses. The long spring day had passed, when and how, she had no idea. She did not feel like going home even now. She remembered that not far from here lived her young friend Katusya; she decided to drop in to see her. Katusya took one look at Sasha and exclaimed:

"What's the matter, Auntie Sasha? Are you ill?"

"No, I'm tired and haven't eaten all day."

"Why not? Have you quarreled with your husband?"

---

52. The church festival on March 25 commemorating the angel Gabriel's announcement to Mary that she would give birth to Jesus (Luke 1:26–38).

"My husband?" Sasha had completely forgotten that she had a husband, a child, and a home, and at first did not understand her friend's question. "No, but I'm tired, very tired. . . . Katusya, tell me why is everything on earth so filthy? Everything, everything . . ."

"What are you saying, Auntie Sasha? Have something to eat; you look so pale. Wait here, I'll bring you some chicken."

"Yes, later. But now listen to me; it's very curious. Look, there's dirt everywhere, and everywhere human passions. . . . You love music and you fall in love with a man—then the music vanishes, defiled by human passion. Kurlinsky loves people, loves life—and they're taking him off to murder, making him a soldier. . . . The water in the river is muddy; the pure earth is covered with stones and human filth, the pure sky is stained by soot and smoke, the pure love of people is sullied by the treachery of one's nearest and dearest; there's no escape, none at all, and I myself am filthy, base, lost . . ."

Sasha burst into tears almost to the point of fainting. Katusya looked at her in horror; it suddenly became clear that Sasha was mentally ill. Katusya calmed her down and brought her back home where Petr Afanasevich, who had been searching in torment all day and in vain for his wife, greeted them with a cry of joy. But, when he looked at Sasha, he realized the state she was in, and fell silent at once in his distressed concern.

16

The Last Sighs of the Song

Sasha woke up the next morning feeling calmer; Petr Afanasevich, after quietly kissing her on the forehead, went off to work. He returned home for dinner and found Sasha playing the piano. But he had some meeting that evening, so he had to leave again. Sasha had been silent the whole day; as soon as her husband left, she got dressed and set off hurriedly to where Ivan Ilych lived. She had not seen him in some time; when she arrived at his house, she began pacing back and forth in front of his gate, hoping without any basis that he would emerge any minute. But lights began to appear in the windows; shadows passed by and someone opened a window. Sasha froze for a moment; then her agitation became so unbearable that she sat down on the porter's bench at the far end of the fence. She was trembling, listening, afraid that someone would see her. Suddenly from the open window came the sounds of her beloved Nocturne in F-sharp Major by Chopin.[53] She had heard it last winter at a symphony concert, brilliantly performed by a professor at the

---

53. Opus 15, no. 2, composed in 1832.

French Conservatory, and she had learned to play it herself. But no one in the world could play it the way Ivan Ilych did. If excitement can kill people, this was such a moment for Sasha. Something ruptured inside her forever. Clenching her teeth, clasping her hands, rigid and numb, she sought Ivan Ilych with all her being. It seemed to her that with all her soul, she had to go somewhere immediately, to take leave of herself; she felt that the life force that had sustained her was insufficient to keep her whole; she stood up and ran along the street with such moaning and wailing that people stopped and stared at her.

When she reached home, Petr Afanasevich had already returned and Katusya had come to see her. Without looking around or seeing them, Sasha ran in and sat down at the piano. At first she began playing the Beethoven sonata that Ivan Ilych had played on her birthday at the dacha. The first arpeggio chord sounded soft and solemn and fell silent. But then came the allegro and her playing was better, livelier, and impressive. She imitated Ivan Ilych's style so faithfully and accurately that in some passages it sounded just like him. But she did not finish the sonata and immediately switched to Chopin's Nocturne. Reaching the end of it, she glanced around, did not say a word, and began playing Mendelssohn's *Song Without Words* in G Major. All of a sudden she stopped playing and cried out in an uncontrollable voice:

"There is no music, no; it's all muddled, dirty, it died . . ." Pale, her face deformed, she collapsed on the floor . . .

Sasha was delirious all night and suffered terribly, repeating that everything on earth had lost its purity, that only Ivan Ilych stood above all this and he would not allow her to get near him. . . . She reached her arms out and begged him to play for her . . .

They sent for the doctor, who found that her heart was overstressed and she was suffering from nervous tension.

Sasha remained in bed all day, pale and quiet; only her fingers moved, as if playing the piano; her large dark eyes expressed such desperate suffering that everyone unconsciously avoided meeting her gaze.

Petr Afanasevich did not leave her side; by the next day Sasha's madness had become even more obvious. Time and again she would sit down at the piano and begin playing first one, then another piece. She expended enormous effort, trying to decipher the manuscript copy of Ivan Ilych's symphony. Exhausted, she would start conversing with some unknown person:

"Is it all right? It's a marvelous piece, isn't it? Enough. Ah, I'm so tired. . . . Stop playing; there's no more music; they've covered it with filth. . . . My God, the sounds are tormenting me . . ."

Sasha would lie down in exhaustion and fall asleep.

On the third morning, when she saw that her husband was still asleep, exhausted from these past few days, she got up quietly, put on her white dressing gown adorned with swan feathers, and went out into the hallway. Taking her white Orenburg shawl from the table, she covered her head with it, and hastily, unnoticed by anyone, went out onto the street.

"Cabby! To the clinic!" she shouted.

"Thirty kopecks," he replied calmly.

"Without delay," Sasha said hastily, glancing around. "I'll add to it."

"Which clinic, madam?"

"The nerve clinic."

Going along Prechistenka, Sasha considered her condition rather sensibly.[54] Her energy was concentrated on not saying or doing anything inappropriate. But she recognized that her willpower was unmistakably weakening, some internal spiritual screw was coming loose, and the wildest thoughts were entering her head uninvited.

"Yes, I'm losing my mind," Sasha suddenly realized. "Any moment now I'll tell the cabby to drive to Ivan Ilych and I'll fall on my knees in front of him, kiss his hands, beg for his love, and ask him to play. . . . No, never!! Obviously that must never be . . ."

"Hurry up, cabby, faster for God's sake . . ."

Here's the Deviche field, and on the left a large building behind a fence. The cabby drove up to the iron gates. Sasha climbed down from the cab and suddenly remembered that she did not have any money.

"Wait a moment. I'll give you a note; take it to that house where you picked me up, and they'll pay you there."

The cabby muttered something in discontent, while Sasha went up to the gates and read the sign: "University Clinic for Nervous Diseases"; below and to the right, for some reason there was a plaque in French: "*Clinique des maladies nerveuses.*"

Walking up to the main entrance, Sasha began knocking at the heavy door. A soldier decorated with medals opened it and looked at her over-wrought white figure in astonishment.

"What can I do for you?" he asked.

Sasha made no reply and rushed ahead, glancing around the inside of the building. Behind a glass door there was a long, bright corridor decorated with

54. Prechistenka is one of the oldest streets in Moscow, where today the Tolstoy Museum is located.

fresh green plants. Nearby was a broad staircase leading up. To the left, there was another long corridor ending in a waiting room. The doorkeeper continued to block Sasha's way, but with curiosity she examined the place where she had voluntarily come to live.

"Please go into the waiting room, madam. You can't stay here . . ."

"Yes, fine. Where's the doctor?"

"I'll inform him immediately."

There was nothing in that room except a few dark wooden couches around a table. A door from the waiting room was opened into the doctor's study. Two women were sitting on a couch; one was quietly sobbing while the other tried to calm her.

Sasha covered her face with her shawl; closing her eyes, she clearly tried to summon up Ivan Ilych's face, hands, and entire presence.

She came to her senses only when someone touched her gently and asked:

"Wouldn't you like to come into my office?"

"Is he in there?" Sasha asked, looking at the doctor insanely. "Oh, excuse me. I was lost in thought. Yes, right away."

Sasha entered the doctor's large study; he indicated an armchair next to an enormous green desk where he sat down.

"Do you wish to be treated yourself or do you want to have someone else admitted?" asked the doctor, examining suspiciously Sasha's white dressing gown, her dark eyes, and her tragic beauty at that moment.

"I ask you to admit me; I'm very ill; I can't sleep or eat; I've lost my self-control and I'm tormenting my family. I need rest and your advice," Sasha said hurriedly, making incredible efforts to be logical and prevent the doctor from guessing that she was mad.

"How can this be? Have you no relatives, no husband?"

"Yes, I forgot. I must write to him; please give me a piece a paper and a pencil . . ."

"Here, take it. But tell me, what's caused you to come here? Are you unhappy?"

"No, no. I'll tell you sometime; now I can't. Is it clean everywhere here?"

"Of course. How do you wish to be admitted, as a paying guest?"

"What?"

"Can you pay sixty or ninety rubles a month?"

"Yes, of course. My husband will pay. Will you cure me? Can you make it so that my soul won't be so distressed at the filth that's inside and all around, everywhere? . . . My God, it's horrible!"

Sasha began to sob. The doctor rang. The soldier with the medals entered.

"Call Mariya Prokhorovna. Open Room 2 for paying guests. Calm down. We'll give you a room immediately and send for your husband. Write down your address."

Sasha began to grow calmer; she thought for a few seconds, and making another enormous effort to control herself, she sat down at the table and began writing to her husband:

> Pay the cabby eighty kopecks. I've entered the hospital for nervous diseases because I have no self-control left and no ability to restrain myself. Come confer with the doctor about my care. Send me clean underclothes, a clean dress, and everything else clean, all clean. . . .
>
> Yesterday I read Dante's *Purgatorio* and suddenly realized that I've been sullied by everything and can't be admitted to the Heavenly Conservatory.[55] You know that Ivan Ilych is no longer in Moscow. The water in the Moscow River is very dirty and there's so much filth at the Moscow Conservatory. He couldn't tolerate it; now he's teaching and playing in the Heavenly Conservatory and is summoning me there as well.
>
> Have another white dressing gown made for me as soon as possible; some mud was splattered on mine today and I'm in despair—yet another unnecessary spot. . . .
>
> I would like to cleanse my soul; however, neither you nor anyone else can take it in hand; no one has clean hands, and my soul is free. . . .
>
> Please, forgive me for this disturbance; when I'm clean and healthy, I'll come back home . . .

"That's enough writing," the doctor said to Sasha, somewhat vexed. "Now write your address."

After Sasha had finished, he summoned his medical assistant and charged her with sending the letter off with the cabby and escorting her to the designated room with a monthly rent of sixty rubles.

When Sasha was left alone in the empty room with only a bed, a table, and a chair, she removed her notebook from her pocket and took out of its side pouch a small amateur photograph of Ivan Ilych, which she had asked him to give her when he had shown it to her.

She stared at it with rapturous eyes and clasped it to her breast.

"Now no one can prevent me from being with you! My dear one! I can feel your soul, your presence; we'll never be parted again . . ."

---

55. *Purgatorio* is the second volume of Dante's *Divine Comedy* (1308–21).

She went up to the bed, lay down on it, closed her eyes, and once more clearly saw Ivan Ilych seated at the piano with his serious, inspired look, not directed at anyone in particular, and she heard his playing that filled her entire being with happiness.

From that day forward Sasha broke with everything in her life. She grew thin and pale, and her lovely face became completely translucent. Her slender fingers were almost always in motion, as if she were playing the piano; her huge dark eyes insanely expressed first blissfulness, then suffering.

The *Song* of her love for Ivan Ilych was sung to the end without words, and this *Song* had destroyed her life.

Having played this entire song in her heart, with all its tender, passionate phrases, Sasha still had three more last sighs ahead with which Mendelssohn's *Song Without Words* in G Major ends, and with which her beautiful young life would end. . . . The first sigh was one of hopeless love, the second of the repose of a purified soul, and the third was one of quiet, eternal joy. Then came the *pianissimo, morendo*—and everything would fade away forever . . . [56]

17

Oblivion

Toward the end of April, Ivan Ilych was sitting at a large desk near an open window, holding the proofs of a musical textbook that he had just completed and was about to publish.

His large head with its hair growing thinner on the crown and grayer at the temples, was bent over some music paper; his face was serious and his expression concentrated. His complicated textbook with its new discoveries of musical laws would prove to be astonishingly useful for instruction at the conservatory, and Ivan Ilych was glad that he had performed such useful labor. He worked for two hours every day with unusual precision and pedantry before his walk, followed by exercise in the fresh air, dinner, a concert in the evening, a visit with friends, or lessons with his pupils.

Everything was correct, serene, and reasonable. . . . Complete satisfaction from the fulfillment of the task he had set himself, service to the younger generation, relations with men only, especially with young men, primarily musicians. No upsets, no excitement . . .

Ivan Ilych occasionally recalled Sasha; his vanity was flattered by her love and, most of all, by her high regard for his talent. But now he was glad that all that had ended.

---

56. The Latin musical notation means "very soft, gradually dying away."

After working his allotted time, Ivan Ilych got ready for his walk. Aleksei Tikhonych handed him his coat and began in a monotonous, tranquil voice:

"That woman, Aleksandra Alekseevna, the one who lived next to us at the dacha, is in a clinic. Their porter recently came to our courtyard to fetch some coal and said that she was wasting away completely and had been admitted for treatment."

"What's wrong with her?"

"God only knows. She took herself off to a nerve clinic."

"Took herself off!" thought Ivan Ilych. "What a woman: energetic to the end!"

For a moment he recollected that evening when his symphony was being performed, when he was conducting that passionate poem to love. . . . Had he really composed it? The melody arose in his head; then Sasha's image emerged in his memory, of her sitting in the first row of the stalls, dressed all in white, with diamonds in her hair and ears, jubilant and triumphant, as she followed Ivan Ilych's symphony and his success with such passionate excitement.

Was this blooming Sasha now locked up in a clinic and had she vanished from his life without a trace?

Ivan Ilych went out onto the street but something had disrupted his spiritual equanimity. He walked quickly, eyes wandering, and made an effort to consign Sasha to oblivion and to concentrate instead on his textbook.

At the turning of the lane he met his cheerful, ruddy, favorite pupil Tsvetkov. They greeted each other. Ivan Ilych's animated eyes expressed joy as he held Tsvetkov's hand and made arrangements with him for that evening to correct and play the short overture he had composed.

Toward the end of the month Ivan Ilych's textbook was published and he received a considerable sum of money. That afforded him great joy. Now he could realize his dream and go abroad with Tsvetkov.

While Sasha was residing and fading away at the nerve clinic, Ivan Ilych was enjoying his travels and the company of his beloved student. He had forgotten all about her and the rest of the world in his epicurean bliss!

Only once more in his life, passing a small house in Switzerland, did he remember Sasha. From inside came the sound of Mendelssohn's *Song Without Words* in G Major being played on a violin. Ivan Ilych stopped and blood rushed to his face. But he soon calmed down and hastened on his walk. He himself never played that *Song* again in his life. "To forget, forget everything except for music; music alone will be my mission, my life, my interest . . ." he thought.

And he did forget everything else, except for his beloved art, which he served to the end of his days.

Chopin's Prelude

LEV LVOVICH TOLSTOY

PREFACE

I WROTE *CHOPIN'S PRELUDE* several years ago and must state that at first it was not written as a retort to *The Kreutzer Sonata* in the least, but simply as an expression of thoughts that had been keenly preoccupying me at that time. The story took the form of an antithesis to *The Kreutzer Sonata* only during its last revision.

Publishing it now in a separate book together with my other stories, I do not renounce the principal ideas it expresses; nor do I renounce the idea that early marriage is a great blessing; that the aspiration for total celibacy does not make sense since the complete celibacy of mankind is impossible and would lead to the discontinuation of the human race; that the goal of our life should not be aspiration for total celibacy but rather aspiration for an early, pure, and chaste marriage.

Therefore, my reply to *The Kreutzer Sonata* and to its Afterword, regardless of how artistically powerful they are and how forcefully they present the negative aspects of marital relations—is only one: their conclusion is erroneous.

They conceive of an ideal that can never be. Abstention from sexual relations cannot be posited as an ideal because it would eliminate the very concept of this ideal and lead to a logical absurdity.

I confess that the tone in which *Chopin's Prelude* was written could have been more serene, and that would have been better; I regret that I yielded to a certain feeling of irritation. But what's done is done.

With another tone, perhaps I could not have been completely sincere when I wrote this story.

May 6, 1900

L. L. Tolstoy

Therefore shall a man leave his father and his mother,
and shall cleave unto his wife, and they shall be one flesh.

Genesis 2:24

Ephesians 5:31

Matthew 19:5

I

One evening Countess Trubova was hosting a farewell ball.

She had arranged it for her three grown nieces who were planning to leave for their house in the country the next day.

Princess Baretskaya, the countess's sister, and her daughters had spent the whole winter in Moscow; she had introduced them into society, entertained guests on their behalf almost every other day, and expended a great deal of money on them, but without achieving the desired results.

Now, as they were leaving tomorrow, of course there was almost nothing left to hope for.

There were even fewer eligible bachelors in Moscow than there were in the provinces. True, there were a few "genuine" young people, with name, position, and means, but it was not easy to catch one of them. They were either lighthearted, merrymaking young men who thought little about marriage, or they were too serious and rarely appeared in society; or, what Princess Baretskaya noticed most often, such a person was just about to turn up, on the verge of making a proposal, and suddenly, for no good reason at all, he would turn his back and disappear into thin air. It was the students in Moscow who were the male partners at a dance. There were as many of those as one could desire. They danced at balls and conducted the music at them. They courted and won the hearts of the young ladies of Moscow; it was only with them that the animation of so-called Moscow society could be maintained.

But what sort of suitors were they? Could the princess want such a frivolous baby, on whose lips the milk had hardly dried, without experience, without position, and most often, without means, as a husband for one of her daughters?

Countess Trubova, however, did not agree with her sister about these students. More than once she had observed that the students or young people in general shouldn't be spurned, that one could expect more constant and sincere attachment to their future wives from them than from older and more experienced men; and that in general one should not impede their relationships with young women because only good could come of them. As proof, the countess offered several examples of happy marriages from her own acquaintances, where the husbands were quite young, recently "fledged," as she expressed it, students. But the princess paid little attention to her sister's words, since she had grown terribly tired of the constant worry tormenting her for almost ten years, namely, her daughters' matches; she dreamed only about marrying them off quickly; naturally she envisioned genuine suitors with more defined status than a student's.

The princess imagined the ideal husband for her daughters as some young Marshal of the Nobility, of whom there were several among their acquaintances, or else a wealthy, young landowner or Land Captain; and, if he were someone from town, then an Official for Special Assignments or a military officer, also, of course, a man of means.[1] But the more urgently she considered this question, the more agitated she became; she paid compliments where needed, flattered, and courted; but the more coolly she treated those who were undesirable suitors, of whom she was always afraid, the less success she had, and the more maliciously, it seemed, fate mocked her, leaving her with daughters on her hands.

One genuine suitor, Count Wostitz, a wealthy man and former military officer, Moscow's most eligible beau, seemed to be much taken with her middle daughter, Princess Manya; but afterward, God knows why, he lost all interest. The elder daughter, thirty-three-year-old Anna, who was almost a beauty, very clever, and, in the opinion of the princess, would have made a wonderful wife, had almost taken up with Shubinsky, a forty-three-year-old bachelor, completely bald; but he suddenly left for his estate in the country, without even bidding them farewell.

The youngest, Sonechka, was always flirting with students who hovered in a crowd around her all winter.[2] The district marshal from B. had begun courting her, and might even have married her sooner than the others, but Sonechka had merely made fun of his long nose and said that he looked like Don Quixote. She was much more attracted to all those beardless young men, the students.

---

1. Marshal of the Nobility: a representative of the nobility in a province or district elected to manage affairs and defend their interests in local government organs; Land Captain: an official appointed by the Ministry of the Interior, usually a former officer or local landowner, involved in all aspects of peasant affairs; Official for Special Assignments: an influential position as personal attaché or troubleshooter on a provincial governor's staff.

2. Sonechka is an affectionate diminutive form of the name Sofiya.

"Well, Sonechka can wait a bit longer. It's still early to fret about her; with her vivacity she'll be able to find herself a good husband. But it would be very nice to marry off Manechka somehow or Anna!"[3]

That's how Princess Baretskaya reasoned, seated now in the doorway of the spacious living room alongside her sister, the hostess, and other highly regarded Moscow mammas arranged in a large semicircle behind them. Perfumed and primped, fanning themselves, many exposing their elderly necks immodestly and, at the same time, wearing false teeth in their mouths and only lifeless hair on their heads, these women sat admiring their own daughters and sons dancing in front of them in Countess Trubova's large, brightly lit hall. Meanwhile, the men, their husbands, congregated in distant rooms at card tables and took little interest in the dancing.

The fourth and last quadrille was coming to an end.[4] The evening was in full swing—the last gala of the season. The next day, when Princess Baretskaya would abandon Moscow, society would be noticeably diminished and becalmed without her and her daughters. Besides, the last three days of Holy Week would have passed, and all the young people, primarily the dancers, would soon be taking their exams.

Almost everyone present that evening knew this and therefore, enjoying their last opportunity, many were dancing with great enthusiasm.

"Oh, oh," Princess Baretskaya whispered nervously, glancing up at the tall figure of Count Wostitz—who had just appeared in the doorway of the hall with a cloak under his arm and a gold pince-nez on his nose—what if it's today! What if he's come for this! Who knows? *Les marriages se font dans les cieux.*[5] The last throw of the dice sometimes pays off. It's just like roulette. But that Manya, my God, what a fool she is, what an inexcusable fool. She says she doesn't particularly feel like getting married now, and that she wanted it much more about five years ago. He was just about to be caught, but managed to slip through my fingers. A little more pressure had to be applied. He was certainly wooing her at the beginning of winter.

With a little smile on his face Count Wostitz looked over the hall with his nearsighted, squinting eyes and went to greet the hostess.

"*Grand rond!*" cried the dance master with all his strength.[6]

---

3. Manechka is an affectionate diminutive form of the name Mariya.

4. The quadrille is an elegant dance of French origin performed by four couples in a square formation.

5. The French sentence means "Marriages are made in heaven."

6. The French phrase refers to the sixth part and finale of a quadrille.

The high-priced, well-known ballroom pianist began playing splendidly the sixth figure of the quadrille.

"*Grand rond!*" repeated the dance master, his voice now completely hoarse.

This was Belikov, a tall blond student, a fashionable philologist, a gallant with right-wing views, but a fine, simple lad, as people described him. He was already in his fourth year of study and had an income; consequently, and as a rare exception to many other students, he was not ignored by the mammas of Moscow. There was little standing in the way of his becoming a genuine suitor, and this was certainly shown by the aplomb and informality with which he behaved. It was usually the case that students in the upper courses almost quit appearing in society and dancing at balls; but Belikov didn't follow that rule; therefore he was held in the highest regard in society, especially by hostesses.

"*Les dames tournent!*" he continued to direct the dance. "*Corbeille!*[7] Kryukov! Kryukov! What's happened to you, my dear fellow, are you lost? *Les dames tournent encore!*" he shouted in anger and with authority. "*Et chaîne double à gauche et plus d'entrain, plus d'entrain, s'il vous plaît!*"[8] Belikov's voice resounded so stridently, his French "r" rolled so raucously that his entire body twitched in time with the music.

There was also sufficient liveliness in all the remaining dancers. Their faces turned red, perspiration was dripping from their brows, and colorful couples flitted by one after another.

After the *chaîne* Belikov devised such an elaborate figure that it seemed impossible to disentangle.

Everyone was crowded into one group. Kryukov, one of the youngest students, not very tall but strong and stocky, with what appeared to be an unusually simple, almost childlike face, had danced with the youngest princess and now was pushed so hard from behind that he was pressed right up against his partner.

Her knees were resting against his legs and her bosom was pressed against his chest. The dance master was trying to unscramble the figure. Belikov's eyes were bulging and he was wiping sweat from his face; he silently dragged his partner, the eldest princess, along with him. She was smiling graciously with her faded, sullen face.

"Well, well, how will the dance master manage to extricate himself?" said Kryukov to his partner, pleased at such proximity to her and wishing that it would last as long as possible.

---

7. The French terms mean "Women turn!" (repeated below with "again") and "Basket"— a figure in the quadrille.

8. "And form a double chain to the left, and more spirit, more spirit, if you please!"

"Are you tired?"

"No," Princess Sonechka replied. "Are you?"

She was like quicksilver, bouncing in place to the beat of the music and swinging his hand in hers, squeezing it softly. Her little round face was beaming with happiness.

"Will you come to see us in the country?" she asked without looking at him, in a low voice, through almost closed lips. "You must come, absolutely. Do you hear?"

"Your mother hasn't invited me," said Kryukov, low enough so that others couldn't hear him.

"I'm inviting you, and mama will, too, I'll tell her to . . ."

"Thank you," said Kryukov.

Continuing to feel the touch of her young, tender, trembling body next to his, he lost his head completely at that moment. Gazing into her particularly lively little face, with its turned-up nose and dark, shining eyes—a face that everyone else found unattractive, but in which he glimpsed so much life, youth, and strength that he could scarcely tear himself away. He couldn't refrain from admiring Sonechka and thinking only about her.

Yes, he was in love with her, and had been desperately for the last three months. He had known this for some time, even back when they were skating one evening at Patriarch Ponds; but now that he knew she was leaving for the country the next day, and that he might not see her again or hold her little gloved hand in his, some new feeling, not quite madness or despair, overcame and dismayed him.[9]

"Why? For what?" he asked himself.

He didn't understand very well at all why it was impossible for her to remain with him forever, since they loved one another and this fact was even clear to other people.

"*Et valse, s'il vous plaît,*" ordered the dance master in a whisper: he had lost his voice from shouting.[10] He was still hoping to untangle and complete the last scrambled figure of the quadrille. Everyone took a step aside to make room. The pianist immediately began playing a well-known waltz by Waldteufel, reworked from the Gypsy song "I feel so happy with you!"[11] Kryukov embraced his partner's slim waist, and, feeling beside himself, took off with

9. Patriarch Ponds was an affluent residential area in central Moscow.

10. "A waltz, if you please."

11. Émile Waldteufel (1837–1915) was a French composer of dance music, best known for his waltzes.

her around the hall. Her arm rested on his shoulder and her warm breath touched his face. They danced two turns of the waltz, and after the last one, when everyone had already returned to their places, he danced Sonechka over to her chair and sat her down.

"Ooh! I'm tired," she said, adjusting a lock of hair that had slipped down over her eye, and shaking her head.

He sat down next to her and said:

"So you're leaving tomorrow? Why? Don't go; stay here."

"What do you mean?"

She smiled slightly, her young bosom rising frequently with her breathing, and she looked into his eyes with her sympathetic, melancholy glance.

At that moment he saw that she was ready, with all her being, to give herself to him, to unite her life with his forever.

"*Regarde un peu ta fille cadette,*" Countess Trubova whispered at the same time to her sister, "*ils s'aiment!*"[12]

"That's all right," said the princess smiling condescendingly and wincing. "Tomorrow I'll be whisking her away. That artist Kryukov, his father, *n'a pas le sou?*[13] Right?"

"As far as I know," said the countess, "but you're incorrigible *dans vos opinions;* for pity's sake, he's a fine fellow, a musician, congenial, and moral."[14]

"Perhaps. But that's even worse."

"I feel sorry for Sonechka," said the countess with feeling (she had no children of her own and therefore both knew and understood young people better than others); "all these crushes—afterward they always leave such a distasteful *rancune.*"[15]

"It'll pass. It happens twenty times over at this age. It doesn't matter. What would you like? *Vous voulez les marier?*"[16]

The princess turned away, waved her hand dismissively, as if it wasn't even worth considering such a trivial matter. Of course, any idea of the serious possibility of a match between Sonechka and this twenty-year-old student could never enter her head—Kryukov, *qui n'a pas le sou,* who was merely one of a number of students who had danced with her daughters this past winter and who had visited them at home.

---

12. "Take a look at your youngest daughter . . . they're in love!"
13. The French phrase means "is penniless."
14. The French phrase means "with your opinions."
15. The French word means "bitterness."
16. "Would you marry them off?"

2

Soon the mazurka began.[17] Kryukov danced it with the unattractive and chubby Mlle Rdevskaya; he failed to amuse his partner and was distracted. He couldn't take his eyes off Sonechka, who was dancing with the Cornet Bukhanov.[18]

Kryukov found this officer, with his minuscule jet-black mustachios curled upward, and his arrogant look, extremely repugnant. He felt terribly jealous of him. Furthermore, he knew that not longer ago than yesterday this same Bukhanov, together with a group of the most irresponsible students and other young men, had visited the darkest, most disgusting places, where they had wasted the entire night. They had set off from Belikov's place, where Kryukov himself had spent yesterday evening, and where everyone had been playing cards and drinking.

But Kryukov himself hadn't been playing cards, hadn't been drinking, and most of all, he hadn't gone off with them afterward. In the first place, he didn't have the means to indulge in these pursuits; second, even if he had had the money, although he associated with comrades such as Belikov when invited, he kept himself somewhat apart and didn't participate in their binges. It wasn't on principle that he refrained from wine, women, and card games; it was simply that he felt disgust at it all, and instinctively feared and shielded himself from this filth. Sometimes his comrades teased him for his moral stance, but they didn't pester him much; and once he had refused to participate in some of their merry activities, they left him in peace, knowing that they would never get him to change his mind.

"And here's this Bukhanov," thought Kryukov now, choking with rage and contempt, "this depraved, dirty little officer, who only last night was wallowing in filth, now wooing Sonechka, my Sonechka. He's bending over her, breathing the same air, looking into her eyes. How dare he? How can he be so insolent?"

Kryukov continued tormenting himself, feeling insanely jealous of this officer who was obviously so sure of himself, of his attractiveness and irresistibility. He wanted to tell the whole world, right then and there, what this Bukhanov was really like, and what was hidden behind his little mustache and his broad chest.

Meanwhile he noted carefully that Princess Baretskaya had several times glanced at Sonechka and her new admirer with a satisfied smile.

17. Derived from a lively Polish folk dance, the mazurka became very popular in European ballrooms during the nineteenth century.
18. The low rank of cornet was assigned to new junior officers in the Russian cavalry.

"Of course, what better suitor could she find for her daughter? Bukhanov has it all: a name, means, position, even looks."

Kryukov grew so angry that his hands began trembling.

Supper was served after the mazurka. Once again Sonechka sat together with Bukhanov, far away, at the other end of the hall. Kryukov continued glaring at them unceasingly.

"What do you find so riveting at that table?" the kindhearted Mlle Rdevskaya asked him unexpectedly. "You seem to be interested in the young princess?"

"What a fool you are," Kryukov wanted to reply, but refrained and said instead:

"No, I'm trying to see whether there's any salad left there."

Supper finally concluded and the cotillion began immediately, the final dance of the evening.[19] Kryukov's torments ended. Now he was dancing with Sonechka again; when he took her by the arm and led her to their previous place in the corner of the hall, he felt that he was reviving again.

But for the first few minutes alone he didn't know what to say to her.

When she sat down, he bent over her and uttered:

"You don't know, Princess, how I've been suffering . . ."

"Why?"

"Why did you promise to dance the mazurka with that . . . ?"

She was surprised, as if she hadn't been expecting such words from him, and answered vigorously:

"I couldn't refuse. He'd invited me a few days ago during our receiving hours. I'm sorry you found it so unpleasant. Please do not be angry with me."

"I'm not angry, but I found it very painful to see you so close to him."

"Why? He's so talkative."

"Because . . ." Kryukov hesitated and finally said: "Because you're so pure and good, while he's the sort of man you shouldn't even know about . . ."

He uttered those last words so forcefully that she involuntarily turned toward him and looked into his eyes.

"And what about you?" she suddenly asked seriously and softly, as if grasping something. "Are you like him or like me?"

"Like you," he replied, also softly. Kryukov blushed deeply.

She glanced at him again with a tender, grateful look; giving his hand a little squeeze, she jumped back to her feet.

---

19. The cotillion is a complicated patterned dance, forerunner of the quadrille, that originated in eighteenth-century France and originally comprised four couples in a square formation.

"Let's go," she said.

A general mazurka had begun.

It was already three o'clock in the morning when the guests began to leave Countess Trubova's house.

The young people were the last who went in a group to bid farewell to the two sisters who were the hostesses, next to whom in the living room sat the three younger princesses, exhausted and a little pale. Old Count Trubov, a short, gray-haired little man, sat near them on the sofa, obviously having had his fill of card games that evening.

Bukhanov, who was standing in front of the others, addressed the princess: "Will you allow me to accompany you to the station tomorrow?" After him came Count Wostitz, the district marshal from B., then Belikov, Sukhodin, Prince Palitsin, and Kryukov; all four of the latter were students. Of these, only Kryukov was not wearing a dress uniform.

"We'd be delighted," said the princess, "and our daughters would be, too. The train leaves at noon. We have everything packed, so all we have to do is get on our way."

"We're going to cry our eyes out," Count Wostitz said in jest, wiping the perspiration from his red face (he had danced the cotillion with Princess Manya, to the old princess's great delight).

"That's up to you—whether you cry or not," said the old princess ambiguously.

Each and every young man kissed the hand of the countess and the old princess, bowed and scraped before the old count and the young princesses, and then left the drawing room.

3

The next day all of them, just as they had planned, arrived at the Kursk Station to see off Princess Baretskaya. She and her daughters were already in their seats.

It was five minutes to twelve and the train was just about to pull away. Count and Countess Trubov stood on the platform; nearby stood the countess's elegant elderly uncle, under the window from which the princess's broad, fleshy face with its triple chin was now protruding. With certain bewilderment she surveyed the crowd of suitors standing a bit farther off, next to the railway brake, where the three young princesses had emerged.

"*Pourquoi est-ce que vous ne les prenez avec vous?*" the elderly uncle asked the princess, leaning over to her ear.[20]

20. "Why don't you take them with you?"

"*Demandez!*" replied the princess. "*C'est tout bonnement bête!*"[21]

"*Elle est trop difficile*," replied Countess Trubova.[22]

"Yes, my dear, *difficile*," the princess teased her in a slightly uncivil manner. "That's fine for you to say when all you have to worry about is your better half," she said, indicating the count with her eyes. "But as for me, I've had it up to here—*par dessus la tête*.[23] And for what reason, if I may ask," the princess lowered her voice completely, "did they hang around here all winter?"

"I wouldn't know. I've had no experience," said Countess Trubova, turning more to her uncle. "However, I think it better not to scorn these youngsters; and the main thing is, not to lose valuable time. I've always said that. She's already wasted time on her elder daughters, and it's going to be just the same with her youngest."

"Nonsense!" the princess said, offended. "You're talking nonsense. Will you be coming to Ivanovka? You must; I'll expect you."

Almost the very same phrase was heard from the other end of the car.

"So, will you be coming? You must, really," said the three young princesses all at once, addressing the young men among whom were all of yesterday's dance partners, not excluding even the district marshal from B. with the long nose who looked like Don Quixote.

"I can't possibly come in July," said Count Wostitz.

"And I can't in August," said Bukhanov, "although it was precisely for that month that the princess invited me."

"And what about you, Ivan Pavlovich?" Sonechka said, addressing Kryukov, who was approaching the train car indecisively when he saw that she wanted to say something to him.

He wanted to reply that he could not come because the old princess had not invited him separately and personally, but had invited them all as a group, but he was too embarrassed to utter this aloud in front of his comrades.

"When will you return to Moscow?" he asked instead.

"I don't know; mama thinks we may go abroad."

Sonechka's face assumed a glum expression.

Just then the chief conductor, who was energetically striding past them along the platform, blew his whistle. Right after that, the steam engine sounded its whistle.

---

21. "You ask! . . . That's just stupid!"
22. "She is too difficult."
23. The French phrase means "as much as one can take."

"So, do you promise to come?" asked Sonechka, leaning hurriedly over the iron rail and extending her hand to Kryukov. "Goodbye. Take care! I'll expect you!"

He dashed up to her, squeezed her hand so hard that she almost cried out in pain, and bowed silently, doffing his cap. The train pulled away.

Without budging, Kryukov stared at Sonechka while she stared greedily back at him, not at all ashamed that her sisters were smiling at her behavior, while Bukhanov was winking to his comrades.

They kept looking at each other until they lost sight of one another.

The train disappeared from view beyond a curve, but Kryukov remained standing in the same spot holding his cap, still staring straight ahead.

"So, old boy, lost in thought. What about?" he suddenly heard Bukhanov's voice next to him and felt someone's hand on his shoulder.

He shuddered and came back to his senses.

All his comrades were standing around him lighting cigarettes.

Kryukov was embarrassed at his absentmindedness, and blushed deeply once more. He put on his cap and said:

"I don't like departures in general."

"Especially when the one departing is . . ." said Bukhanov.

"Such a nice family," said Kryukov to complete his phrase.

And he thought that the whole Baretsky family, especially the young princesses, were really very nice people with whom he wished to live forever.

Leaving the station, the young people said their goodbyes and dispersed in pairs into carriages heading off in various directions.

Only Kryukov, who lived at the other end of Moscow and who was poorer than the rest, returned home on foot. His classmate Sukhonin offered to give him a lift, but Kryukov refused, feeling the desire and the need to walk and to be alone. He realized that something very important and very sad had just taken place in his life, and that only he understood and, as expected, could understand this calamity.

Sonechka had left and he would not see her again. She had invited him and was hoping that he would visit them in the country, but he could not go simply on the basis of her invitation. How could he not realize that the old princess deliberately had not invited him personally, as she had Bukhanov and Wostitz, because she did not wish to continue the friendship and was afraid of it? In other words, Sonechka had left for good and, perhaps, he might never see her again for the rest of his life.

And meanwhile?

Meanwhile, from the moment he had first met her, when he felt that she regarded him affectionately, and perhaps could become his wife someday, his life had changed dramatically. It had become meaningful: a purpose had appeared that immediately raised his spirit and his strength.

Since the time he had become acquainted with the Baretsky family, Kryukov had become bolder, more animated, more cheerful. He began studying, forgot about other women, and was completely content with dreams of Sonechka.

And now?

Now he was left alone again, completely alone, with a hole in his heart. Once more there was nothing bright or joyful left in his life, nothing at all lay ahead.

But why had he lost her? Why hadn't he kept hold of her? Why didn't he marry her, if she occupied his thoughts so completely?

What? He, Vanya Kryukov, a poor second-year student, still living like a boy in his father's house in some hole at the end of a hall, marry the young Princess Baretskaya?[24]

How could that be? Did it mean that he would marry her and bring her home to his parents to live with her in his own room? Or leave the university? Or what? And what would his family members say to this idea—his father, mother, and sister? And Sonechka herself: would she really agree to marry him, against the wishes of her own mother and sisters, his parents, and the whole world? What then? Accordingly, would he have to carry her off secretly and by force, and then marry her? Besides, did students even have the right to get married? They had to obtain permission; for that, you had to spend time and take steps. Where would he get the strength to do all that? How and where would he begin?

"No, no," Kryukov repeated to himself. "It's obvious that the situation's such that it's completely impossible to get married. 'He's' still a child; 'he' hasn't grown up yet."

"How can it be that 'he' hasn't grown up yet?" Kryukov asked himself. "What kind of child is 'he' if he loves her, loves her passionately, when, from the springtime air and sunshine, from an excess of strength, this feeling took his breath away. He knew that only Sonechka, only being close to her, could both moderate and invigorate him. Could all this merely be the caprice of his idleness and imagination? Was it really impossible for him to live without the thought of a woman? He might be able to, but how? By what? What's left to

---

24. Vanya is the usual diminutive form of the name Ivan.

him? A family in which all its members live their own separate egotistical lives and no one has any interest in others? And the university, his studies, his comrades? Those studies that he finds repulsive, with few exceptions? His comrades, not one of whom had he grown close to and befriended, as he had previously expected, and who held such different views and habits about everything? His music? Yes, perhaps only music remained as something good, joyful, and comforting. He would certainly take up music again that summer when he was finished with his exams. But Sonechka? Was it really necessary to forget her?"

This idea caused him great distress.

He walked along familiar streets swiftly, occasionally hopping over puddles on the pavement; anxious, gloomy thoughts whirled around in his head.

4

Upon arriving home, Kryukov locked himself into his little room and read the most boring lectures on comparative linguistics until five o'clock. Then he had dinner; after everyone had left the dining room and moved into the living room where a card table had been prepared, he sat down at the piano.

He opened one of Chopin's Notebooks at random and began playing the first piece he came upon, no. 15 of the *24 Preludes, sostenuto*.[25] He played it with great feeling and elegance.

At that moment his father walked through the dining room holding a deck of cards.

"What a splendid prelude that is," he said. "What simplicity, and at the same time what power. Your playing today is excellent."

"Really? Do you like it?" asked Kryukov.

"Have your young princesses left?" his father asked.

"Yes."

"Are you sad? It's not worth it, my son. There are plenty of fish in the sea. After all, this is no time for you to get married."

With these words Kryukov's father went off to the next room.

"Plenty of fish in the sea," Kryukov repeated after him. "So that's the kind of help and support I get from my father at such a difficult time. Besides, could he ever really understand me?"

---

25. Chopin's *24 Preludes*, opus 28, are a set of short pieces for the piano, one in each of the twenty-four keys, originally published in 1839. The Italian musical term *sostenuto* indicates a manner of playing that is sustained as long as, or beyond a note's full value.

"This is no time for you to get married," he repeated his father's words to himself. "Of course. How else could he see things?"

To calm himself down, Kryukov began playing the next prelude, no. 16, *presto con fuoco*, which he knew by heart."[26]

When he felt agitated, nothing calmed him down the way music could; he was able to convey everything he was feeling in the notes, without worrying about whether someone was listening to him, as happened when he played without real necessity.

He remained at the piano for almost an hour. Then he came back to his senses and returned to his lectures.

But after playing, he was too overwrought and his memory was not working at all. Therefore he decided to leave the house and go out for a walk.

He glanced into the living room where a game of vint was now in full swing, with its assorted exclamations: pass, three spades, four no trump; even his sister was playing.[27] He went into the hall and began dressing to leave.

The maid Matresha, pretty and fit, with a smooth face and bold movements, popped out of her room to help him.

"Going for a walk?" she asked casually, chewing on something and wiping her mouth with her hand.

Kryukov merely looked at her resentfully and ran down the stairs. He turned hurriedly to the right, feeling the need to move as quickly as possible.

It was almost 7 in the evening. Springtime twilight was closing in with its light chill and its very fresh air.

"Where to go? Talk to whom?" To whom could he tell everything he felt in his heart? Complain to?

Kryukov searched in his memory for someone close to him, but did not come up with anyone.

"Those closest to me, even people related by blood, don't understand me and won't. Tell all to my mother or sister? If they didn't laugh at me, they'd try to dissuade me; they wouldn't believe in the seriousness of my mood and thoughts. Talk to my father?"

"He's just shown his approach. My father's a sensitive man and understood my situation; on the other hand, no one can be as coldly cruel and indifferent in practice."

26. No. 16, the so-called *"Hades" Prelude*, is considered the most difficult of the series. The Italian *presto con fuoco* means "very fast, with fire."

27. Vint is a Russian card game similar to bridge and whist, sometimes referred to as Russian whist.

"Should I write directly to Sonechka, who might be the only one to understand me? Consult with her? But about what? Tell her I love her but that I can't marry her?"

Emerging from the little lane onto one of Moscow's grand boulevards, Kryukov recalled that his comrade Komkov lived not far from where he stood.

It had been a long time, perhaps some three months, since he had last dropped in to see him; on some previous occasions there had been no one else with whom he could talk so simply and honestly.

"How's he doing?" Kryukov wondered. "How are his affairs and his mood?"

He turned off from the boulevard into the next familiar lane.

Komkov was a medical student in his third year, the son of a gymnasium teacher who had died several years ago.[28]

The clever and capable Komkov enjoyed great popularity in the university and at one time, namely last winter, had been passionately involved with a student organization from his hometown. He had become implicated in some incident during his first year, but lately had calmed down and begun applying himself more diligently. Last spring he had managed to use some small funds to travel abroad; he was ecstatic as a result of his trip.

"Is Aleksandr Ivanovich at home?" Kryukov asked, when the familiar maid opened the door to the small apartment in which the Komkov family lived.

"Yes, he is. But he doesn't live here with us," she replied. "He got married and moved into the separate annex. Over there."

"Really? When?" Kryukov asked in surprise.

"A month or so ago. He married the young Miss Puzikova. Do you know her?"

"No, I don't," said Kryukov.

"She's a merchant's daughter, but she's educated and a good girl. This way, please."

The maid pointed to the gray wall of a dilapidated and lopsided one-story annex in the courtyard, looking more like a caretaker's hut than a house.

Now Kryukov wanted to see his comrade in this new setting even more than before. He wondered why he had moved from the larger apartment where, probably, only his mother lived and his older brother, who was also

---

28. A gymnasium is a type of school providing secondary education, comparable to English grammar schools and American prep schools.

recently married. He approached the door of the annex and rang the simple bell by pulling the chain.

A moment later a young woman appeared on the threshold; she was thin and pale, dressed simply in a plain black dress.

Kryukov asked her if Komkov was at home.

"Ah, it's you!" a loud voice rang out from the little room across the tiny hallway. "I recognized your voice. You haven't been to see me in quite a while."

Then Komkov himself, tall and broad-shouldered, with disheveled blond hair, wearing a student's double-breasted jacket, came out to meet his old friend. His face had changed noticeably and acquired a healthy glow since Kryukov had last seen him.

"Am I disturbing you?" asked Kryukov.

"Disturbing me? Why would you? Let me introduce you: this is my wife. This is Kryukov, my old friend from the gymnasium," he said simply.

"I'm so surprised to find you married. I never expected it."

"Yes, yes. Well, brother, *tempora mutantur et nos cum illis.*[29] And as for you, I've heard that you've entered society, become an aristocrat, and attend all sorts of 'dances.' Is it true? Well, are you thinking of following my example?"

"You mean, getting married?"

For some reason Kryukov started laughing, as if wanting to show by his laughter that he could never have conceived of such an inappropriate act. But his laughter sounded unnatural; Komkov noticed that.

"That's too bad, my friend," he said seriously. "Why don't you think about it? Is it too early or just too difficult?"

"Both," replied Kryukov, following his hosts into their neatly furnished small room, where a samovar was boiling and where bread and jam were on the table.

In the next room, curtained off from the one they had entered, two beds placed next to each other could be seen through the opening.

"You ask permission from the authorities, go to a priest, and that's it," said Komkov, sitting down on a small sofa and setting about rolling cigarettes— the activity from which he had most likely been torn.

"Nothing more?" asked Kryukov.

"What else do you need? As you can see, we've arranged our living quarters and we're living splendidly. We eat whatever God sends us; we study and

---

29. The Latin sentence means "The times change and we [change] with them."

we're happy for the time being; as for tomorrow, what will be, will happen, or rather, what has to be."

"Why did you move here from your apartment?"

"We have our own life," said Komkov. "My elder brother also got married. Why should we stir up trouble? No, it's better that each of us lives separately."

"Are you content?"

"Completely."

"That's how well you've pleased him," Kryukov said, turning to the young woman who, with a gentle smile, was now offering him a glass of tea. For some reason at that very moment he thought about Sonechka; he found that this Puzikova woman resembled her, especially in her eyes and her figure. But Sonechka was somehow much more animated.

"She has nothing to do with it," said Komkov, nodding at his wife. "Any other young, healthy, pretty, pleasant woman, if fate had deigned to send a different one to me instead, would have pleased me just as much. They're all the same. Don't you agree?"

"Doesn't this offend you?" Kryukov asked Komkov's young wife in astonishment.

"Me? No. Good Lord! Why should I be offended? He's only saying that in jest."

"What do you mean, in jest? No. That's what I really think," said Komkov. "There's nothing offensive in it. My wife's a young woman like any other; she completed the gymnasium; she reads and speaks some French, and she tickles the 'ivories'—but that's not the point. It's not what sort of wife she makes—it's a matter of luck: one person does better, another, worse. The main point is in us, our relation to marriage, and in the correct solution of the sexual question. Only then can a man settle down; only then can he feel that he's assumed his proper place and begun to live fully, to act, and to be useful. Only from that time can he continue to grow and develop as a moral being.

"In my opinion, an unmarried man is like a hungry dog; he bustles, fusses, rushes around, and merely makes a fool of himself, doing nothing sensible on earth, or else he's like a depraved ape, who's lost all his human qualities. There's nothing in between; then he's no longer a man, but a limp rag."

"You're expressing yourself harshly," Kryukov said with a laugh.

"It's the honest truth," Komkov resumed heatedly. "How can we be distinguished from animals, if only from apes, if not by a rational and conscious attitude toward our own nature and its demands. How is it that we know that when we're hungry, we have to eat, but we don't know that when the time comes, we have to get married? We have yet to acknowledge that fundamental law and we don't follow it very well. People often starve; they do various stupid things out of hunger; they get angry, they fall ill, and seek salvation not in food but in medication or God knows what else. When you're a bachelor, you're starving—both physically and, the main thing is, you're starving spiritually."

5

"Yes, my friend," continued Komkov. "It's essential that we get married. It's not in vain they say that. Once married, you're changed. I'll say more: once married, you sober up; it's as if, once married, you calm down and grow stronger. You acquire a completely different view of the world and of other people; an entirely different soul emerges. 'A bachelor's only half a man,' as the old Russian proverb says."

"Oho," said Kryukov, "I can't believe you're saying all this!"

"I should've married when I was a gymnasium student!" Komkov exclaimed. "If I'd known the secret of life earlier, which is simply hidden and obscured from us in every possible way, would I really have married so late?"

"Obscured how?" Kryukov asked, failing to understand.

"In every way possible. Even in our early youth they teach us to regard sexual questions in secret and surround them with mysterious prohibitions; even in reading about man's Fall, we're used to regard sex as a genuine sin, something forbidden, when, in fact, it's only an unavoidable physiological necessity of the human organism, without which man would no longer exist on earth, and on which his mental equilibrium and even his development depend. Why, just think how ridiculous it is to consider the way we came into being as a sin, that most holy thing in the world that gave you life and breath, instilled your holy, divine soul in you. Meanwhile, we treat it as something shameful; we mustn't talk about it; we make decisions about it on the sly, when nothing else on earth demands such frank, open discussion everywhere—in the family, in society, and in our legislatures. It's no accident that in India they consider this power that created life to be a superior divinity, and people worship it everywhere. It's no accident that among ancient Roman lawyers marriage was recognized as a right, a natural right (*ius naturale*), which followed from the physical attraction of the sexes for one another.[30] It's no accident that the ancient Persians considered it as a shame and a disgrace

30. The Latin *ius naturale* means "natural law," a law common to all beings.

to be unmarried, and the laws of the *Zend-Avesta* threatened punishment for it in the afterlife.[31] This I understand."

Kryukov smiled. Komkov's young wife also smiled condescendingly and continued listening to her husband; she behaved in such a natural and simple way that Kryukov immediately felt at ease with her, as if he had known her his whole life.

"You smile," Komkov continued heatedly, "well, listen to me. I'll share all that's been stored up in my soul on this subject; of course, it's more tragic than amusing. I think that as soon as the time of sexual maturity occurs, either for a man or a woman, at the moment questions arise in his or her soul as a result of this maturity, these questions must be resolved immediately, in one way or another. A person who hasn't resolved this issue in a natural and correct manner, that is, with a marriage beginning at the time I just indicated and lasting until the end of his days, then this person will be an unhappy, insecure, and unfulfilled human being. Someone once said, I think it was Leskov, that you don't know a person completely until you know the sexual side of his life.[32] There's great truth in this. On earth there's not one single healthy unmarried man—one with blood in his veins and not whey—even though his hair's turned white, who's completely chaste, free from thoughts and concerns about women. Such a man would be a saint—and there aren't many of them."

"Thus it means that early marriage is necessary," said Kryukov. "Then all would be well. But this is so difficult. There are so many obstacles—worries about material well-being, the family's attitude, and the future. Is it really possible to marry while still a student? I think that person's betwixt and between. After all . . ."

"It's precisely the opposite," Komkov said, interrupting him. "As soon as you get married, you begin studying in earnest and realize how little you've been able to accomplish before then. You know, people say, 'I don't want to study, I want to get married!'[33] In my opinion, this should not be understood

---

31. The *Zend-Avesta* is the primary collection of sacred texts of Zoroastrianism, the religion and philosophy of the ancient Persians based on the teachings of the prophet Zoroaster or Zarathustra.

32. Nikolai Leskov (1831–95) was a Russian short story writer, novelist, and journalist who in his later years took very seriously his moral responsibility to teach virtue through his art. He eventually "converted" to Tolstoyanism and placed even greater stress on the didactic function of literature.

33. A famous quotation uttered by the young hero in Denis Fonvizin's comedy *The Minor* (1782).

as an indication that a young man wants to marry to avoid studying; on the contrary—he wants to marry so that he'll be in a position to study harder. I'd change the proverb to say: 'I can't study until I'm allowed to marry.' I know from my own experience that since I took her as my wife," once again he indicated his wife with his eyes, "I simply don't recognize myself when it comes to studying. Where did all this come from? A clear mind, a good memory, mental acuity! My mother says that it's all right when there are no children, but just wait, they'll fuss and run about and bother you; then you'll sing a different tune. . . . But that'll be even better," Komkov continued confidently. "There may be worries, it's true, and they may even increase; on the other hand my strength will grow by a hundredfold. This also holds the secret of marriage, that is, of a genuine, honest marriage; it's a secret that bachelors, for example, don't even suspect. The fact is that after getting married, a man matures tremendously; even though his struggle for existence may increase, his individual strength expands, since the vital bonds that connect him with real life and reality deepen."

"It's not the same for everyone," said Kryukov. "Perhaps I'm even worse than you; for example, it seems completely impossible for me to marry, even if I wanted to. Is it really that simple?"

"What? You're afraid you won't have anything to eat?" asked Komkov. "You might have to give up the university, a diploma? That's the whole point, my friend. First of all, you must reach the point where you recognize the complete necessity of getting married, no matter what. Once you're convinced of this, the rest no longer matters. Well then? Leave the university, if you can't continue, become a clerk, a railway man, an office worker; go ahead and starve, not alone, but with your wife. That's where the difficulty lies— one must have the courage to part with everyone, to break with every convention, and to pursue one's own path. On the other hand, there lies the only salvation. Isn't it better to sacrifice the university and what it will give you, but manage to preserve your soul's freshness and boldness? Is it really better to indulge in debauchery, be depressed, and engage in drudgery for a salary of one and half thousand rubles and spiritual coldness?"

"No one would agree to that," said Kryukov. "Who'd be willing to risk something certain for the sake of something unknown and wind up with one's wife on the street with not even a half-kopeck in his pocket? Of course, if one could be certain of assistance from one's family, even one's own people."

"Well, you'll have to wait a long time for that," Komkov said loudly, interrupting him. "Help, my friend, you can expect only from yourself. When you rely on yourself, you're in charge. It's all the more so with marriage.

"Of course, it's hard to swim alone against the tide, against society, parents, and traditions; but what else is there, when no other path is open?

"I reached the conclusion that there's no one who understands and sympathizes less than one's own people; there are no greater egoists. It's sad and unfair, but that's the case. I observe the same situation everywhere in our society. While they should be concerned about us, help us get established at the right time, married at the appropriate age the way peasants do; our parents, don't you see—once they've given birth to us, afford us complete freedom, while they sit down calmly to play a game of vint, just as you always say that your family does. That way it's more comfortable, more peaceful. Meanwhile they should be obliged to provide for us and our wives for a number of years, support us until we've gained strength and are able to stand on our own feet. Then it would be easy for everyone to get married at the right time. You know, my mother's a wonderful old lady, yet for some reason she suddenly objected when I declared that I was getting married, and she tried to dissuade me. I simply couldn't understand a thing. At first she didn't want it to happen at all—it's too early, she said, what are you doing—then it was all right, she softened. Now she helps us, rents us this small apartment, and gives us twenty-five rubles."

"Aha! You see, she's helping you nonetheless," said Kryukov. "Many wouldn't even get that amount of support."

"Everyone gets help. All people are human beings," said Komkov. "Do you think that a person's heart wouldn't soften when two young people, joined to one another in the name of a sacred task—the prolongation and upbringing of the human race—would starve and suffer deprivation? There's no reason to fear the future—another day will dawn and food will be provided; you must be bold and resolve these present issues, without any more thought and without further delay."

6

"In order to marry, one must first fall in love with a nice young woman," Kryukov said. "You seem to be forgetting that completely."

"Fall in love?" Komkov said with a smile and sighed deeply. "You keep asserting such wonderful things. What exactly does 'love' mean? Can you explain that to me? Of course, you won't fall in love with a monster of a girl or one lacking a nose; everyone understands that. Of course, it's better if you choose a girl for yourself who's of the same age, habits, and upbringing as you are. But then, God knows what.

"I repeat: they're all more or less the same inside and out. Besides, there're no difficulties whatsoever in this matter and won't ever be. Every man and woman has right before their eyes every day and every hour of their lives another woman or man they desire. It's the mutual attraction of the sexes, nothing more. Why assign such words to it as 'love,' 'amorousness,' and so forth? Really, it's high time to dispense with all that. Do you honestly think that love really exists? For the simple-hearted, perhaps; in the imagination, yes."

"No, in my opinion, there's still something called 'love,'" Kryukov observed modestly.

"Is there?" asked Komkov.

He fell silent unexpectedly and began reflecting. Then Komkov continued thoughtfully, without hurrying, staring fixedly at Kryukov, whose face turned dark red once again after he had uttered those last words:

"Well, what do people generally understand by the word 'love'? What's the strongest, craziest love, as they say? You've become a man, reached sexual maturity; you need a woman who would complement your personality and continue your bloodline.

"You search for her and right away you see millions of them all around. But people have arranged things so badly in our society that for thousands of reasons it's not easy to connect with the one you've selected. The first reason is that the woman you've chosen is dressed.

"Well, so you fall in love with this woman who's wearing a dress; you long for her as much as you will, until you're nearly insane; you dream about the possibility of uniting with her—in a word, you're in love—the degree depends on you. Usually the more obstacles there are to your uniting with her, the stronger your love. If you remove all obstacles, the love vanishes. In its place comes marriage, that is, the cohabitation of a man and a woman for the purpose of continuing the human race and for mutual fulfillment.

"Once this cohabitation's begun, only then can real love take root.

"Love for one's wife, for the future mother of your children, for your friend and life companion—is almost a fraternal love. I understand this kind of love; it must exist and it does. But sexual love, that amorousness, is created only for debauchees, people who're half-unwell, feeble of mind and body, who deserve to be treated, not imitated. Sexual love should not exist, just like the love of food or wine should not. And so, when you become intimate with the young woman you've chosen, and who, as I've said, fate has ordained for you from the beginning of your manhood, then you say to yourself, to the whole world, and to that young woman: 'I take you as my wife and I promise never to be with another woman besides you. I promise to take care of you and our future children and demand the same promises from you.' That's the religion of marriage. It's clear and simple. It seems to me that the earlier a man realizes its necessity, and thus puts himself in the proper relationship to the world, then the stronger he'll be, the healthier and smarter. The more chaste we are before marriage, the more content our life will be."

Komkov began to grow excited, and his large, serious eyes started to gleam. He continued speaking, feeling that both Kryukov and his wife were now listening to him attentively.

"I don't understand how our wives agree to marry us men—stained, soiled, and depraved as we are! How is it that they don't demand of us the purity we demand of them? How do they, so pure and fresh, decide to become the wives of those who've already wasted half their strength and health? Few people shout about this crude and incomprehensible inequality! Few are those young women who punish us, make demands of us, and throw down Bjørnson's gauntlet in our faces!"[34]

"Yes, I often think about this, too," said Kryukov.

"Well then," continued Komkov, "thank heavens this is gradually entering our consciousness; we still have a long way to go to its practical realization. Meanwhile, I sometimes imagine what would happen if all of us, all young people were married! Even if only our Moscow students were married? Just think how much more intelligence, purity, and energy they would have. Not only would the students themselves be invigorated and renewed, but all humanity would be rejuvenated from this change. One must realize that all of us, although only some four thousand students in Moscow, young and healthy, the so-called best people of our age, all of us are living, with rare exceptions, without having resolved the sexual question, or else, having resolved it in the most disgusting manner. We frequent brothels; we're a bundle of nerves, we engage in debauchery, drunkenness, and ill humor; we play cards, even conceiving of devices for dealing cards; and finally, we fight duels, suffer from all sorts of diseases, are often tormented by longing and discontent, the source of which is the sexual side of life which we ignore or resolve artificially. It seems to me that all these student disturbances, episodes of disorder, attrac-

34. Bjørnstjerne Bjørnson (1832–1910) was a Norwegian author whose play *The Gauntlet* (or *The Glove*) (1883) criticized the difference in the sexual mores applied to men and women, respectively. He posed the demand that not only women but also men should remain chaste until marriage.

tion to different ideas that are reduced to dust as soon as they're applied to real life, all this would vanish, or at least half of it would, if those producing it now were to be married and thereby become sober and active. Our common people possess such strength, vitality, and morality simply because they're made to marry at a very young age. I'm convinced that it would be the same with our society, if it recognized the importance of early marriage. In the future people won't understand why we agonized, wasted the best years of our lives, languishing idly and suffering, when such a simple remedy exists. What can explain all this suffering, longing, discontent, yearning, and so on, of our youth at this particular time of their lives? The simplest, most materialistic of all materialist laws of human nature. Yet no one seems willing to acknowledge this for anything on earth. Instead, they invent all sorts of new words; novelists build the most intricate and idealized plots that bewilder stupid humanity, when it would be more appropriate merely to follow the instructions of mother nature or mother physiology, as happens in the animal world and among our common people, which stand closer to the truth than we do, having muddled and obscured it less."

Komkov now stood up and began pacing in the only free space of his tiny room. His face was entirely flushed and he had begun shaking his head with a nervous gesture, tossing back his hair that had flopped down onto his high forehead.

"If people engaged less in fantasies," he continued with a sore, painful note in his voice, "if people did more, worked, or studied; if they treated life's questions more simply, more honestly, yes, more honestly, and solved them, instead of retreating from them into unknown heights and depths, where life itself ceases—then humanity would become so much happier, so much smarter, and it would move forward."

7

"There are people," Komkov continued, getting more and more agitated, now constantly tossing back the hair that kept falling over his eyes, "there are strong people, important people, who want to persuade us that marriage is an abomination, and that our ideal must be celibacy!"

Komkov's voice suddenly fell, as if he could not find enough inner strength to speak.

"In other words, the ideal and goal of life must be death," he uttered with difficulty, as if yielding to the agitation overwhelming him. "You know, I simply don't understand this; my poor head can't accommodate such wisdom!"

he cried suddenly, such that Kryukov and young Komkova both shuddered and a look of surprise appeared on their faces.

He fell silent for a moment, stood in one place, and then began pacing again in the vacant space of the room.

"Our ideal must be annihilation," he continued in a muffled, angry tone. "The termination of the human race, because that's what clever people have always thought—the Buddhas, Schopenhauers, Hartmanns, and us![35] So what if the human race ceases; it will get what it deserves. Everything on earth must cease; there's no doubt about that and it's nothing new. Why should we be so upset about it? It would be bad faith on our part to fear the human race will end, when the point in question is not our pleasure but our purity.

"The goal of our life must be to aspire toward the ideal of purity. When people reach it, they will beat their swords into plowshares, lie down, embrace each other as brothers, and they will die.[36] Then the heavenly kingdom will be established on earth.

"For whom, permit me to ask, will it be established, this heavenly kingdom? Besides, what, in the last analysis, is this heavenly kingdom?" asked Komkov, smiling maliciously. "Why should we strive for it, suffer for it, and attain this ideal purity, when our only reward is death? Who would pursue such pleasure? Who, what rational, thinking man would be captivated by such a philosophy that urges us to strive for annihilation?

"However, people do get captivated by it, many people, even," he said sadly, adopting a softer and more serious tone. "Unfortunately, people are unable to think and act creatively and sensibly; in a majority of cases they seek outside help and advice; unfortunately, there's no one left except weaklings and fools. And they perish, these feeble, simple-minded people who've been attracted to such sublime teachings: they perish!"

"Why do you say they perish?" asked Kryukov. "On the contrary, I think that the story you're telling has brought much good to people."

"Perhaps, but it's also produced even more harm, suffering, and evil," Komkov said, almost shouting again. "I know this from many examples."

"In what way?" Kryukov asked in surprise.

"Because after hearing this story, people don't get married and won't when it's time for them to do so; they want to be pure, perfect," Komkov replied with irony. "Because they want to be chaste; they preach celibacy, while at the

---

35. Nikolai Hartmann (1882–1950) was a Baltic German philosopher who developed his own philosophy described as a variety of existentialism or critical realism.

36. "They shall beat their swords into plowshares": Isaiah 2:4.

same time they themselves, nearly always, are engaged in debauchery on the sly, and they're engaging in sexual fantasies hundreds of times worse than the most flagrant debauchers; because if they really want to vanquish carnal life and its demands in themselves they drive themselves to illness, to the insane asylum, or to the cemetery; because they futilely destroy their own strength, youth, life, and all the best things given them by God, all for the sake of this absurd idea!

"What else could come from this preaching? How else could one relate to it? If you follow it, believe it, you must perish; if you understand its essence and immediately recognize its consequences, you must reject it as something incomprehensible, irrelevant to life, and therefore unnecessary.

"It's impossible to follow such obvious falsehood. It's impossible to tell a young man who's burning with a thirst to live, with passions and desires, that all these passions are unlawful, and that he must attempt to eradicate them in himself. It's unscrupulous and wrong. Can one advise a hungry man or a thirsty man to wait until his hunger or thirst passes of its own accord, or advise him to struggle without satisfying them?

"It's a sin because it's also murder! Of course, both hunger and thirst will pass, if you bury yourself alive in the earth, as they did in Ternovskie Khuto-ra.[37] Then it would be better to behave as they did—it's much more understandable. The sect of Skoptsy resolved this question in an even simpler and more reliable fashion, having conceived of a way to combat the temptations of the flesh.[38]

"But we're cultured people, after all," Komkov continued confidently. "We reason rationally and soberly; we're not crazy fanatics. After all, we study the laws of nature to know that life has no end, as the Buddhas, Schopenhauers, and Hartmanns preached; on the contrary, it goes on forever, as eternal matter, just as sunlight and the entire world have been endlessly eternal in the past and will continue to be in the future!

"We're alive and therefore will defer not to death but to birth; not to cold, lifeless chastity but to marriage, pure, honorable marriage.

"They say, 'No, death won't occur because there'll always be people who'll somehow inadvertently perpetuate the human race for us, but for those who can embody the ideal, let them do so! One must merely strive for the Christian

37. In 1897 a fanatical group of Old Believers "took a short cut to immortality" and buried themselves alive, along with several young children in a town in southern Russia.

38. Skoptsy was a secret sect in imperial Russia known for practicing castration of men and mastectomy of women in accordance with their preaching against sexual desire.

ideal, for the ideal of Christ in general, and the ideal of chastity in particular, to be guided by it as if by compass, to know the direction, which way to head, just like a ship at sea—then everyone and everything will be fine. An ideal is not an injunction or a rule; an ideal is an ideal only if it's eternally unattainable; therefore there's no reason to fear that we'll ever reach it. We must simply know the right direction to go.' These words may contain some beauty; perhaps one can even blindly believe in them and fall under their hypnotic trance, but as soon as you investigate the meaning of these words with a clear head, you'll see what sort of contradiction they contain.

"Strive for the ideal. It's unattainable. This ideal is chastity. That means, strive for unattainable chastity while others perpetually propagate the human race for you.

"You ask, who are these people who are perpetually propagating the human race for you?

"It turns out, they're ordinary mortals, all of humanity. But why then won't they, these people, ever attain chastity?

"Because it's unattainable. Then for whom and for what is the ideal of chastity being preached so insistently? It's not for anyone or anything.

"It's astonishing," said Komkov, sighing so deeply that it took him a whole minute to exhale all the air from his broad chest. "It's astonishing, how one can be so taken by this barren idea, forgetting everything else on account of it, sacrificing certitude, logic, and truth!

"Such a way of thinking is simply incomprehensible to our generation. It's fine to say that our ideal should be the teachings of Christ—who would argue with that? That our life should entail work to establish brotherhood, equality, and happiness on earth. But why affix the ideal of asceticism to life, to the sexual question, when it leads to such absurdity?

"The concept of an ideal marriage can exist, an ideal solution to the sexual question, the notion of a chaste marriage—all these ideas can be clearly defined and expressed without contradicting logic or truth; but the concept of an ideal death or annihilation, or the ideal nonexistence of life and the world is incomprehensible to everyone.

"Yes, yes, that's the primary error of *The Kreutzer Sonata* and its Afterword, since it's already clear that I'm referring to them.[39] It's the error in their conclusion: an ideal is posited that can never be realized. The ideal of Christ is understandable, of its own accord, and in no way does it contradict marriage; the ideal of marriage in and of itself is also very clear and understand-

39. Lev Tolstoy's story was published in 1889; the Afterword a year later.

able and doesn't contradict Christ. The ideal of Christ consists of humility, forgiveness for all, and love; the ideal of marriage is purity and fidelity. Following the demands for chaste marriage one must marry young; one must do so not for the sake of pleasure but for the generation of children. Hence it follows that one should not sleep with one's pregnant or nursing wife. All that's understandable. Why then isn't it possible to combine these two ideals—the ideal of marriage and the ideal of a love life for people on earth? Is it really the case that one excludes the other? If so, then something is wrong.

"Could it really be the case that life is possible only where Christian love is impossible? Or, on the other hand, is Christian love possible only where life is impossible and where it comes to an end?

"The ideal of marriage, that is, of chaste marriage, that's what should be posed in the discussion of sexual relations; and this ideal is not unattainable but attainable, although, perhaps, centuries and entire millennia will pass before humanity achieves this goal.

"I recently met with a Tolstoyan," Komkov said, smiling condescendingly, "and my God, how he flew into a rage when I started explaining what I'm telling you now. Poor things, they believe so fervently in their idols that it's simply a shame to overturn them. He immediately began preaching to me about a ship and its compass, of course. I asked him: what sort of ship is it on which you sail the seas? Is it not, perhaps, that very same institution of marriage that you now seek to drown, forgetting that you yourself are sailing on it? What good will your compass do, or your general direction, when all that will sink to the bottom along with you?

"One can say we're not pure, that we regard sexual matters incorrectly, that we're depraved in all sorts of ways; and one may, even must, speak about all this; but to say that marriage is an abomination, that this supreme divine law is an abomination that must be abolished and, in the process, abolish all of humanity at the same time—that cannot and must not be said. It's impossible because, I repeat, only marriage, and marriage alone, can resolve the sexual question correctly. And I'm not talking about polygamy, polyandry, or free love—that goes without saying—but about strict and conscious monogamy.

"I didn't understand this for a long time and also reasoned in every way possible, according to our Russian weakness for reasoning; but, thank the Lord, fate deigned to enlighten and instruct me.

"As you know, last year I happened to travel abroad."

Komkov fell silent once again, lit a cigarette, and sat back down in his previous place on the sofa. It seemed that he had already stated everything that was disturbing him so deeply; now the look in his eyes and the expression on his face became more serene.

"And there was the West, the rotten West," he continued, tossing his head back and stretching his long legs out in front of him. "It rescued me from the Russian fog in my head, and knocked some sense into me. Had I lived in Russia a hundred years, I'd never have learned as much as I did abroad in one month. The first thing I learned was this—it's necessary to act, not to reason. It seems a simple truth, but we still don't understand it here.

"I realized that one does not move forward and enable others to do so by means of the barren, immature discourse that we've all known for so long and are so fed up with; that produces only boredom and makes it harder to live. One makes progress by taking action—constant, insistent, and reasonable. That's the only productive path. I realized that in the West that truth has long since been absorbed into people's flesh and blood; it's become everyone's religion; people live by it and are satisfied with it. No teaching, no sermon could teach me more than what I observed in the living practice of the West. It sobered me up. To become even soberer, to get even closer to life and to understand it, to fulfill myself, and become more of a genuine person, I got married when I returned to Russia."

"I see," said Kryukov with a smile.

"Yes, but you wouldn't have seen it if I hadn't spent some time living abroad. God knows to what mysterious heights I might still have ascended! We all strive to think things out and get to the bottom of something that no one else has ever conceived before. Mysticism still predominates in our realm, in various forms and manifestations. It's not in vain that we're considered children who think and live childishly.

"We want to achieve equality and brotherhood on earth; yet to do so we conceive of a means that will annihilate us.

"We want to become perfect—that's splendid, but why is the cessation of life necessary to achieve that?"

Komkov stood up once again and now paced the room more slowly. He moved to the chair where his wife was sitting; taking hold of it from behind, he paused.

"I think," he said thoughtfully. "This is what I think: the goal of our life is reasonable service to life, not death. Service to the infinite perfection of life and the happiness of people on earth. Achieving this perfection is possible only by moving forward, but moving forward merely by following the immutable laws of this movement bestowed on us by nature. We'll achieve brotherhood and the equality of all people on earth, and perhaps even higher levels of human social perfection, but the laws of nature will unalterably remain the same. Our job is merely not to corrupt them, to understand them correctly, and to illuminate them with our universal and divine reason."

After remaining at the Komkovs' until late that night, Kryukov finally stood up and began taking leave of his hosts.

"So," said Komkov, escorting his friend to the outer door so he could lock it behind him, "that's quite a sermon I preached to you. Now I have the same advice for everyone."

"As a result, you're very happy," said Kryukov, standing on the steps of the wing where the Komkovs lived.

"No more, and perhaps even less, than others," said Komkov. "But I feel happy knowing that now my conscience is at rest; I doubt everyone feels that way. I'm happy, you see, inasmuch as I've resolved the issue that was tormenting me; there'll be both grief and misfortune, it doesn't matter, whatever fate brings—but now I'll bear it all and live fully, not exist halfway."

8

Kryukov walked home, carefully mulling over in his head everything he had heard that evening spent in such an unexpected manner. But strange to say, even though Komkov had advised him so ardently to get married, and although he himself had represented a model of a happily married young man leading a full and active life, just as he preached—his overly shrill speech was of little help to Kryukov as he tried to cope with his own situation and merely seemed to make him more distraught now. He could not agree with his friend.

All of that was splendid in words, but so far from action and practical fulfillment, for him, at any rate, that might it not be better not to think at all about the impossible?

"It's fine for Komkov to talk, when he's already married; he has a small apartment free of charge, his mother helps him, and perhaps his wife's parents do, too. It's fine for him, when his wife, most likely, isn't accustomed to luxury and is content merely with what there is. Could I ever settle Sonechka into such a hovel? I don't have even a place like that.

"And besides, simply, well, how could he, Vanya Kryukov, ever marry Princess Baretskaya?"

For some reason this last phrase kept entering his head.

Vanya Kryukov!!

"So, wait for her five or even ten years? Is it even possible to sustain oneself and one's feelings unscathed for so long? Could one possibly vouch for oneself and resist all the temptations that surround us, all the while quenching the flame that constantly burns within?

"No, no," Kryukov repeated to himself over and over. "I can't possibly think about Sonechka; I must forget her soon, very soon; that's my only hope. Why did I let myself be attracted to her? Why did I think and dream about her so much, with the only result that I came to be mocked by other people?"

He suddenly recalled Komkov's words about love: "There's no such thing as love; there's only sexual need at the time of maturity." Is it really that simple? Could his feeling for Sonechka, his longing—is all that nothing more than the necessity of resolving and satisfying the sexual side of his being? Could all these poetic dreams of his merely be explained coarsely and crudely?

"No, it couldn't be, it couldn't," Kryukov kept telling himself.

"What? And the feelings he had experienced yesterday while dancing with her, and what he had felt today as he escorted her to the station—wasn't that genuine, ardent, sincere love? Of course, it was! And now? Now she's gone, and even though he was still thinking about her, remembering her, he could no longer love her so passionately. Why should he think about her when it would result in nothing but torment? He must purge her completely from his memory, and do it as quickly as possible!"

The closer Kryukov came to his house, the gloomier, more complicated, and more hopeless his situation seemed. He was aware of only one thing with a dull ache that would not release its grip on his heart, namely that he was unhappy and lonely, inexpressibly lonely in the world, and that he had to forget Sonechka, whether he loved her or not.

Arriving home, he stopped on the stairs to their apartment; pressing the electric button, he rang the doorbell.

"Tomorrow I have to read ten more pages of linguistics and review half the history of Rome," he mused thoughtfully.

The young servant Matryona came shuffling down the stone stairs. She was in her soft slippers, a sign that all guests had already departed and everyone had gone to bed.

The long iron hook clinked and Matryona stood to one side and allowed Kryukov to enter the low, cold room. She was wearing a short, white, unbuttoned shirt that did not quite cover her ample bosom. Her lustrous face was shining, as always, and her ruddy lips were curled in a smile. It was obvious from her clothes that she, too, had just bedded down for the night.

"Gone to bed already? It's so early!" Kryukov said.

"Yes, sir It's after midnight."

Kryukov ran upstairs into the crowded front hall, tossed his coat on a chair, and walked briskly through the dark corridor to his own room. He sat down at his desk and opened the first textbook he happened upon. It was Tacitus.[40] He also had to prepare a slew of chapters from him for the examination. What on earth for? Why?

Tacitus had tormented and angered Kryukov of late. It turned out that in the university, even though he had chosen the literary department of the philological faculty instead of classics, he had still found it necessary to return to the Latin he hated. Not only did he have to read Roman authors, but he also had to complete written exercises, the same *extemporalia* from which Kryukov had hoped he had freed himself for the rest of his life after his last school examination.[41]

He did not feel like sleeping at all. Having inhaled so much fresh air during his walk home, he found it very stuffy in his little room. He stood up and opened the little window vent. Cool night air smelling of spring and fresh oil paint rushed in at him. He took a very deep breath and sat down at his small desk again, tossing the book away onto the windowsill.

9

It was utterly quiet in the apartment; only the loud ticking of a clock could be heard in the corridor.

The sound of a night cab could be heard rumbling across the roadway; it was drawing closer, obviously, at a slow pace. Somewhere in the distance a train hooted; at that moment a depressing, lonely, bitter feeling grew even stronger in Kryukov's soul. The approaching sound of wheels on the roadway, coming closer and closer, the fresh air, the train whistle in the distance, and the silence all around—all this disturbed him inexplicably.

What was happening to him? Why was he so bored, so ill at ease?

Suddenly Matryosha's soft, shuffling steps could be heard in the corridor outside his door; the next moment she entered his room without the least embarrassment and closed the door behind her.[42]

"I came to bring you some water," she said in the simplest way. Coming right up to Kryukov's chair, her blouse brushed his shoulder and for a

40. Roman historian (c. 55–120) whose precise and vivid prose style was a major influence on later writers.

41. *Extemporalia* is discourse that is offhand, not premeditated or studied.

42. Matryosha is a diminutive form of the name Matryona.

moment he smelled the scent of her warm body; she approached his bed and placed the decanter of water on his night table.

"You'll get cold. You've opened the vent."

"No, it was stuffy in here."

Matryosha began to arrange the bed and tuck in the blanket, although there was absolutely no need to do so. Then she began to smooth and fluff the pillow.

"I made up your bed with clean linen today."

"Fine, thank you. You may go now."

Kryukov sat motionless, staring at the dark windowpane, which reflected the light burning on the table. All of a sudden he felt that from the moment Matryosha had entered and closed the door behind her, from the second he had inadvertently glanced into her eyes and understood immediately what it was, obviously, that she so passionately wanted from him with all her being—some incomprehensible inner tension stirred within him and turned upside down all the desires, thoughts, and dreams that had filled him to that point.

Where did it come from? How could he have allowed that horrible, forbidden feeling suddenly to erupt in him? What was happening to him? Good God, had he really fallen so low, had he arrived at the time, reached the point that Komkov had described, when he was no longer able to struggle against these animal instincts in himself, and was unable to stifle his sexual needs?

What about Sonechka? And his love for her?

After these unspoken thoughts he had kept to himself, an inner terror overpowered his soul. His palms broke out in a cold sweat, his knees started trembling, just as if someone had struck him. Kryukov was really frightened. How could he, a vile, base man, allow even the slightest trace of such a criminal desire to arise in him? How on earth, from where does such diabolical temptation dare to perturb him?

A strong springtime breeze continued flowing through the window vent; the smell of fresh oil paint particularly upset Kryukov.

Matryosha still had yet to straighten up and was still smoothing out the pillow, turning from side to side.

She was a married woman, but her husband, a drunk and a boor, had deserted her about three years ago and had vanished without a trace, leaving her with a year-old child on her hands. The Kryukovs, who spent last autumn at their dacha near Moscow, had taken in Matryosha and treated her kindly. She had recovered and grew appreciably more attractive with their care. Quite a while ago, when she first began living in their house, Kryukov had noticed her unusually slender, pink feet when she was barefoot washing the floors. But he did not allow himself to pay it much attention.

"I made up your bed with clean linen," she repeated now in some strange, breaking voice, "and it wasn't even for any holiday."

Kryukov turned to look at her and once again met her eyes with their moist, impure glance, filled with impudent daring.

At that very moment something struck his heart with a wave of uncontrolled force. Everything began to surge and heave within him: he lost his serenity and self-control.

He jumped up and without giving himself any account of what he was doing, he ran headlong out of his room without looking back.

His soul was aching and his heart was bleeding. He ran down the long corridor, quickly turned right at the end, went into the dining room, and closed both double doors tightly behind him.

It was almost dark in the dining room; only the weak light from the street lamp flickered and trembled on the wall next to the window and on the black piano.

Kryukov rushed over to it and sat down in front of it on the piano stool. He was breathing deeply and his eyes shone in a fever.

"What filth, what horror, what horror this all is," he repeated in despair. "How on earth, how do I behave? Why, only a little weakness is needed, and it's over, all over, and I'll become just like Bukhanov! Did I summon her? Did I really do anything to invite intimacy with her? Have I looked at her even once with impure eyes? She came to me and practically offered herself. My God, what if Sonechka were to know all this? Pure, lovely Sonechka. But I'll definitely tell her; let her know what dangers and temptations we're constantly subjected to."

A multitude of feelings and thoughts that suddenly became unusually consequential and powerful, now boiled up in Kryukov's soul. Never before in his life had he thought and felt so decisively and clearly.

He recalled the entire conversation with Komkov down to the smallest detail. Only now did he come to understand the real meaning of what his old friend had said to him.

"Yes, yes," Kryukov affirmed to himself, sitting motionless on the piano stool, staring with eyes wide open at the window through which the light from the street had entered. "When the time of sexual maturity arrives, one must resolve the sexual question in one way or another. I don't want to suffer or pine away; I don't want to engage in sexual fantasies or be aroused mentally; I don't want to become depressed or fall ill; therefore, I must get married. That's the only rational solution to the sexual question. 'Strict, conscious monogamy,'" he repeated Komkov's words.

"It would be better to quit the university and get a job as a clerk or an office assistant; it would be better to starve," he continued repeating fervently and decisively, "better to be driven away from home, to be poor and live on the street, than to remain in such tormenting uncertainty, in constant loneliness, agitation, and anguish, and finally, to fall inevitably into sin!

"So what if we're poor?" Kryukov asked himself, getting more absorbed in a new train of thought. "So what if I leave that boring university, that damned Tacitus, linguistics, and all that useless learning? I'd only become freer, much more at peace. Why do I need a diploma, when I can attain more sublime happiness, get a higher diploma about which I only dare to dream—Sonechka?

"Yes, there's only one thing left for me to do: that is, just as Komkov said: break with everyone and everything, go against convention, and achieve this first goal, the most important one—marriage." For its sake he would have to sacrifice everything. But would Sonechka even have him? How could he ever convince her mother, her family? How could he possibly deal with all those obstacles?

But now Kryukov felt great strength and energy within him; at that moment nothing seemed terrible or impossible to him.

He understood that he must accomplish this intention no matter what; there was no place left in him for reluctance or faintheartedness. For some reason he was confident of success.

Sonechka loves him, he knew that; she would do anything he wanted. That means, it all depends on him. He could wait a year or two, even more, if only everything could be clarified and decided. Then nothing would seem terrible.

These last thoughts unexpectedly occasioned wild, unbridled joy in Kryukov's soul.

That was the way, precisely the way for him to decide and act. How was it he had not understood it all before? What was he so afraid of? Why did he want to wait? It was not without reason that Komkov had been so agitated when he spoke about this matter. In fact, how was it possible not to be agitated when this was the question on which all life depended? But now he, even he would be calm, once having decided what must be done. What a fine life he would lead with Sonechka! They would struggle, work, and love one another. They would be so happy together!

Kryukov glanced at the Chopin score that had been left in place on the piano since he had last played; it was now lying open before him on the music rack; all of a sudden he really felt like playing once more that stormy and passionate *Prelude presto con fuoco* that he had played that evening after his brief conversation with his father.

The first intense, nervous, spirited chords already resounded decisively and powerfully in his imagination.

"Will it be audible in my parents' bedroom? What if I wake them?" Kryukov wondered.

"So what," he replied in an angry, irritated voice, one both immodest and unfamiliar to him. "So what if I wake those egotists? They've tormented me in all sorts of ways, prevented me from sleeping, studying, or preparing my exams when they had the singer Klimentova crooning here or the violinist Bauer sawing away until three o'clock in the morning.[43] Did they ever think once that I might be studying, or that I was tired, and that I might not really appreciate what they were doing? Play the *Prelude,* have no fear; you have the right to do it." Kryukov opened the lid of the piano and struck the keys with all his might!

The passionate, powerful sounds of Chopin's *Prelude* rang out in the dining room, disturbing the night silence and filling the space all around.

"Tomorrow I'll write to her," Kryukov repeated after the *Prelude;* "tomorrow I'll tell her everything, and that will be the end of my anguish; I'll visit them this summer, even though the old princess didn't issue me a separate invitation. I'll quit the university, leave my parents, my father, my mother, my home; and I'll get married, I'll marry Sonechka no matter what, and let the whole world learn about my decision!"

He played the *Prelude* as he had never in his life played it before: chills ran from his temples across his head and up and down his spine.

43. Mariya Nikolaevna Klimentova (1856–1946) was a Russian soprano and singing teacher who performed at the Bolshoi Theatre in Moscow and the Mariinsky Theatre in Petersburg. Harold Bauer (1873–1951) was a noted pianist who began his musical career as a violinist. During 1893–94 he traveled through Russia giving recitals and concerts, after which he returned to Paris.

Part Two

REFLECTIONS

Ruminations on Tolstoy's
The Kreuzter Sonata

"I picked mushrooms and thought about
'The Kreutzer Sonata' and about art."
LEV NIKOLAEVICH TOLSTOY, diary entry, August 11, 1889

"You have not written anything stronger than
this work, nor anything darker."
NIKOLAI STRAKHOV, letter to Tolstoy, November 6, 1889

"He [Tolstoy] belongs to the twelfth century rather than to the nineteenth
century. He is a compound of a monk of the Middle Ages and a modern
Slav, with the mysticism of the one and the romanticism of the other."
ÉMILE ZOLA, *New York Herald,* August 24, 1890

"I never expected that my train of thought would lead me where it did.
I was horrified at my own conclusions, I didn't want
to believe them, but it was impossible not to."
LEV NIKOLAEVICH TOLSTOY

"Yes, it [publication of *The Kreutzer Sonata*] can be allowed as part of
the collected works; not everybody can afford them;
it won't be a matter of a large circulation."
TSAR ALEXANDER III to Sofiya Andreevna Tolstaya

"Volume 13 sold so well that within the same year it was reprinted in both a
second (20,000 copies) and a third edition."
PETER ULF MØLLER, Postlude to *The Kreutzer Sonata*

"In Buffalo, Montreal, Boston, New York—in all of the large towns the salesmen stood on the street corners with enormous baskets filled with your books, and all day long they scarcely had time to deal with one customer before the next was ready."
ELLIS D. ROBB, letter to Tolstoy, April 3, 1894

"Have you read Lev Tolstoy's new tale 'The Kreutzer Sonata'? I heard it read yesterday. Not even Shakespeare could have produced something so strong, so artistic. What exceptional, almost divine insight into the human spirit!"
KONSTANTIN FEOFANOV, letter to Aleksandr Zhirkevich, January 1890

"No wonder the Countess was often near the end of her patience."
GEORGE BERNARD SHAW, "Our Bookshelf," May 6, 1911

"'The Kreutzer Sonata' is a nightmare, born of a diseased imagination. Since reading it I have not the slightest doubt that its author is cracked—*qu'il y a une petite fêleur dans sa tête.*"
ÉMILE ZOLA, *New York Herald*, August 24, 1890

"Do you mean you really don't care for 'The Kreutzer Sonata'? I won't say it's an immortal work or a work of genius . . . but in my opinion, among the mass of what is presently being written here and abroad, you won't find anything to match it in importance or beauty of execution. Even without mentioning its artistic achievements, which are in certain passages astounding, you must be grateful if only because the work is extremely thought-provoking."
ANTON PAVLOVICH CHEKHOV, letter to Alexei Pleshcheev, February 15, 1890

"[People] were struck, however, by 'The Kreutzer Sonata' and especially by the 'Afterword,' in which a man who had fathered thirteen children rose up against conjugal love and even against the continuation of the human race itself. They said that 'The Kreutzer Sonata' could best be explained by the fact that Tolstoy was old and that he 'hated his wife.'"
IVAN BUNIN, *The Liberation of Tolstoy*, 1937

"So long as we are alive, nothing that Mother writes will be published."
TATYANA LVOVNA TOLSTAYA

"'The Kreutzer Sonata' has been put into the hands of several unmarried young ladies of high social position in Russia. . . . Many of them have thoroughly assimilated the main idea of the book, and in proof of their conversion have discarded low[-cut] ball dresses . . . which, they are now convinced, serve only to arouse animal passions."
E. J. DILLON, "The Kreutzer Sonata," *Universal Review*, March 1890

Epilogue to *The Kreutzer Sonata*

LEV NIKOLAEVICH TOLSTOY

TRANSLATED BY HUGH MCLEAN
AND REVISED BY MICHAEL KATZ

I HAVE RECEIVED, and continue to receive, a great many letters from people I do not know, asking me to explain in clear and simple language what I think about the topic of the story I wrote under the title *The Kreutzer Sonata*. I will try to do that, i.e., in brief words to explain, insofar as that is possible, the essence of what I tried to say in that story and the conclusions which in my opinion can be drawn from it.

I meant, *in the first place,* that in our society a firm conviction has taken root, common to all classes and supported by false science, that sexual intercourse is an act essential to health, and that since marriage is not always a possible solution, sexual communion outside of marriage, one that obliges a man to nothing more than a money payment, is something completely natural and therefore to be encouraged. This conviction has to such an extent become general and firm that parents, on the advice of doctors, arrange fornication for their male children. Governments, the only justification for which lies in concern for the moral well-being of their citizens, organize debauchery, i.e., they set rules for a whole class of women obliged to perish in body and soul in order to satisfy the supposed requirements of men, and unmarried men with a clear conscience engage in fornication.

And I wished to say that this is wrong, because it cannot be moral for the sake of the health of some people to destroy the bodies and souls of others, just as it cannot be right for the sake of some people to drink the blood of others.

The conclusion, which, it seems to me, follows naturally from this, is that people should not surrender themselves to this error and deception. And in order not to surrender to it people should not, in the first place, believe immoral teachings, even when they are supported by false science, and in the second place, should understand that to engage in sexual congress in such a way that they are freed from its natural result, namely, children, or to cast the entire weight of consequences onto the woman, or to take measures to prevent the conception of children—such sexual communion is a violation of the basic requirements of morality, an abomination, and that therefore unmarried men who do not wish to live in wickedness must not do this.

In order to be able to refrain, they should lead a natural way of life: not drink, overeat, eat meat, or avoid manual labor (not gymnastics, but real, wearying work, not play), not permit themselves to think about the possibility of intercourse with women they are not related to, just as no man admits the possibility of intercourse with his mother, sisters, relations, or the wives of his friends.

As proof that abstention is possible and less dangerous for health than indulgence any man can find hundreds of examples all around.

That is the first point.

The *second* is that in our society, in consequence of the view of sexual intercourse as not only a necessary condition of health and a pleasure, but as something exalted, something lofty and good in life, marital infidelity has become the most usual phenomenon in all classes of society, especially among the peasantry, because of conscription.

And I maintain that this is bad. The conclusion that follows from this is that we should not do it.

In order not to do it we must change our view of sexual love so that men and women are educated in their families and by public opinion not to regard, both before and after marriage, falling in love and the fleshly love connected with it as an exalted state, as they regard it now, but as an animal state degrading for a human being. Violation of the promise of fidelity made at the wedding should be deplored by public opinion at least as much as it deplores violations of financial obligations or swindles in trade, and not celebrated, as it now is, in novels, poems, songs, operas, etc.

That is the second point.

The *third* is that in our society, as a consequence again of that false significance attributed to carnal love, the birth of children has lost its meaning, and instead of being the purpose and justification of conjugal relations has become an obstacle to the pleasant continuation of amorous relations. Therefore, both outside of marriage and within it, on the advice of practitioners of medical science, the use of methods that deprive a woman of the possibility of childbirth has become widespread; likewise widespread is something that used not to occur and even now does not occur in patriarchal peasant families: continuation of marital relations during pregnancy and breastfeeding.

And I maintain that this is bad. The use of methods to prevent the conception of children is bad in the first place because it frees people from the cares and duties associated with children and serves as a justification for carnal love; in the second place because it is something very close to the act most abhorrent to the human conscience, namely murder. And failure to abstain during pregnancy and breastfeeding is bad because it destroys the bodily and, chiefly, the spiritual strength of the woman.

The conclusion to be drawn from this is that we should not do it. And in order not to do it we must understand that abstention, which is a necessary condition of human worth in the unmarried state, is even more obligatory in marriage.

That is the third point.

The *fourth* is that in our society, in which children constitute either a hindrance to pleasure or an unfortunate accident, or a certain kind of pleasure when a particular number of them agreed upon in advance are born, those children are brought up not to anticipate the tasks of human life which face them as rational and loving beings, but only with an eye to the pleasures they can give their parents. And because of this, children of human beings are brought up like children of animals, in such a way that the chief concern of parents consists not in preparing them for activity worthy of human beings but rather (in which the parents are supported by the false science called medicine) to feed them as well as possible, further their growth, make them clean, white, well fed, and good-looking (if in the lower classes they do not do this, it is only out of necessity; their views are the same). And in present-day children, as in any overfed animals, irresistible sensuality develops unnaturally early, the cause of the terrible torments suffered by these children in adolescence. Clothing, reading, music, dancing, sweet food, the whole surroundings of life, from the pictures on boxes to novels, stories and poems excite this sensuality even more, and in consequence the most terrible sexual vices and diseases have become common accompaniments of the maturation of children of both sexes, and they are often continued even in maturity.

And I maintain that this is bad. The conclusion to be drawn from this is that we must stop raising the children of human beings like the children of animals, and for the education of human children we should set different goals than a good-looking, well-tended body.

That is the fourth point.

The *fifth* is that in our society, love between a young man and a young woman which has carnal lovemaking as its basis has been elevated as a lofty, poetic goal for the aspirations of people, evidence of which is the entire body of art and poetry of our society. Young people devote the best part of their lives to it: men, to picking, seeking, and taking possession of the best objects of their love in the form of love affairs and marriages; and women and girls, in luring and ensnaring men for love affairs or marriage.

And from this the best energies of people are wasted not only on unproductive, but also harmful activity. This is the source of the greater part of the insane luxury of our life, the idleness of men and the shamelessness of women who have no qualms about exhibiting themselves in fashions derived from known depraved women, exhibiting parts of the body that arouse sensuality.

And I maintain that this is bad.

It is bad because to attain the goal of unification with the object of love either in marriage or outside it, no matter how poeticized it has been, is a goal unworthy of a human being, just as it is unworthy of a human being to represent to many people as the greatest good the acquisition for oneself of sweet and abundant food.

The conclusion to be drawn from this is that we should stop thinking of carnal love as something particularly exalted, but rather understand that a goal worthy of a human being, such as service to humanity, one's country, science, or art (not to mention service to God), no matter what it is, if we consider it worthy of a human being, it is not attained by union with an object of love, either in marriage or outside it, but that on the contrary, falling in love and union with one's object of love (no matter how hard people try to demonstrate the opposite in verse and prose) never facilitates the attainment of a goal worthy of a human being, but always hinders it.

That is the fifth point.

That is essentially what I wanted to say and thought I had said in my story. It also seemed to me that one could argue about how to eradicate the evil these points indicated, but that not to agree with them is quite impossible. It seemed to me that it is impossible not to agree with these points, in the first place, because they are in full agreement with the progress of mankind, which has always moved from dissoluteness toward greater and greater purity, and with the moral sense of society, with our consciences, which have always condemned dissoluteness and valued morality; and in the second place, because these positions are only the inescapable conclusions to be drawn from the teaching of the Gospel which we profess and at least unconsciously acknowledge as the basis of our concepts of morality.

But it turned out otherwise.

No one, it is true, directly disputes the prescriptions that one should not engage in debauchery before marriage nor after marriage, that one should not artificially prevent childbirth, that one should not make playthings out of children, and one should not place the love union higher than everything else—in a word, no one disputes that chastity is better than dissoluteness. But people say: "If it is better to be unmarried than married, evidently people must do what is better. If people will do that, the human race will become extinct, and therefore the ideal of the human race cannot be its own annihilation."

But to say nothing of the fact that the extinction of the human race is not a new idea for people of our world but is an article of faith for religious people, and for science-minded people it is the inescapable conclusion from observations of the cooling of the sun, in this objection there is a big, widespread, and long-standing misunderstanding.

People say: "If human beings attain the ideal of complete chastity, they will be annihilated. Therefore this ideal is invalid." But those who talk this way are consciously or unconsciously confusing two different things, a rule or prescription, and an ideal.

Chastity is not a rule or prescription, but an ideal, or rather one of its preconditions. An ideal is an ideal only when its realization appears to be attainable only at infinity and therefore the possibility of approaching it never ends. Not only if the ideal could be attained, but if we could even imagine its realization, it would cease to be an ideal. Such is the ideal of Christ—the establishment of the kingdom of God on earth, an ideal foretold by the prophets saying that a time would come when all people, taught by God, would turn their swords into ploughshares and their spears into pruning hooks; the lion would lie down with the lamb and all creatures would be united in love. The whole meaning of human life consists in movement in the direction of this ideal; therefore striving toward the Christian ideal in its entirety and toward chastity as one of the conditions of this ideal not only does not exclude the possibility of life, but on the contrary, the absence of this Christian ideal would destroy forward movement and consequently the possibility of life.

The reasoning that the human race will become extinct if people strive with all their might for chastity is like the claim that people have made (and still do) that the human race will perish if instead of struggling for existence people will try with all their might to demonstrate love for friends and enemies, for everything living. Such arguments come from a lack of understanding of two modes of moral instruction.

Just as there are two ways of giving directions to a traveler who seeks them, so there are two ways of giving moral instruction to a person who seeks the truth. One method consists in listing for him the landmarks he will encounter: he will be guided by these landmarks.

The other way consists in giving the person only direction by the compass he carries with him. On it he always sees a single direction and therefore can always be aware every time he deviates from it.

The first means of moral guidance is a method of external precepts and rules: human beings are given precise descriptions of the acts, which they must perform and those they must not.

"Keep the Sabbath, get circumcised, do not steal, do not drink intoxicants, do not kill a living being, pay a tithe to the poor, do not commit adultery, wash and pray five times a day, get baptized, take communion, etc." Such are the prescriptions of external religious teachings: Brahmin, Buddhist, Moslem, Jewish, and the church falsely called Christian.

Another means is the practice of providing human beings with a goal they can never attain. In striving toward it, a person thinks to himself: man is given an ideal by comparison with which he can always measure his distance from it.

"Love thy God with all thy heart and all thy soul and all thy mind and thy neighbor as thyself. Be perfect, as thy heavenly Father is perfect."

Such is the teaching of Christ.

To measure the fulfillment of external religious doctrines is to measure to what extent one's deeds fit the definitions prescribed by these doctrines, and they may fit perfectly.

To measure the fulfillment of Christ's teaching is to perceive the degree to which one's behavior does not fit the ideal of perfection. (The degree of proximity is not apparent: all that is evident is the failure to reach perfection.)

A person who confesses the external law is like a person standing in the light of a lantern hung on a pillar. He stands in its light, sees light all around him, and need go no farther. The person who confesses Christ's teaching is like the man who carries a lantern in front of him on a more or less long pole: the light is always in front of him and always beckons him to follow it and again reveals to him new, well-lit space that lies ahead.

The Pharisee thanks God that he is fulfilling everything.

A rich young man has also fulfilled everything since his childhood and does not understand what more he could do. And such people cannot think otherwise: ahead of them there is nothing toward which they could continue to strive. The tithe has been paid, the Sabbath observed, parents honored, adultery, theft, and murder have not been committed. What more? For one who confesses the Christian teaching, the attainment of any degree of perfection evokes the need to attain a higher degree, from which another still higher is revealed, and thus without end.

The person who confesses the teaching of Christ is always in the position of the publican. He always feels himself imperfect, cannot see behind him the path he has traversed, and always sees ahead the path he must still follow and which he has not yet walked.

This is the difference between Christ's teaching and all other religious doctrines, consisting not in differing requirements, but in different means of instructing people. Christ gave no life formulas; He never laid down any requirements, just as He never instituted marriage. But people did not understand the peculiarities of Christ's teaching. They were used to external doctrines and wanted to feel themselves in the right, just as the Pharisee, feeling himself in the right, going against the whole spirit of Christ's teaching, and taking His words literally, constructed an external doctrine of rules called Christian church doctrine, and substituted this doctrine for the true teaching of the Christian ideal.

The churchmen calling themselves Christian in place of the teaching of Christ's ideal concerning all manifestations of life postulated external definitions and rules that are contrary to the spirit of the teaching. This was done in relation to the state, the courts, the army, the church, and the divine service; it was also done in relation to marriage. Despite the fact that Christ not only never established marriage, but if you seek external evidence, He rather rejected it ("leave thy wife and follow me"); the church doctrines which call themselves Christian have established marriage as a Christian institution, that is, they define the external conditions under which for a Christian carnal love may supposedly be without sin and fully lawful.

But since in the true Christian teachings there is not the slightest basis for the establishment of marriage, the result has been that people in our world have pushed off from one shore and have not yet reached another; that is, they essentially do not believe the church definitions of marriage, feeling that these definitions have no basis in Christian teachings. But at the same time they do not see before them the ideal of Christ, which has been hidden by church doctrine, the ideal of striving for complete chastity. Thus they remain without any guidance in relation to marriage. The result of this, which at first seems strange, is that among Jews, Moslems, Tibetan Buddhists and others who profess religious doctrines of a much lower level than the Christian one, but who possess precise external definitions of marriage, the family principle and marital fidelity are much more strictly adhered to than among so-called Christians.

These religions practice concubinage and polygamy, but limited by definite rules. With us we have complete dissoluteness and concubinage, polygamy, and polyandry not subject to any limitations, all hidden under the guise of fictitious monogamy.

Only because for money the clergy perform a ceremony called church matrimony, a certain number of cohabiting couples of our world naïvely and hypocritically imagine that they are living in monogamy.

There is no Christian marriage and never has been any, just as there never has been and cannot be any Christian divine service (Matthew 6:5–12; John 4:21), nor Christian teachers and fathers (Matthew 23:8–10), nor Christian property, nor a Christian army, nor Christian courts or governments. This has always been understood by true Christians of the first and following centuries.

The ideal of Christianity is love for God and one's neighbor, renunciation of the self for the sake of service to God and one's neighbor. Carnal love and marriage constitute service to oneself and therefore in any case are a hindrance to service to God and other people; therefore from the Christian point of view they are a transgression, a sin.

Getting married cannot promote service to God and man even when marriage has the purpose of continuing the human race. Instead of entering into marriage for the production of children's lives it would be much simpler to rescue and support those millions of children's lives that are perishing all around us from the lack of not just spiritual, but even material food.

A Christian could enter into marriage without consciousness of transgression and sin only if he saw and knew that all existing children's lives were provided for.

One can reject the teaching of Christ, a teaching with which all our life is infused and on which our morality is based, but if you accept this teaching, you cannot deny that it professes the ideal of complete chastity.

For in the Gospels it is stated clearly and without any possibility of misinterpretation in the first place, that a married man must not separate from his wife in order take another, but must live with the one with whom he was first joined (Matthew 5:31–32; 19:8); in the second place that for men in general, and consequently for married and unmarried men alike, to look on a woman as an object of gratification is sinful (Matthew 5:28–29); and in the third place, for an unmarried man it is better not to marry at all, in other words to remain completely chaste (Matthew 19:10–12).

For a great many people such thoughts seem strange and even contradictory. And they really are contradictory, but not within themselves; these thoughts contradict our entire way of life. Necessarily one wonders: who is right? These thoughts or the lives of millions of people, including mine? I also experienced this very feeling to the highest degree when I arrived at the convictions I now proclaim. I never expected that the course of my thoughts would bring me to the place it did. I was horrified at my conclusions, wanted not to believe them, but it was impossible not to. No matter how contradictory these conclusions are to the whole structure of our life, no matter how they contradict what I used to think and even proclaimed, I had to accept them.

"But all these are general arguments which are perhaps valid, but they concern the teaching of Christ and are obligatory for those who profess Him; but life is life, and one cannot, after pointing out to people the unattainable ideal of Christ looming ahead of them, leave people beset by one of the most burning and universal problems, those that generate the greatest misery, with only this ideal and without any guidance.

"A passionate young man is at first captivated by the ideal, but he cannot hold out; he lets go, and without knowing or recognizing any rules, he becomes completely dissolute."

This is the way people usually reason.

"The ideal of Christ is unattainable; therefore it cannot serve us as a guide to life. One can talk about it, dream about it, but it is not applicable to life, and therefore must be abandoned. An ideal is not what we need, but rules, guidance fitting our strength, the average level of morals in our society. An honorable church marriage, even if it is not completely honorable, since one of the partners, namely the man, has already had commerce with many women, or marriage with the possibility of divorce, or simply civil marriage, or (following that same route) Japanese temporary marriage—why not go all the way to houses of prostitution?"

People say that is better than street vice. The trouble is precisely that if people are allowed to compromise the ideal out of weakness, the limit can never be found where they must stop.

But actually this reasoning is fallacious from the beginning, primarily in asserting that an ideal of absolute perfection cannot provide guidance in life, and in view of that one can only throw up one's hands and say that I have no need of such an ideal since I can never attain it, or to debase the ideal to a point consonant with my weakness.

To reason like that is exactly like a navigator saying to himself that since I cannot follow the line indicated by the compass, I will throw the compass overboard or stop consulting it; in other words I will discard the ideal or fix the compass needle at a point corresponding to the present position of my vessel, that is, debase the ideal to the level of my weakness. The ideal of perfection provided by Christ is not a dream or a topic for rhetorical sermons, but a very necessary and accessible guide to moral life, just as a compass is a necessary and accessible guide to navigation for a sailor. But you must believe in the one just as you believe in the other. No matter in what situation a person finds himself, the teaching of the ideal given by Christ is always sufficient to provide true guidance to those acts which must and must not be performed. But you must fully believe the teaching, and that teaching alone; you must stop believing in any others, just as the navigator must believe his compass, stop looking around and being guided by what he sees on both sides. We must learn how to be guided by Christian teachings, how to use its compass, and for that the main thing is to understand one's own position, to learn not to be afraid to measure exactly one's deviation from the ideal direction it provides. No matter what position a person is in, it is always possible for him to draw nearer to the ideal, and he can never be in a position where he could say that he had reached the ideal and had no need to strive to draw closer to it. This is the nature of a person's striving for the Christian ideal in general and for chastity in particular. In relation to the sexual question, if you think of the most various attitudes of people toward it, from the innocence of childhood up to marriage, in which continence has not been maintained, at each stage between these two situations, the teachings of Christ with the ideal He presented, will always provide clear and definite guidance as to what a person must and must not do.

What is a pure young man or woman to do? Keep themselves free from temptations, and in order to maintain themselves in that state, devote all their strength to service to God and man, and strive for greater and greater purity of thought and desire.

What is a young man or woman to do if they are beset by temptations and are absorbed by thoughts either about love in the abstract or love for a particular person and, because of this, have lost to a certain extent their capacity to serve God and man? It is the same: not push themselves toward loss of innocence, knowing that such indulgence will not free them from temptation, but only strengthen it and despite the temptation, keep striving for greater and greater chastity for the sake of complete service to God and man.

What are people to do who did not intensify their struggle and who have succumbed? They should look at their fall not as legitimate gratification, as people do now when it is legitimized by the ceremony of marriage, nor as an accidental pleasure which can be repeated along with others, nor as a misfortune when the fall took place with a person not one's equal and without a ceremony; rather they should regard this first fall as the only one, as entering into an indissoluble marriage.

This entering into a marriage along with its consequences, the birth of children, defines for those entering it a new, more limited form of service to God and man. Before marriage a person can serve God and man directly in the most various ways; entering into marriage restricts the sphere of activity and demands nurture and education of the offspring produced by the union, making of them servants of God and man.

What are a man and woman to do who live in marriage and who perform that limited service to God and man possible in their circumstances by nurturing and educating children?

It is the same: strive together to free themselves from temptation, to cleanse themselves, and cease to sin by changing those relations which impede their common and individual service to God and man, by substituting for carnal love the pure relationship of sister and brother.

It is therefore untrue that we cannot be governed by the ideal of Christ because it is so lofty, perfect, and unattainable. We cannot be governed by it only because we lie to ourselves and deceive ourselves.

For if we say that we need more attainable rules than the ideal of Christ and that otherwise without attaining the ideal of Christ we will fall into debauchery, we are saying not that the ideal of Christ is too lofty for us, but only that we do not believe in it and do not want to regulate our behavior according to that ideal.

By saying that once we have fallen, we will fall further into debauchery, we are only saying something we have already decided, that to fall with a woman not our equal is no sin, but an amusement, a distraction which we need not correct by what we call marriage. If we had understood that to fall is a sin which can and must be expiated only by an indissoluble marriage and by all the activity that comes with the upbringing of children derived from that marriage, then the fall could in no way be considered a cause of degeneration into dissoluteness.

For this is just like the situation of a farmer who did not consider a true crop the particular one that did not succeed, but sowing in a second and third place, considered a crop only the one that did succeed. It is evident that such a man would waste much land and seeds and would never learn to farm. Only establish chastity as your ideal and consider that the fall of any person with any other person, no matter whom, constitutes a unique marriage, indissoluble for one's entire life, and it will be clear that the guidance provided by Christ not only is sufficient, but is the only one possible.

"Man is weak; you must assign him tasks within his powers," people say. This is just like saying, "My hands are weak; I can't draw a straight line that would be the shortest distance between two points, and therefore, to make things easier, though I want to draw a straight one, I take as a model a curved or crooked line." The weaker my hand is, the more I need a perfect model.

We cannot, after recognizing the Christian teaching of the ideal pretend that we don't know it and replace it with external prescriptions. The Christian teaching of the ideal is revealed to mankind precisely because it can govern us in our present age. Mankind has already outgrown the period of external, religious prescriptions: no one believes in them anymore.

The Christian doctrine of the ideal is the only doctrine that can govern mankind. We cannot and must not replace the ideal of Christ with external rules, but must firmly keep that ideal before us in all its purity, and most of all, believe in it.

To a navigator not far from shore you can say, "Steer by that promontory, that cape, that tower," and so forth.

But the time comes when the sailors have moved far away from the shore, and their only guide can be the unreachable heavenly bodies and the compass that shows direction. Both of these have been given to us.

"The Wife Murderer"

A FRAGMENT BY LEV NIKOLAEVICH TOLSTOY

(LATE 1860S)

EVERYTHING THAT COULD BE DONE (in that situation) was done. Without pitying others or himself, he surrendered himself to the passion that had filled his heart. He did much that was difficult and terrible: he kept watch over them, sneaked up on them, and he killed her, killed her for certain, and disfigured him—punished them, showed them they couldn't fool with him; and, what was even worse—he wasn't afraid of other people's judgment and told everyone without fear: "Arrest me, judge me. I killed my former wife, that lewd bitch, and I know that I did a good job of it. Now arrest me and judge me, just as you like. You won't understand me. And I don't want to understand you." He did all this, and it seemed to him, he should have been at peace (and proud of what he'd done). Everything he'd done, he did to relieve his anxiety. But sitting alone in the police station, he was not at peace. That state of mind from which he had sought relief by doing all that he had done, was just as burdensome, squeezing the life out of him like a heavy stone lying on top of him and crushing him.

There was one change in him: before this it had seemed that he had to do something and that after he had done it, he would feel better, that the fire would cease scorching him. But now he knew that there was nothing more to be done; yet the burden was still crushing him, and fire was still scorching him, and he was exhausted.

He sat on his cot and looked at the small barred window in the door, heard footsteps, doors slamming in the wing, and conversation in the neighboring cell:

"What gentleman?"

"A gentleman, a landowner. He totally disemboweled her, they say. He's repented. 'Arrest me,' he says. 'I killed my wife.'"

"What will happen to him, Uncle Ivan?"

"It's well known. Can they just allow him to commit murder? Same as would happen to you or me. Just because they're masters, does that mean there's no judging them? No, brother. Nowadays the law demands order."

"Well, uncle, has he greased some palms, or what?"

"Far from it! Damned duty, believe me!"

"A trial," he thought. "So be it. The knout, Siberia—so be it. If only she could see how that butcher slashes crisscross on my plump back. She won't see. She's lying there, her disheveled head bent over her white arm, sobbing her last dying sobs. So be it—but it's no easier for me. There's nothing more to be done. To judge me? The police superintendent? The public prosecutor?" He moaned from shame and spiritual torment at the thought of having to listen and to reply.

The doors creaked in the wing, footsteps [were heard], bustling, whispering, and the loud voice of a gentleman asked where the prisoner was.

"In a secure cell, Your Excellency."

The tall stately superintendent, with his dyed mustache and topknot, came in the door with a reprimand about the disarray.

"Are you retired Captain Zhelyabovsky?" he asked.

He made no reply. He looked at the superintendent, at his satiated, supercilious face, at his decoration, at the officer's haste as he took the superintendent's overcoat, and at the serene confidence of the free and happy superintendent. He recalled the repulsive cheerfulness of his teacher who'd been whistling a little song when Zhelyabovsky, then a child, was being punished. And just as he did then, he felt his powerlessness and wanted to cry. He glanced at him twice, dropped his eyes, and made no reply because he was afraid that his voice would quaver and he'd be ashamed. But in not replying, he decided that it was unnecessary and impossible to reply.

"You're a prisoner and must answer me as part of our interrogation," said the superintendent.

"I've said everything. I murdered my wife.[1] Put me on trial."

"You're distressed, upset. I understand that and sympathize. Try to calm down. I'll ask you to answer our questions tomorrow. Believe me, I feel sorry for

---

1. The following words were crossed out: "and I regret that I killed <<him>>. The word "him" is struck out and this reading is presumed.

you. Can I be of any use to you? Your valet asked me to allow him in. Would you like something to eat? Tomorrow I'll ask you to reply to all my questions."

"I don't need anything."

"Your valet?"

"Vaska? Why on earth?"

"You, master, Mikhaila Sergeevich, father!" The valet came in and began to kiss his shoulder and hand.

The superintendent left.

~~The valet, Vasilii, stood by the door and for a long time was silent. But when everything had quieted down, the large man fell flat on the ground and began sobbing.~~

~~"Father, forgive me! I did it. Why did I tell you?"~~

~~"Shut up."~~

~~"No, I won't. Father, forgive me; listen. I'll get you out of here. Only listen to me."~~

~~"I have nowhere to go. Only help me to—kill myself."~~

~~"Good gracious, Mikhaila Sergeevich! I've destroyed you! Forgive me. Listen to me. Your sin is great, and mine is even greater. Listen to me; run away. I've brought you some money; everything's ready. Let's go. I've destroyed one soul; don't destroy me and yourself."~~

~~"Where will I go?"~~

~~"We'll go abroad."~~

~~"Shut up. I'm going to sleep."~~

He lay down on the cot and remained there for a long time. Vasilii[2] sat there quietly and dozed.

The same Anastasya Dmitrievna, sobbing her last dying sobs, lay there before the eyes of Mikha[ila] Serg[eevich], and the same burden and same feeling of powerlessness tormented him.—

He tried to pray, but in his soul there arose only spite against God. Yet at the same time he felt as if he were in His hands. He didn't sleep for two nights and couldn't fall asleep. For a moment he'd drift into oblivion then suddenly jump up:[3] Guard, guard . . .[4]

---

2. Crossed out: "fell asleep and began to snore."
3. Crossed out: "Vaska, Vaska! How can we leave?"
4. Crossed out: "How much do you want . . . let me go."

. . . .
. . . . . . .⁵

The guards were drunk. A veteran soldier went out to buy some food.

⁶M[ikhaila] S[ergeevich] left the courtyard and turned at once into a vacant lot behind the merchants' courtyard. All night he walked through the woods or along the road. Toward morning, parting stalks of grain, they entered a field of rye and fell fast asleep and slept all day long. Toward evening they came back to the road. He approached a river.⁷ There were carts near the river, wagons, women, children and peasants. Everyone regarded him in astonishment. M[ikhail] S[ergeevich] ~~undressed and entered~~ the water.

5. There is a line of dots in the original. In the margin is written: "The guard came and began saying how the prisoner had escaped."

6. Crossed out: "Vasilii and."

7. Crossed out: "I feel like bathing."

Excerpts from
Lev Nikolaevich Tolstoy's Letters,
1889–91

LETTER TO G. A. RUSANOV[1]
Moscow, March 12, 1889

STILL, SOMETIMES I do want to write, and just imagine, most often it's a novel, broad and free, something like *Anna Karenina*, which would easily include everything that now seemed clear to me from a new, fresh perspective, and useful to people. The rumor you heard about a story by me has some foundation. About two years ago I wrote a draft of a story that did examine the theme of sexual love, but it was written in such a careless and unsatisfactory manner that I won't revise it, and if I were to take up that subject, I'd have to start all over again.

LETTER TO N. N. STRAKHOV[2]
Yasnaya Polyana, November 17, 1889

I very much valued your opinion and received your criticism that was far more generous than expected. As a work of art, I know that this piece is beneath any criticism: it was the result of two devices, each incompatible with the other, and that accounts for the awful things you've heard. Nevertheless, I'll leave it just as is, and I don't regret it. It's not a result of laziness, but I

---

1. Gavriil Rusanov (1845–1907) was a landowner in the province of Voronezh who was disabled by illness and became one of Tolstoy's most faithful correspondents.

2. Nikolai Strakhov (1828–96) was a Russian philosopher, publicist, and literary critic and long-time friend and correspondent of Lev Tolstoy.

can't correct it: I don't regret it because I know for certain that what I've written is not without utility, and is without doubt very useful to people and in part innovative. If I were to write something artistic, and I don't promise to do that, I'd have to start over again and do it right now.

LETTER TO V. G. CHERTKOV[3]
Yasnaya Polyana, January 15, 1890

My wife has made a copy of the last version of "The Kreutzer Sonata" and given it to Storozhenko[4] who'll deal with it. Masha's making all the changes in your copy and we'll send it to you so you can give it to dear Hanson.[5]

After America, the country that's most sympathetic to me is Denmark. I received such a wonderful letter from a schoolteacher there.[6] In addition, my wife's sending a copy to de Vogüé;[7] his wife's asked to translate it, and my daughter Tanya's making a copy for Hapgood.[8] So then, let them [all] translate it, and the Russian version will probably appear later.

LETTER TO V. G. CHERTKOV
Yasnaya Polyana, April 15, 1891

My wife returned from Petersburg where she saw the Tsar and spoke with him about me and my work—completely in vain. He promised her to allow "The Kreutzer Sonata" [to be published], which doesn't make me happy. There was something nasty in "The Kreuzter Sonata." I find any mention of it terribly unpleasant. There was something bad about the motives that guided me in writing it; it occasioned such malice. I can even see what was bad about it. I will try not to let that happen again if I manage to finish writing anything else.

---

3. Vladimir Chertkov (1854–1936) was the editor, publisher, and publicist of Tolstoy's works, one of his disciples, and his closest collaborator. He had written that the author's ideas about the sexual question were so integrated into the passenger's narrative that it "lost its vitality and naturalness."

4. N. I. Storozhenko (1836–1906) was a Russian writer and critic who was given a copy of Tolstoy's story for inclusion in an anthology, but the censor prevented its publication.

5. P. Hanson published his authorized translation of Tolstoy's story into Danish in 1890.

6. A reference to a letter from a Danish teacher, I. Sorensen (October 23, 1889), expressing his sympathy for Tolstoy's views.

7. Vicomte Melchior de Vogüé (1848–1910) was a French novelist, critic, and translator who wrote an influential book on the Russian novel in 1886. His wife did not translate Tolstoy's story into French.

8. Isabel Florence Hapgood (1851–1928) was an American writer and translator of Russian literature. She visited Yasnaya Polyana in 1891 and left an account of her stay.

Excerpts from
Lev Nikolaevich Tolstoy's Diary,
1889–1900

JULY 2 [1889]

I FEEL A LITTLE BETTER. The Hapgoods have left. I walked to the village and the haymaking. Nothing's going well. Everyone's arguing. I worked on "The Kreutzer Sonata." Not bad. Finished it completely. But now I have to revise it all from the beginning. Prohibiting her from having children must be made the central idea. Without children she's reduced to the point where she must fall. More about the mother's egoism. The mother's self-sacrifice is neither good nor bad, just like work. Both are good only in the presence of understanding and love. But work for oneself and self-sacrifice only for one's own children—that's a bad thing. Went to bed early.

JULY 4

Got up at 6 A.M. Mowed, now it's 11:30, I'm tired. This morning and last night I thought long and hard about "The Kreutzer Sonata." Sonya's recopying it; she's upset and last night talked about the young woman's disillusionment, the sensuality of men, alien to her at first, and their lack of sympathy for children. She's unfair because she wants to justify herself, and in order to understand and speak the truth, it's necessary to repent. The whole drama of the tale, which has been continually escaping me, is now clear in my head. He taught her sensuality. The doctors forbade her to have children. She's well fed, well dressed, and there are all the temptations of art. How can she keep from falling? He must feel that he himself drove her to it, that he'd murdered her earlier when he'd come to hate her, that he was searching for a pretext and was glad when he'd found one . . .

JULY 7

I thought: for "The Kreutzer Sonata." 1) The distinction in the wife's moods—she is two women. 2) The seducer-musician considers it his duty to seduce. And besides: it's better if I don't go to a bordello, I might get infected.

JULY 24

. . . Began working on "The Kreutzer Sonata."

I thought: 1) I'm writing "The Kreutzer Sonata," even "On Art," and both of them are negative, evil, while I want to write something good. . . .

Slept during the day. Worked a bit on "The Kreutzer Sonata." I finished a rough draft. I realized how to rework the whole thing, introducing love and compassion for her. Went for a swim . . .

AUGUST 11

. . . Didn't do anything all day. I went mushrooming and thought about "The Kreutzer Sonata" and about art. "The Kreutzer Sonata"—I have to make the dying woman delirious, as she begs for forgiveness and can't believe that he's the one who killed her . . .

AUGUST 19

I thought of something for "The Kreutzer Sonata." Fornicator is not a swearword, but a condition (I think the same is true for a woman fornicator), a condition of restlessness, curiosity, and a need for novelty that arises from having intercourse for the sake of pleasure not with one woman, but with many.[1] Just like a drunkard. One can abstain, but a drunkard's always a drunkard, and a fornicator's always a fornicator; at the first lapse of attention, he'll fall. I'm a fornicator.

AUGUST 28

I woke up early and sat right down to work on "The Kreutzer Sonata" and wrote for four hours. I finished it. It seems good, but I went mushrooming and felt dissatisfied with it again—it's not what's needed.

---

1. The Russian root is *blud*—lechery, fornication.

AUGUST 29

I thought that I'm fussing over my writing "The Kreutzer Sonata" out of vanity; I don't want it to appear before the public as less than finished, clumsy, even bad. That's disgraceful. If there's something useful, necessary for people, they'll find it in what's bad. A story that's perfectly finished won't make my conclusions any more convincing. I must be a holy fool even in my writing . . .[2]

SEPTEMBER 7

Yesterday Sonya read "The Kreutzer Sonata" aloud, and Tanya made some valid observations: 1) that one doesn't feel sorry for her; 2) that she won't repent and ask forgiveness.[3] Her sin is so small compared to her punishment . . .

SEPTEMBER 21

Late. A nightmare: a mad woman, raving, who's being held from behind. I read and wrote a little. I decided to rework it ["The Kreutzer Sonata"] once and for all; there's no need for the murder.

SEPTEMBER 23

. . . I began working on "The Kreutzer Sonata," which is no longer really "The Kreutzer Sonata." Everything's pointing toward the murder simply as the result of a quarrel. I read an account of a man who killed himself and his wife who'd killed their children, and that confirmed my intention even more . . .[4]

OCTOBER 6

In the morning I wrote a new version of "The Kreutzer Sonata." Not bad, but sluggish. I'm doing it for everyone, and that's why it's so difficult . . .

OCTOBER 16

Dejection, sorrow, remorse; if only I can avoid doing harm to myself and to others. I wrote a great deal, correcting "The Kreutzer Sonata." I haven't experienced such a dispirited state in a long time.

---

2. Tolstoy is referring to the Russian institution of the *yurodivyi*—holy fool, or "fool in Christ," an idiot believed to possess the gift of divine prophecy.

3. Tanya was Tolstoy's eldest daughter (1864–1950).

4. Tolstoy read the report in the newspaper *Nedelya*, November 17, 1889.

OCTOBER 31

Yes, and yesterday I received a long letter from Chertkov. He criticizes "The Kreutzer Sonata" very fairly; I'd like to follow his advice, but I don't feel like it. Apathy, gloom, dejection. But I don't feel bad. Death lies ahead, that is, life; how can one not rejoice?

NOVEMBER 2

I received a letter from my sister Tanya about the reading of "The Kreutzer Sonata."[5] It is producing an impression. Good, I feel happy.

NOVEMBER 7

I'm getting news that "The Kreutzer Sonata" is making an impact, and I'm glad. That's not good.

DECEMBER 6

I woke up at 7 A.M. and set right to work. . . . I looked through all of "The Kreutzer Sonata," made deletions, corrections, and additions. I am terribly fed up with it. The main thing is that it's not right artistically and it rings false.

JANUARY 18 [1890]

Work was interrupted by Butkevich, who'd arrived from the country.[6] I had a talk with him. He told me that many people hated "The Kreutzer Sonata," saying that it was the description of a sexual maniac. This distressed me at first, but then I found it pleasant that in any case it had stirred up what needed to be stirred up. Of course, it could have been better, but I did what I could . . .

FEBRUARY 11

I also thought there's no need to write an afterword to "The Kreutzer Sonata." There's no need, because it's impossible for people who think differently to be convinced by arguments.

---

5. Tatyana Kuzminskaya had written to Sofiya Andreevna Tolstaya from Saint Petersburg about the success of the reading that had taken place on October 28 in her house in the presence of guests.

6. A. S. Butkevich (1869–1942) was a local beekeeper and the son of a Tula landowner.

MARCH 8

A lot about "The Kreutzer Sonata." People ask: what next? I must write an afterword, but I can't . . .

MAY 9, PIROGOVO

1) Many of the ideas that I have been expressing lately belong not to me but to those who feel a kinship with me and turn to me with their questions, doubts, ideas, and plans. Thus the main idea, or better to say, the feeling behind "The Kreutzer Sonata" belongs to a woman, a Slav, who wrote me a letter that was comical in its language, but in its content, about the oppression of women by sexual demands.[7] Later she came to see me and made a strong impression on me.

JUNE 4

Articles and letters all about "The Afterword" and "The Kreutzer Sonata." It's astonishing the contempt for the written word, what abuse of it!

I'm suffering from the fact that I'm surrounded by such people with deformed brains, such self-assured people, with such ready theories, that's it useless to write anything for them: there's no way to reach them . . .

AUGUST 15

Yes, some articles yesterday about "The Kreutzer Sonata." The scandal in America and abuse from Nikanor.[8] I didn't find it unpleasant.

MAY 22 [1891]

An afterword to the afterword: Whether I explained properly or not why the greatest sexual continence is necessary, I don't know. But I do know for certain that copulation is an abomination that can be regarded or thought about only with revulsion under the influence of sexual desire. Even in order to have children you wouldn't do this to a woman you love. I'm writing this at a time when I myself am possessed by sexual desire, which I can't fight against . . .

---

7. In February, Tolstoy had received an unsigned letter sent from a monastery, probably written by a Czech woman. There is no record of her having visited Yasnaya Polyana.

8. The postmaster general of the United States had declared *The Kreutzer Sonata* obscene and prohibited it from being distributed by mail. Nikanor, archbishop of Kherson and Odessa (1827–90), launched a vitriolic attack on Tolstoy's work.

JUNE 5 [1893]

I'm going to Tula now. On the way I thought:

1) I was struck by the thought that one of the main reasons for hostility be-tween husband and wife is the rivalry in how they manage the family.

The wife mustn't acknowledge the husband as reasonable and practical because, if she were to do so, she would have to do as he wished, and vice versa. If I were writing "The Kreutzer Sonata" now, I would advance that idea . . .

DECEMBER 15 [1900]

I walked past a bookshop and saw "The Kreutzer Sonata." I recalled that I had written "The Kreutzer Sonata," and *The Power of Darkness,* and even *Resurrection* without any thought of preaching to people, or about being of use to them, meanwhile these works, especially "The Kreutzer Sonata," have brought a great deal of good.[9]

9. *The Power of Darkness* (1886) is a peasant tragedy constructed in the classical manner. *Resurrection* (1899) was Tolstoy's third and last long novel.

Excerpts from
Sofiya Adreevna Tolstaya's Diary

EDITED BY O. A. GOLÍNENKO, S. A. ROZANOVA,

B. M. SHUMOVA, I. A. POKROVSKAYA AND N. I. AZAROVA

TRANSLATED BY CATHY PORTER

DECEMBER 28 [1890]

YESTERDAY IN THE DRAWING-ROOM he was telling Lyova about the narrative form he was trying to create when he started writing *The Kreutzer Sonata*. This notion of creating a genuine *story* was inspired by that extraordinary story-teller and actor Andreev-Burlak.[1] He had told Lyovochka about a man he had once met at a station who told him all about his unfaithful wife and how unhappy she was making him, and Lyovochka had used this as the subject-matter of his own story.

JANUARY 10 [1891]

I have observed a connecting thread between Lyovochka's old diaries and his *Kreutzer Sonata*. I am a buzzing fly entangled in this web, sucked of its blood by the spider.

JANUARY 25

It occurred to me this evening, as I was correcting the proofs for *The Kreutzer Sonata*, that when a woman is young she loves with her whole heart, and gladly gives herself to the man she loves because she sees what pleasure it gives him. Later in her life she looks back, and suddenly she realises that this

---

1. The actor V. N. Andreev-Burlak visited Tolstoy and first told him the story that served as the basis of "The Kreutzer Sonata."

man loved her only when he needed her. And she remembers all the times his affection turned to harshness or disgust the moment he was satisfied.

And when the woman, having closed her eyes to all this, also begins to experience these needs, then the old sentimental, passionate love passes away and she becomes like him—i.e., passionate with her husband at certain times, and demanding that he satisfy her. She is to be pitied if he no longer loves her by then; and he is to be pitied if he can no longer satisfy her. This is the reason for all those family crises and separations, so unexpected and so ugly, which happen in later life. Happiness comes only when will and spirit prevail over the body and the passions. *The Kreutzer Sonata* is untrue in everything relating to a young woman's experiences. A younger woman has none of that sexual passion, especially when she is busy bearing and feeding children. Only once in every two years is she a real woman in fact! Her passion awakes only in her 30s.

FEBRUARY 12

I do not know how or why everyone connected *The Kreutzer Sonata* with our own married life, but this is what has happened, and now everyone, from the Tsar himself down to Lev Nikolaevich's brother and his best friend Dyakov, feels sorry for me. And it isn't just other people—I too know in my heart that this story is directed against me, and that it has done me a great wrong, humiliated me in the eyes of the world and destroyed the last vestiges of love between us. And all this, when not once in my whole married life have I ever wronged my husband, with so much as a gesture or glance at another man! Whether or not I ever had it in my heart to love another man—and whether or not this was a struggle for me—is a different matter, and that is *my* business. No one in the world has the right to pry into my secrets, so long as I have remained pure.

I don't know why, but today I decided at last to let Lev Nikolaevich know my feelings about *The Kreutzer Sonata*. He wrote it so long ago, but he would have had to know sooner or later what I thought about it, and it was after he had reproached me for "causing him so much suffering" that I decided to speak up about *my* suffering.

MARCH 10

I read an extraordinarily sensitive and intelligent article on *The Kreutzer Sonata*, by M. de Vogué.[2] He says, amongst other things, that Tolstoy had

---

2. Eugène Melchior de Vogüé (1848–1910) was a French diplomat, writer, and literary critic whose book *Le roman russe* (1886) aroused considerable French interest in Russian literature. His article on "The Kreutzer Sonata" was published in a Russian journal in 1890.

taken his analysis to extremes (*"analyse creusante"*), and that this had killed all the personal and literary life of the work.

[MY VISIT TO SAINT PETERSBURG]

Early that morning I checked that I had paid all my bills, asked Tanya to settle the rest for me, got dressed and sat waiting for the time when I had to leave. I had on a black mourning dress I'd made myself, a veil and a black lace hat. At a quarter to eleven I set off. My heart was pounding as we approached the Anichkov Palace. I was saluted at the gates, then at the porch, and I bowed back. I entered the ante-chamber and asked the doorkeeper whether the Tsar had instructed him to receive Countess Tolstaya. No, he said. He then asked someone else, and got the same reply. My heart sank. Then they summoned the Tsar's footman. A handsome young man appeared, wearing a bright red and gold uniform and a huge three-cornered hat. "Do you have instructions from the Tsar to receive Countess Tolstaya?" I asked him. "I should think so, Your Excellency!" he said. "The Tsar has just returned from church and has been asking about you." (The Tsar had apparently been at the christening of Grand Duchess Elizaveta Fyodorovna who has just converted to Orthodoxy.) The footman then ran up a steep stairway, covered in an ugly bright green carpet, and I followed him up. But I had not realised how fast I was running, and when he left me with a deep bow at the reception-room my heart was pounding so wildly that I thought I should die. I was in a terrible state. The first thought that came into my head was that this business was not worth dying for. I imagined the footman coming back to summon me to the Tsar and finding my lifeless body. I should be unable to say a word, at any rate; my heart was beating so violently that it was literally impossible for me to breathe, speak or cry out. I sat down and longed to ask for a glass of water, but could not. Then I remembered that the thing to do when a horse has been driven too hard is to lead it about quietly for a while until it recovers. So I got up from the sofa and took a few paces around the room. That did not make it any better though, so I discreetly loosened my stays and sat down again, massaging my chest and thinking about the children. How would they take the news of my death, I wondered. Fortunately the Tsar had not been informed of my arrival and had received someone else before me. So I had time to rest and get my breath back, and I had fully recovered by the time the footman returned, and said: "His Majesty begs Her Excellency the Countess Tolstaya to enter." I followed him into the Tsar's study and he bowed and left. The Tsar came to the door to meet me and shake my hand, and I curtseyed slightly.

"Do forgive me, Countess, for keeping you waiting for so long," he said. "It was impossible for me to receive you earlier."

I replied: "I am deeply grateful to Your Majesty for doing me the honour of receiving me."

Then the Tsar began to talk about my husband (I do not remember his exact words), and asked me the precise nature of my request. I then spoke, in a quiet but firm voice:

"Your Majesty, I have recently observed that my husband seems disposed to resume his literary endeavours. Only the other day he was saying to me: 'I have moved so far beyond these philosophical and religious works now that I think I might start on some literary work—I have in mind something rather similar to *War and Peace*, in form and content.' Yet with every day that passes the prejudice against him grows stronger. Volume 13 was banned, for instance, although it has now been decided to pass it. His play *The Fruits of Enlightenment* was banned, then the order was given for it to be performed on the Imperial stage. *The Kreutzer Sonata* was banned . . ."

"Surely, though, you would not give a book like that to your children to read?" the Tsar said.

I said: "This story has unfortunately taken a rather extreme form, but the fundamental idea is that the ideal is always unattainable. If the ideal is total chastity, then people can be pure only in marriage."

I also recall that when I told the Tsar that Lev Nikolaevich seemed disposed to write *literary* works again, he said: "Ah, how good that would be! What a very great writer he is!"

After defining what I took to be the main point of *The Kreutzer Sonata*, I went on to say: "It would make me so happy if the ban was lifted from *The Kreutzer Sonata* in the *Complete Collected Works*. That would be clear evidence of a gracious attitude to Lev Nikolaevich. And who knows, it might even encourage his work."

To this the Tsar replied: "Yes I think it might very well be included in the *Complete Works*. Not everyone can afford to buy it, after all, and it will not have a very wide circulation." . . .

A letter arrived for me in Yasnaya from the Minister[3] while I was away, announcing that he had given permission for *The Kreutzer Sonata* and the "Epilogue" to be published in the *Complete Works*. In Moscow I learnt of this at the press where it was printed. I cannot help secretly exulting in my success

3. I. N. Durnovo (1834–1903) was the Russian Minister of Internal Affairs from 1889 to 1905.

in overcoming all the obstacles, that I managed to obtain an interview with the Tsar, and that I, a woman, have achieved something that nobody else could have done! It was undoubtedly my own personal influence that played a major part in this business. As I was telling people before, I needed just one moment of inspiration to sway the Tsar's judgement as a human being and capture his sympathy, and the inspiration came, and I did influence his will—although he is a kind man anyway, and obviously quite capable of yielding to the correct influence. Anybody who read this and thought I was boasting would be quite wrong and unjust.

Volume 13 will come out any day now, and I should dearly love to send the Tsar a copy, enclosing a group photograph of my family, in whom he showed so much interest.

JUNE 1

Everybody is so terribly interested to hear about it! Yet nobody knows my real motive for visiting St Petersburg. It was *The Kreutzer Sonata* that was at the bottom of it all. That story cast a shadow over my life. Some people suspected that it was based on our life, others felt sorry for me. Even the Tsar said: "I feel sorry for his poor wife." Uncle Kostya told me when I was in Moscow that I had become "*une victime*," and that everyone pitied me. So I wanted to show that I wasn't a victim at all; I wanted people to say that my visit to St Petersburg was something I had done instinctively. I knew in advance that I would be successful and that I'd be able to prevail upon the Emperor, for I have not yet lost my powers of winning people's sympathy; and I certainly made an impression on him, with my words and my demeanour. But it was also for the sake of the public that I had to vindicate the story. Everyone now knows that I *pleaded with the Tsar* for it. If that story had been written about me and my relations with Lyovochka, then I would hardly have begged him to let it be published. Everyone will see this now. I have had various reports of the Tsar's flattering comments about me. He told Sheremeteva that he was sorry he'd had urgent work to attend to that day and had been unable to spend longer with me, as he found our discussion so interesting and enjoyable. Countess Aleksandra Andreevna Tolstaya wrote to tell me that I had made an *excellent* impression. And Princess Urusova said that Zhukovskii had told her that the Tsar found me sincere, simple and sympathetic, and that he had not realised I was still so young and pretty. All this flatters my female vanity, and avenges me for all the years in which my husband not only failed to promote me in society but actually did his utmost to drag me down. I can never understand why.

JULY 21

I am haunted again and again by thoughts of *The Kreutzer Sonata*. Today I again told him I could no longer live with him as his wife. He assured me this was exactly what he wanted too, but I did not believe him.

JUNE 3 [1897]

Taneev came, and Turkin, to teach Misha.[4] All other feelings are over-shadowed by the dread of scenes over Sergei Ivanovich's visit . . .

My husband's *strength* has been the death of me, and has broken both my spirit and my personality—and it's not as though *I* lacked strength or energy! My heart is happy and at peace at present. But it was deeply painful to see the horror on Lev Nikolaevich's face when he heard of Taneev's arrival. He is morbidly jealous, and his suffering is unbearable to me too. And as for my own . . .

JUNE 7

I long desperately for music; I'd like to play myself, but I never have the time. I did play two of Mendelssohn's "Songs Without Words" today, how-ever. Oh, those songs! One of them in particular moves me to my very soul.

JUNE 8

I was proof-reading *The Kreutzer Sonata* today, and again it made me so sad. How cynical it is, how blatantly it exposes the evil side of human nature. Pozdnyshev is always saying it's *we* who indulge our swinish passions, it's *we* who feel sated—*we* do this, *we* do that, it's always *our* fault. But a woman's emotions are quite different from a man's, and besides, one should never generalise about feelings, even sexual ones: there is far too much difference between a man's experiences and those of a pure woman.

JULY 23

They were attacking me over Sergei Ivanovich too. Well, let them! This man has brought such richness and joy to my life; he has opened the door to the world of music, and it was only through hearing him play that I found happiness and consolation. His music brought me back to life after Vanech-ka's death, when life had deserted me. His gentle and happy presence has soothed my soul, and even now I feel so peaceful, so comfortable, after I have

---

4. Sergei Ivanovich Taneev (1856–1915) was a Russian composer and pianist who served as the model for the character of Ivan Ilych in Sofiya Tolstaya's story "Song Without Words."

seen him. And they all think I am in love with him! How quick they are to cheapen one's feelings. Why, I'm far too old—it would be quite inappropriate.

JUNE 14 [1898]

I played the piano for three hours non-stop today, and I tried to learn Chopin's A Major Polonaise; it is hard, but oh, what a magnificent piece it is! Later Nadya Feret arrived and sang very pleasantly for us. I read my son Lyova's short story "Chopin Prelude" in the *New Times*. He has no special ability—it's a small talent, sincere and naïve. I finished the day with L.N. and we behaved like children.

JULY 4

The day before yesterday I sat up until three in the morning happily writing my story "Song Without Words." I played the piano for about three hours both yesterday and today. I was thinking about Taneev's songs today, for Sasha was humming them on the way to the swimming pool, and I then began to sight-read them. . . .

I am unforgivably depressed, and I seem to smell corpses everywhere, and it's sheer torture. Only music can save me from melancholy and from this terrible stench.

AUGUST 31 [1909]

This morning we had a visit from a 30-year-old Romanian who had castrated himself at the age of 18 after reading *The Kreutzer Sonata*.[5] He then took to working on the land—just 19 acres—and was terribly disillusioned today to see that Tolstoy writes one thing but lives in luxury. He was obviously very hurt, said he wanted to cry, kept repeating, "My God, my God! How can this be? What shall I tell them at home?" and questioned everyone, seeking an explanation of this contradiction.

---

5. The Romanian was named A. Marukhin. Tolstoy's comment on him in his *Diary* was that he was "an exceedingly interesting man."

Excerpts from
My Life

SOFIYA ANDREEVNA TOLSTAYA

TRANSLATED BY JOHN WOODSWORTH AND ARKADI KLIOUTCHANSKI

EDITED BY ANDREW DONSKOV

IN THE CARRIAGE

AND HOW COULD I NOT BE AFRAID? After Birjulëvo, and even there at the station, the torments began which every young wife must go through. Not to mention the terrible physical pains, and just think of the shame! How torturesome it was, and unbearably shameful! All of a sudden there awakened within me a new, crazy but involuntary feeling of passion which had been dormant in the young not-yet-developed maiden.

It was good that it was dark in the carriage, good that we could not see each other's faces. It was only close, very close that I could feel his breath, which was fitful, quick and passionate. His whole strong and powerful being overwhelmed my whole self, which was meek and loving, but suppressed by tormenting pains and unbearable shame.

Again and again, the whole night the same trials, the same sufferings. In his novella *The Kreutzer Sonata* Lev Nikolaevich describes Pozdnyshev's disenchantment on the first night of his so-called honeymoon—the very beginning of married life.

This feeling of disenchantment and dullness was something Lev Nikolaevich experienced himself. It was an unfamiliar phenomenon, something new, this communication with a society girl. He told me himself that before marriage he had lived with a high-spirited, beautiful peasant woman named Askin'ja at Yasnaya Polyana. Earlier he had paid a visit to various "houses," and different women had come to him in hotels to sell their bodies. He looked upon his relationships with them as the satisfaction of a need, and nothing more, though sometimes as a pleasure. In this area everything came easy to him.

And now all at once here was this frightened, innocent little girl, initially dispassionate, suffering physically and morally, and only later infected by her husband's passion, which had not yet managed to awaken in the girl I was back then.

Lev Nikolaevich himself once said, through the lips of one of his characters, that the feeling for passion and debauchery, as well as a response to it, must be *educated* in a woman. And he was right.

THREE SIGNIFICANT PERIODS

I shall conclude my confession by talking about the third period which significantly influenced my life. I shall write about it in more detail, if I live long enough, when I come to 1895. For the moment I shall offer but a brief sketch.

This was the time following the death of my little son Vanechka.[1] I was in a state of extreme despair—the kind that happens only once in a lifetime. Such a state of sorrow is usually fatal, and those that survive are not in a condition to endure such heart-wrenching suffering a second time. But I did survive, and for that I am obliged to chance, as well as to the mysterious medium of . . . *music*.

At first after the death of my beloved boy I kept praying, went around to various monasteries and churches and lived completely in God. In one church I caught cold, took seriously ill and almost died.

In the spring I managed to pull myself together and my health began to improve. I decided to go see my sister in Kiev, again in the same prayerful mood.

One day in May, after recovering and returning to Moscow, [where we were living at the time,] I was sitting on the balcony. It was a warm day, and the whole garden had already turned green. Sergej Ivanovich Taneev dropped by—someone I hardly knew and felt rather uncomfortable with. To make conversation, I asked him where he would be spending the summer. He replied that he didn't know, that he was looking to rent some kind of *dacha* [cottage] on a country estate.

And then all at once it came to me that our annexe at Yasnaya Polyana was empty, and I offered it to him on the condition that I must first consult with my family. I myself was morally reaching out for anything that would take my mind off my life with Vanechka, and the presence of someone who was

---

1. Ivan L'vovich Tolstoy (1888–1895), affectionately known as Vanechka.

completely oblivious of my sadness to date—and was a pretty good pianist to boot—seemed quite desirable to me.

But fate has a hand in everything, and our own will counts for so little in comparison with God's.

And so, one way or another, Taneev came to us at Yasnaya Polyana and took up residence in the annexe along with his dear old nurse, Pelageja Vasil'evna.[2] He did not want to impose on us and insisted that we rent the annexe to him and that he pay us in full. He and Tanja agreed on a payment of 100 roubles for the summer, and I at once put this sum aside for the poor—it was too hot for me to hold for any length of time.

Taneev had quite a bit of contact with the young people. You could often hear his strange, jolly laugh when [the residents of Yasnaya Polyana] went for walks all together or played tennis. He studied Italian along with Tanja and Masha, played chess with Lev Nikolaevich, and they had a wager: whoever lost a match was obliged to carry out his opponent's wishes. In other words, if Taneev lost, he would have to play something suggested by Lev Nikolaevich, while if Lev Nikolaevich lost, he would have to read something he had written, according to Sergej Ivanovich's request.

I recall the strange inner awakening I felt upon hearing Taneev's wonderful, deep playing. My sadness and heartfelt longings somehow disappeared, and my heart was filled with joy and serenity. Each time the playing stopped, my heart was once more overwhelmed by sorrow, despair and a lack of desire to go on living.

But then Sergej Ivanovich would lose a match, and start playing a Beethoven sonata, or Chopin's *Polonaise in A-flat major*, or the Freischütz overture,[3] Mendelssohn's *Songs Without words*, variations by Beethoven and Mozart and many, many more wonderful pieces. As I listened, I felt more and more often a tinge of delight within me, and my heartaches would grow lighter, and I would wait for the healing music with agonising anticipation.

And then Taneev might invite us to his rooms in the annexe to hear his opera *Oresteia*, which he played and tried to sing, even though he did not have a voice, but this came across as rather strange and not very pretty. And I gladly listened to this music, which exuded so much beauty, as I sat serenely in my chair and allowed my sadness to dissipate.

2. Pelageja Vasil'evna Chizhova (1825–1910), nanny to Taneev in his youth; later cook, housekeeper, secretary and care-giver.

3. *Der Freischütz* [The marksman], an opera composed between 1817 and 1821 by the German composer Carl Maria von Weber.

Sometimes Taneev would play over a particular scene time and again, un-aware that I was listening, while I sat on the annexe's porch, listening to him play through the open windows, and I felt at ease.

This went on for two summers, and for part of the winter, too. I became intoxicated by music and got so accustomed to hearing it that I found myself no longer able to live without it. I subscribed to concerts and listened to music wherever I could, and even started taking lessons myself.

But Taneev's music affected me most and best of all. It was he who first taught me, through his marvellous playing, to listen to and love music. I made every effort to hear his playing wherever and however I could, and would arrange to meet him just for this purpose—just so that I could ask him to play. Occasionally, when I did not manage to do this for some time, I felt sad, tormented by the burning desire to hear him play once more, or even just to see him.

His presence had a beneficial effect on me whenever I started feeling a long-ing for Vanechka. I would weep and feel the energy drain from my life. Some-times all it took to calm me down was to meet with Sergej Ivanovich and hear his quieting, dispassionate voice. I had already got accustomed to being calmed by his presence and especially his playing. It was a kind of hypnosis, an invol-untary influence on my aching soul—one he was completely unaware of.

It was not a normal state to be in. It happened to coincide with my change of life. For all my moodiness I remained virtually unaffected by Taneev's per-sonality. Outwardly he was nothing to look at. He was always even-tempered, extremely closed in, and an utterly inscrutable person, as far as I was con-cerned. One often imagines that behind a person's inscrutability lies some-thing deep, special and significant, and, indeed, that was how Taneev could sometimes appear to me. It seemed as though in his daily life he repressed any trace of the impulse and passion which his music bestowed so beautifully, ir-repressibly and fascinatingly upon his listeners, revealing the inner world of the performer. I shall be writing more about my relationship to him and our further acquaintance when I come to the year 1895 in my memoirs.

For healing my sorrowful soul unintentionally through his music—he didn't even know about it—I have remained forever grateful to him, and I have never stopped loving him. He was the first to *open* the door for me to an *understanding* of music, just as Lev Nikolaevich led me to the understanding of the literary arts, just as Prince Urusov gave me an understanding of and love for philosophy. Once you enter upon these scenes of spiritual delight, you never want to leave them and you constantly come back to them.

What feelings I experienced during those twelve years of profound delight from concerts and listening to music! How many times, when tormented by various unpleasantries at home, complications in family and business affairs, etc., I would go to a concert and hear fine music, or even play myself, and I would all at once feel a sense of peace, joy, serenity, and come to terms with life's challenges.

As far as any kind of romantic relationship to the *performers* of musical works was concerned, I refused to entertain such a thought. I would always deny it and was actually afraid of it, even though there was one time when the influence of Taneev's personality was very strong. Once that kind of feeling surfaces, it kills any sense of importance in the music and art. I wrote a long piece on that.[4]

ANDREEV-BURLAK

A few days after Andreev-Burlak's departure, our son Serëzha, together with Ljasota, played a Beethoven sonata dedicated to Kreutzer.[5] This sonata left a tremendous impression on all of us. I wrote about it as follows:

"How powerful and how expressive of all the feelings in the world!"

Andreev-Burlak's stories and the sonata dedicated to Kreutzer were the first catalysts leading to the story Lev Nikolaevich eventually wrote under the title *The Kreutzer Sonata*. I recall Lev Nikolaevich saying that he ought to write a first-person story for Andreev-Burlak [to read], with someone playing [Beethoven's] Kreutzer Sonata simultaneously, and have Repin[6] paint a picture to go with the content of the story.

"The impression would be overwhelming from this confluence of three arts," said Lev Nikolaevich.

THE CHILDREN'S ILLNESSES

That same day, the 31st of August, we all asked Lev Nikolaevich to read us his *Kreutzer Sonata* in the presence of the Kuzminskij family and Nikolaj Nikolaevich Ge, which Lev Nikolaevich did. This reading uplifted everyone. It was impressive, and some of us were quite excited by it. I had been familiar with it for a long time, having transcribed this vexing story more than once. I did not like it, as I recognised in its hero the same traits of animal jealousy that I had seen so many signs of in my husband, and which I so little deserved back then.

---

4. *Song Without Words*.

5. Vasilij Nikolaevich Andreev-Burlak (1843–88), Russian actor and master of dramatic reading; one of the organizers of the First Russian Actors' Guild (1883). He is also the author of *Volzhskie stseny* [Scenes of the Volga].

6. Il'ya Efimovich Repin (1844–1930) was a celebrated Ukrainian-born artist and memoirist. He was a close friend of Lev Tolstoy's and did several portraits of him.

After the reading Lev Nikolaevich still did a lot of re-working on this story. He wrote in his diary:

"I have to write the nonsense that would be uttered by a delirious dying woman asking forgiveness for her infidelity."

He conveyed this thought to me, and I said he ought to make her *not* guilty, otherwise it might be wrong from a literary standpoint. At first he argued, but in the long run listened to my advice and came to the same [conclusion regarding the] ending on his own.

WINTER AT YASNAYA POLYANA—*THE POWER OF DARKNESS* AND *THE KREUTZER SONATA*

During this time I was busily transcribing *The Kreutzer Sonata* to send to Monsieur Vogüé to be translated into French.[7] Vogüé was not terribly fond of the story, and when he realised how successful it had become, he said:

"C'est un succès de scandale."

Back then in Petersburg people were reading it in manuscript form. It was also read at my sister T[at'jana] A[ndreevna] Kuzminskaja's before a huge crowd.

Lev Nikolaevich wanted to include it in the *Festschrift* for Jur'ev, but the censors forbade it.[8] Gajdeburov, too, wanted to publish it in his magazine *Nedelja*, but, again, it didn't work out, and Gajdeburov wrote Lev Nikolaevich:[9]

"Pity your story was read in Petersburg to satisfy a few curious people; they've spoilt the whole thing, and I received an official notification saying that the Count's story will be banned and the books recalled."

Petitions were submitted to the censorship board by both Aleksandr Mikhajlovich Kuzminskij and Nikolaj Nikolaevich Strakhov, but to no avail, as K. P. Pobedonostsev, who was in power then, strongly protested.[10] Strakhov wrote [to me] about him on 22 January 1890:

---

7. Eugène Melchior, vicomte de Vogüé (1848–1910), was a French writer and literary historian who discovered Russian literature for French readers.

8. Sergei Andreevich Jur'ev (1821–88) was a prominent literary figure, translator, and editor, who was trained as an astronomer before devoting himself to literature.

9. Pavel Aleksandrovich Gajdeburov (1841–93) was a political commentator and journal editor.

10. Aleksandr Mikhajlovich Kuzminskij (1843–1917) was a state councillor and the husband of Sofiya Andreevna's sister. Nikolaj Nikolaevich Strakhov (1828–96) was a philosopher, librarian, literary critic, and longtime editorial associate of both Lev Nikolaevich and Sofiya Andreevna. Konstantin Petrovich Pobedonostsev (1827–1907) was the senior procurator of the Holy Synod of the Russian Orthodox Church and a conservative political activist and commentator.

I was recently over to see Pobedonostsev. It turned out he hadn't even read *The Kreutzer Sonata,* just that Feoktistov had recounted to him a host of horrors.[11] I defended it, explaining to him the moral content of the story. Someone told me that Pobedonostsev had afterward said, referring to me, that he didn't know whom to believe—Feoktistov or me. "I haven't read it, and I shan't read it," he told me. "Why?" I enquired. "Why should I fill my imagination with difficult and repulsive images?" [he replied].

LEV NIKOLAEVICH'S AFTERWORD AND OTHER WRITINGS

At that time, after hearing so many different reactions to *The Kreutzer Sonata* from all sides, Lev Nikolaevich decided to outline his thoughts [on it] and began writing an Afterword to *The Kreutzer Sonata* [*Posleslovie k «Krejtserovoj Sonate»*]. This project moved along quietly, but it was challenging, and the Afterword caused Lev Nikolaevich a great deal of mental and spiritual stress.

MY ACTIVITIES

Of special interest in connection with the banning of *The Kreutzer Sonata* are the letters written by N. I. Storozhenko, the publisher of the Jur'ev *Festschrift,* who strongly petitioned for the clearance of *The Kreutzer Sonata* for this collection. He made a special trip to Petersburg for this purpose. Pobedonostsev said that *he* would not have dared lay a hand on a work of such high art. It was the Empress and Minister Durnovo who banned it, fearing its success and influence.[12]

Storozhenko wrote, for example:

Not one of Lev Nikolaevich's works has so swayed the human soul as *The Kreutzer Sonata.* Students copy it at night and discuss it in their classrooms. Recently one student read a whole paper on it in the anatomy laboratory, which provoked a noisy discussion.

The story was circulating everywhere in copies.

AGAIN *THE FRUITS OF ENLIGHTENMENT* AND
THE KREUTZER SONATA

N. N. Strakhov also wrote Lev Nikolaevich concerning *The Kreutzer Sonata* in April 1890, after the story was banned once and for all by the censors:

---

11. Evgenij Mikhajlovich Feoktistov (1829–98) was a writer, journalist, and liberal politician.

12. Tsaritsa Marija Fëdorovna, wife of Tsar Alexander III.

What is striking is that, more often than not, no notice is taken of the moral aim, nor of the condemnation of egotism and wantonness—so accustomed have people become to these habits of egotism and wantonness, that they feel offended directly by you, [wondering] why you attack the inevitable, attack what we manage to get along with very well. It is only the smart young people, only the smart, keen women who have fathomed your exposé, recognised the evil you are protesting against, and support your preaching of chastity. I was amazed at Countess Aleksandra Andreevna Tolstaya's reaction—she blurted out simply: "What?! Does he want to put an end to the human race?" As though it were somebody's responsibility to argue for the continuation of the human race. Maybe start up some breeding stables?[13]

In Petersburg, as everywhere else it was put on, *The Kreutzer Sonata* stirred up considerable reaction. It was the talk of the town and everyone, upon meeting their relatives or acquaintances, would ask right off: "Have you read *The Kreutzer Sonata*?"

THE KREUTZER SONATA AND MY STORY

While I was proofreading *The Kreutzer Sonata* for Volume XIII—a story I had never liked on account of its coarse treatment of women on the part of Lev Nikolaevich, it made me think about writing my own novel on the subject of *The Kreutzer Sonata*. This thought kept coming to me more and more frequently, to the point where I could no longer restrain myself. I did write this story, but it never saw the light of day and is now lying among my papers at the Historical Museum in Moscow.

MUTUAL RECRIMINATIONS

There was a good deal of bitterness in our relationship of that period. Whenever he reproached me for hanging onto private property, for copying his diaries, for the way I raised the children, I would berate him for his lack of love for the family, as well as for *The Kreutzer Sonata*, which the people who read it in manuscript copies for some reason associated with our family—with the result that this story humiliated me in the eyes of the whole world and destroyed whatever love remained between us ... In any case, I felt greatly offended by

---

13. From Strakhov's letter to Tolstoy dated April 24, 1890, published in Leo Tolstoy and Nikolaj Strakhov, *Complete Correspondence*, 2 vols., ed. Andrew Donskov (Ottawa: Slavic Research Group at the University of Ottawa; Moscow: State L. N. Tolstoy Museum, 2003), II: 813–15.

the shadow this story had cast over me, and here I was feeling so chaste in all my marital relations! There was not a word, not a single movement or even a glance at another man that would have made me blameworthy before my husband.

It's strange, but for some reason both Lev Nikolaevich's brother Sergej Nikolaevich and his friend D'jakov took pity on me, and even the Tsar himself, upon reading *The Kreutzer Sonata*, said how he pitied "his poor wife."

VOLUME XIII DETAINED

Upon hearing of the banning of *The Kreutzer Sonata*, which had been anticipated earlier, Stakhovich strongly urged me to petition for its clearance with the Tsar himself. He said that just as Nicholas I had taken it upon himself to act as censor for Pushkin's writings, so I should ask Alexander III to personally censor the writings of Lev Nikolaevich Tolstoy.

I had the vague feeling that this didn't make any sense, that Lev Nikolaevich would never agree to it. But vainglory on the one hand and, on the other, a fighting impulse to vigorously stand up for my cause and feel the power of my own energy and perseverance, overshadowed my heart and prompted me to go to Petersburg, straight to the Tsar.

I didn't make any final decision then and waited for this question to mature by itself at the proper time.

THE REASON FOR MY TRIP

Nobody knew the principal reason for my trip to Petersburg, which was this: the *Kreutzer Sonata* story had somehow cast a shadow over me. Many suspected that [Lev Nikolaevich] had taken it from our own lives, while others saw it as depicting the humiliation of wives and of women in general. My uncle Kostja Islavin told me that society considered me *une victime,* and that the Tsar had said: "I pity Tolstoy's poor wife . . ."

And so it was [at least partly] to show how little I resembled a victim that I went to petition for this story. The fact that I was petitioning for it meant I could not have been the model for its subject; it meant I was innocent and not a participant in the events depicted in *The Kreutzer Sonata*. I also wanted to raise Lev Nikolaevich's *prestige* and to show to the highest circles of society the true meaning of Lev Nikolaevich's teachings and writings, which had been falsely interpreted in a revolutionary sense. All of which I fully achieved, even though I was terribly depressed in Petersburg. I wrote to my daughter Tanja:

"I am vexed by my waiting situation. After all, my heart is breaking with impatience at wanting to go back home . . . I can't leave, since the Tsar has said he was looking forward to receiving me *with pleasure . . . !*"

EMPEROR ALEXANDER III

In the Tsar's study stood two black Africans in native uniforms. The runner once again bowed to me, opened the door and left.

The Tsar met me right at the door, and offered his hand. I curtsied to him, and he began with the words:

"You must pardon me, Countess, for making you wait so long, but circumstances made it impossible for me to receive you earlier. I hope the stairs didn't wear you out? They're pretty steep."

And I responded to the Tsar:

"I myself am deeply grateful that Your Majesty has extended this courtesy to me by receiving me."

The Tsar gestured to an arm-chair beside his desk, while he himself sat down at the desk. He began talking (I don't remember his exact words) about Lev Nikolaevich, and asking what I specifically wanted from him. Since Feoktistov had already allowed me to publish Volume XIII of Lev Nikolaevich's writings, the only thing left for me to petition for was *The Kreutzer Sonata,* and perhaps this reason might seem too insignificant a request for an audience. But I showed no sign of embarrassment and began speaking altogether firmly and calmly from the start. The Tsar's kind, pale-blue eyes looked at me so gently, then he himself showed such a touching bashfulness that it was quite easy for me to talk with him. And I began:

"Your Majesty, in recent times I have begun to notice in my husband a disposition to write in his former, belletristic genre. He recently told me that he has retreated from his religious-philosophical works to the point where he can write fiction [again], and that something has been coming together in his head on the order (and of the magnitude) of *War and Peace* . . ." (This was the honest truth.) And I went on:

"Nevertheless, warnings against him are still springing up. You see, for instance, Volume XIII of his writings has been detained. Just the other day they managed to clear it, for some reason. They also banned *The Fruits of Enlightenment,* yet now an order has been issued to stage it at the Imperial Theatres . . .

"Yes, *The Fruits of Enlightenment* will now be staged," said the Tsar. "This was put on by an amateur troupe at Tsarskoe Selo, and I laughed my head off. It was a splendid performance. But there's no serious motif there, it's just a farce."

"Excuse me, Your Majesty, the serious motif lies in the fact that for us of the nobility, land is an amusement, a toy, but for the peasants, it constitutes their daily bread."

"Yes, but the farce lies in the fact that the chambermaid outwitted her noble masters and turned out to be smarter than they."

After a brief pause, I then began speaking about the detention of *The Kreutzer Sonata*. On this point the Tsar said to me:

"You see, the way it's written, you probably would not want to give it to your children to read. After all, the Count is writing against marriage."

And I said:

"How could the Count write against marriage, when he has been proving by his entire life that he is in favour of marriage? We have nine children. It is unfortunate, though, that this story is written in such an extreme form, but the underlying thought is that the ideal is forever unattainable. If extreme chastity is held up as the ideal, people in a wedded state can only be pure."

I also recall that when I told the Tsar that Lev Nikolaevich seemed to be [now more] disposed to writing fiction, the Tsar exclaimed:

"Oh, how good that would be! He's *such* a good writer, such a good writer!" He put special emphasis on the word *such*.

After my definition of the ideal in *The Kreutzer Sonata*, I added:

"How happy I would be if the ban on *The Kreutzer Sonata* in the *Collected Works* were lifted! This would be a clear sign of favour toward Lev Nikolaevich and, who knows, it might even encourage him to work [on his fiction]."

Whereupon the Tsar replied:

"Yes, it could be cleared for the *Complete Collected Works*. Not everyone's in a position to afford them, and there could be no talk of wide distribution."

WITH MY SONS

No matter how brave a face I put on, however, when I learnt that Lev Nikolaevich would be going off with his daughters for the whole winter to [help] feed the famine victims while I, tied to my four youngest children, was obliged to live alone in Moscow, I became very upset and cried so much that I brought upon myself an extreme case of neuralgia. Later, long haunted by the thought of writing a story on the Kreutzer Sonata [theme] from a wife's point of view, I set out at once to draft an overall plan, and then assiduously got down to writing this novel.

A NOVEL IN RESPONSE TO *THE KREUTZER SONATA*

In addition to my family duties and my activities for the famine relief, in the evenings I would work on my novel in response to *The Kreutzer Sonata*, which I had long had in mind and which had now piqued my interest once again.

I was always troubled by Lev Nikolaevich's attitude toward women. This misunderstanding [he displayed] of the possibility of sheer feminine purity, this disrespect and unceasing suspicion of an affair or betrayal—all of this I experienced first-hand and wanted to give voice to in my novel. Lev Nikolaevich also lacked any ability to really *love* a woman. . . .

Had Lev Nikolaevich's heart really dried up? Or did he love me for all those years we lived together? This will remain a mystery to me, too. As it will to everyone . . .

In my novel I wanted to point out the difference in the love that lives in men and women. With men love, first and foremost, is on a material level; with women it is first and foremost an idealisation, the poetry of love, tenderness, and only after that comes sexual arousal. Of course, as an inexperienced writer, I did not fulfil my task very well, but I wrote with considerable enthusiasm, always keeping in mind the background of Lev Nikolaevich's *Kreutzer Sonata*, which served as a pattern for my story.

MY STORY AND MY SON LËVA'S REACTION TO IT

Just as in the country, so too in Moscow, where I was living, I filled my long, lonely evenings with writing the long story I had started in response to Lev Nikolaevich's *Kreutzer Sonata*. My son Lëva, upon hearing of its contents, strongly criticised me for it and even wrote to me from Petersburg on 27 November 1892:

> As Papà's wife, as the mother of us all, someone who couldn't possibly carry out her appointed task better than she does and is still not finished with it, you have earned the right to high praise indeed. But if you should begin to corrupt this position of yours through various outpourings of your groundless and unfair annoyances in [the form of] a poorly written story, you will be departing from your chief, exalted purpose as a wife and mother, since there will no longer be any love here, and you will knock yourself off track.

I don't know whether my son was right or not. I do know that I began writing this story because, without any provocation, all eyes of the public, from the Tsar's right down to Lev Nikolaevich's brother Sergej Nikolaevich's, were focused on me. They began to feel sorry for me as the victim of a jealous husband, and a few of them began to suspect something. I wanted to give a more accurate portrayal of an honest woman and her ideals of love, in sharp contrast to male materialism.

SERGEJ IVANOVICH TANEEV

Back in the spring I was lying in semi-pain on a day-bed on the balcony of our Khamovniki home when Sergej Ivanovich Taneev came to see me. During our conversation I asked him where he was planning to spend the summer. He said that usually he spent his summers with his friends, the Maslovs, in a village in Orël Gubernia, but this year they had a sick child with them and he didn't feel right about imposing on them, so he was looking to rent a private room somewhere on a nobleman's estate. At once the thought came to me of renting him our Yasnaya Polyana annexe, but we didn't yet know whether it might be occupied by our sick son, Lëva, as he had proposed earlier, or whether he would stay at Hanko. In any event I offered Sergej Ivanovich the annexe on condition that Lëva declined to spend the summer there.

It seemed that my proposal was very much to Taneev's liking. We parted with the agreement that he would think it over, and that I would talk about it with my family and get in touch with Lëva. The upshot was that Sergej Ivanovich, along with his elderly nanny, moved into the annexe for a total payment of 125 roubles. I didn't want to take any money, but Taneev would not agree to live at our place rent-free. This money I donated to a charitable cause, since Taneev's stay and his amazing piano playing gave us nothing but joy.

After dinner he would usually play chess with Lev Nikolaevich, and later, in the evenings, he would do a lot of practising on the piano, and everybody was in ecstasy at his playing. Lev Nikolaevich and he had an agreement: if Sergej Ivanovich lost a game of chess, he was to play for Lev Nikolaevich whatever Lev Nikolaevich desired. And if Lev Nikolaevich lost, he would have to read for Sergej Ivanovich from his latest writings. This agreement was most advantageous for all of us, since we all were an audience and our evenings were greatly enriched.

I recall the feverish impatience with which I waited for these evenings and Taneev's marvelous playing, which relieved my acute emotional struggles for a time. Sometimes I would go to the annexe where Taneev was staying, and sit unnoticed on the porch and listen through the open windows while Sergej Ivanovich was rehearsing a Chopin Polonaise that Lev Nikolaevich had asked for, or a Beethoven sonata or some other piece. During these moments I would be oblivious to my grief, carried away as I was into another realm, relaxing in my soul and acutely anticipating again and again the repetition of this blissful condition.

Truth be told, it was not until that moment that I had a clear understanding of what music was all about. I rarely went to concerts and was not acquainted with any good musicians, especially pianists. Taneev's playing was special. When it came to music, he was a philosopher, too. Sometimes he performed with such passion that it was eerie—all the more so since in life he was rather placid, and seemed to be completely devoid of passion. He liked jokes and satire, he liked to eat, and in his outward appearance he was plain to the extreme. One had to get to know him more closely to understand his inner substance and the very essence of his nature and spiritual life. One thing was for certain: more than anything else in the world, he loved music and his old nanny Pelageja Vasil'evna.

Sometimes I would go for walks with Taneev, Sasha and her dear English [governess], Miss Welsh, but frequently, if something should remind me directly of Venechka, I would run off alone home in tears. It was even harder to go for walks with my immediate family. I recall one time Lev Nikolaevich inviting me to go for a walk with him, and I felt such joy at his tender invitation, but along the way I burst into tears and upset my poor husband, who said rather depressingly:

"There's nothing out there, there's no real summer. It's as though a new era in life [has begun] which is altogether unfamiliar and, in my view, extremely difficult."

All day long each of us would stay in our respective corners and come together only at dinner-time, supper-time and tea-time. I was often sad, too, over the absence of my sister's family, with whom we had spent almost twenty-five consecutive summers together.

As I describe these facts, I greatly regret not having noted down Lev Nikolaevich's conversations at the time, or anything about his spiritual life. Personally, I was always interested in his career and his mood. It's just that it never entered my head to write it down. At the time I had no idea that in my advanced years I would be writing the whole story of my life.

LEV NIKOLAEVICH'S SUFFERINGS AND MY OWN

I wrote a story on this theme—namely, that love for music should never be overshadowed by any other feeling. It should be *pristine*, like Nature. The thought of writing this story was kindled by the uncivilised behaviour of some young ladies toward the pianist Hofmann. They actually *kissed* his galoshes and wouldn't let him pass. Falling in love with a musician or artist, by its very nature, excludes love for the art itself. Having realised this and written about it, I found it all the more impossible to allow this to happen within myself.

Excerpt from
The Truth About My Father

LEV LVOVICH TOLSTOY

TOLSTOY'S VIEWS ON THE CONJUGAL QUESTION

WHEN I WAS SEVENTEEN or eighteen, my mother asked a young pupil of the Moscow Conservatoire to come to Jasnaia, for the purpose of giving me some lessons on the violin. After dinner my young teacher was asked to play, and as my elder brother was an excellent pianist, we enjoyed classical music nearly every evening.

Of all the works that were played, the one that made the greatest impression on my father was *The Kreutzer Sonata*, by Beethoven. He was then nearly sixty. It was at this period, perhaps a little before *The Kreutzer Sonata* was written, that he wrote his posthumously-published work, "The Devil." All who have read these two novels will be well aware that both dealt with the sexual question.

Beethoven's *Kreutzer Sonata* was heard in our house at Jasnaia during the period when Tolstoy began to feel that his married life was coming to its end, and that the mode of existence that had pleased him for so many years no longer satisfied him. He suffered from the contradiction between his ideas and the realities that surrounded him while he was seeking the true road to take for the purpose of developing his spiritual life.

Marriage and the family were the greatest obstacles to that development. It was for this reason and at this period that he furiously inveighed against these responsibilities with all the strength of his passion.

The ideas of Posdnicheff, the hero of *The Kreutzer Sonata*, were Tolstoy's own ideas, and the conclusions from all these uncompromising ideas are not only conclusions with which the author was in sympathy but were distinctly approved by him in an appendix to the novel.

"I did not anticipate," Tolstoy wrote, "that when I was writing this work a rigorous logic would lead me to the point to which I arrived. My conclusions have terrified me. I did not wish to believe them, but I could not help doing so."

We all know what those conclusions were. "When the passions shall have disappeared, then humanity will have no more reason to be: it will have fulfilled the law."

In other words, sexual life is an evil that must be suppressed.

In looking back to-day on those wonderful evenings at Jasnaia, when my father, sunk in his armchair, listened to Beethoven's sonata, I understand thoroughly what was passing in his mind. His grey eyes filled with tears, fixed in front of him, he thought, felt, and created.

He then discovered for himself and for humanity one of the greatest truths of life: the falsity of modern marriage. This was a revelation to him, and he was happy to be able to communicate it to others.

The music of Beethoven affected him so much that very often he could no longer stand it. He would get up suddenly from his chair and go to the open window, and a hasty but particular sound came from his mouth, like that made by Posdnicheff when he told his story in the railway carriage.

The famous *presto* movement of *The Kreutzer Sonata*—the *presto* that was the great cause of bringing Posdnicheff's wife and her lover together—convulsed Tolstoy's heart every time he heard it.

The reader remembers, perhaps, that last atrocious scene between the murderer and his wife: "She clung to the dagger with her hands and cut them, but could not keep hold of it. . . . I heard, and I still remember, the resistance due to her corsets," etc.

All these scenes, each of an incomparable strength, like all the ideas in *The Kreutzer Sonata,* filled the head of my father while he sat without moving in his chair, listening to the music.

In the mornings, during the hours he usually devoted to his work, he wrote the thoughts that had been inspired by the music of the night before.

Day by day, as this immortal work was created, my father read to us aloud what he had written.

The whole family and our friends met in the drawing-room to hear these readings, and I do not believe any reading has ever interested any of us more. For all of us, as for the author himself, the thing that was being born was something entirely new and fresh, something of the greatest importance, and the impatience with which we waited the development and the climax of the story can easily be imagined.

Immediately after these intellectual feasts, warm disputes arose, and Tolstoy took advantage of this to continue his story the next day by giving his hero further new ideas that were still more striking, more clear and more true.

"But," would object my aunt, Mme. Kouzminsky, for instance—she was always very frank in expressing her opinions to my father—"do you mean to say you would bring mankind to an end? That would be contrary to nature. All animals follow the law of nature in order to reproduce themselves on earth."

On the following day we would hear Posdnicheff state emphatically: "As long as humanity exists it will have before it an ideal, and that ideal will certainly not be that of the rabbits and the pigs, to propagate themselves as much as possible; nor that of the monkeys or even of the Parisians, to take advantage of and enjoy the sexual passion as much as possible; but it will be an ideal of good, which is to be realised by chastity and abstinence."

In another part of his monologue Posdnicheff, in speaking of his wife, says: "Charcot would have described my wife as being hysterical, and myself as abnormal, and perhaps he would have begun to treat us scientifically. Nevertheless, there was nothing to treat."

This retort of Tolstoy was based, no doubt, on his deep-rooted antipathy towards modern medicine and modern science, which he held neglected and confounded the moral laws of life, which alone can save humanity.

It is very agreeable to recognise that in no part of the world is *The Kreutzer Sonata* more appreciated than in Europe. All that I have read or heard here in regard to this work confirms this view. It is at the same time also true, however, that perhaps in no part of the world are the great truths expressed in the book no longer followed to such a small extent as in Europe.

It is not going too far to say that, for the purpose of bringing about a simple improvement in the health of the French nation, for example, the application to everyday life of some of the principles laid down by Tolstoy in this book would have an enormously salutary effect. . . .

Here are some of my father's thoughts on women, which he often expressed under different forms. I mention them according to his own words, as I recall them to memory:

(I) There are three kinds of women. The first is that kind of woman who becomes a mother and attaches herself more to her children than to her husband; that is the best type of woman. The second is she who is more wife than mother, and thereby becomes a woman of average quality. Then there is the third type—the kind of woman who attaches herself neither to her children nor to her husband, which is the most abject type.

(II) A sound and healthy woman is a wild beast.

(III) The most intelligent woman is less intelligent than a stupid man.

A very severe judge of women, Tolstoy was nevertheless surrounded all his life almost entirely by women, and women of the finest types. It must be admitted that he had extraordinary good fortune in this respect, for all the women with whom he was in relation incontestably approximated to the ideal woman, as defined by himself.

"Such a woman will demand from her husband real work, which requires energy, and she will fear no danger. She knows that children, the generations to come, are the most sacred things men can look upon, and that she exists for the purpose of serving this holy work with all her being. Such women develop in their children and their husbands the strength of sacrifice, and by this they dominate men. O women who are mothers; in your hands lies the salvation of the world!"

Excerpt from
Tolstoy: A Life of My Father

ALEXANDRA LVOVNA TOLSTAYA
TRANSLATED BY ELIZABETH REYNOLDS HAPGOOD

IT WAS SPRING and they were in their house in Moscow. Among a group of guests gathered there were the painter Repin, the actor Andreyev-Burlak, a student at the Moscow Conservatory, the tutor of the Tolstoy boys Andryusha and Misha, and Lasoto, a violinist. Seryozha and Lasoto were asked to play.

Seryozha was different from all the other Tolstoys because of his great shyness and reserve. He often concealed his emotions, his outbursts of tenderness or passion, under a cloak of deliberate rudeness, or brusqueness. The most serious-minded and industrious of all the Tolstoy brothers, he had his own separate existence; he did not lean toward either his mother, or his father, and he rarely confided his thoughts to the members of his family. It was only when he sat down to the piano and for hours played his beloved Chopin, Beethoven, Bach, Grieg, or attempted to compose something himself, that everyone listened to him. It was said that Seryozha had a remarkable touch. As a matter of fact it was only to the piano that he laid bare his heart: in sounds that were tempestuously passionate or tenderly singing one sensed the sadness, the inner struggle of this ill-favored and reserved youth.

It must have been that on this spring evening the young man played the Beethoven sonata dedicated to Kreutzer with especial verve. The first part, which Tolstoy particularly liked, strongly affected everyone present. They spoke of how fine it would be if Tolstoy wrote a story on the theme of the Kreutzer Sonata, and Repin illustrated it and Andreyev-Burlak acted it. This idea was never realized; Andreyev died shortly afterward. But in Tolstoy the idea continued to mature. It is difficult to say exactly when the theme of *The*

Kreutzer Sonata first entered his head—that evening, under the influence of the music, or very much earlier, when in the 1870's he sketched out and then abandoned a story called "The Murderer of His Wife."

On April 3, 1889, when Tolstoy was visiting his friend S. S. Urusov in his country place, he jotted down in his diary: "It is early, I intended to write something new, but I reread just the beginnings and settled on *The Kreutzer Sonata*." And on the 5th of April he wrote: "I wrote a great deal on *The Kreutzer Sonata* and it was not bad."

But Sofiya Andreevna wrote in her diary in December, 1890, that "the idea of making a real *story* was given to him [Tolstoy] by Andreyev-Burlak, an actor and wonderful storyteller." Then Sofiya Andreevna added: "It was he who told about how once in a railroad train a man confided in him the misfortune of his wife's unfaithfulness and this was the subject used by Lyovochka."

In creating his main character, Pozdnyshev, there is no doubt that Tolstoy drew upon various aspects of his own relations with his wife: the periods of tenderness and coolness, the discord, the quarrels, and faithfully described some of Sofiya Andreevna's more annoying characteristics fully aware of this, she did not care for *The Kreutzer Sonata*.

"There were words and expressions of hatred because of the coffee, the tablecloth, the carriage, a lead in a card game—all things without any importance to either of them," Tolstoy has Pozdnyshev say in *The Kreutzer Sonata*. "In me, in any case, hatred toward her boiled furiously. I watched her sometimes as she poured tea, swung her foot, carried her spoon to her mouth, noisily sipped the liquid, and I hated her as much for this as for the worst kind of act. I did not notice at that time that the periods of resentment came over me quite regularly and at equal intervals and corresponded to the periods of what we called love. A period of love—a period of bitterness—a spirited period of love—a long period of bitterness—a weaker manifestation of love—a brief period of bitterness. . . . We were two prisoners who hated each other, fastened to the same chain, ruining each other's lives and trying not to see it. I still did not know at the time that nine-tenths of married people live in this hell in which I lived and that this cannot be otherwise."

Tolstoy's ideas about marriage and continence were upsetting to Sofiya Andreevna.

"You are harassing and killing yourself," she wrote him on April 19, 1889, to Yasnaya Polyana. "I . . . have been thinking: he does not eat meat, nor smoke, he works beyond his strength, his brain is not nourished, hence the drowsiness and weakness. How stupid vegetarianism is. . . . Kill life in yourself, kill all impulses of the flesh, all its needs—why not kill yourself altogether? After all you are committing yourself to *slow* death, what's the difference?"

The writing of *The Kreutzer Sonata* took almost two years. Tolstoy wrote in spurts; at times he lost interest in it and then he would take it up again with enthusiasm. In a letter to his friend G. A. Rusanov, he wrote (March 14, 1889): "The rumor about a novel has some foundation. As early as two years ago I wrote the rough draft of a novel dealing with the theme of sexual love, but I did it so carelessly and unsatisfactorily that I did not even revise it, but should I become interested in the idea I would make a fresh start." Earlier Tolstoy had written in his diary: "Have been revising *The Kreutzer Sonata*. . . . Have gotten bored by *The K. S.*"

When Tolstoy wrote that he was "bored" by one of his works it meant that he was nearing the finish of it. Before he had quite concluded the novel he began to write the Epilogue, and meantime the novel was being passed around. Tolstoy received varied reactions: bewilderment, condemnation, friendly criticism, enthusiasm.

In his Epilogue he attempted to reply to the many questions he had been asked.

"Given the ideal of chastity," he wrote, "one must consider that the only departure from it on the part of any two people must be to form a unique, indissoluble union for life, and then it will be clear that the guidance given by Christ is not only sufficient but also the only one possible."

In a letter to V. I. Alexeyev Tolstoy wrote: "The contents of what I have written are as new to me as to those who have read them. In this respect the ideal revealed to me is so far from my own actions that at first I was terrified and said nothing, but then I became convinced, repented, and rejoiced at the joyful advance in store for others and for me."

N. N. Strakhov, although he criticized *The Kreutzer Sonata* from the point of view of the external handling of the novel, wrote Tolstoy an enthusiastic letter about its substance.

Tolstoy replied: "From the artistic point of view I am well aware that the writing is beneath all criticism: it was based on two mentally inharmonious methods, hence the formlessness you sensed. Nevertheless I am leaving it as it stands and have no regrets, not because I am lazy, but I cannot correct it. I also have no regrets because I know somehow that what is written is true, and not only not useless but surely beneficial to people, and in part it is new. If it were to be written in artistic form, which I do not repudiate, I would have to start all over again and at once."

Chertkov criticized it: "The novel in its present state can do no more than arouse in the reader questions, doubts; it does not clarify them to the degree which you are capable of clarifying them, by injecting into the novel the core of Christian convictions which so far is lacking. . . ."

This reaction on the part of his friend evidently distressed Tolstoy, who noted in his diary: "He makes a valid criticism of *The Kreutzer Sonata*, and I'd be glad to follow his advice, but I have no urge to do so. I feel only apathy, sadness, despondency."

Was Tolstoy really in need of such criticism? He was more severe on himself than anyone else. "I am writing on *The Kreutzer Sonata* and 'What Is Art?' and they are both negative, wicked, and I want to write what is good," he said in his diary for June 24, 1889.

During this period of artistic creativeness any polishing of his writing, his style, seemed a superfluous luxury to Tolstoy. To him the important thing was to have time to express thoughts from which readers might benefit.

His main concern was his own conscience. "All I want is to be in a state of cleanliness, that is to say, clean of all lustful appetite," he wrote to the elder Gay, "of all delights, wine, smoking, sexual lust and human fame, to be humble, that is to say, be prepared to have my work scored and myself slandered."

And Tolstoy was both scored and slandered. Now, people said, after having enjoyed a stormy life, in his old age he preaches chastity and abstinence.

"To struggle, that is one's very life," Tolstoy wrote in his "Thoughts on the Relations Between the Sexes," and later on he said: "Man must not make chastity his goal, but an approach to chastity."

The Kreutzer Sonata was banned, despite the fact that everyone everywhere was talking about it and it was being passed from hand to hand.

"It is difficult to imagine," wrote Alexandrine in her memoirs, "what happened when *The Kreutzer Sonata* and *The Power of Darkness* appeared. Although they were not yet licensed to be printed, these works were copied by the hundreds and thousands, they were passed from hand to hand, they were translated into all languages and were always read with incredible emotion; it seemed as if for the time being the public abandoned its private cares and lived only on the writings of Count Tolstoy."

When on February 25, 1890, the whole of Volume XIII of the complete works of Tolstoy, the one in which this novel appeared, was held up, Sofiya Andreevna appealed to Durnovo, the Minister of Internal Affairs. Her request that the ban be lifted was refused; but Sofiya Andreevna was not one to give up easily. The greater the obstacles, the greater her energy. After consulting with Granny and with A. M. Kuzminski, she decided to go to

St. Petersburg and in person request the Emperor to allow the publication of the novel. The Emperor proved to be more liberal-minded than any of his subordinates, and he granted Sofiya Andreevna permission to issue Volume XIII. By now it was April, 1891. Sofiya Andreevna came back from St. Petersburg gay and satisfied. The ban on Volume XIII had been the cause of serious financial loss. Moreover, she appears to have been flattered by the reception and attention accorded her by the Emperor, for she enjoyed talking about it to all her relatives and acquaintances.

Many people missed the deep significance of *The Kreutzer Sonata*. They made it trivial, they distorted it. One of the states in the United States proved to be less liberal than the Russian Tsar; it banned the novel as being pornographic, and in Germany a publisher, hoping to make money, launched a vile advertising campaign and printed a naked woman on the cover of the book.

All during this period Tolstoy was absorbed by the question of sex. Having wrestled with the temptations of lust all his life, he was well aware of its great power which leads men to crime and sometimes to complete moral collapse.

Afterword

ANDREY TOLSTOY

AFTER *ANNA KARENINA* (1877), whether Lev Tolstoy would write again was a question akin to that of my parents' generation of whether the Beatles would ever get back together. Unlike the Beatles, Tolstoy did go on to write again, but as happened with John Lennon, his work largely became a form of activism, direct and unambiguous. Lennon wrote "How Do You Sleep?" about Paul McCartney's rock star myopia and political nonengagement; the existential crisis that debilitated Tolstoy's art was in the same vein. The part of him that despaired at the vanity of earthly pursuits (present also in his alter ego Konstantin Levin) eventually prevailed. A personal struggle that had been dramatized in complex binaries like Pierre Bezukhov and Prince Andrei in *War and Peace* (1869) turned into the single-minded locomotion of *The Kreutzer Sonata* (1889), a virtual monologue where the counterpart to its insomniac protagonist is not another character but we the readers. We stand accused and have to ask ourselves: are we part of that culture Pozdnyshev describes? And if we are, can we continue to live as we do?

Pozdnyshev decries the pervasive misogyny of Russian and European culture. Women, he claims, are taught to be chaste, intellectual, artistically inclined, well dressed, pleasantly mannered—all in order to be more sexually appealing to men, who, after years of philandering around brothels and such, finally decide to settle down and won't do it with just any woman, but only with a perfectly groomed, innocent girl. Until women know better (and they get to know better only after marriage, at which point it's too late), they accept this state of affairs and exploit their sexuality for gain, picking the most profitable of countless suitors—and when there is nothing left to gain, they prepare their own daughters for the same fate. Marriages made this way are based on primitive sexual desire, which is shameful to some men and all women, and which, once satiated, is replaced by lifelong resentment: his, because he is forbidden from reigniting his appetite with a different woman; hers, because she realizes there is no such thing as romantic love. This leads to cycles of violence, infidelity, depravity, guilt, child abuse, and other domestic horrors.

Through Pozdnyshev, Tolstoy argues that until society stops treating women as sexual objects, political movements seeking greater rights and medical advances improving contraception or diminishing infant and maternal mortality rates will be meaningless. But—this is where Tolstoy-the-philosopher seems like such a maddening burden to Tolstoy-the-artist—his conclusion is that we ought to abolish sexual relations altogether, rather than reform them.

As long as we are operating under what Roland Barthes called the readerly paradigm, we will sense that *The Kreutzer Sonata* is a limited work. We might sense that, almost unconsciously, it takes place inside the very train that crushed Anna Karenina years earlier, and that we are witnessing a runaway plot. We might remark on the irony that it was on a train that Tolstoy caught a fatal case of pneumonia, having left home at the age of eighty-two to practice at last the complete asceticism he preached. We might wonder whether Tolstoy, writing late in life, having enjoyed his women, wealth, and fame, is proposing something even remotely viable.

But if we turn to what Barthes called the writerly paradigm, in which a text is incomplete without a reconstructive, critical operation by the reader, then the project of *The Kreutzer Sonata* becomes a far more interesting, polemical one. Its dialectics will not be balanced out by another character (some sort of anti-Pozdnyshev), and Michael Katz's new translation has this point in mind. By situating the work next to responses in prose by Tolstoy's wife and son, as well as excerpts from memoirs about the writer by two of his children (with different and opposing loyalties), Katz sets up a model for our own engagement with the novella. The rich cast of characters that creates the cosmic breadth of Tolstoy's earlier works has been replaced by the vastness of our own lives and the characters who populate them. *The Kreutzer Sonata* is not a monologue, but a dialogue lying in wait, on a train that never stops with a companion who never sleeps.

Selected Bibliography of Works in English

WORKS BY LEV NIKOLAEVICH TOLSTOY

Tolstoy's Diaries. 2 volumes. Edited and translated by R. F. Christian. New York: Charles Scribner's Sons, 1985.

Tolstoy's Letters. 2 volumes. Selected, edited, and translated by R. F. Christian. New York: Charles Scribner's Sons, 1978.

Tolstoy's Short Fiction. Edited and with revised translations by Michael R. Katz. New York: Norton, 2008.

WORKS ABOUT LEV NIKOLAEVICH TOLSTOY

Bartlett, Rosamund. *Tolstoy: A Russian Life.* New York: Houghton Mifflin Harcourt, 2011.

Dillon, E. J. "The Kreutzer Sonata: Count Leo Tolstoy's Latest Unpublished Work." *Universal Review* 6 (1890), 291–311.

Golstein, Vladimir. "Narrating the Murder: The Rhetoric of Evasion in 'The Kreutzer Sonata.'" *Russian Literature* 40 (1996), 451–62.

Gustafson, Richard. *Leo Tolstoy: Resident and Stranger.* Princeton: Princeton University Press, 1989.

Hapgood, Isabel. "Tolstoi's Kreutzer Sonata." *Nation* 50 (April 17, 1890).

Herman, David. "Stricken by Infection: Art and Adultery in *Anna Karenina* and *Kreutzer Sonata.*" *Slavic Review* 56 (1997), 15–36.

Isenberg, Charles. *Telling Silence: Russian Frame Narratives of Renunciation.* Bloomington: Indiana University Press, 1993.

Jackson, Robert Louis. "Tolstoj's *Kreutzer Sonata* and Dostoevskij's *Notes from Underground.*" *American Contributions to the Eighth International Congress of Slavists.* Edited by Victor Terras, 2: 280–91. Columbus, OH: Slavica, 1978.

Kramer, Lawrence. "Tolstoy's Beethoven, Beethoven's Tolstoy: *The Kreutzer Sonata.*" *Critical Musicology and the Responsibility of Response: Selected Essays,* 145–61. Aldershot, England: Ashgate, 2006.

LeBlanc, Ronald D. *Slavic Sins of the Flesh: Food, Sex, and Carnal Appetite in Nineteenth-Century Russian Fiction.* Durham: University of New Hampshire Press, 2009.

McLean, Hugh. "The Tolstoy Marriage Revisited—Many Times." *Canadian Slavonic Papers* 53 (2011), 65–79.

Møller, Peter Ulf. *Postlude to The Kreutzer Sonata: Tolstoj and the Debate on Sexual Morality in Russian Literature in the 1890s.* Translated by John Kendal. Leiden: E. J. Brill, 1988.

Rancour-Laferriere, Daniel. "Lev Tolstoy's Moral Masochism in the Late 1880s." *One Hundred Years of Masochism.* Edited by Michael C. Finke and Carl Niekerk, 155–70. Amsterdam: Rodopi, 2000.

Rischin, Ruth. "Allegro Tumultuosissimamente: Beethoven in Tolstoy's Fiction." *In the Shade of the Giant: Essays on Tolstoy,* ed. Hugh McLean, 12–60. Berkeley: University of California Press, 1989.

Weir, Justin. *Leo Tolstoy and the Alibi of Narrative.* New Haven: Yale University Press, 2011.

WORKS BY SOFIYA ANDREEVNA TOLSTAYA

The Diaries of Sofia Tolstoy. Translated by Cathy Porter. New York: Random House, 1985.

The Diaries of Sofia Tolstoy. Revised and abridged. Translated by Cathy Porter. New York: Harper, 2009.

My Life. Edited by Andrew Donskov. Translated by John Woodsworth and Arkadi Klioutchanski. Ottawa: University of Ottawa Press, 2010.

Song Without Words: The Photographs and Diaries of Countress Sophia Tolstoy. Translated by Leah Bendavid-Val. Washington, D.C.: National Geographic, 2007.

WORKS ABOUT SOFIYA ANDREEVNA TOLSTAYA

Donskov, Andrew. Introduction to *Sofia Andreevna Tolstaya: Literary Works.* Ottawa: University of Ottawa; Moscow: State Tolstoy Museum, 2011.

Popoff, Alexandra. *Sophia Tolstoy: A Biography.* New York: Free Press, 2010.

———. *The Wives: The Women Behind Russia's Literary Giants.* New York: Pegasus, 2012.

CPSIA information can be obtained
at www.ICGtesting.com
Printed in the USA
BVHW032136141219
566618BV00004B/39/P

9 780300 189940